Paganini Agitato

A Novel
by
Ann Abelson

Edited and Revised by Lenny Cavallaro

with an Afterword by Stephanie Chase

Fomite
Burlington, VT

ISBN-13:978-1-959984-02-3
Library of Congress Control Number: 2023934767
Fomite
58 Peru Street
Burlington VT 05401
www.fomitepress.com
08-02-2023

To my daughter, Maya, and son, Jacob, with the hope that they will develop a greater appreciation for the literary talent of their paternal grandmother.

Acknowledgements

I wish to express my sincerest appreciation to Ken Atchity and David Angsten for their contributions to and assistance with the completion of this novel.

I must also express deepest gratitude to Don Frank and Angela Smith for their exemplary editorial assistance with the final preparation of the manuscript.

Last and certainly not least, my gratitude to Donna Bister and Marc Estrin of Fomite Press for bringing my mother's manuscript to print.

Contents

PREFACE

M Y MOTHER, THE LATE ANN ABELSON, began this novel more than forty years ago. The incomplete manuscript earned her a National Endowment for the Arts grant in 1978, but because of poor health she had to put it aside and turn to more readily accessible subjects for her writing. *Paganini Agitato* is the story I believe she would have wanted published.

I was always curious about my mother's fascination with Paganini. Perhaps it was the operatic drama of Paganini's life that appealed to her. Although she was not a musician herself, she adored opera and continued to travel to New York for productions of the Metropolitan Opera until the last year of her life. She attended local concerts with far less frequency and passion. Moreover, I never sensed she was especially enamored of the violin; the piano was her favorite instrument.

Ironically, she married a violinist—an Italian, at that! My father certainly had no pretensions as a second Paganini and was more talented as a composer than a performer. So apart from a superficial coincidence, there seems little by way of autobiographical influence in the ultimate evolution of *Paganini Agitato*. [Her earlier novels had drawn extensively from personal experience.]

❋ ❋ ❋

THIS IS THE story of the legend and legacy that was Niccolò Paganini and the terrible price one man paid for fortune and glory. "Superstar," notorious rake, reckless gambler, loving father, and alleged dallier with the Devil who was denied a Christian burial, Paganini was perhaps the greatest violinist of all times. Today the Paganini saga continues to fascinate as much by his life as by his virtuosity and artistic accomplishments.

As a composer, Paganini left behind a respectable legacy, including a number of works that remain part of the standard repertoire. Many who followed him borrowed material from these compositions; Liszt's *Paganini Etudes* and Rachmaninoff's *Rhapsody On A Theme By Paganini* are but two of the better-known masterpieces derived from his music.

In this novel the reader will journey with Paganini from the squalid streets of Genoa, his birthplace (where his house on the "Street of the Black Cats" is marked by a plaque to this day), to the grandeur of the European courts, the splendor of Venice (where a caravan of gondolas made their way to the Lido, conveying thousands of passengers to hear Paganini's graveyard recital at midnight under a sickle moon), and even to the pomp of the Vatican.

Paganini was a man of immense contradictions who still appears larger than life. His music is wonderful, and I hope those who have not yet heard his greatest works will want to listen to them after reading this novel. *Paganini Agitato* has been written for all readers—musicians and non-musicians—who enjoy painstakingly researched, lively historical fiction about a truly remarkable character.

Lenny Cavallaro

PROLOGUE

Upon receipt of the proper ecclesiastical documents, the Baron Achilles Paganini made hasty arrangements for still another journey of his father's bones. They were to be removed from the improvised graveyard on the family's estate in Parma to the Catholic cemetery several kilometers away.

He hoped it would be the final journey. Thirty-six years, massive bribery, and the indignation of the rich had at last infused justice with compassion.

"Must we?" pouted the Baroness Paola. Even after bearing twelve children, she continued to remind her husband of an irrepressible duckling.

"I'm afraid so."

"Sometimes good things come too late," she philosophized. "Do we have to wear black?"

"Only for a few hours. In the church and at the graveside. Both gravesides."

"I look comical in black."

"So you do."

Andrea was in France pursuing a Russian lady twice his age; Niccolò, swollen with mumps; and Giovanni had fallen from a horse. Only Attila, at nineteen, seemed vaguely interested in the proceedings. His little brother, Riccardo, merely sulked and obeyed. It was difficult, apparently, to impress children, even with their own pedigree.

"Does this mean Grandfather was not a sinner?" Attila wanted to know. Half imp, half theologian, he had been offering only token resistance to his mother's decision that he need not become a Jesuit.

"Don't be irreverent," yawned the Baron, scratching.

"Well, then, what does it mean?"

"It means that the decision of the Bishop of Nice, promulgated in 1840, has been revoked. We may now bury my father in hallowed ground."

"But that was more than thirty years ago. I wasn't even born."

"Fortunately," said Achilles, "*I* was born."

THE LEATHER-LINED BERLIN rambled up the carriage road, its foggy windows muffling the swish of rain and wind. Paola told her husband that if the storm did not subside, she would under no circumstance step outside at the improvised graveyard on the grounds of the Villa Gaione. The Baron glanced at the bald and bespectacled priest, who shrugged obligingly. Achilles conceded there was no reason why she ought to.

The tomb lay in a grove of towering elm trees near the crumbling outer wall of the estate. Several carriages awaited them there, the occupants invisible. Accompanied by the priest, the Baron, Attila, and Riccardo stepped into the driving rain and huddled by the open grave during an abbreviated prayer of commitment. They did not linger, leaving the gravediggers to raise the coffin and the priest to conclude all decencies.

Attila led his father to the family carriage. Then, noticing a rich black brougham parked nearby, he dashed toward it across the watery pathway.

"I am Attila Paganini," he shouted into the carriage, for the rain roared like surf. "Permit me to thank you in the name of my father, the Baron Achilles, for your kindness. Are we acquainted?"

A very ancient lady, heavily scented, looked down upon him. "A grandson?" she queried in a deep, melodic voice that cracked slightly.

"Yes, *Signora.*"

"I knew your grandfather, of course."

"Your name, *Signora*?"

"But then, many knew him after a manner. That was so long ago."

"He has been dead thirty-six years."

"Well, do not stand there like an idiot getting chilled to the bone!" scolded the old woman. "Isn't someone waiting for you?"

In a single, imperious gesture, she waved him away and ordered the coachman to proceed, lurching forward as the carriage started, its wheels spattering mud over Attila's elegant mourning.

"You're filthy!" cried the Baroness when he rejoined them. She wiped her son's face with her lace shawl. "Oh, we'll never wring him dry! Who was that?"

"A very old woman."

Baron Achilles nodded. "Of course. When the body lay in the pest-house at Nice, neatly embalmed and covered with canvas but without a resting place, droves of women came to visit. They bribed the guards….Which one?"

"She didn't leave her name."

The Baron stared out at the gravesite. The bald priest stood beneath a black umbrella, mumbling prayers in Latin as the soaked gravediggers hauled on their ropes. "And at Saint-Ferréol, a small mound between rocks and ocean, unmarked—they left flowers. Was she an Italian?"

"At that age, it's impossible to tell. She must have been a hundred."

Paola laughed. "That means upward of forty."

"No, no, she is much older than you."

"And in Genoa," continued Baron Achilles. "I was there when the little pirogue arrived, bearing his remains—the *Maria Magdalena.* No fewer than a dozen ladies stood at the water's edge."

"Oh, nonsense!" declared his Baroness. "You are becoming mawkish and sentimental."

"And when negotiations with the Vatican broke down, and I had him removed to the villa—"

"More ladies, I suppose?"

"The Grand Duchess Marie Louise herself, may her soul rest in peace. But it is no use talking to any of you. I have spent thirty years petitioning for a few feet of consecrated earth for my father's remains, and you—and you—" Baron Achilles looked from one bland countenance to another; only Attila seemed attentive.

"Why all these women, Father? Were there none he truly loved?"

The Baron glanced at his son, a vague and distant look in his eyes. "My father had a mistress, but not of flesh and blood."

"Oh please, don't start!" snapped the Baroness, fussily arranging her skirts.

"My dear. We must give the Devil his due."

Attila's eyes nearly burst from his head. "Is that why the Bishop of Nice—?"

"I will not tolerate these fabrications!" the Baroness insisted.

They heard voices quarreling outside. With his little hand, Riccardo wiped fog from the window and peered out into the rain.

At the tomb, something appeared awry. The priest was arguing with a long-faced official while the three mud-smeared gravediggers looked on, the disinterred coffin at their feet. "What is it?" the Baron inquired.

Attila jumped out of the carriage into the rain. His mother called after him, but to no avail. "That boy will be the death of me," she lamented.

A moment later Attila returned, his eyes bright. "The authorities demand that the coffin be reopened. The magistrate must be called. It will be at least an hour, maybe two. There are some papers …" His father frowned. Always the authorities. Health or taxes, or the church.

Paola searched the windows of the waiting carriages. "We certainly don't need to open it here."

Achilles agreed. "At the church, then." He climbed from the carriage, opened his umbrella, and walked out to talk with the men. Attila followed him.

"Do they open the graves of all heretics, Father?"

"Your grandfather was not a heretic."

"But you said—"

"I said his—" The Baron stopped, looked at his son. He could see the boy was genuinely curious. "Wait here, Attila."

He walked out to the men, exchanged some words with them. The official shrugged, showing open palms, and the priest, gruffly wiping the fog from his glasses, marched back toward the carriage. The Baron nodded to the gravediggers and then followed the priest, gesturing for Attila to join him.

"Come, my fine one. It's time you heard the truth about your grandfather. I've a good long story to tell."

❉ ❉ ❉

"Walk?!" cried the Baroness when she heard of their plans. "You cannot walk! It is too far—and the rain!"

"Merely a drizzle," said the Baron, scanning the clouds.

The priest pulled the door shut, but the Baroness threw open the window. "He might be getting mumps—everyone hereabouts has mumps!"

"I'll be all right, Mother. I promise."

The Baron laid his hand on the shoulder of his son. "We'll see you at the cathedral," he told his wife. His fluttering palm dismissed the carriage, which lurched up the road.

The Baroness craned her head out the window. "Don't you listen to those stories of your father's!" she pleaded. "Nonsense! All nonsense!"

The black berlin rolled off into the rain, and the two began their walk beneath the sheltering umbrella.

PART ONE
THE PRINCESS OF LUCCA

1
THE COURT FIDDLER

Lucca had changed. Lucca had been crossed by a meteor. Only a few years ago, the phenomenon had appeared over Parisian rooftops; soon, all Italy disintegrated in homage. Was the trail of light a sign from Heaven? Or was it an omen of evil, a fiery portent of Hell? Time would tell; history alone gave face to the Devil.

Little Lucca, as was fit, seethed with freshly minted revolution. Bloodless, merry, strewing oleander and roses, and gushing fine rhetoric, Lucca had thrown herself into the arms of the conqueror, in this instance Elisa Marianna Bacciochi, born Bonaparte. Erect and imperious, the Emperor's sister reviewed the troops of her petty principality astride a horse (alas for the Jacobins!); she outswore and outshouted her frenetic workmen; she set herself to the task of founding a new Athens and perpetuating her brother's, if scarcely her husband's, name.

Niccolò Paganini remembered the old Lucca that had vanished in the night: sedate, patrician, full of studied graciousness and gracious ways. He had come for work; the musician is neither Jacobin nor royalist, freeman nor slave. He follows the good clink of francs and scudi, and keeps his own counsel—if he can. Lucca had basked in a late summer splendor. Niccolò would never forget his first heady draughts of the city, the dappled facades, twittering balconies, vast, unexpectedly sumptuous churches, and above all, the festivals, for Luccans celebrated their relics as well as their saints, always with pomp and processionals, candles, torches, fireworks, the shuffling of sacerdotal feet, the medieval garb exhumed, mended, and hastily adapted to aristocratic haunches. And, of course, the inevitable music competitions, which fertilized Lucca with new names, songs, and faces, as all Italy's aspirants came to vie for purse and honors.

He had competed—Niccolò Paganini of Genoa, third of twenty-seven. Well, enough of that. Contests are never wholly fair, because they are never wholly free, always tethered to a chain of persons, conditions, and considerations. The hurt had healed, though for a time it seemed incurable, and Niccolò emerged with something better than the plaudits of a single victory: a permanent chair in Lucca's finest orchestra, the *Capella Nazionale*, and one for Carlo, his brother. He had had to bargain for Carlo, the weaker, already virtually a bridegroom; their father, Antonio, had insisted, threatening not to surrender his immature younger son without the watchful accompaniment—Niccolò viewed it as spying—of the elder.

Lucca had brought success of a sort, even before the boot-thump and the drumbeat of the new century. Twelve scudi a month—relative riches; opportunities to be heard and known, to make one's uniqueness felt; freedom in all its sweetness and ramification.

Lucca had given him friends: the easy, envious camaraderie of musicians. And best of all, he had found here a substitute family, the Quilici—not, unfortunately, of the great musical dynasty of Lucca, though somewhat distantly related—a gay, hearty, unstrained, unstraining band who loved him not for his promise of accomplishment, but because he was Niccolò and of their world.

The father was a mere postilion, but (unlike Antonio Paganini) not embittered by his hard, irregular life and affluent relatives. Daughter Anna Bucchianeri and her family made their home in the parental quarters, facing the side entrance of the church. Scarcely a dozen years older than Niccolò, Anna conveyed a lusty maternal affection, which he could accept and relish without the sense of unworthiness his own mother provoked in him. Bartolomeo, the son, had been a captain in the grenadiers—dull, charming, more elegant than his station condoned, pursued by errant wives, unwed girls, and enterprising mothers. Another married daughter lived with her immense brood on the other side of the square.

For a time, Paganini made his home with them. Even after leaving, he sustained a strange, not too clearly defined friendship for the Quilici and Bucchianeri. They were his own, his nearest and dearest, yet presenting none of the abrasions that somehow attend family life. He loved them, in truth, more than Carlo or Nicoletta or Domenica, though with these there was the blood-tie to be reckoned with, deeper than affection or passion, as all the world knows.

The child, Eleonora Quilici, had lifted huge, densely fringed, habitually downcast eyes upon him, shyly, yet with a certain slyness and unutterable longing and love. But the complexity of his bond, imagined or real, with the family had confused Niccolò. For the first time in his life, he was ashamed of his own spurt of lust, for she was too little, too very much his own, to despoil. He had contented himself with stroking her, consoling her, running hot, moist fingers through her tangled hair, whispering silly, half-remembered truisms about eternal love and the dedication of the artist. A tear had zigzagged down the thin, little cheek to the mouth's corner, and the child (how old could she have been? Fourteen?) raised herself to brush his lips with her own and utter a great, hollow, resigned sob before turning swiftly away.

Thereafter, she had viewed him furtively, always in sorrow, contriving never to confront him. Desire chafed, and pity; and pity proved the stronger. After all, the world overflowed with willing women; one need not stoop to pluck one's very nest. Yet one paid a price for the withholding of love, as for its indulgence. And Eleonora's abundance of love, pure, unasked for, sealed forever within the velvet of her small person, continued to undermine him. He was moved and at the same time repelled. He was angry that love was, in the final analysis, so inherently meaningless. He had not willed it so, but it was so. Like the gift of his talent, like the meteor that had soared over Lucca, her love had arisen on the whim of the gods—or of the Devil himself. Lust degenerated into a guilty tenderness. Niccolò amused the company by improvising on the guitar and inscribing florid dedications to Eleonora. "But I prefer the violin," she declared.

She became a mild reproach, an indebtedness he could never shed. A thin film blurred his bond with the second family. A great honor had been accorded him—to be godfather to the Bucchianeri male infant who was to bear his name. Niccolò cringed. He did not know how to refuse, and he meekly consented, standing properly beside the heavy, affluent aunt who shared his spiritual obligation, and trying not to look at the babe. Because his feelings were unresolved, both as to religion (he, too, had been singed, if but briefly, by the Goddess of Reason) and the family, he found the experience disconcerting. But there followed gaiety and feasting, gluttonous delicacies, and dancing, clapping, and song in the narrow, crowded house opposite the *Piazza San Michele*. Eleonora laughed and looked into his eyes with her great, sad eyes, then quickly away, and Niccolò wondered whether he would always be aware of her as of a chafing chain beneath his underclothing, or a pinching shoe, or a mark upon his brow.

THE NEW SOVEREIGN was annoyed. She detested the nearly perpetual pealing of the bells from Lucca's seventy-five churches. Dawn to eventide, the hours were marked and fragmented by high, low, tinkly, mellow, or most solemn proclamations from more or less concerted belfries.

The princess was a woman with an imperial vision and a proclivity for headaches. Moreover, Elisa was violently anticlerical. She resented the delicate tension of quarrels, proclamations, severances, and rapprochements, which she designated—fiercely—her brother's "temporizing" with the Pope. Even Niccolò's fiddling, incorporated into the Luccan court as soon as the revolutionary regime had taken over, often invoked extremes of scratchiness or sensitivity. "Peace, I must have peace!" she would bellow in the sarcastic yet ingenuously frontal manner she had perfected. Or piously, in the style of a rejected text, "Let there be air!"—*air* being Elisa's familiar term for freedom, serenity, and an end to theological darkness and cant.

Yet the phosphorescent quiet of Lucca's evenings and nights made her restless. She would seek diversion in travel throughout her tiny domain, excitement in the *Bagni di Lucca*, the nearby watering place, or bed-pleasure, at which, as Niccolò well knew, she was brusque, marvelously competent, and indiscriminate. Niccolò reveled in her favors yet disapproved of her. He found her outrageous and masculine when she designated a consort for an hour or a night among the baseborn. In ecstasy, she reminded him of the dock girls of Genoa, eager to snare a few coins, a crude meal, or a few moments of titillation. A true princess, Niccolò supposed, mated ceremonially, with a meticulous regard for pedigree. But Elisa surely recalled hard times in Ajaccio or, more recently, plebeian Marseilles in a war-ravaged land. She had not always been Princess of Lucca and Piombino.

The position of chief musician to the court proved no sinecure. True to their bourgeois origins, the Bacciochi were never lavish, save to themselves. Niccolò had frequent occasion to lament the old days, when he had but to play pages of music set before him. Now, there were concerts three times a week, music to ferret out or compose, mutinous professors to flatter, cajole, and rehearse, and operas to prepare. The princess doted on opera, but found its Italian manifestations gross, naive, and wanting in the modern spirit.

And, most onerous of all, there was Prince Felix to teach. Elisa's husband proved a violinist of boundless enthusiasm and energy, and an infallibly bad ear. In his absent-minded way, he seemed a decent fellow, preferring the society of books to the amusements of Elisa's miniature Versailles. Legalities of the Napoleonic legacy, however, had relegated him, in and with respect to Lucca, to the subsidiary role he already enjoyed within his own household.

Elisa Marianna held court, ruled the small, somnolent principalities Napoleon had grudgingly granted her, and played her diverse roles. She might be, as the spirit moved, severe and intellectual, a desexed blue-stocking of uncertain age, and founder of the new Academy dedicated to the moral and aesthetic uplift of Lucca and its people. The following day might find her soft, teary, nervous, and reduced to cruelty or hysterics over an imaginary slight by a younger or prettier woman. She was Napoleon's deputy, avenging angel of the revolution, closing down the monasteries, equalizing all men before the law, establishing schools that all might understand the correct nature of things, courageously mustering and drilling her armies of righteousness. She was queen of the revels, presiding at sumptuous dinners and balls, or bending fervently with small screams of joy, anger, or frustration over her game of faro or roulette, until the dawn broke.

Luccans were shocked when Elisa demolished the ancient church of Santa Magdalena to create the *Piazza Napoleone*. The aristocrats grumbled as she courted them assiduously on the one hand and curtailed their comfortable feudal privileges on the other. Her zoological gardens and fountains (for which the very course of the Frago had to be diverted) amused a populace heady with freedom from immemorial levies and nuisance taxes, and intoxicated by the notion, if not the fact, of liberty, equality, and fraternity.

Elisa loved her likeness and the likenesses of her family on coins and busts, mosaics and murals; the little city buzzed with artistic endeavor. She had roads built, because she had to get about; reopened the neglected quarries of Carrara to provide marble for her projects; imported from the land of Marco Polo trays of strange worms to excrete silk for the well-born, the well-married, and those whose revolutionary fortunes had turned over safely and well.

She had acquired summer palaces in Viarregio and Piombino, but these did not satisfy her. She wanted something more: an ultimate in terms of beauty, value, novelty, capacity to impress and startle. She nagged poor Felix, whose opinions and decisions could not have been more optional. She wrote plaintively, tragically, insistently to the Emperor. Eventually, she procured Marlia, the villa of a defunct count: a venerable estate that had fallen upon lean years. The transformation of Marlia from weeded acreage, cobwebs, and mold to the first country seat in the world (in the English manner, to be sure; Elisa detested the British, but not their landscape artistry) absorbed the princess's energies for more than a year. Closeted with the distinguished Bienaime, Napoleon's most generally acknowledged contribution to the Bacciochi, and several of his Italian architectural colleagues, the Princess of Lucca found contentment of a sort and the conviction that she, too, was a creator.

"Tell me, Paganini. Do you ever burgeon, or swell, when you perform?"

She pointed to his genitals, her meaning clear. It could have been mere intellectual curiosity.

"Never, *Principessa.*"

"Why, then. What would happen to this glorious Italian sausage if I asked you to play for me right now?"

As if you aren't asking me to play right now, he thought. But he answered, "I'm sorry, *Principessa*, but I can play only one fiddle at a time."

"Then play it right here. Here. At the very gates of paradise, no? How do you say that on the streets? Is it *purchiacca?*"

"That's as good a term as any," he said sliding into her steamy body with ease. "We Italians…The Neapolitans say *fessa* or *cecca*. In Calabria—"

But his regal mistress was no longer listening. Her mouth was open, her eyes lasciviously glazed; she thrashed about like a bitch in heat.

Oddly, he felt like holding back his momentum and intensifying her desire till it turned to agony. He bit into her neck, unconcerned about tomorrow's evidence. He gently teased the erect nipple of her left breast. But he was himself terribly aroused. Not the princess herself— God, no, he had certainly known better—but the sheer triumph of circumstance. He, Niccolò Paganini, attached to the Luccan court for its careless amusement, scarcely more than a servant, bedding down with the sister of Napoleon Bonaparte! How could he tell *that* to his father, who grumbled about his failure and inadequacy?

But no, he mustn't crest too soon. Last time, she had forced him to continue through the little death—*le petit mort*, in the French she preferred—coaxing him to utter exhaustion. And on other occasions, the noble princess had ordered him to eat her after his own climax. The smelly essences in his mouth trickled down his chin. No, she was a very whore! And the glory of being her musical stud led nowhere. Of this he was becoming certain.

He pumped savagely, trying to inflict hurt. How she shuddered! How guttural! What a pig, this would-be goddess!

But Elisa was ahead of him. Blasphemies and oaths in both French and that abominable Corsican dialect announced her fulfillment. Whereupon Niccolò likewise catapulted to climax, feeling diminished, humiliated, and used.

Regaining composure quickly, Elisa dismissed him with hardly a glance. "And don't play those insipid variations again tonight."

* * *

Paganini had come to the Bacciochi court with trepidation. Scarcely had he established himself within the old Luccan world when it disintegrated. The new *Capella Nazionale* dissolved, as did the older orchestra, the players scattering to find a living elsewhere. Gone was the warm, relaxed patronage of the church; the churches trembled for their lives as Napoleon grappled with the Holy Father. Niccolò's first Luccan performance had been at a solemn pontifical mass celebrated by Archbishop Sardi; he had been censured for performing a sonata of half an hour's duration, unprecedentedly florid and full of pyrotechnical bravura, after the Kyrie.

Niccolò scorned the simple piety of women and children; it used to embarrass him when Teresa, his mother, informed all who would listen that musical genius had been guaranteed her second son, shortly before his birth, by an angel in a dream. But the Church, true or false, seemed an indispensable and comforting backdrop, the natural setting of Italy. And in Italy, one could live with contradictions. One could embrace all gods, pagan, Christian, revolutionary, and those yet to appear in the ferment of the churning times. One did not need to be consistent.

The court, at first, had awed him; then, he was amused. From first to last, however, he felt insecure, conspicuously the upstart. Perhaps this was due to the princess's unpredictability, her swift decisions and precipitous reversals, her fine Napoleonic talent for rewarding and punishing at nearly the same time. Toward the end, contempt—quiet, repressed, always concealed from others—made the burdens perfunctory and light. He knew himself superior to any task assigned him and grew reckless with the knowledge.

But before that there had been much to learn. *Politesse* first; Elisa was a product of St. Cyr, the aristocratic school established by *Mme.* de Maintenan. It was said that Napoleon regarded it as the source of all her pretensions. Whatever the cause, Elisa's insistence upon etiquette was formidable. Niccolò resisted briefly but then began shrewdly to imitate his betters. To make one's way in the world—and he fervently hoped to—one could not employ the jargon of the Genoese waterfront. And even in the quarters of the professors of music—in Lucca every half-educated trumpeter called himself professor and felt it his right to be so called—one heard little of value.

Niccolò had long used French and Italian currency interchangeably, as did everyone he knew. He now began to shape neat French phrases and deliver them in a tolerable accent. Here and there his speech was splashed with a French word or sentence or epigram. French was not difficult; it was but garbled Italian spoken through the nose. Prince Felix, despite his excruciating intonation once he tucked a violin under his chin, proved a fine mentor. Of a naturally pedagogical nature, he corrected all errors with automatic amiability and a genuine desire to share. Like the Bonapartes, he was a Corsican, neither French nor Italian, but surely a little of both.

It was rumored that Felix Bacciochi (or Pasquale, the name given him by his family) had been acquired by Elisa after several earlier affairs, some scandalous, others purely ambitious, had come to a dead end. There was little doubt that in the Napoleonic scheme of things, Felix would remain a nonentity. Elisa possessed, and proudly, the cavalier manner of her brother. She resembled him in face and ambition, in temperament and in love. Were she a man, she, too, in boots and tricorne, would fling women to the floor of carriages. Not being a man—and the princess often deplored this—she ordered men to her chambers with a total absence of coyness and mystery. She had varied appetites, Niccolò learned, and was even more erratic in her pleasures than in presiding over the affairs of her modest territory. Like a man, she quaffed out of sheer thirst; whether from a sweet spring or a muddy one, it did not seem to matter. Yet she could be sugary and yielding, almost girlish, when the spirit moved; or scornful and contemptuous as a man with a woman whose favors he has bought; or as indifferent in the act of love as in blowing her nose.

None of this enhanced her to Niccolò. After the novelty of cohabitating with a Bonaparte princess had worn thin, he aspired to her favor only because it represented security of a sort, a sign that he was rendering satisfaction. He resented being her quarry, deprived of the joy of the chase and the glory of manly conquest. He was Elisa's sometime lover, not by his own longing or choice, but by her royal designation. He was no lover at all, but a lackey ordered occasionally to give of his substance, and the mate of a queen bee or a devouring mantis. At any moment, this bizarre woman might weary of her prey and regurgitate it.

Against that day, he must be prepared.

❊ ❊ ❊

"It is not that I long for Genoa," Carlo explained in his earnest, plodding way. He bit into an overripe plum, then wiped his chin and waistcoat with his handkerchief. "But Annina is again with child. The others, as you know, were born in my absence."

"Well, you are no midwife." Niccolò indulged a gigantic yawn. He argued with his brother solely for the sake of form. It was a nicety both were observing, one that would eventually be conveyed to their father. For Antonio would expect, as a matter of decency and kinship, that Niccolò do all in his power to keep Carlo with him.

"True, I am no midwife," Carlo repeated unsmilingly. He reasoned further, "But it is seemly that a father attend the birth of his sons. And daughters, even. Barring war and disaster, of course."

"Of course."

"What I mean to say …" Carlo had a veritable genius for not getting to the point. "The new austerities will, I am informed, drastically affect the size of the orchestra."

"I know."

"You know?"

Niccolò shrugged. He had sensed the forthcoming reduction in his forces for months and had been wondering just when the blow would fall. It would have been too much to expect that the princess call a halt to the building ventures and monuments. The Emperor's bounty had long been dissipated, and the Bacciochi continued to flourish by means of an intricate system of credit coupled with genteel confiscations.

"I know, I know—you might suppose it would be customary to inform me," Niccolò said crossly. He was aware of his deliberate ambiguity, intending Carlo to suppose he had been advised of the dismissals, which was not actually the case. The director of orchestra had not been consulted on the staffing of his forces. Elisa was given to consulting no one.

"You put in a good word—you tried?" Carlo asked pathetically.

Niccolò grimaced. "I didn't say I was asked."

"No, of course not, of course not." Carlo moistened his lips, gone parched since the plum pit had been deposited. "Father will be disappointed."

This was an understatement. Antonio Paganini would be wrathful. He might, moreover, be convinced that Niccolò had played some sinister part in the ousting of Carlo, if only by failing to fly to his defense or designating another victim in Carlo's stead.

"One cannot create conditions of life to gratify him," said Niccolò. "He has no right to expect that."

"He has sustained many sorrows."

"The world is unpredictable."

"From me he expected nothing," Carlo said flatly. "My talents are meager. Always he wished he had a more reliable trade to teach me." It was difficult to decide whether Carlo harbored bitterness. Could one thus accept mediocrity and the low assessment of others without even a small struggle? "But for you I think he had great hope."

"I trust I shall not betray it."

"I mean—" Carlo gestured. Thought and gesture dissolved in prudence.

"Yes, you mean. You mean what he meant. That even as a child, Wolfgang Amadeus Mozart enriched his father."

"The name still an open wound," Carlo deplored.

"Ground into my flesh," Niccolò agreed. "Remind Father, when you return, that Mozart lies in an unmarked pauper's grave. It is good for him to remember occasionally."

"I did not say the name."

"And that there is little likelihood that this is going to happen to Niccolò Paganini."

"Calm yourself. I am not Father," Carlo reminded him.

In a more controlled voice, Niccolò completed his thought, grinning. "Tell him his second son will yet be the Bonaparte of violinists."

Carlo laughed at the analogy, which seemed to annoy his brother.

"Does it not seem plausible? Will he demand a dukedom, perhaps, or will mere money suffice?"

"It is I who am returning home a mendicant, not you."

"I'll give you what I have," Niccolò sighed. "Arrive in triumph. At least enjoy a few days' peace." Carlo's weak, watery eyes stabbed Niccolò with a confusion of feelings: affection, pity, exasperation.

"It is not Father who concerns me," Niccolò continued, his voice rising. "It's Mother. She suffers for him. And for us. And for herself."

"She believes you have been touched by God."

"Oh, at least," muttered Niccolò.

He paused. The story of Teresa's vision would always annoy him; and from Carlo's flat, cautious statement, he recognized that it annoyed Carlo, too. "I do not like to think of her in *Passo del Gato Moro*."

Alley of the Black Cat. Memory of his Genoese boyhood welled up in him, sharp, racking, horribly luminous: the crooked up-and-down stairs of the streets, the stench, the cooking odors, the encrusted poverty and dirt. He remembered the hot summer cobblestones under his feet, the lowing dock sounds drifting hazily over the squalor, the eerie Mediterranean fog so swiftly and serenely lifted, the profusion of slithering black cats that gave the alleyway its name. Surely there were witches nearby: hideous, toothless hags who sent forth their creatures to be fed, or at least so ran the old wives' tales of the district. Otherwise, why so many cats, all sinister, marauding, belonging to no one, dark as night and evil? Perhaps *Passo del Gato Moro* rose upon the rocks that concealed Hell itself, or some anterior land peopled by Hell's weird sisters.

Niccolò's tortured recollections of childhood appeared inevitably in an aura of cat smells, slow, sinuous cat movements, mating sobs, jungle howls, viscous cat languor. More lacerating, though he acknowledged his indebtedness to them, were his parents' hopes: Antonio's subtle cruelty and Teresa's conspicuous, compounded martyrdom. He, Niccolò, had been singled out to enrich the house and to give it a great name and an upsurge in fortune that genius alone renders conceivable. And here he was, after the early acclaim, the promise, the prophecies, the obsessive discipline, the discoveries: a jester in a petty court, precariously favored, buried within tapestried walls, performing pretty antics for a handful of effete men and scented women.

Niccolò rose and placed his hand on Carlo's shoulder. "Return safely," he murmured. Niccolò extracted his drawstring purse and handed it in a lordly manner to his brother. "My love to our mother."

"I shall tell them of your successes, Niccolò."

Niccolò nodded. "Tell them, but not too specifically, that I enjoy many favors from the *principessa*."

"Of course."

"And may Annina be safely delivered of a healthy son."

"As God wills."

"One must occasionally pit one's will against God's," Niccolò suggested. "It is the spirit of our age."

"For some of us," Carlo floundered.

"Yes, you are right. For some of us," said Niccolò.

The Bonaparte of violinists, he had said, with just a trace of uneasy levity. And yet, even as Carlo's footsteps echoed down the stairs, he was pervaded by an overwhelming certitude.

He saw himself alone on a wild crag, glory in his heart, defiance in his fists, and knew with marvelous clairvoyance his singularity and power and strength.

For here, out of the amorphous ages, rose a new century, a time of infinite hope and possibilities. And all the old stances would wither: all notions of the good, the just, the beautiful, the fixed order of things. Earth and the heavens had but dissembled; now the truth burst forth from the cadaver of ancient days in torrent and in flame. And everything was possible. Yes, yes, this would be the miracle of the new century; everything *would* be possible.

Europe was ripe for the worship of the human will.

The old gods had died; God himself seemed shaken into an uneasy dependence on Man. Resolutely, the Corsican had shown the way. He had appeared from nowhere and had bent the world—monarchies, peoples, boundaries, armies, the Holy See itself—to his will.

The will, Niccolò thought. The will, the wings to will. The recognition was swift and instantaneous.

He, too, would appear from nowhere and bend the world to his purpose. He would possess vast power over the hearts of men and women. This, after all, might prove the sturdier hegemony. This was the bone-marrow of his strivings: to know power and to wield it.

And gold, he thought, remembering that he had flung away a purse. *And gold!* For suddenly he was sick of poverty and hunger. And of his grubby beginnings. And of the fawning, ingratiation, and unease of the Bacciochi court.

Power. Fame. Fortune. For these he would give his very soul. Niccolò felt a sudden, strange uncoiling within him. With a shriek of pain, he doubled over, staggering against the wall of his candle-lit chamber. For a moment, he thought it a recurrence of his childhood weakness, that clamping, perpetual hurt in his chest that his father had thought perverse and deserving of beatings. But the abrupt violence of this attack was altogether different. The spasms felt like a birthing in his breast, a paroxysmal liberation of some long-hidden dark power. A creature clawed within, ravenous, insatiable, feeding on the blood that surged through his heart, sucking the air from his lungs, gripping his limbs with tentacles of pain. Niccolò fell to the floor, helpless, his consciousness swiftly slipping away. The room was swallowed into a black void, infinite, impenetrable. Out of this darkness, nightmares emerged.

When he awoke, hours later, a heap of sweating flesh on the cold floorboards, he could not remember how long he had been there, or what he had dreamed. The nightmares were gone; only a vague uneasiness remained, a sickening feeling that some transgression had taken place, some evil undoing. He felt a faint dripping in the hollow of his heart, and something else—a burning coldness, like swallowed ice. He ripped open his shirt, rubbed his hand over his chest to warm his blood. He was alone in the room, yet he did not feel alone. Something stirred inside him, restless, embryonic, locked in the prison of his rounded ribs.

As if it were waiting, he thought. Waiting for sleep to set it free.

2
I Capricci

THE PYRAMIDS OF EGYPT could not have been undertaken with greater fanaticism and urgency, or with less regard for the expendables whose blood and brawn went into the mortar. Reconstructed Marlia appeared, a roseate pearl against the intense blue sky and the shrill green and russet hills. Once the princess had committed herself, once content with the plans, her impatience for results became the nightmare of those condemned to her energetic presence.

The great of the world bestir themselves frequently, Niccolò learned. It was but a diversion for Elisa, Felix, and the court to move from one seat to another, transporting cooks and food and clothing and servants and the remnants of the former orchestra. Decisions were made hastily, with little regard for the seasons. "Oppressive!" became Elisa's cry of liberation: meaning, she must rush forth to yet another dwelling, survey her rutted roads and her people going about their business as though there had been no revolution, and compile an inventory of specific abuses. The bourgeoise sovereign could be depended upon to encounter indolence, thievery, and neglect on the part of the house servants. Every gardener and every chambermaid knew her ire and recognized that wealth recently accrued is wealth most assiduously guarded; after a few generations, it ceases to matter whether a plant has quietly withered or a whiff of scent vanished.

The clowns and jesters, as Niccolò secretly thought of his pitiful band of remaining musicians, found themselves transplanted at whim and compelled to provide novelty and amusement for a fickle court. And in the providing, Niccolò learned another thing: What is gratuitously given is held cheaply. It seemed often that he was scooping out the very possibilities of sound itself; that in his quest for the new, the unfamiliar, the hitherto unrealized, he was pouring out upon these painted marionettes all the aural treasures of time past and of the unborn centuries. He might have been dozing in a stable like any sodden groom for all that they noticed.

The princess, of course, knew his worth and sometimes even condescended to admit it. "You are Italy's first fiddler, my funny one, and perhaps the world's," she would murmur amorously. "But what's a fiddler?" and she would smile like a sated, uninquisitive cat playing idly with a mouse. "You should have found your way to the military college. These are times for generals."

"There are many kinds of generals," Niccolò bantered.

"No," said Elisa. "Only the victorious and the vanquished."

Child of the city streets, bred on Genoa's cobblestones and steep alleyways, accustomed to the briny wharf odors and the bustle of the rough port, Niccolò was unprepared for Marlia. He had traveled to and from the cities of the north—Florence, Pisa, Livorno, Bologna (always guarded by the greedy Antonio)—and viewed with impassivity, for his concerns lay elsewhere, the close-tufted hills and sparkling waterways and yielding, over-worked Italian earth. But Marlia was different. Marlia was no mere glory of generous and fecund nature. It was Nature's tribute to the conqueror. It was affluent man's final and definitive victory over Nature itself.

The broad avenue flanked by magnificent, perfectly symmetrical poplars—rows upon rows of poplars, beyond one's imagining of them for sheer height and strength and numbers—led to an arched gateway where old stone blended in dignity with the ironmonger's craft. Entrance was discreetly guarded; within her cushioned carriage,

Elisa nodded correctly to the tricorne standing in ramrod salute and passed on, her entourage following. Prince Felix might be taking his exercise alongside the carriage on horseback; more often, he sat opposite his wife, knees akimbo, dozing over a volume of philosophy.

About Marlia, there was an iridescence, a flawlessness that transcended accident or art. The ancient structure rose fresh and new in the filtered sunlight, polished as a rare and precious gem. The lake, man-made, stocked with brilliants, streaked and shimmered with the lyrical movement of black and white swans. Varied and intricate, the gardens sprawled in vast geometrics. Here and there, a few deer nibbled, or gazelles; a lethargic, blazing peacock might strut casually among a profusion of lesser birds. The floral groupings were marvelously precise, matching the symmetry of trees and hedges, and calculated to bloom the greater part of the year, often in affined groups of contrasting textures and colors. In late February, when Paganini first accompanied his mistress to Marlia, the vision of a grove of blossoming magnolia, pink, wounded-white, and fierce purple, proved more than the street urchin of Genoa could absorb with equanimity. Marlia's beauty was assaultive.

As was, in her unpredictable way, the Princess of Lucca.

"What do you really think of Marlia?" she demanded gruffly of the gentle, self-effacing *Madame* Laplace, wife of the mathematician/ astronomer infelicitously turned minister.

"Most exquisite, *Madame*," murmured that lady with deep sincerity and a certain guardedness, for Elisa did not really care what anyone thought.

"How does it compare with, say, Malmaison?"

Madame Laplace began to understand. "They—they are different, one from another," she said.

Elisa offered a gelid stare while her anger mounted, and *Madame* Laplace continued to explain patiently, "Each supernal, each in its own way."

"You are a liar!" screamed Elisa. "You are secretly smirking, all of you! You are saying that Josephine has exquisite taste!"

The blood drained from the good, honest countenance of the astronomer's wife. "No, *Madame*, you do us both an injustice," she whispered with difficulty.

"*I!* I commit an injustice!" Elisa was beside herself. "Out of my sight! Out, before I dispatch you to Paris in disgrace!"

Yet she would tolerate no fawning, nor the dishonest flattery she secretly yearned to hear and whose falsity never failed to offend. She begged for it, presented traps to the unwary; but once the offering was made, she smothered her victims in self-righteous rage.

The Marchesa Camilla Mansi, an erstwhile favorite, praised the new estate in her flamboyant, south Italian way. Camilla began sincerely enough but was carried away by her rhetoric and her sovereign's initial glee. She found Marlia insultingly superior to all the more-or-less-alike villas of Italy. Versailles, by comparison, might be viewed as a dusty mausoleum, and Malmaison as beneath contempt. The Empress was indeed *reputed* to have good taste; but in such matters she displayed a discernible provincialism or, at any rate, an absence of the worldliness and originality of the Princess of Lucca.

From the best our world had to offer, the Marchesa progressed to the Garden of Eden, surely a rough, thrown-together affair in comparison with Marlia, which was far better arranged and tolerated no serpents. Elisa became visibly edgy, but Camilla was determined to rave on to the ultimate absurdity. Paradise, she declared devoutly, could but echo Marlia in details of loveliness. Either the princess, in conceiving the place (the landscape architects were forgotten), had experienced a beatific vision of our final reward, or Heaven itself would need rearrangement.

"Imbecile! You should be horsewhipped!" Elisa shrieked.

But an hour later, she demanded to know—and with apparent humility—how a certain dress of green-gold damask "looked." Poor

Olimpia Fatinelli panicked at the query. Young as she was, she sensed the consequence of every possible reply.

"Well?" bellowed Elisa. "What's wrong with it?" She paraded haughtily before the stricken girl to better display the dress. She seemed genuinely to want to know, but one could never be certain.

"N-nothing, *Principessa*," stammered Olimpia. "It is very beautiful."

For this, she was rewarded with an hysterical slap on the cheek, as Elisa proceeded to rip the gown from her narrow shoulders and yell opprobrium and obscenities at her dressmaker.

❈ ❈ ❈

HE WOULD HAVE PREFERRED that she be less assaultive, too, in bestowing her favors upon him.

He could not, of course, pursue her as he might a woman of the lower classes, view her dotingly, draw upon the entire arsenal of obvious pursuit. Yet the etiquette of the palace admitted countless manifestations of mock-courtly love, and Niccolò would have been glad to offer these as respect. With a mistress such as Elisa, this was impossible.

She made no obeisance to niceties, even before people. Her appetites, she made promptly clear, were as capricious as her temper or her ambition. St. Cyr had given her pretensions. The Napoleonic coup had endowed her with authority. But the revolution had emancipated Elisa, not so much from notions of female chastity as from the proprieties that attend the exercise of unchastity, the muted delicacy and furtiveness that prevailed elsewhere at court.

Elisa did not find it necessary to conceal her purposes. She flirted outrageously when the spirit so moved her, with an assortment of employees and hangers-on whom she might angrily cuff, dismiss, or ignore a day or two later. Her more blatant favors were bestowed in an atmosphere of gossip and fanfare; before one could properly step out of one's trousers, the news had filtered from ballroom to private apartments to kitchen and stable. Niccolò resented this: not the envy, smirks, the inferences that he was advancing himself by means of special privilege, but the garish light that made his pleasures public. He would have preferred to come circumspectly in the night, with everyone pretending not to know.

And the princess could be, and usually was, crude as a pack-carrier. She panted, she heaved, she exposed herself, she bit and scratched, she emitted cries of satisfaction or impatient instructions. But a moment later, her face clouded with thought in the very act of love, she would talk of other things. There was a devastating harmony about the Princess of Lucca; she knew no conflicts. Lust, ambition, vanity, the fires of intellectual energy: all conditions blended in her person. Her very forthrightness offended.

"My brother has tossed me a bone," she muttered, aggrieved, pressing her boyish nakedness upon him. "Lucca and Piombino. The *principalities* of Lucca and Piombino, no less! This is a toy realm, Paganini, a toy realm. Why am I less worthy than Caroline the goose? She is Queen of Naples! Or Joseph, cabbage-headed Joseph?" Her fingers slid beneath her small breasts, which she cupped delicately for his delectation and her own.

"This is not the end," she whispered, her arms tightening urgently about him as she separated her thighs and made her purpose immediate and clear. "He will yet hear from me."

For a time, the inequities of distributing the Napoleonic loot simmered quietly as the princess groaned and gurgled in quickly achieved ecstasy.

"He is uneasy with me," she continued as though there had been no pause in the plaints. "I do not bow and scrape and sing hosannas to his omniscience, as does Pauline. That one was always the favorite. She is impossible. She infuriates him; her immorality is a public scandal!"

Elisa had turned bluestocking, one of her occasional guises, forgetting utterly where she was and with whom. "But she so very prettily combines repentance with flattery, and in his Augustan presence this pays off. They say she even sleeps with him," she concluded bitterly, reaching for a sheet to cover her nakedness.

Occasionally, she displayed curiosity about her paramour and bombarded him with questions.

"Your father—what does he do?"

One does not, in bed, tell a princess one's father is a carter and owns but a single horse. Or is an abominable violinist. "A Genoese merchant, *Principessa*."

"He let you become a fiddler?"

"He wanted me to astonish the world. Like Mozart."

"You are no Mozart," she decided. "But you may yet astonish the world. Who taught you?"

"My father. And Antonio Rolla of Parma, but very briefly."

"Who else?"

"I have taught myself," Niccolò said.

The princess seemed skeptical. "All those tricks? The human voices; the weird, otherworldly noises; the guitar and cello sounds?"

"I looked for them, and I found them."

"What is it you really want?" Elisa looked at him boldly, curiously.

He returned her glance. "To be great."

"You are arrogant."

"Yes," he admitted.

She whispered, "That is what I want, too."

"I know," he said.

Elisa laughed heartily, a low, uninhibited belly-laugh. "I shall make you a present," she decided. "You are so very like me, it is a pity you are a mere fiddler and must stand attention in the hallways and the kitchen when not occupied."

Niccolò could almost hear the sedate clink of gold coin and visualize the small, clearly-defined features of Elisa Marianna on the liberating discs. "Your Grace is too kind."

"I shall make you a captain of my guard and give you a fine scarlet uniform," Elisa continued happily. "Honorary, of course, but with all the privileges, so you can mingle with our guests."

Niccolò was puzzled. The donor seemed intoxicated by her generosity. Perhaps, after all, there were unseen advantages in such a gift? He would have preferred money, less difficult to understand and use. He realized suddenly that for him power, renown, and success would never be abstract. They would always be substances to be measured between thumb and forefinger.

But he concealed his disappointment. "I can never thank you adequately, *Principessa*," he said.

HE WAS TROUBLED by his dreams. The twisting convulsions he had suffered on the day of Carlo's departure had not recurred, but the disturbing, inscrutable night world he had fallen into had continued to plague his sleep, leaving him on even the brightest mornings with a dark and bitter aftertaste of nausea and loathing. Though nothing could be recalled of the nightmares, he felt a lingering presence and a vague, ominous sense of violation, as if a boundary deeper than flesh had been crossed, his very soul invaded. What was this thing that came in the night, mysterious and unnamed? Had some deep, hidden part of himself split off, emerging into the dreamworld with a power and identity all its own? Or was it truly "Other," a spectral creature from a place beyond the natural world? If so, it was a demon, certainly; this was not the sweet angel of his pregnant mother's dreams.

Niccolò came to fear his sleep, holding dearly to the light of day, and to his music, and to the endless distractions of the Bacciochi court. Despite restless nights, he found his energies undiminished; indeed, the creature seemed to provoke within him an urgent, fiery power, erotic in its intensity. It fed his musical endeavors, fueled his growing ambitions, and inevitably spilled into the corridors of the court.

Dalliance flourished in the passages, amorous intrigue in every corner. The elite had expanses of time to squander—time to mope on love, longing, deprivation, satiety, fickleness, constancy, that whole gamut of sentiment, earnest or synthetic, dealing with the tender affliction.

Young, by no means overworked after the diminution of his musical staff—he had the improviser's ready gift and had conquered his technical problems—Niccolò found the life of the court an intoxicating brew. He discovered how easy it was to enchant, to titillate, to lay waste, whichever his current purpose; he discovered his own careless magnetism. The violin wooed, and eloquently. The world was a wonderland—flesh, beauty, softness, promise—asking little save amorous stances of him.

Madame Laplace of the expressive, intelligent eyes, and apparently unassailable virtue, for instance; surely the lady was worthy of a sonata or two, some plaintive pleading of the G-string, some pyrotechnical celebration of love victorious (a mere disembodied notion of love, to be sure, neither reciprocal, spurned, articulated, nor demanding of him) in double harmonics and chords. And *Signora* Bernadini, second wife of the former president of the Luccan senate, half her husband's age, restless, too patently afflicted by her lot as battle prize of the Bonapartes; Olimpia of the merry, crinkled eyes and too, too giddy tongue; and earnest Rosa Trebiliani, headmistress of the Institute of Elisa, a formidably beautiful Roman aristocrat, scornful or unaware of her loveliness…

How could one live unmoved in this vibrant vortex of female activity, surrounded by the sight and smell of women who spent half their lives adorning themselves, making themselves desirable? Niccolò complained in a letter to his Genoese friend, Luigi Germi, of the "sweet heat" of the Bacciochi court; there was a hothouse muskiness here that seeped into his efforts, blending uneasily with the real business of life.

Which, after all, was music.

Lean, bony, and aquiline, he stood fondling his violin before the courtly audience, his glance tentatively subdued till alighting upon plump Adelaide Sarti, uncomfortable in her high-heeled gold slippers. Adelaide blushed. She did not want to offend her princess or her betrothed, both of whom were in the salon, and she was unused to juggling escapades.

"*Scena amorosa*," Niccolò said quietly, raising his bow arm. His eyes were glued to Adelaide's pink, blinking countenance, which she was rapidly fanning. And like a lovesick adolescent, he blurted one by one the titles of the brief movements: Flirtation, Request, Consent, Timidity, Gratification, Quarrel, Reconciliation, Love Token, Leave Taking. He had removed the two inner strings so that the dialogue was unmistakable: the high, pure E-string voice of Adelaide Sarti, sighing, pleading, scolding vivaciously, for she did, and his own mellow-voiced, conveniently ardent utterances.

"Venus and Adonis," whispered Rosa Trebiliani, somewhat too loudly. A suppressed giggle found its way to the very platform.

The coda, of course, provided the inevitable bravura demonstration, and amid murmurs and nudges and brisk applause, Niccolò bowed, surely aware of the fragility of his situation.

Princess Elisa was reserved. "Very beautiful," she announced, smiling with her mouth.

"I am grateful, *Principessa*."

"And with only *two* strings," Elisa murmured, rather too appreciatively. "That is no small feat."

He bowed again, very low. It was not Paganini's custom to protest that his accomplishments were commonplace.

"Can you perhaps compose something—eh, let us say, a little more substantial?—for *one* string?"

"If it would please the *Principessa*."

"It might please her," Elisa snapped. She added as an afterthought, with an excess of zeal, "A sonata, perhaps. For the Emperor's birthday."

Her smile was rapidly extinguished as she noted Adelaide Sarti backing prudently, with a series of little bobbing bows, from her presence.

❄ ❄ ❄

THE CREATURE GREW RESTLESS, crowding his sleep. Niccolò tossed upon his bed, unable to succumb, his mind reeling.

Perhaps he was slipping from grace. Perhaps he was tiring of the pleasant bondage of court life, a kind of death in honey. Perhaps, as distant rumbles of Napoleonic adventures and misadventures trickled into Lucca, it became clear that the new empire would by no means endure forever, and the patterns of Paganini's quest would have to be radically altered.

For in the final analysis, it made little difference which petty tyrant or beneficent lawgiver won or lost whichever coronet. Kingdoms would be born and would wither. His own realm was of sturdier stuff: sound. Trailblazing sound, such as had never before held in thrall ear, attention, and emotion. It died as it came into the world yet was indestructible. Insubstantial, it changed history. Impalpable, it altered the human heart.

This is what mattered: to do with a small stringed shell and a tenuous bow what no other had assayed. To succeed. To change the scope of instrumental music forever after. To perform, and in performing, to deify the performer, set him apart from ordinary men, make him a hero, a titan, a creature endowed with supernatural powers. To be the greatest violinist of all times.

There were two major problems. The music itself—where to procure it?—and the devices to astonish, bedazzle, and conquer. He had learned as a child that even the wee scratch of a bit of glass on the cobblestones might cause Teresa to shudder violently; that the sudden yelp of one of *Passo del Gato Moro's* dark felines, in bliss or agony, would send his sisters rushing into one another's arms as at the crash of thunder or oceanic lightning. And as a child, he had appeared on several programs with the revered *castrato* Marchesi, perhaps the last of the great male sopranos, noting with shivers of excitement the impact, the thrill of recognition with which an audience discovers emotions larger than life, beyond the confines of its imagination.

For this, Niccolò fumbled. This is what music meant to do. Not merely to amuse and to please, but to shatter the very husk of self, so that everything becomes possible—extremes of joy and rage, fear and hope, ecstasy, despair, and that element beyond the merely human: something suggested by the *glissando* of glass upon the cobblestones, stabbing one's inner organs, by the impossible juxtaposition of notes, rapid, diabolical, weirdly slashed and shaded, leading, if only for a moment, to a land outside things known.

The sedate, careful, finespun literature of the great precursors did not offer such possibilities. Corelli had performed a vast service to the violin, yes; he had freed it from medieval tavern and trampdom, brought it into the warm, hallowed bosom of the church, and established a great school. But what had the master's grave nobility and overcautious elegance to do with what he, Niccolò Paganini, wanted to say to the world?

Vivaldi, too, the Venetian priest to whom surely the angels had sung in dreams and visions. Vivaldi, prolific as a mountain spring, had extended the possibilities of the instrument, created a great body of work that would evoke adoration and respect as long as there were ears to hear. But there was little for Niccolò to retell. Vivaldi had not said enough.

Tartini, the stormy Paduan who engaged in jousts of violinistic skill and was reported to have made a pact with the very Devil? Tartini, too, had folded his aspiring wings under his coat and stopped short, safe in the great loft of St. Anthony, content to surrender his audacity and fire to the *sonata da chiesa*, the churchly concerto, the methodical studies on the art of the bow. He remained a parochial Prometheus, Tartini. His Satan was but a mischievous fellow, incapable of real malevolence: never a coiling serpent, never the very core of evil, never presiding genius of the Dark Land. Tartini had seen Hell, but without passion.

All of them—Veracini, Pugnani, Somis, even the crackling, eccentric Pietro Locatelli, who flung deliberate executant difficulties into the path of performers—all were known and loved, studied, performed, and in the end, rejected. How innocent they had been, the great precursors! How young and undefiled their world! He, on the other hand, had been born to a bloody legacy; he inherited turbulence, contortions, war, and plunder, demolishing change. He was a child of the revolution. And he had come to believe that all Italy's violinistic great comprised an ancient regime of music, a noble historical backdrop for the destiny of his own genius.

Music, then, had to be created for his needs, and in one sense he had done this each day, albeit with half a heart and more wit than effort, to serve the bottomless appetite of the court for amusement. The *Napoleon Sonata* was a feverish success; Elisa wrote in her own hand to the Imperial Majesty in Paris, who may or may not have taken notice. Numerous short and long works, arrangements, transcriptions, shocking *tours de force* poured from his pen or, more often, directly from his bow. The guitar, too, remained an old love and not forgotten.

He labored, he experimented; he had done so intuitively since boyhood, discontented with the limited scope of string music. He had mastered harmonics, long out of fashion, and now worked to refine the mathematical division of strings, with the resultant octave-scaling; and to emit tones that, while true, produced precisely that eerie, inhuman, disembodied sound he needed. And he discovered he could double and triple these effects, creating otherworldly chords, solid and broken.

Routine tuning bored him. He found he could produce tuning effects by deliberate mistuning—*scordatura*, he called it—tightening his strings to achieve greater brilliance, dazzling his listeners with a piercing, penetrating tone all the more effective because most minutely awry. Perhaps he paid a small price in purity and volume. But no matter: Niccolò learned to render audiences as taut as gut strings. One could ask no more.

Old Monteverdi himself, of sacred memory, had introduced the plucked string, delighting with pleasant *pizzicati* suggestive of languid strummers of yet more languid guitars. But Paganini transferred this device to the left hand, presenting rapid-volley impressions, very dazzling and bold, calculated to produce little cries of pleasure from the ladies.

A residual portion of his talents remained unreleased, however; a lurking inner mystery for which he had survived childhood and youth, endured beatings and deprivation, journeyed restlessly to and from the northern cities. His message to the artists—*to the artists*!

For years, he had nurtured these strange caprices in a new voice and language, performing them infrequently in public. Some dated from his boyhood, some were but lately fashioned, and all grew suddenly urgent, crying out for acknowledgement. He rose from his bed in a feverish haste, and wrote them out without an accompaniment, without revision or revaluation, or patience to seek out the felicitous phrase. The pieces had long been fully shaped within him; he could neither add nor subtract a note. And before the night was through, here they were on paper in his rapid, nervous hand, a blob of candle wax in an upper corner, all twenty-four of them, caprices all (for he knew no more inclusive nomenclature), neatly inscribed "to the artists." Now and forever, for he had said it all, and those who feared to scale these heights, who could not transcend such perils, were no artists!

At last, Niccolò fell into sleep, having sated the demon that clung to his ribs.

3
SATANIC PACT

ELISA'S LOYALTY TO THE FAMILY would always burn steadily within her, despite bickerings, rivalry, and grievances. It was primitive and central to her being, but it was scarcely uncomplicated. Pauline, the infamously beautiful younger sister, had always been a rebuke to Elisa. Her very want of striving, her voluptuous unconcern, her uncanny ability to manipulate people without extending herself, the genuine love and adulation heaped upon her…At a very early age, Elisa realized her own course would have to be a more strenuous one. She would labor, scheme, petition; she would sow and reap. Nothing would come to her unbidden, and many bidden things would fail to come.

Pauline's first marriage to the lionized General Leclerc, their brief reign in distant Haiti (seething with black rebellion), the warrior's death of yellow fever, and the return of the exquisite young widow, literally shorn, immobile in her deep grief, had elicited a wave of popular sympathy for the Bonaparte princess. That her sorrow was short, her blotting out of sorrow wayward, and her extravagances gargantuan did not alter the loyalty of the Parisians.

It had been Elisa, the struggling *salonnière* in the vestments of a latter-day Sappho, who on more than one occasion brought Pauline's indiscretions to the attention of their brother. "We must have no scandal," she declared firmly, as though no trace of scandal had ever been associated with her own person. She failed to impress Napoleon, although he, of course, agreed with her.

Widowhood, indeed, seemed an improper state for Pauline; obviously, she needed a husband to deceive. The elderly Prince Borghese was hastily procured, the nuptials accomplished, and in short order the Duchy of Guastalla bestowed upon the old nobleman and his bride. "And what is Guastalla? Where is it?" Pauline had pouted, shrewdly aware that her new husband was no general and she but a woman, both severely limiting factors in the order of Napoleonic destinies. But Elisa counted her sister's hectares and pouted, too, aware of the absence of justice in this world.

Paganini speculated for many months about Pauline Borghese, wondering whether wider opportunities might be forthcoming under her patronage. One might surely, in her territories, move about more freely—perhaps give concerts in nearby cities, a practice Elisa had expressly forbidden. And he had heard rumors—Lucca thrived on whisperings and rumors—that the younger princess was genuinely enamored of music.

This could scarcely be said of Elisa, whose economies were first and increasingly felt by the court players. The orchestra that had begun to be whittled away with Carlo's departure became, in time, a mere string quartet uneasily augmented by local talent as the infrequent need arose. Elisa regarded court music as an inescapable expenditure, but she held no particular attachment to it or to any of her possessions, only to the notion of possession. Her first violinist and director of orchestra— he still carried these titles—was fancied for reasons distinct from his musical prowess. He could have been, for all that it mattered, majordomo; indeed, Elisa occasionally favored her majordomo.

Moreover, Pauline was reputed to be genuinely extravagant, particularly with respect to artists and musicians. Her generosity to Blangini, surely more to her than a music master, was legendary. And Elisa's expenditures, while exorbitant to the distant Napoleon and his treasurer, were always calculated, thoughtfully doled out, and most often represented real and palpable chattel acquisitions. For the Princess of Lucca was wary of the insubstantial, preferring Marchesini mosaics, which could be shown, held, and put away as an investment, to Paganini sonatas which, once heard, no longer existed.

Yet it required strategy and a measure of anguish to procure a leave of absence from the Bacciochi court. For many months, Niccolò petitioned and waited, then petitioned again, only to be dismissed with a pretext—that Prince Felix, for instance, could not be parted from his music instruction! This the princess proclaimed before half a dozen smiling women, all of whom knew the regard in which Prince Felix's musical efforts were held.

Niccolò could not understand her reluctance but knew she harbored some peculiar reason for wanting to detain him. It then occurred to him—one could be certain of nothing—that Pauline might be the reason. If he was, indeed, the first of Italy's violinists, bound cheaply to the Bacciochi court, why hand him over to a rival? Niccolò began to appreciate Elisa's astuteness. Prudently, he had said nothing of Pauline or of his hope for crumbs from the Borghese bounty, mistakenly supposing his motives concealed.

"I AM TOLD you have been seen walking the streets at night," said the princess. She caught Niccolò's eye in the mirror as the chambermaid unlaced her corset. "Have you so tired of the ladies of the court that you must seek your pleasure in the alleys?"

"I serve only one lady of the court, *Principessa*."

"And thus you serve the Emperor. It is unseemly for a captain of the guard to be so flagrant in his indiscretions."

"I assure you no indiscretions have taken place," said Niccolò. "And most certainly not while in uniform."

"Of course. It would have to be removed, would it not? Tell me: Is this why you are so desperate to absent your duties? Do you imagine the court of my sister to be a company of harlots?"

Niccolò feigned bewildered surprise. "I am desperate only for sleep, *Principessa*. It has been difficult to come by of late. For that reason, alone, I walk at night."

The princess examined her naked reflection, drawing a hand across her breasts. "Perhaps your days are not as full as they ought to be," she mused.

"It is not a fault of my days but of my nights. I am haunted by dreams."

Ensconced in her red silk *robe-de-chambre*, Elisa dismissed the maid with a flick of her hand. "Tell me about these dreams."

"There is little to tell, for there is little I remember. But they are unholy; of that, I am sure. They leave me in a most wretched state."

"You are ill upon awakening?"

"Yes. Quite so, and then—"

"You are invigorated?"

"Why, yes. But how did you know?"

"Because, I, too, have been beset of late. The wages of sin, I suppose."

"Do you dream of transgression, *Principessa*?" Niccolò was genuinely curious.

Elisa arose abruptly and crossed to the bed. "My dreams are my own concern. As is my vigor. Now take off your clothes. As much as you may prefer it, I will not undress you like your Luccan whores."

❊ ❊ ❊

AND WITH CHARACTERISTIC abruptness, Elisa relented. Her energies were occupied elsewhere, in a most critical project: a final bid for the extension of territory. As her machinations began to seem promising, as her intermediaries grew emboldened and Napoleon listened, Elisa's fear of losing an unimportant palace ornament relaxed to a point of utter indifference. "Of course," she agreed blithely, as though there had never been excuses, denials, and contrived obstacles.

"Thank you, thank you, *Principessa*," Niccolò murmured in an excess of zeal, for he was growing desperate.

Elisa added ironically, her smile accepting all his aspirations and her own more solid ones, "Go with God."

He had always detested travel. It drained him, crunched his bones, brought the bitter taste of death and decay to his mouth. The roads were winding wounds upon the body of earth, and all seasons were infelicitous. The joggling made him wretched and ill. The nausea, the bodily tenderness, the sheer dislocation of getting from one place to another taught him his own and man's fragility.

But this, too, must be his portion. He must be a wanderer if he would be heard, and he must be heard. He dreamed of distant places: melodious Paris, Vienna of the Holy Roman Empire, bizarre Russia encrusted in ice and snow. Between himself and all of them, he acknowledged a jagged network of muddy or frozen or fragmented roads, chilly coaches, the sickening smells of food, vomit, children, his own lassitude, and the very trickling away of life. But there was no solution. Go he must; go he would.

Fortunately, he recovered quickly. He was no sooner out of the coach than his sickness began to dissolve. Unsteadily, Niccolò might find his way to the theater, enjoy the opera (or a portion of it), find a clinging little singer to love briefly and frenetically on her own practiced pallet. And on the morrow, his own problems: work and destiny.

But destiny proved elusive. Every charlatan in Italy conspired against him, or so it seemed. The weather itself turned hostile. Rain fell in a needling, icy drizzle day and night, piercing the very marrow. Niccolò hawked and coughed, knew himself in the clutches of a fever, nursed watery eyes and a clogged nose, but did not dare take to bed. Surrender might have put an end to his ventures. Surrender meant lackeydom, he decided.

Good lodgings were difficult to find in Turin. He moved frequently, sometimes from day to day, outraged by noises or filth or fleas, and usually after a bitter battle concerning his indebtedness. The food, too, he found abominable, despite its widespread acclaim. Niccolò would never believe that dysentery was not concocted in the unappetizing sauces of generations of Turinese cooks, who exported it to the world. He contented himself that his bout was slight and not too debilitating.

But the most acute problem proved his need to be heard. Not a theater or hall in Turin was available. Niccolò pleaded, wheedled, dashed from one faint hope or clue to another. He sought unpopulous churches and villas and palaces whose owners had died or followed the Napoleonic fortunes elsewhere. He groveled before petty officialdom, waiting respectfully in cold anterooms for authorities who failed to materialize. He wrote eloquent letters which disappeared, bringing no replies.

Niccolò was perturbed but not astonished by these difficulties. He was, after all, venturing forth alone, without patronage, without the blessings of a noble house, a priestly one, or a municipality. He had no intermediary to represent him to the world, no impresario to spread repute and whet curiosity and eagerness. It was unheard of to arrive alone, unknown, uninvited, determined to leave one's imprint upon a place. And such was truly Niccolò's purpose, supported by little more than animal tenacity.

He floundered; he raged silently till his intestines ached with frustration and rebuke. Yet the freedom of being his own master, if but for an interlude, rendered no other course possible. One pays dearly for a protector, Niccolò had learned. The price is servility; one becomes a cipher. Beholden to no power, he felt power roaring within him. Because he was incapable of doubting himself, the vision of a shining future sustained him, softening obstacles and rage.

Eventually, through a network of complex, clawed-for felicities, Niccolò procured his auditorium. Then came the tedious yet delicate burden of finding auxiliary talent. One could not, after all, appear alone. The public expected a professor of violin to present himself surrounded by the semblance of an orchestra, no matter how incompetent, bumbling, and inadequately rehearsed. A female singer had to be engaged for the usual intermezzo, although her gait, décolletage, and costume were of greater interest than her vocalizings, provided the latter were not so unpleasant as to call forth catcalls and evil mob laughter. Niccolò had seen such persecution in Genoa years before. He would never forget its quick contagion. Within minutes, he, too, burned to whistle and howl and drive a poor player from the stage. He chose his singer carefully: neither young nor old, not too gifted lest she outshine him, but in all ways adequate.

He triumphed, and he failed. Overnight, Niccolò Paganini became a great name in Turin, gateway to Italy. The audience was ecstatic; competitors, aflame with awe and envy; and the coffers overflowed with French and Italian currency, a most beautiful sight. Niccolò, who had trembled with anxiety lest not a soul appear to listen, experienced no doubt of his ability to overwhelm and conquer once he confronted an audience.

Yet he crawled to his lumpy bed at the inn inconsolably grieved, convinced he had wasted himself. Pauline Bonaparte Borghese, reposing in Turin between more strenuous pleasures, had not, albeit ardently solicited, chosen to come hear her sister's *maestro di capella*. Niccolò knew the taste of ashes, even as he was acclaimed.

❊ ❊ ❊

BUT HE POSSESSED what cynical Genoese called the hard face. He would not be deflected. He had come to Turin to be heard by the younger Bonaparte princess, and he would not leave Turin without accomplishing his mission.

"Who, then, is this Paganini?" Pauline inquired of her wizened little music master, Felice Blangini, as Niccolò stood by, trembling.

"You do not know him, *Principessa*, but you will," Niccolò ventured. He realized immediately that the remark had failed to enchant.

Pauline stared coldly, as if appraising a new adversary. Her beauty, at close range, was almost disconcerting. Not the classical flawlessness of form, the chiseled perfection of her features, the whiteness of her throat and shoulders, her coloring—not these alone or together, but a vibrant emotional transparency instantly agitated, troubled, moved.

"He is a professor attached to the Luccan court," Blangini pronounced carefully in a high, somewhat nasal voice, emphasizing the interloper's connection with the Bacciochi.

Pauline's pencil-thin eyebrows acknowledged that fact while conceding the complexity of her own relationship. "Did *she* send you to me—the Princess of Lucca?"

"By no means," Niccolò said. "I was very persistent, and I told her nothing."

"You play well," Pauline decided, quite in the manner of a child accepting an unwanted toy. She added, "And you *are* very persistent."

Since she had risen, and Blangini, who had been standing by her side, stepped forward to escort her, the audition was terminated.

Niccolò bowed. Scarcely concealing his disappointment, he murmured, "Thank you for your graciousness."

Pauline turned to go but paused. Her clear, shining gaze turned interrogatively upon him, with a touch of guardedness or petulance.

"Why, then, did you want to come here? Why did you want to play for me?" she asked.

And as Niccolò, violin in one hand, bow in another, confronted her shimmering loveliness, he realized that Pauline was distrustful of him, that she viewed him as a seductive tool of the Bacciochi, and that her recoil was so genuine and so great that his mission was doomed to failure.

"Your generosity to musicians, *Madame*," he bowed, prepared for dismissal.

"Oh, but I already have a musician, *Monsieur* Paganini," Pauline protested, entirely in earnest. She slipped her arm into that of the hideous Blangini, bestowing upon him a smile of intimacy and amorousness and a secret shared, one of corrosive weariness with the world. For such a smile, Niccolò would have lopped off an ear or years from his allotted lifespan.

The Princess of Guastalla departed on the arm of her paramour. A tightly buttoned lackey stood attention, ready to usher Niccolò from the premises.

THAT NIGHT HE DREAMED and knew he was dreaming. Though he fell into the nightmare like a stone through water, powerless to rupture its stranglehold, he remained intermittently aware of what he was and where he found himself, of the blurred outlines of chair and bedpost and washbowl, and of the humiliating sickness that scooped out his very intestines, leaving him helpless and vulnerable.

He dreamed of the breast's solace and of Teresa, his mother, gentle, maternal-foolish, unquestioning. Pain curled him into the womb's suspension, his knees approaching his face; then relaxed him till he lay limp and wounded, parched lips sucking the air. Teresa nourished and understood and accepted. But he was torn from her—he felt the very ripping of his flesh, heard his lost shriek of deprivation—by the rough, greedy hands of Antonio, whose blows fell impartially on mother and child.

He dreamed of the Princess of Lucca, transformed into a winged harpy gnawing fiercely at his manhood yet sheltering him beneath great, unassailable, protective wings whose shadow he dared not leave. The dream-Elisa smiled craftily, reading his irresolution. Her fangs tore into his heart; he heard the noise of bestial mastication. Scorpions clawed at his toes; he wrestled with plaited serpents. And throughout his tossing, he feared the exertion would deplete him once again, leaving him helpless, disgusting, sprawled in the mires of his weakness and shame.

Princess Pauline appeared out of a crimson effulgence, beckoning and taunting. Naked, wet, shining as from a night-sea bath, she rose before him in pearly splendor, and as he leaped to pursue her, she vanished altogether, turning into a bald, leering little gnome, hideously gnarled, with a nasal voice and a protruding belly. Niccolò moaned helplessly and tumbled down the precipice. The stones cut his face and hands and body; descent was swift as a waterfall. The peaks had been too dazzling, too steeped in terror, to scale.

Niccolò lay broken and charred in a burning pit of slime. Out of the fiery darkness, the pounding echo of familiar laughter rapped upon his skull. Niccolò raised his eyes and peered out into the blazing inferno. He braced himself. This time he was aware; this time he would *remember*. Slowly, out of the flames, the creature emerged.

Niccolò froze, struck dumb in astonishment. The specter that had long haunted his nightmares was not the dreaded demon, not some cruel fiend lusting for torture, but the stunningly familiar figure of a young and slender maiden.

Eleonora Quilici, his virgin love.

Sheathed in pearly satin, a shapely silver silhouette in a sea of golden fire, her body moved like an undulate flame slowly drifting toward him. Gone was all pretense of innocence, of girlishness or puerility. Her eyes were lined in Egyptian black; her lips, painted the color of blood. Her bearing and demeanor exuded cruelty and grace, a beguiling threat of sinful pleasure.

Niccolò lifted his body from the muck and kneeled like a mendicant before her. "Eleonora," he said, his voice trembling. "Why do you come to me?"

Her eyes glimmered darkly in the flickering light. "Your ambition is your prayer," she replied. "That which you ask for, so shall you receive."

"You may grant such favor?"

"I, and I alone."

Something flashed at her feet. A coil of flesh, glistening, lizard-like. It quickly retreated beneath her gown.

"Tell me your deepest desire," she commanded.

Niccolò's heart rattled in his chest. "Fame," he said quickly. "Riches. I want…I want to conquer the world."

Eleonora laughed. "Can a man conquer the world with a fiddle?"

"Perhaps," answered Niccolò. "With a little help…"

"Certainly with *my* help," she said. "But to conquer the world, you must wear the colors of the conqueror. That is why I made you a captain of the guard."

"You? But the princess—"

"Princess Elisa is ruled by her dreams," said Eleonora. "As are you."

She held out her hands. Niccolò took them and rose to his feet. Locked in her burning gaze, he felt his limbs awaken beneath him, his pain dissolve into lust. He longed for once to touch her, to taste her, to enter her…

She scowled and bent back his hands, forcing him down again, down to his knees in the boiling mire. "You will conquer the world," she told him. "You *will* uncover the deep power of music. You will amass a magnificent fortune. The glory of your name will be revered for centuries. All this, all of it, *I* will give to you."

Niccolò looked up at her, his eyes swelling with a glowing inner vision. Glory, fame, riches: the world. "All mine," he said aloud. Groveling at her feet, he pressed his lips to the hem of her gown.

She lowered her eyes imperiously. "There are, however, two sides to any bargain."

"Why, yes…of course. What is it that you wish of me?"

"Your love," she replied.

He waited. Surely there was more. "You have it," he said.

"All of it?" she asked.

He swallowed dryly, his throat burning. He felt a creeping unease. "Yes. All of it," he said finally.

"Then you will never be able to love another," she told him.

"Never?" Niccolò hesitated. "Surely—"

"No love—except your love for me—will be possible."

A shadow of fear crept over his heart. He swallowed hard, calculating and feeling desperate.

Eleonora gazed upon him with an inveigling smile; she reached across her shoulder, unclasped the gold medallion that held her satin gown.

Niccolò stared in awe at the goddess revealed. She is more than beautiful, he thought. What need have I for any other?

"As you say, then."

Eleonora moved toward him, naked as Eve. "Indeed," she said, sliding her long white fingers through his tousled mane of hair. "*As I say.*" Her hands tightened, grasping his locks with a startling strength. She pulled him to her, burying his face in the coolness of her thighs. His mouth opened, his lips and tongue moved like a slithering sea creature, blindly feeding in her rosy wet flesh. Her eyes closed with a sigh and then opened abruptly. She yanked his head back, his mouth dripping, his throat exposed. Her long, leathery tail dropped down between her legs, then rose like a silver cobra, snaking up his body, wrapping around his neck. He choked, his face turning crimson as her tail squeezed tight. Niccolò's bulging eyes locked on her in terror.

The fire rose up; flames danced around her. "Return to Lucca," she commanded. "The Princess is now a Duchess, and the Duchess will set you free."

NICCOLÒ AWOKE KNEELING ON THE FLOOR, gasping for breath, his bed-clothes soaked in a stinking sweat. Moonlight greased the window above him; rough-hewn beams cast shadows across the wall. He looked around the unfamiliar room, seamy, squalid, but *real*, nonetheless. He touched the floor, the bed, the wall: wood, cloth, stone. He was back in the world of things, the world of flesh and blood. He rubbed his neck, relieved to be alive, relieved to have survived—but survived what? He shuddered with a sudden, terrifying thought.

Had Niccolò Paganini made a pact with the Devil?

FINALLY, AFTER YEARS OF PLEADING, tantrums, and eloquent if unorthodox diplomacy, Elisa's efforts met with sudden and unexpected success. The Tuscan state was absorbed into the Promethean empire and, for want of a more suitable heir or a more urgent suit, Elisa designated its Duchess.

Niccolò was stunned. Was this not what the nightmare succubus had foretold? On the journey back to Lucca from his failure in Turin, he had berated himself for indulging in naive superstitions. Pact with the Devil? Ridiculous. These were enlightened times, and he was an enlightened man. To think that for days he had worried about it, pondering at one moment her golden promises, the soft well of her flesh, and in the next, stroking his throat with a chilling apprehension. Nothing more than a bad joke of a bad dream, he had thought, an inflammatory mixture of wishfulness and desperate fatigue. Nauseous and pallid in the teetering carriage, he had seen what a truly pitiful creature he was, inventing a demon in the guise of a young girl, a pink parody of the Devil, a false god offering fame and riches like tinsel and candy.

And yet, within hours of his return to the city, he found the first part of her promise had come true. *The Princess is now a Duchess.*

But what of the rest? Never had he felt so keenly aware of his dependence on the court and his want of status. Indeed, Elisa in her ambition seemed temporarily to have forgotten him. The bread of patronage stuck in his throat, yet no road beckoned. He had, throughout the years, created a stir here and there, evoked perishable compliments and fanfare. But he possessed, as yet, no substantial reputation, no devotees, scarcely a musical connection upon which to lean. He longed for liberation yet recoiled from the thought of liberty. One might stifle in captivity; one might, by the same token, starve in freedom. It was a gambler's choice. The Napoleonic Empire would either last a thousand years or quickly disintegrate. Either fame, fulfillment, and the gold of the world awaited his genius, or he would lie in the anonymous dust of his ancestors.

And the Devil? He had not heard from her again.

He waited. He loitered in palace corridors and dispensed inane compliments to whichever foolish women chose to pause and listen. The court busily prepared to remove itself to Tuscany. Elisa issued daily stratagems for the display of imperial pomp, and no conqueror of ancient days could have planned a more impressive entry into a captive city than she intended for Florence.

"Quiet! The dead are turning in their graves!" Stefano, the crippled tailor, shouted from across the moonlit *Piazza San Michele.*

He was greeted by a cascade of laughter as the revelry within rose to a still higher pitch.

"Alas, it is too warm, with so many dancing, to shut the windows," Anna Bucchianeri noted, though with scant regret. To her neighbor she called out good-naturedly, "We are having a private gala ball."

"For all the whores of Lucca," screamed the sleepy tailor.

Anna banged shut the window despite the interior warmth. She flashed a warm, matronly smile upon Niccolò, in whose honor the party was being held, for he was to leave for Florence on the morrow. "I am sure old Stefano thinks we've gone raving mad."

Niccolò poured wine into empty glasses. "Perhaps we have," he mused, his words lost in the whirl of sound from the raucous troupe of street musicians banging out their tune.

"You do not dance, Niccolò," called out Orlando Grassi, the bass player.

"Not visibly."

Grassi's toast was pronounced with such flourish that wine trickled down upon his sleeve. "To Florence."

"Amen. To Florence."

Anna said, "You are troubled, Niccolò. All evening, Eleonora tells me …"

Niccolò bowed, gazing across the room into the huge, clairvoyant eyes of Eleonora Quilici. "Your sister reads my mind as though I were a sheet of music."

"It is unfortunate that you do not understand her in so sympathetic a manner," Anna began.

"I do not plan to remain long in the service of the Bacciochi," he said abruptly, his eyes on Eleonora. She had risen to dance, scarcely aware of the identity of her partner. And he felt her watchfulness, a great, invisible net, and knew that she could, somehow, see him though turned to face another, and hear him distinctly across the tumultuous, swarming room.

"Then what will you do, Niccolò?" cried the good Anna, fearing he had provoked a disaster at court.

"I shall become a virtuoso."

"But you *are* a virtuoso."

"I shall endeavor to earn my living without patronage."

"Is that possible?"

Niccolò shrugged. "With the blessing of the Devil, anything is possible."

"Ooh, Niccolò has visited the Devil," cried Minetta, Bartolomeo Quilici's fiancée.

"No, the Devil has visited me. And I am deeply indebted to her." The wine had begun to loosen his tongue.

"To *her*?" Minetta giggled. "The Devil is a *woman*?"

He was watching Eleonora float across the dance floor. "Most assuredly," he said.

"And for what are you indebted to her?" Minetta asked.

"For dark secrets."

"Ooh, Niccolò has dark secrets!"

Someone slipped a guitar into his hands, and he caressed it vaguely, releasing soft, wailing sounds in tune with the troupe.

"What are they, these dark secrets?" Orlando demanded loudly, for the wine had dulled him. "Can I learn them?"

"How to make you laugh, and how to make you cry," answered Niccolò. "And no, you cannot learn them."

"Why not? You have no monopoly on the Devil," Orlando shouted above the laughter and the din. "I can drive as hard a bargain with him—or her—as you can. I am from Naples."

The women exclaimed over this, nodding sagely.

"She would but look at you and say, 'Go back to Naples, little archangel!'" Niccolò scowled at the guitar, improvising weird, provocative cadenzas that brought the revelers to their feet.

The motley troupe picked up the tune and the dancing recommenced. Anna's youngest child sobbed from an attic cradle. Minetta shrieked over some boorish quip, and the baker arrived with two great trays of sweetmeats. Poor Stefano the tailor, still unable to sleep, banged his cane on the pavement and shouted for silence, now threatening the merrymakers with gendarmes.

Looking up from his guitar, Niccolò peered across the steamy, crowded room into the grave face of Eleonora Quilici, who sat fingering the little crucifix on her bosom.

4
Freedom

Almost from the start, it became evident that the acquisition of new domain would prove a Pyrrhic victory for the Princess of Lucca. Lucca and Piombino might very well have been, as she periodically labored to prove to the Emperor, small, insignificant, and unworthy of her talents. But as titular head of Tuscany, her powers were at once enormously curtailed. She had been sovereign in Lucca. Now, she was reduced to a figurehead, a Bonaparte functionary who happened to be Napoleon's sister.

Elisa could not bend the Tuscan cities to her will as she had the smaller principalities. She could not effect her reforms, drill her little army, close down nunneries, open secular schools, organize learned bodies of local pundits and sages, revise laws and industries, abolish ancient practices. In reality, she possessed no independent authority. By becoming Duchess of Tuscany, she became literally the Emperor's representative, invested with power merely to exchange courtesies and act as a reminder of the imperial tie.

With a precipitate change of tactics he did not feel necessary to justify to his sister, Napoleon himself appointed all key functionaries—treasurer, police chief, administrative heads of state—who were accountable to him, not to the superfluous duchess and her consort. He presented her, moreover, with a bevy of experienced ministers through whom her complaints, suggestions, indeed, her very sisterly affection had to be routed. Her responsibilities were ornamental and meager, and her budget to accomplish these was very meager.

And Florence, beautiful Florence, did not fling itself gratefully into the arms of the conqueror, as Lucca had done. Italian cynicism and apathy had set in; and in certain high quarters, so had a conviction that the Napoleonic order had begun to overreach and would soon start to totter.

For revolution and empire blend uneasily, and the claims of empire are surely the more urgent. The Little Corporal, as Emperor, became conservative and legitimist, anxious to found a dynasty, sending out exploratory feelers to the Hapsburgs, whose last queen of the French had fared badly and whose more recent relationship with that people had been far from cordial.

Elisa, less flexible and more politically consistent than her brother, could not at first follow these peregrinations. She found herself aggrandized yet shorn of authority, mouthing obsolete sentiments that but a short time ago had smacked of eternity. Almost the sole gratification provided her by the Parisian mutations, compromises, and tightening of central authority came with the unexpected news of the Emperor's divorce from Josephine. Elisa was jubilant; only the prudent pleading of Felix deterred her from dispatching a congratulatory letter to Napoleon.

Early in her reign, the new Duchess of Tuscany decided she would reside, whenever possible, in Pisa and Livorno, thereby avoiding the arrogant Florentines altogether. However, affairs of state required her occasional presence in that center. There were public duties to be performed, and some basic pageantry seemed in order if the Empire was not to be regarded by its subjects as fraud or myth. From the start, Elisa encountered epic humiliations. The old Luccan families had closed ranks with the conquerors, contributing the most personable and promising of their youth to the royal service. Florence, in turn, provided snubs, rebuffs, and frustrations.

The reception of the Grand Duchess Elisa had been carefully arranged, but to no avail. The prefect lay conveniently dying, the mayor had absented himself from the city, and the resistant aristocracy conspired to be unavailable. When it seemed that no more than fifteen horse guards and twenty-four foot guards could be mustered, Elisa, after expletives and vague threats, announced that she would enter the city at night, unescorted. The dundering old crones and ancient chamberlains designated by the mayor to serve the new duchess proved a further effrontery. Most of these were dismissed with little kindness or ceremony.

Nor did the municipality's ball in honor of the duchess afford even conventional satisfaction. Elisa had learned to identify and prize gentility. Now, amid the glories of Florence, whose very stones suggested majesty, she found herself surrounded by the greedy, the sycophantic, the newly arrived. Everyone hoped for gain through her or sought recognition among the vulgar by exploiting her presence. Elisa remained for half an hour, festering inwardly though maintaining her regal composure. Then she quit Florence altogether, determined to spend as little time there as her responsibilities permitted.

Paganini's diminishing role in the Bacciochi court trickled away to a negligible one. Elisa had little use for him. Ardor was the occupation of indolence, and she was far from indolent; moreover, she had long ago tired of her fiddler. Her political affairs and the concomitant local frustrations kept her in a perpetual upheaval. She longed for the Emperor's ear. When she learned of an imminent Hapsburg alliance, she decided peremptorily to journey to Paris, more as a means of advancing herself than to celebrate the union of Napoleon and Marie Louise.

SINCE ELISA WAS OCCUPIED with weightier matters, the time seemed ripe to Niccolò for an agreeable rupture of their relationship. He had kept it no secret, where it seemed safe to discuss frankly, that he felt bored, weary, and rebuked under court patronage. He became convinced that the protection of the Bacciochi had seduced him, offering an illusion of security when what he needed was the struggle for glory and rewards. He had accepted the mite of a petty courtier. He had become so dependent on his morsel during the Luccan years—four for the municipality, nearly five for the Bacciochi—that he found it terrifying now to start out unknown, as in the beginning. He was no stripling—at twenty-seven fame should have long been his portion and not just an intoxicating dream—and the greedy paw of Antonio Paganini demanded its tribute regularly, while teary tales of illness, calamity, urgent dowries, and economic misfortune continued to pour in from Genoa.

He was annoyed by the expectations of his family, whom he hesitated to advise of his plans. From the beginning of the Luccan residence, he had sent money regularly to Antonio Paganini and sporadically to his sisters, to Carlo, to the various progeny. More often petitioned than thanked, Niccolò felt himself gradually pushed into the role of tight-fisted Croesus. Antonio remonstrated and bargained, wrote tragic exaggerations of the family's circumstances, and upbraided his second son for parsimony, selfishness, and want of compassion.

Still, the greater weight had to be lifted. Niccolò was nearly twenty-eight, no longer young, nearly alone. The time was overripe for that bold thrust: not, as he once mistakenly thought, of substituting one patron for another, but for becoming a free man, an artist, and forcing the miracle of his powers upon an unbelieving world.

Had this not been the Devil's promise? *And the Duchess will set you free*…But how? Niccolò sulked, and plotted, and prayed to his dark mistress for a means of escape.

Princess Elisa returned from Paris determined not to leave the Florentines to their indifference, no matter how outraged her sensibilities. Perhaps she had conferred with a higher intelligence. More than pride and peace were at stake, she had learned; by accepting ostracism, she conceded the tie between Paris and Florence an insecure one. This Elisa could not risk. Very cautiously, taking pains to be neither conspicuous, extravagant, nor discourteous to local traditions, she set herself to the task of wooing one prominent family at a time. One small sinecure followed another, each favor concealing an invisible knot. Enhanced dowries were made possible for daughters of down-at-the-heel nobility. Minor posts were filled, involving several generations of Florentines in a relationship of gratitude to the new regime. More and more beautifully modulated Italian was heard at court. Tuscan colors and customs went bravely on display, despite Elisa's genuine belief that Italians were backward and could be civilized only by the benefits of French enlightenment.

While her participation in the affairs of Tuscany had been severely limited by imperial fiat and her physical presence in Florence rendered minimal by choice, Princess Elisa now tried astutely to soften the abrasion of an alien conqueror. In her hard-headed, Corsican way, she was able to understand the impact of the French gendarmerie upon a proud and ancient people, and the onus of foreign restrictions on a city historically proud of its freedom. It now became her wish to ingratiate herself. And unexpectedly, after massive curtailments and the near elimination of his public function at court, Paganini was ordered to provide music for an imperial ball, to which all the great Florentine families had been invited. Here, hopefully, the conquered might condescend to mingle with the conqueror.

A demon stood at the foot of the bed.

Niccolò recoiled, trembling, the perturbations of a fading nightmare still crawling through his flesh. He pulled the covers up and peered into the dark.

"Is it you?" he asked, his voice cracking.

The spindly creature loomed like a shadow, silent as Death. Niccolò waited, the only sound his own fevered breathing. Slowly, he leaned forward, straining to see.

This was not the demon at all, but only Niccolò's scarlet captain's coat, draped carelessly over the bedpost! The fiddler fell back into the sheets, laughing in relief.

Then he grew silent. Why, he wondered; why had the succubus made a gift of this uniform?

To conquer the world, you must wear the colors of the conqueror.

Niccolò propped himself up on his elbows and stared again at the crimson coat. His eyes suddenly lit up the room.

"The very color of the Devil!" he thought.

❈ ❈ ❈

THE DANCING HAD BEGUN; the carriages crowded one another in the courtyard. It was the last day of the year, and a cold, fine rain caused ladies to step mincingly upon the courtyard stones, fretting for their gowns and slippers.

Niccolò, presiding over the cousinly mingling of French and Italian music, turned from the musicians' dias and made his obeisance to the Grand Duchess and her consort as the royal couple appeared on schedule, dispensing smiles. The princess had never seemed so prepossessing and splendid. She wore deep blue and silver brocade upon which her dressmakers had labored as under the whip till that very morning. A small, glittering tiara (pirated by the Emperor), as well as constellations of smaller brilliants on her bosom, arms, and earlobes, presented a vision of almost unbearable majesty. She might have been a little uncomfortable under the bones and stays and tight white gloves and precarious fastenings, but even the illusion of power brings fortitude.

Abruptly, she summoned Paganini, in the middle of the Lully overture, which he defiantly completed before surrendering leadership to an elderly violist. When he appeared, he found her in a fury, her silent glare savage as lightning.

Prince Felix's smile was warm and comradely. But with one glance at his spouse, the situation became clear to him, and he gesticulated ineffectually, unsure of what was expected. Within moments, consternation had infected the ladies of the court hovering behind Elisa; and from the eyes of Olimpia Fatinelli there darted a warning plea for caution. This was, clearly, no occasion to offend Elisa Bonaparte.

When she spoke, it was very coldly, very quietly, as one would correct an insufferably ignorant domestic.

"Withdraw and do not show yourself until you are properly dressed," she commanded hoarsely.

Niccolò bowed, acknowledging that he understood her meaning, but conveying a determined recalcitrance. "I am dressed, *Principessa.*"

Elisa bristled. She was aware of many eyes upon her, of that undercurrent of amusement with which the rages of the great are viewed by subordinates. In Lucca, Elisa could afford to scream, "*Merde!*" or to slap a disquieting chambermaid. In Florence, the empire was on trial, and the duchess was subject to replacement.

"My dear Paganini," Prince Felix ventured in a most conciliatory tone. "Perhaps black court dress might—"

Elisa interrupted, "You are under no circumstances to appear before my guests in the uniform of a captain of my guard of honor." The victor of Austerlitz could not have put it more decisively.

"My brevet does not state," Niccolò retorted, "when I might and when I might not wear this uniform."

And he could discern from Elisa's pallor, tightened mouth, and involuntary twitch that had it been possible to order his immediate decapitation, she would have done so without a scruple.

"I forbid you to show yourself in this uniform," she hissed.

"I wear it legitimately," Niccolò maintained. "Need I remind the *Principessa* of the occasion of its bestowal?"

"My dear—" Felix pacificated vaguely, appealing to none and both. He could understand his wife's sensitivity. In the face of Florentine apathy, after the humiliation she had experienced in recruiting an acceptable guard of honor from among the families of the wellborn, she could scarcely permit a mere violinist to show himself so exalted. The news, colored with scandal and derision, would resound through all Tuscany by morning.

"Perhaps the good Professor Paganini—" Felix began tactfully, preferring to humor. An artist, after all, is half divinity, half madman; precipitating an imbalance can prove very dangerous.

"Perhaps *Signor* Paganini does not understand," Elisa interrupted. "He may appear at court properly dressed, or he may quit Florence. And now he may consider himself dismissed."

She was, after all, the sister of Napoleon.

Niccolò's silent plea, a truncated little gesture of acceptance and fidelity to his own gods and demons, was for Felix. He wanted not intercessions but understanding, for he was about to abandon the good prince to wretched intonation and inept tutelage. Bewildered, unbelieving, unable to understand the complexities of so absurd a rupture preceded by so absurd a quarrel, Felix watched Niccolò's withdrawal with stunned horror. And as befitted a Bonaparte consort, seed-bearer, instrument of legitimate bliss, he stood silent, unheeded.

Niccolò remembered little that followed save motion, urgent walking in the cold Florentine night, world without sky, slant, erratic rain borne by raw winds from the Tuscan hills, the Ponte Vecchio suspended from nowhere, the churning, inky-black Arno…and the exhilaration that freedom had wrought, the naked, unencumbered, floating mastery achieved this night for all time.

No homeless hound prowled about the city on such a night. No one accosted him in his gaudy uniform. No voice greeted, blessed, cursed, or acknowledged the enormity of what had been done. He fell heir to an abandoned, nocturnal Florence, to its monuments and bridges, its loveliness, its eternal glory. Florence, the soul's city. Florence, vulnerable and magnificent.

Niccolò walked restlessly around the *Piazza della Signoria*, recognizing the silhouettes of the youthful David, of Perseus, of the flawless Apollo Belvedere, intense black upon the black of night. The wind formed small, rolling spirals and howled briefly, mutedly; rain fell in tiny pebbles upon the old stones. He felt supernaturally clean, all irresolution's impurities burned away, healing waters pouring over him. The knots of conflict had been sliced asunder, leaving sweet relief and a strange rapture.

"Gone to the Devil," he whispered in glee.

On these words, midnight struck, a glorious affirmation from a dozen bell towers in gold and mellow bronze and labored, leaded voices. Another year of the Christian era, 1809, had drawn senselessly to a close. Niccolò stood alone, unencumbered, miraculously free. Servitude was done. The great world waited.

Part Two
The Devil's Pact

5
A Barnyard Fantasy

Luigi Germi, long-time friend and attorney of Niccolò Paganini, followed the fiddler's expanding career with loyalty, astonishment, and increasingly high-pitched complaints.

The lawyer's work in settling estates brought him often on the road and far from Genoa. Unlike his itinerant friend, however, he did not consider travel an inconvenience. To the contrary, Germi regarded the joggling coaches and execrable roads as offering rare opportunities for thoughtful reflection. If not on wheels, where could one cogitate in this frenetic, nineteenth-century world? Gone were the serenity and leisure of a happier time, with its established order of things. Man now found himself fragmented, severed from his heritage, from his very thoughts. A journey removed him from the press of duty. He had but to sit, to withdraw from the world's whirl, to return himself to himself.

So it was with no great hardship, though often an adventure, for Germi to find himself in Modena, Parma, Rimini, Ancona, Livorno, or wherever Paganini had contrived to play (and this, the attorney conceded, must have called for elaborate strategies on the part of that eccentric player, voluntarily cut off from protection).

Some of the ventures proved profitable for the wraith-like pearl of players; some did not. The performances, on the other hand, were invariably dazzling, pyrotechnical, calculated to astound. And everywhere,

Paganini was rapturously received by the expansive Italians, who recognized genius and viewed it, since it was their own, uncritically. As a civilized Italian of aristocratic lineage, Germi knew his palate more discriminating. Having heard a number of performances in the Bacciochi court, he had deplored Paganini's devices, usually of the most questionable taste: showy cadenzas superimposed upon classical concertos, imitations of barnyard sounds, spooky capers, strings deliberately broken, superfluous arpeggios and double stops, and unearthly pizzicati. Now, these were given untrammeled rein; indeed, Paganini's recitals were often crass exhibitions of violinistic bravado, clowning, and stunts.

Germi was not alone in his criticism. But unlike the scattered malcontents seeking fine flaws, he loved and admired Niccolò and argued passionately with him not to debase the nobility of his art. The attorney harbored no doubt that this new voice would be heard, recognized, and—if possible—widely imitated. For better or worse, Paganini would change music, and as things looked, Germi felt it might well be for the worse. The contagion of the few would soon become the fashion of the many. There was no doubt of it. Paganini unleashed an almost hypnotic spell upon audiences. His tricks, surely so unsubtle and obvious, moved the fiddler's listeners to tears. Dragging his high art and divinely bestowed talents into the gutter of popular taste, Paganini transformed popular taste and the very gutter into high art. It was confusing, the counselor felt; diabolical and somehow disorderly. Art meant progression, a series of mathematically graduated revelations. Not revolution. Revolutions, for all their prating of progress, are retrogressive and inherently self-destructive. Anyone who had been around Europe these last twenty years should have memorized that. And when one has genius in one's soul, bow-arm, and fingertips and a great Italian violinistic tradition to boot, one should not stoop to clowning and animal noises.

So thought Luigi Germi. And being an open, giving, communicative fellow, he shared his misgivings with all who would listen, including

Niccolò Paganini. But the latter's eloquence lay in his bow, not in his tongue. He smiled, he seemed to concur, but he never explained himself. And, needless to add, he never mended his ways.

❀ ❀ ❀

NICCOLÒ KNEW HE WAS IN LEAGUE WITH THE DEVIL; he could no longer doubt it. The goddess of the underworld was feeding his talent, inflaming his audiences, spurring his triumphs. Her presence took form in the brilliance of his music—and in the sweet terror that plagued his sleep.

Night after night, in one strange city after another, he would lie awake for hours, unable to sleep. Haunted by the sounds and shadows of the unfamiliar rooms, he would struggle to surrender, to overcome the fear that lurked in his heart. When finally he would drift off, she would come to him, slipping as easily into his dreams as a lover into his bed.

Whatever happened then was lost to him. He would awaken before dawn, exhausted, sickly, coughing phlegm and blood, his bones aching and his body bruised as though he'd ridden with a fury to the very edge of hell, and he would remember nothing. He might find a cold pool of semen, his bedclothes sopped and sticky, or his body soaked in sweat, tremulous and itching. Of the dreams, however, only vague and troubling memories remained, pale shades parading in mist.

Still, the darkness offered gifts. Deep in some hidden chamber of his soul, a string was plucked, a chord was played, and the sound of it resonated to the core of his being. He knew this was the source of his power, and he poured it relentlessly into his art and work.

He started with contempt for ordinary accomplishments and ordinary goals. It was not his destiny to be merely another Italian violinist. Italy and the world were cluttered with them. They begged at courts and churches, taught rebellious children, hired themselves out as orchestra scrapers, foraged for affluent weddings, christenings, funerals.

Although most were blatantly mediocre, touches of greatness could be found among them.

Instrumental music had grown respectable. Fiddlers no longer squeaked for their suppers at rural taverns and inns; nor were they stoned in the villages for their diabolical connections. But respectability has its price: he who turns his back upon the Devil is forever deprived of her magic.

To break all boundaries—to do with the violin more than the violin was meant to do—such was the purpose of Niccolò's wanderings. Fame first: not mere repute, not hollow applause from the galleries and the grudging acceptance of the learned, but a name so fiery that it burned itself into the consciousness of the race. And wealth: not mere comfort, not humdrum affluence, but an epic treasure that all would view with awe. Wealth enough to endow a great dynasty, perhaps.

And glory, without which nothing mattered.

Niccolò studied the singers. He had always loved the mystery and magic of the opera house. He respected the frankly false. Its very artifices enthralled him. Theater was the vicarious in life, hence life liberated from the husk of pure truth. And with the liberties so obtained, one worked not for imitation but for effect. Indeed, effect was all.

The great singers reached out to grasp and consume the emotions of their hearers. They laughed, they wailed, they slobbered over vast griefs, they engaged in acrobatic displays, they followed stately *legati* with ornate roulades and scintillating vocalises. Theirs was a cunning far removed from the dull respectability instrumentalists had at long last obtained. A paltry thing, respectability. No one lionized fiddlers, Niccolò observed. Violinists were not borne to their carriages on subservient shoulders or pelted with flowers by their admirers. No one dedicated impassioned verse to the sedate professors and their dignified eighteenth-century tunes, all so peculiarly reminiscent of one another, as though the very language of music had become atrophied.

So much for purity!

He remembered a performance in Genoa as a boy of eleven. He had appeared in public from the time he could wield a bow, but this was his first paid concert, after a brief tutelage by Rolla (who had taught him nothing), in the lavish *Teatro Sant'Agostino*. Through Antonio Paganini's managerial wiles, the child had been engaged, after much haggling, to play during the entr'acte. Antonio had unwrapped his son's talents as one would have brought fish to market, clamoring that they be noted, examined, bought. The day's hero had been Luigi Marchesi, greatest of the great *castrati*, darling of Genoa and of all Italy.

Already the noble art of the male soprano had begun to wane. The Holy Father frowned, if belatedly, on surgery's cruel assistance to *bel canto*; the revolutionary doctrine of the godliness of nature, it seemed, had paradoxically won ecclesiastical acceptance. And foreigners, alas, viewed the desexed treble voices of men, however beautiful, with incomprehensible squeamishness.

But in 1793, there had still been great *castrati*—Velluti, Crescentini, and the inimitable Marchesi—to teach Niccolò an indelible lesson. Not moderation, not harmony, not balance, not taste; none of these things really mattered. What mattered was impact: the shock of irresistible assault, the final victory. Marchesi had circus tastes. Irrespective of the needs of his role, he appeared in helmets and plumes, ludicrously arrayed, clutching sword and shield and lance, and refused to show himself without a fanfare and the martial rolling of drums. One would have thought, a Genoese nobleman had been heard to grumble, that his poor brain had been arrested, not his reproductive organs. And worse: whatever the work being performed, the idol Marchesi started with a favorite aria, appropriate or not, and would not turn from it until the audience had shrieked itself hoarse in appreciation.

But when he sang—in an ethereal, strangely sweet voice not at all resembling a woman's save in range and compass—when the pure, free, disembodied bird-sound floated, in ecstatic lightness and magnificent florid embroideries, into the ornate loges of the theater, over the faces of the groundlings, into the swarming galleries, Niccolò knew there was grandeur here transcending the small insincerities that were, perhaps, the castrate's defense against a heartless world. When Marchesi sang, only the singing mattered. Time, stunned, had truly stopped.

❋ ❋ ❋

"WE HEAR ONLY ENVIABLE THINGS OF YOU," said Girodigiani, a first-rate cellist and one of Niccolò's few friends in Ferrara.

"For instance?"

"That you are rich."

"That rumor, alas, has found its way to *Passo del gato moro*," Niccolò deplored. "My father pelts me with sarcastic letters. He calls me *Signor Figlio* and wonders whether I am his son."

"He should know that better than you."

"As long as he imagines me with money in my pocket, I am the son of his loins and of my most virtuous mother. What else do you hear?"

"That you are the greatest violinist in Italy."

"Of course."

"Rolla claims he taught you."

"Little or nothing, and only briefly."

"Europe has not your equal."

"Oh, quite likely Europe hasn't. But what's the need, since I, the original, am quite available?"

"The *Principessa* Bonaparte gave you the sack."

"Not at all," Niccolò bristled. "It would not be gallant of me to publish who gave *whom* the sack."

"And the Dark One is your current patron."

Niccolò bowed modestly. "Let us say that he has evidenced an interest in my career."

"You have a pact with him, like Tartini."

"I have a pact with him—unlike Tartini. But now I have troubles."

"A woman!" exclaimed Giordigiani.

"After a manner. Benedetta has walked out on me."

"When?"

"Today. After a long speech."

"The day before the concert," moaned the sympathetic Giordigiani. "Why?"

"She concluded that I do not love her."

"Isn't it enough that you pay her?"

"Apparently not. Or apparently, I do not pay her enough."

"Can you procure someone—now?"

"In Ferrara? Where in Ferrara can one find a woman with both a voice and an acceptable bosom?"

"Not, surely, among the Ferrarese. The only divine bosom—you know I never exaggerate, Niccolò—presently gracing this—" Giordigiani paused for precision—"this aggregation of asses, belongs to my fiancée."

"Again?" murmured Niccolò. "My most cordial congratulations. Who is she this time?"

"Antonietta Pallerini. A dancer."

"Would she grace our boards with a song or two?"

"She is a dancer. I don't believe she has ever sung in public."

"No matter. She has a bosom. And if you are engaged to her, she is not tone-deaf. I shall myself teach her a few simple ditties. Without a singer, these bumpkins will stone me. Worse, they will demand their money back."

"I doubt whether she would—" Giordigiani began.

"Let's go tell her," said Niccolò. "I'm sure she will consent, for your sake. And remember, not a word about my satanic connections. Dancers are so superstitious."

La Pellerini proved to be a small, tense, somewhat swarthy girl whose assets Giordigiani had not exaggerated.

"Me? Sing? *Bello*, you are teasing. I shall be a laughingstock."

"You don't have to be too good," said Niccolò by way of encouragement. "Merely not unpleasant. And ornamental, which the *signorina* already is to an extent undeserved by these Ferrarese louts."

Antonietta giggled. "My father used to say I sing like a crow."

"My father used to say I play like a glass blower," said Niccolò. "Annihilation is the sacred duty of fatherhood. Let us find a few simple old tunes—'*Lungi dal caro bene*,' that's safe—and perhaps some droopy old aria, an easy one."

La Pellerini was a woman of the theater. She learned quickly and could rise to the demands of an emergency, particularly since her delightful *bello* pleaded so nicely on his friend's behalf. But no measure of good will could make her a singer. The voice proved thin, vibrationless, somewhat wiry; it would have seemed an ordinary voice in any parlor and not an especially sweet one alongside a cradle. Niccolò hoped the occasion itself would carry her: his own virtuosity, her poise and décolletage, the clever guitar accompaniment he would improvise for her. Makeshift, yes, but nonetheless fortuitous. The vagabond fiddler learns to make a blessing of adversity. Tomorrow, next month, next year, things would be better. But things were not at all bad today.

THE EVENING SEEMED DESTINED FOR DISASTER, and Niccolò played gleefully and to the hilt, as though disaster were his purpose. The theater was cramped; the stage lights, flickering and garish. He preferred a spacious auditorium, for his tone, while not large, was extremely penetrating, heard to advantage when there was scope for expansion and flow.

At the outset of the concert, one of the orchestral musicians (nearsighted, no doubt) tripped over a chair while making his entrance upon the crowed stage. For a few stunned moments, he lay sprawled before his viewers. Then he rose, grinned stupidly, and found his place. The music lovers of Ferrara, who had come to gawk and be astonished, laughed idiotically at the possibility of bodily injury and broke into obscene handclapping.

Niccolò waited in the drafty wing, annoyed with the player and the audience. He could not help noting, as the concert progressed, that the applause rewarding his own most dazzling efforts scarcely approached the ovation the bumbling old dolt had brought upon himself by falling flat on his face. Anger made Niccolò's fingers nimble. He tossed off violinistic fireworks with a rusty taste in his mouth. His skinny, wraithlike figure bowed to his listeners with exaggerated humility. And the makeshift orchestra played well, displaying unexpected vitality and discipline: as though its members sensed an audience gathered truculently for some sort of proof, and almost as though they had become defiant.

"No, no; I don't think I shall sing," wailed La Pellerini, splendid in red and black lace with an array of scintillating Spanish combs in her hair.

"What? And waste such loveliness upon your *bello* and myself? When I am in league with the Devil—" (it had slipped out; Niccolò clasped his hand dramatically over his mouth)— "and Giordigiani, poor fellow, is already so enamored, you might appear in a sheet, for all that it matters."

"Oh, a sheet would be delectable," said Giordigiani. "But Niccolò *mio*, don't you think—"

"I think they are panting to hear the new soprano," said Niccolò. "And if they aren't, they should be. Come."

He seized his guitar and pushed the trembling girl before him. Confronting the audience, Antonietta's poise was outwardly restored. She moved proudly, with the regal gait of a dancer, bending gracefully in a deep bow of magnificent homage. The Ferrarese whistled, leered, applauded; someone shouted that the *signora* ought to be good for something, wisdom widely echoed and again applauded.

Antonietta struggled bravely with her small, timid voice and want of conviction. At the guitar, Niccolò embroidered fanciful cascades, delicious broken chords, and bizarre arpeggios to embellish her efforts. He muttered encouragement. Antonietta wavered. He cued her softly, imperceptibly. She heard only the inattention, the laughter, the mocking whistles, piercing and persistent. By silent agreement, her offerings were curtailed. Niccolò bowed gallantly to her, but Antonietta ran past him, sobbing, from the stage. The audience clapped wildly.

Soon, Niccolò appeared alone, violin and muscles flexed blood-thirstily. His mien was so lordly and so terrifying that the auditorium quieted suddenly. The audience sat as if smothered by noxious fumes or to learn of a great disaster.

"My next offering," he announced quietly, "was composed for the music lovers of Ferrara. 'A Barnyard Fantasy.' You should recognize friends."

This proved the sort of stunt Luigi Germi found most execrable and so loudly deplored. With the utmost intensity, as though unveiling a new and original masterpiece, a work whose wonders he himself approached with awe, Niccolò raised his bow and emitted a series of cracklings, crowings, neighings, barkings, mewings, and quackings. The Ferrarese sat hypnotized. Each series of imitations was greeted by cries of pleasure, wild, spontaneous applause, and demands for encores.

Niccolò halted from time to time—the work was arranged rondo-wise around a rustic little tune he had heard as a child—to accept the accolades with a great show of gratitude.

But the scorn in his eyes and in his smile promised a memorable finale. Raising his bow arm in a gesture of contemptuous finality, he called out, "This is for the braying donkey who whistled!" For a moment, paralyzed silence, as the hee-haw, hee-haw, North Italy's colloquial symbol for the Ferrarese, rasped out, bold as life, from the catgut and Paganini's fingertips.

Hotheads rose and dashed toward the stage, screaming curses. "Oh, they are sensitive, the asses, and don't want to be called asses!" he cried running for his life. The dressing room was barricaded; he had to push the door in. He found Giordigiani attempting to offer the supreme solace to the weeping Antonietta, who was clinging to him. "Come," he called out. "There will yet be a massacre!" More than modesty inspired their haste.

The friends found sanctuary in a waiting fiacre. The horses, frightened, tried to rear and set off in panic, for stones and rotten fruit had begun to pelt side and wheels. The postilion's frantic interrogations—the old fellow imagined himself trapped in an invasion or revolution or war, perhaps actually a prisoner, and was uncertain as to who the combatants were—could be heard above Pellerini's hysterics and Niccolò's not too lucid account of what had transpired on the stage. The moon smiled a thin, sickle smile, unreal as a painted moon on a sky of mottled canvas.

They were pursued by Ferrarese gendarmes who ordered Paganini to quit the city within twelve hours. This Niccolò was prepared to do, reflecting with satisfaction that he had gathered his receipts before indulging his indiscretion, and that both had been gratifying.

6

TRIUMPH OF *LE STREGHE*

FERRARA, IF A FIASCO, could be viewed as a mere anecdote. The northern provincial cities had capitulated, one after another, with wild public acclaim, an immoderate press, and no end of eerie rumors. But the successes, Niccolò calculated, while generating a crude fame, were anecdotes, too—rehearsals, one might say, for the inevitable siege of Milan.

Milan, like Paris, was hub, tastemaker, cultural crucible, parade ground of *le monde*, and capital of Enlightenment. It was brilliant; it was fashionable; it was lavish and amoral, witty and learned. And more than Paris, with which it was frequently compared, more than Vienna, about which one could only speculate, Milan was cosmopolitan. All tongues could be heard in its streets and squares.

None of these things particularly moved Niccolò. While his tastes were distinctly urban, any city—given a theater, an audience, a few willing actresses—seemed as good as another. But he knew that his reputation, no matter what subsidiary triumphs he gathered, lay stillborn without recognition from Milan. And in Milan, all his previous accomplishments—as wonder child of Genoa, as courtier to the Bacciochi, as fingerboard wizard of Ancona, Turin, Rimini, Parma, and the rest—would scarcely help at all. Milan did not inherit judgments.

From the first moment of his arrival, disheveled and indisposed after a midwinter journey, Niccolò succumbed to the enchantment of the city. He was inebriated with its worldliness and sweet license, its cynicism, its cunning. And Milan was rich; its public life reflected this, and its squalor lay cleverly concealed, unlike other cities, where beggars lurked under carriage wheels and swarmed in front of theaters, and the civic sores, as it were, went assaultively on display. Milan, too, had made its pact with the Devil, Niccolò concluded. The perfumed trollop, Vanity, had replaced the revolutionary Goddess of Reason, who had, in turn, overthrown the Italian Madonna.

But where, where, where could one procure a theater? And what ought one present to bedazzle Milan, bringing it into his obedient, yea-saying retinue? Here he could not afford the luxury of failure or even the luxury of a modest success. Milan might indeed prove gateway to the world.

His old teacher, Alessandro Rolla, was discovered to be a musical force in the city: conductor of its leading orchestra, pundit and policy maker at the new conservatory, well-entrenched friend of the French, who thought here, as everywhere, that they had come for a thousand years. Niccolò sought him out, patiently endured his reminiscences, and played for him. Rolla remembered the small Genoese who had come to him in Parma and sightread an immoderately difficult concerto that lay in manuscript on the music stand. Loyal, sentimental, and incapable of meanness, the old fellow welcomed his former pupil with open arms. If he had been apprised of Niccolò's cruel assessments and frequent denials, he now chose to overlook ingratitude, applying himself with touching parental benevolence to arrangements for a hearing in the most discriminating city in Italy. The debut, he maintained, must leave nothing to chance; the presentation must be as flawless as the performance.

Rolla himself decided to conduct the accompanying orchestra. Niccolò would have been content to do without such a costly courtesy, but acquiesced, aware of some advantage in humoring the old man. Rolla's notions of a suitable orchestra, unfortunately, had little in common with Niccolò's casual gathering in of available hands. Alessandro Rolla auditioned and scolded, drove the inept from his presence, and hushed the parsimonious protests offered first apologetically and finally in anguish by Niccolò.

"A miser can launch only a miserly career," he decided energetically. And when Niccolò wailed that he had not the money to pay so many musicians—a transparent lie—Rolla ordered him loftily, in that case, to steal it. "Is Napoleon cautious?" he shouted. "Did Caesar hoard his *soldi* for his old age? Did Alexander the Great hesitate to risk a few more men? Remember, you are in Milan, not among the rustics who have yet to hear a real orchestra!"

At the end, over Niccolò's protests, he assembled eighteen violins, six violas, six cellos, four basses, paired flutes, clarinets, and oboes, and enough brass to wage war. "The Milanese dote on Janissary music," Rolla confided. "It makes them feel imperial."

"How will I be heard above the artillery?" Niccolò moaned.

"That is your problem," said Rolla. "I am inclined to think you will make yourself heard. Our Scala is large but acoustically perfect. There is nothing in the world to compare with it. We shall schedule four rehearsals."

"Four rehearsals! *Ohimè!* They will expect to be paid?"

"It is the custom."

Niccolò rocked back and forth, aching with constraint. He seldom held even a single rehearsal and never more than one. He expected and tolerated a degree of ineptness from an orchestra.

"The program."

"Something conventional at the start," Rolla suggested.

"Beethoven? Kreutzer?"

"Good, let it be Kreutzer," said Rolla. "This Beethoven of yours grows each year more erratic and dissonant. He is now nearly unplayable. I shall amuse them with the orchestra during the entr'acte. And then something…something à la Paganini. What do you have?"

"Old things, mostly. Millions of unsuitable things. And the *Caprices*."

"I do not mind a caprice or two. But half a program of caprices, and unaccompanied, smacks of the conservatory."

"Not at all. They are for artists."

"Hold your peace. At your age, a violinist knows nothing. He lacks judgment; he still needs a wet nurse."

"My *maestro* is gruff." Niccolò was tempted to drive him from the premises.

"My pupil is impertinent and stubborn. I told your father, and not once, that you were not yet ready to leave me in Parma. I'm sure it was money he was thinking about, not you. Yet, considering your lack of education, you have not turned out too badly. Of course, there are the occasional rough edges."

Niccolò sneered. "Truly?"

"No matter," Rolla decided. "If there are better violinists in the world, I have yet to hear them." And as Niccolò began to bob gratefully, "Don't thank me. I by no means say that you could not improve yourself. Your *legati* are sometimes quite…quite …"

"Yes, *Maestro*?"

"Quite unastonishing. Now, at once prepare something suitable and thoroughly *à la* Paganini with which to close your program. Else your audience will go home remembering only the big drum and the Janissary music."

Niccolò needed a simple melody upon which to focus. He acknowledged himself a leech, a pirate, a tune snatcher. He borrowed seedlings and fragments wherever he found them—from folk songs, revolutionary airs, a popular opera—transmuting them by his own peculiar alchemy into highly developed, intricate, above all, garishly original works. But he needed now the germ of an idea.

He thought, he discarded. Morbidly, he began to ponder his long neglect of composition. Since the early court years, he had brought forth virtually nothing; he had, indeed, permitted his native fluency to become clogged. Indolence, perhaps other kinds of battles, the gift of rapid improvisation that bypassed labor, the backlog of youthful work now seldom heard or played or thought about…Oh, already there was so much music in a world inundated with music!

Still, necessity stared him in the face, and all clocks menaced. None of the older compositions would do. The court work, however scored, was too inconsequential, too commonplace, too wanting in impact; most of it was frankly derivative. The caprices, which he continued to regard respectfully as the testament of his young manhood, failed to please; even Rolla had quibbled. Perhaps the pieces could not, after all, be presented in their entirety. Perhaps they were not sufficiently of the theater.

He tore paper, he uttered abominations, he spoiled a fine quill. Always, in the past, a work had evolved serenely, methodically, as he willed it, without agony and doubt. His inability now to find an immediate solution troubled him. Had his gift shriveled? Had he succumbed to lassitude? While he had never written with the self-consciousness of professed composers or with the thought of creating works that might live apart from his execution of them, the writing had poured out freely, shrewdly, and uncomplicatedly. Now that it mattered, now that his efforts would be part of the measure of the world's judgment upon him, he was afraid. The flowing sources could not be located. He fluttered timidly for an idea. Weeks passed. Nothing came.

Sickly cognizant of the shrinking calendar, half shattered by Rolla's nagging, Niccolò fell into a most profound depression. Had the demon deserted him? Had some thoughtless escapade been taken as a slight, a transgression of his pact? That casual afternoon hour with a red-haired whore in Turin? As soon forgotten as the meal he'd eaten afterwards.

The fawning young vocalist in Modena? He had thought she'd be a balm to his sleeplessness. She was anything but.

Perhaps it was that brief encounter with the woman in Rimini? Walking back to his quarters after a late evening concert, he had spied her in a dim pool of gaslight on the narrow street; she had been following him. Her satin dress whispered delicately as she approached. She stared at him openly, eyes wide, lips glistening, breathless in the dark. He took her right there, against the cold stone wall of an ancient church. Then he left her abruptly, hurried back to his rooms. Not a word had been spoken by either of them.

The Turinese trollop, the myrmidon in Modena, the idolizing wife of a wealthy Rimini burgher: these and half a dozen other liaisons had largely been forgotten. Certainly, love had been no part of them. Niccolò had done nothing to break his pact. He had been faithful to his dark Eleonora. Where was she now, when he needed her most?

For days he could not sleep. He wandered the streets, racked with fatigue, unshaven, disheveled, unrecognizable. He lost all track of time and place; day and night and candlelight, the streets, the *piazze*, his cell-like chamber: all intermingled in his fevered mind. Resting in twilight at the rim of a fountain, he drifted into a dreamy reverie, a trance that found no passage to the underworld of sleep.

"Eleonora," he heard himself whisper. "Why have you forsaken me?"

"Oh ye of little faith," she replied, her voice like the laughter of tumbling water.

Niccolò opened his eyes. He was lying at the writing table in his rented room. Discarded sheets of paper littered the floor. The door creaked open and the candle blew out.

"Eleonora?"

The musky scent of her filled the air.

"Where are you?" he asked, searching the shadows.

A cold breeze rustled the papers on his desk. Niccolò shivered. He heard the clatter of horse hooves echoing out on the street. Dragging himself from the table, he crossed the room to the open window. The full moon shone brightly over turreted roofs. Three floors below on the cobblestone street, a carriage rolled to a stop at his doorstep. In the moonlight, the black brougham gleamed like a lacquered casket, its horses snorting steam into the bracing night air. The black-caped coachman slipped from his perch like a serpent, swung open the door to the carriage, then turned and held out his gloved hand. Niccolò watched as a woman in red exited the door of his building. Taking the coachman's hand, she raised her ankle to the step and, sensing Niccolò's watchful eye, turned to look up toward him. Her face glowed like a porcelain moon. Niccolò's heart leapt into his throat. The succubus had come to life!

"Eleonora!" Niccolò shouted.

She turned away and climbed into the carriage.

"Eleonora—wait!"

The coachman shut the door and glided back to his seat. With a tart snap of the quirt, the pair of horses bolted forth, and the carriage rattled away.

Niccolò raced out of his room, down the winding stairs and out to the curb. The carriage was turning a corner at the end of the deserted street. He ran after it, shouting wildly. The horses continued at a trot, and the carriage disappeared.

Niccolò sprinted to the corner as the brougham turned onto a busy thoroughfare. Infused with a peculiar and unexpected vigor, Niccolò continued his chase, drawing astonished stares from passersby. The sight of the bedraggled man racing idiotically up the street was apparently too much for even the abiding citizens of Milan.

Niccolò dashed alongside the speeding carriage, grabbed hold of the window sill—the window was open—and pulled himself up onto the running board. The carriage continued at a relentless pace, hurtling through the crisscross of pedestrians and coaches. Niccolò unhooked the door latch and slipped inside.

Eleonora grinned as though she'd been waiting for him.

"You *are* determined," she said.

Catching his breath, he fell into the seat beside her. "Why? Are you leaving?"

"No one's *leaving*, Niccolò. I'm only going out for the evening." She sighed and looked out the window. "This *is* Milan, is it not?"

"It is, indeed." Niccolò felt his gaze drawn to her, to the warm glint of moonlight in her eyes, the creamy swell of her young breasts, the vast folds of her crimson gown glimmering like an ember. The sight of her exhilarated him.

"I can't let you forget me," he said.

She turned from the window. "How could I ever?"

Niccolò reached out, gently touched her cheek. "I need you," he said.

"I know," she replied. She kissed him wetly on the mouth; her tongue slipped easily through his lips, slithering like a viper over sharp teeth. Niccolò pressed himself to her, his hand searching beneath her skirts. She tore at the buttons of his trousers and quickly found her prey.

"Niccolò *mio*! And you thought you were all dried up!" She tightened her grasp, her long fingernails biting into his skin. Niccolò caressed her neck with his lips, his nose tipping the scarlet ruby that dangled from her ear. The scent of her sharpened his senses, honing his passion to a razor's edge. He would have her now, in full consciousness, awake and keenly aware. The horses snorted, their hooves pounding as the carriage bounded on. Night air whirled through the open windows, quickening the lovers with its cold embrace. Gaslights passed like shooting stars, bright flames burning the cloak of darkness. Niccolò's calloused string fingers tore through layers of silk and lace. He grabbed her buttocks in his strong, dry palms, and pulled her body against him. The she-devil licked his ear, whispering silken words in some ancient tongue, words that strangely infected and inflamed him. He thrust himself upon her. She bit his ear and threw him off, and the carriage came to a halt.

Niccolò found himself sprawled on the floor. He looked up at her, breathless and confused. Eleonora sat regally above him, bright queen of the succubi. The door flew open. Several white-gloved, red-uniformed attendants stared in at him from the sidewalk.

"Sir?" asked a short, portly one, tilting his head.

Niccolò hastily buttoned his pants. He looked to Eleonora in confusion.

She took pity. "I'm sorry we haven't more time, my love. But this is *not* a dream."

The round attendant coughed politely. His scarlet uniform looked disturbingly familiar. "Where are we?" Niccolò asked him.

"Why, the Opera House, sir."

Niccolò turned to Eleonora. "Opera?"

"Ballet. You've heard of *Herr* Süssmayr?"

Franz Süssmayr was a composer and a friend of Mozart's. His novel compositions had grown wildly popular in recent years.

"Of course. You know him well?" Niccolò asked.

"Intimately," she replied.

Niccolò stared at her. What was this feeling? Jealousy?

"They're waiting, Niccolò."

The attendants grinned with forbearance. Niccolò picked himself up and climbed out of the carriage. The fat little imp shut the door. Niccolò stood at the window, his hands like the paws of a dog on the sill.

"When will I see you again?"

"Why?" she replied, "I see you every night." She tapped on the glass, and the coachman cracked his whip. Niccolò watched the carriage disappear down the street.

Other carriages were pulling up, disgorging Milan's *beau monde* onto the steps of the marble-domed opera house. Niccolò tucked in his rumpled shirt, straightened his jacket, and walked in with the crowd.

It quickly became apparent why she'd brought him to this place. Scarcely had he seated himself when his problem vanished. Hope and promise literally confronted him in the form of a trite little tune that opened "*Il Noce di Benevento*"—an innocuous, so-called witches' dance. Witches, of course: hoarse, leering hags dancing about their sinister cauldrons. Murky clouds, flashes of lightning, feline yelps and yowls issuing from under their very footprints: the net of evil, vague and invisible.

He saw nothing; he heard no more. Before the act had ended, he dashed like one stricken to his room and began to rule paper. The set of brilliant variations superimposed upon the modest tune poured out of pen, brain, and fingers, without a backward glance or searching or constraint. It must have been lurking there, in the recesses of consciousness, waiting.

His dark mistress had delivered him to it.

Variation on variation, the work would present excruciating technical difficulties to shock and astonish. Imitations, yes, fantastic imitations; charlatanism elevated to high art. He, Paganini, would be outrageous and wicked and macabre, telling what none are meant to hear, yet he would defy them to withhold adulation and homage.

He would project sounds never before emanating from violin and bow—a keening nasal oboe tone, dry reediness, shrill supernatural voices, high and low, raucous and feeble voices, voices of aged crones, errant spurts of laughter, the grotesque swish of broomsticks, guttural sounds, weird and slithering, angular sounds. It was here, it was all here in these notes that poured from pen onto the lined paper almost more rapidly than he could think. The scintillating *staccati* were here, the bizarre distortions, the galloping roulades, the explosions of arpeggios—all the "fireworks" so decried by Luigi Germi—and harmonics more eerie and dazzling than any yet heard.

To scoop out their inner organs, he thought fiercely.

Niccolò called the composition *"Le Streghe"*—"The Witches"—and on his knees gave thanks to his succubus queen.

❀ ❀ ❀

"You are famous!" Rolla announced, shattering Niccolò's weak, feverish sleep.

He stomped into the shabby, disorderly room, sniffed the fetid air, and brandished his newspaper. Unable to find a place to sit, he removed Niccolò's cloak and greatcoat from the bed with his cane. "Those witches, those witches! You are the greatest violinist in Europe, it says so, and I am your master."

"I am sick," Niccolò moaned from his bed. "I am spitting up my lungs, and you are a liar and a fool."

"The Viceroy commands you to appear at court," Rolla shouted exuberantly. "Each of you a fine feather in the other's cap."

Niccolò sat up, choked, then spat into a knotted rag.

"Eugene Beauharnais," explained the old conductor. Receiving no answer, he continued loudly and deliberately, as though Niccolò were deaf. "Josephine. The Empress Josephine. Her son, Eugene."

"I don't care whose son, Eugene."

"The Princess Bacciochi was the arch enemy of the Empress," Rolla gossiped. "Even at the coronation she was rude; she was heard to say, '*merde*'; she would not hold the train of Josephine's robe."

"Who is the Princess Bacciochi?" Niccolò yawned.

But Rolla had unfurled the newspaper and begun to wave his hands, brandish his stick, and jump up and down on his spidery legs, as though conducting, while wild, hyperbolic phrases flew from his lips.

"Your purity of intonation is sheerly incredible—that is what he says, sheerly incredible—"

"I shall be evicted from this stable if you don't stop shouting," Niccolò complained, over an attack of coughing.

"You are a Titan, he says. You are *inexplicable*—"

"That was my left leg you struck with your cane."

"…foremost and greatest in the world—"

The landlady thrust her head in the doorway, wondering whether the *gran' signor* wanted anything.

"Yes, yes," Niccolò moaned, pointing to his visitor. "Get this old fool out of my room."

"Such levity before the lower classes," Rolla began to lecture.

"That's not my job," declared the landlady indignantly. "This is a respectable place!"

"Go, go," commanded Rolla loftily.

"We'll see who goes," she threatened. "To be ordered from one's own house! Even the French, even the invasion…I and the old man, may his soul rest in peace, we kept our own chamber, even with the house requisitioned. Now, there is no war—"

"Quiet," groaned Niccolò. "I have concerts to give, I am dying, and these vultures will not allow a man to suffer in peace."

The landlady withdrew, muttering about the respectability of her house.

"Why do you stay here, in such squalor, with this old sack of meal?" Rolla inquired indignantly. "You are rich, or will be. Do you know who wrote so glowingly of your violinism? Not a local hack. Not even a Milanese, though the Milanese are beside themselves singing your praises."

Since Niccolò had turned to the wall, clutching his chest, the old teacher continued in a high, declamatory voice, "Lilienthal. Peter Lilienthal. *The* Lilienthal. You know where this report will be read in a week, two weeks?"

Niccolò squirmed, aware of the eternal gulf between the suffering and the healthy; aware that his own art would always rise upon ashes of disease, decay, the muted anticipation of nonbeing that haunts all living men; aware that if he truly possessed a future as an artist, it would be in defiance of pain and malaise, and that death would be his mother, his lover…He closed his eyes and tried not to listen, for even words, good, uplifting, encouraging words, cut into him like whiplash and festered feverishly.

"In Munich! In Berlin! In Vienna!" cried Rolla, shaking his inert pupil. "Lilienthal is exultant; we need not say a word. You are a success, *figlio mio*. Your struggle is ended. Spohr will kill himself." The old man smacked his lips delicately, beaming at the very notion. "Lafont will kill himself, too, but particularly Spohr, that fussy German stuffed *Strudel*. Italy has recovered her ancient glory."

Niccolò did not answer. Everything the old fool said was probably true, but one could not afford to celebrate in advance, let money trickle away, and gloat over one's good fortune. Fortune was a beast, a bear to be tamed and trained to do somersaults. One could never relax. Meanwhile, there were these miseries to endure, to wait out with patience and forbearance.

"Will you play at court? What shall I tell the viceroy?"

Niccolò scarcely heard him. He thought of the strange sunsets of Genoa, the blazing summer sun a pool of blood in the darkening harbor waters, and the slithering cats, black and gray and dappled, beginning to emerge from their lairs. And his heart was heavy, and he knew an inexplicable yet familiar constriction: not love, not longing, but sadness that things are as they are, that victory is joyless, that to live is to struggle without surcease.

"… play at court?" he heard vaguely. Rolla had banged out each syllable to the accompaniment of his cane.

Niccolò nodded.

"Can't you see the professor is sick?" rasped the landlady from the hallway. "Who are you, the fiend himself?"

"Bah! Go comb the cobwebs from your hair, slattern," Rolla replied.

He descended the squeaky staircase, wondering aloud why the youth of the land were so weak, flabby, self-indulgent, and wanting in character. "Sick! Sick! I am an old man and do not allow myself to be sick!" he informed no one in particular.

❉ ❉ ❉

Niccolò lay a while longer in his warm and lumpy bed, trying, as he did every morning, to coax out the fevered images that had plagued his night's sleep. Distorted fragments flashed in his mind: the stroke of a whip on the back of his thighs, wrists tied and hung, blood on the bark of a white birch, the reptilian tail climbing up his leg, a breast pierced with the tusk of a boar, arms and necks torn and twisted, yellow-eyed wolves in a feeding frenzy, bizarre insects crawling over flesh. These were his disturbing visions, at once strange and familiar, enticing and repugnant; they left him sickly and wretched, yet aroused.

The Devil was a goddess; the Devil was a whore. He welcomed the guilt and the suffering she brought him, for he knew she would make him the greatest virtuoso in the world. It was something he'd always known, even before she had appeared that night in Turin. He had never doubted it, even in the early Luccan days, even as a boy. In return for the secrets, for that organic knowledge close to other men but revealed to him alone and incorporated as instinct, he must give in return. His soul? His strength? Himself?

For he believed in that balance of the scales of good fortune and calamity, which is justice. He would have fame; therefore, he must be made to suffer. He would be ravaged by disease; therefore, he would amass wealth. He was the incomparable, the incredible, beyond which neither art nor imagination dare venture; therefore, his satanic master dug fiery fangs into him and gnawed quietly upon his life.

When he felt better, Niccolò left his bed and crawled to the washstand, rubbing his palms over the stubble of his chin. He paused to regard himself in the mirror. Too feeble to laugh aloud, he began to chuckle foolishly at his reflection.

"I am possessed," he muttered, rubbing his pale jowls. "I have begun to resemble my master."

His landlady screamed, "Don't fall, *Signor*! You will hurt yourself! They will think you have been done violence here—" She rushed to his side and supported him with her massive arms.

"A moment's dizziness," he explained.

"Cupping is best of all. There is nothing better than to drain off the bad blood. The doctors, they want only money; they do not care if one dies." She helped him into bed and pulled the dirty blanket over his haunches.

"Whom…whom do I resemble?" Niccolò implored in a weak, disembodied voice.

"Why, you resemble *Signor* Paganini," she boomed. "How could you resemble anyone else? Your honorable parents I do not know; perhaps you indeed favor one over the other." She teased the dust with her broom, then closed the heavy shutters with an air of finality.

"The fever, I think it's back," she said. "And you are skinny as a skeleton as it is. What would they say if I had a stranger die in this house? The finest people have been here, no deaths, no nonsense. *Madonna mia,* you never know who it is you let in, or what harm may be done you. Life is hard."

❈ ❈ ❈

THE PAGANINI RAGE waxed lustily: eleven concerts within six weeks at the Scala or the *Teatro Carcano* or the *Teatro Re,* all screaming ovations, all so promptly sold out to avid speculators that the Milanese were forced to battle one another for seats. And speculation trickled throughout the city, from court to cafe to parlor to kitchen. Was he, indeed, diabolical, this weird fiddler? Had the Evil One a role in producing these delectations? Was it injurious to listen?

His fortunes spiraled wildly upward as the great meteor, blood-red and desperate, began its final downward course. The Napoleonic Empire had begun to disintegrate. Whispers and wild rumors trickled slowly into the awareness of ordinary men, only half-believed by those who provoked them and vehemently denied by others. The Russian campaign was advancing; it was not advancing. Casualties were light and heavy. Left and right, the generals were betraying the Emperor; Bernadotte had called him a mad dog. Austria had not consolidated peace with the French upstart even after sending him a Hapsburg princess as a burnt offering. And all Italy seethed as hope, aspiration, and conspiracy splintered the peninsula. Everywhere, the rumble of a changing order could be heard. The new thrones tottered. The British were reported to be massing forces. Legitimacy was on the march.

Niccolò thought vaguely of Prince Felix and of his dear friends, the Quilici, when the British occupied Lucca in the spring. But his more urgent thoughts were of himself, of the strategies he must exercise and the conquests that awaited him. The Revolution was dead; of that he had long ago convinced himself. The Napoleonic era would soon be mentioned only by reminiscing ancients and children reciting their lessons. Hero, savior, or tyrant, the Corsican was doomed. New loyalties were in order.

Paganini learned a few words of German, a most execrable tongue. He suffered himself to perform for Eugene Beauharnais, a foppish young man with an outrageous sense of self-importance, but he allocated even more time to the Austrians, suddenly everywhere, who joined him in quartet playing and promised him a conqueror's welcome in Vienna.

7

ANGELINA

IT WAS NOT TO Vienna that he hastened, however, but to Genoa and his father's house. Homecoming is bitter. A sure formula for disenchantment, one anticipates. And when memory betrays us, it is ourselves we hate.

Genoa seemed small, smaller than he had remembered. It was not the grandeur of the places visited during the separation, but that he recalled with a child's eye, which sees everything clear, definitive, larger than life.

One swift, loving embrace from the family, and he was sick with impatience to be off, to abandon them once again, to seek peace in turmoil. Only the wars deterred him. He did not want to be where there was rioting and pillage. Old Rolla had shut himself up in his studio at the first Milanese disorders, declaring that he would not flee, since the house was his, nor come forth until the populace behaved more sensibly. But Niccolò had rushed from the city. Unwittingly, he had come to regard himself as guardian of something precious that must not be imperiled.

His mother, Teresa Paganini, had grown frail. There seemed a deliberate martyrdom about her, perhaps foil to Antonio's tyranny, that at once distressed Niccolò and angered him. She whimpered, caressed his cheeks, clung to him, begged him never again to depart. He tore her hands from his face. It had always been so, Niccolò reasoned bitterly. Love, exasperation, remorse: such had always been his bond with his family. He would never be able to endure them, and he would never be free of them.

Domenica and Nicoletta, his sisters, danced attendance, arraigned their progeny, and presented doltish, plebeian husbands who could not wait to talk of money. Carlo seemed genuinely glad to see his brother, but Niccolò could hardly believe this stolid provincial the same Carlo who, after all, had shared his early wanderings, had known Lucca, the court, the volatile princess, the ferment of that golden age. Time is vicious, Niccolò thought; we turn into devils or brutes.

Antonio Paganini viewed his son's homecoming as the enactment of a judgment and sentencing, his own role being that of wrathful deity. There had scarcely been time to break bread before he thundered out the preliminary denunciations. He had been robbed of a father's due, gratitude. His second son wallowed in wealth; reports of his triumphs had reached Genoa from the four corners of the earth. But had he remembered his poor family? Had he been prompted by a sense of duty, since love seemed too much to expect? Had he—nurtured, protected, comforted, educated, launched in an uncertain world by the world's most selfless father—felt obliged to share a pinch of his bounty with his family? Did he know his father suffered the pains of rheumatism in both legs? Did he care to know? Did he realize his mother had thin, weak blood? Did this move him? No, no; it was more pleasurable to scatter money over gaming boards, to squander it on pampered living, to stuff it into actresses and whores.

Niccolò reminded his father that seldom had a month gone by without a contribution conveyed through his friend and advocate, Germi, who would be glad to verify these sums; and that he had sent money to his parents even when he had been in need, far from comfortable, and ill.

Antonio snickered. "There is no end to these lies and fabrications," he advised his wife and Carlo, as though Niccolò were not present. "And he is so glib that, as he tells the lies, he begins to believe them."

"Germi has the reckoning."

"Aha, he keeps a reckoning! He cannot send his poor family a pittance, a bone, without arranging for the generosity to be recorded by a lawyer. And trumpeted from the housetops, no doubt. I suppose it has been proclaimed to all Genoa that you are supporting your father."

"Since it is so obviously untrue, I don't see how all Genoa could accept such a proclamation," Niccolò said. "You must decide with which reproach to flay me. Either I am starving you, or I am boasting of my generosity."

"You are doing both," Antonio shouted roughly. "Do not try to trip me with your fancy reasoning. I am no fool." He wiped his mouth and eyed his son guardedly. "You will give a concert here in Genoa?"

"At the Sant' Agostino."

"The Sant' Agostino?" gasped Teresa with awe.

"I shall be there. I shall count every coin in the till. Oh, you will be unable to deceive me with your mock poverty, my fine son."

Niccolò shrugged. "I do not believe I have ever practiced deceit, Father. And I know I have been as lavish as the circumstances permitted."

"Yes, yes," Teresa corroborated.

"Quiet," shouted Antonio Paganini, and pounded on the table.

Niccolò raged at the injustice. His words of refutation had been mild, but the charges grated. Did Antonio actually believe what he said? How could he tell such lies, with the entire family present? He looked at his mother, foolish and loving, at his sisters with their distended bellies, squalling infants, and sordid domestic cares; at Carlo, kind and ineffectual, but scarcely talented enough to eke out a living as a musician; at his stormy, frustrated father, who expected not an errant wanderer still securing his reputation at thirty-one, but the very goose of the golden eggs.

And Niccolò knew that he was trapped. Habit and guilt, pity and the need for approbation, formed an uneasy amalgam. Antonio would get a tribute, quite beyond his due, but Niccolò would find neither ease nor comfort here, not pride in his accomplishments, but the serpent of dissatisfaction and the slow poison of resentment.

His Sant' Agostino concert was a huge success, a regal homecoming, an exercise in delirium for the placid Genoese. The sometime patrons of his childhood, the Di Negri, cheered him from the doges' box, sharing in the fanfare and glory; and beside them, Sir William Bentinck, commander of His Majesty's regiments in Genoa, and his aide-de-camp, Colonel Maxwell Montgomery, beamed their satisfaction with the progress of Britannic history and Italian music. Niccolò clasped violin and hand to his heart and bowed nearly to the floor. All audiences are royalty, he seemed to say, and the only royalty are paying audiences.

He experienced in the excitement of the moment—perhaps because of the eruption of early memories and a realization of hope and longing fulfilled—his first and last twinge of political guilt. How easily he had shed his convictions! How painlessly, with what apathy, he now acknowledged new masters! Had not the Corsican, after all, stood for something? Had he not brought, in his time, liberating visions, ideals, promises? Had he not ushered in the age of man, making possible even a Paganini?

No matter. The Corsican had failed.

The Genoese screamed themselves hoarse hailing their native son. In an anguish of dizziness, fear of falling, and anxiety lest his fiddle slip from his hands, he was carried from the theater on the shoulders of leading citizens. He concluded cynically that there were more comfortable ways of getting about. *Signora* Di Negro kissed him on the mouth, invited him to her villa, and did not, as in the early days, send him to the kitchen to eat with the servants. Sir William conveyed the felicitations of His Majesty's government and hoped Niccolò would soon be heard in

London. And Antonio Paganini, blissfully counting and recounting the receipts, knew the meaning of filial gratitude.

Niccolò was pleased, but scarcely prepared to sit still. All the world beckoned. All the world awaited his revelations and his plunder. Yet travel was impossible. No one knew where the next disorders would flare, where a last stand would be taken, where one set of conquerors had yet to be exchanged for another. Bored, chafed, bristling with impatience, Niccolò realized he could do nothing but wait for the turbulence to subside.

In the meantime, his nightmares had mysteriously abated. It had begun the first night of his arrival in Genoa. He had lain awake, as always, warily awaiting the fall into sleep, but when it came, no dreams came with it. For the first time in over a year, he slept for hours without waking, and in the morning, felt deeply rested and revived. The following night was the same, and the next, and so it went for weeks on end.

He found it, at first, a great relief. The coughing, the pallor, the weakness in his heart: all began to fade. A healthy vigor returned to his life. He experienced a long-forgotten surge of physical power—not the sinister and erotic impulse that had impelled his music, but the brimming force of life coursing through his veins, the tingling sensation of being alive in the bright light of day. In the city of his youth, he began to feel young again.

But not without concern. For though he was glad to be rid of the nightly horrors, some sunless part of himself longed for enticement. The Devil, it seemed, had succeeded in corrupting his soul. He feared her yet yearned for her. And in this state of anxious paradox, he obsessed over the question of when—if ever—she would return.

It was a question he could not answer. Niccolò realized he had no control; the Devil's love—if it could be called such—was like a force of Nature: capricious, indifferent, occasionally indulgent, and totally out of Niccolò's hands. His career was at the mercy of a merciless she-devil. And yet…Perhaps she had left him only because, at the moment, he had no need of her. The fate of nations had intervened. Perhaps this was merely a restorative reprise from the incessant hell he'd been living in, a chance to recover before riding headlong back into his battle with Destiny.

If so, why not take advantage of the opportunity? Niccolò soon felt himself in the grip of fresh temptations.

❀ ❀ ❀

Germi had cautioned him to avoid the waterfront.

"Even angels flying over the Genoese waterfront find their halos tarnished," he said. "It is inevitable. In broad daylight, one is likely to find himself in a pool of blood—his own, mind you—minus cloak and purse. At night, anything can happen. One may awaken in chains, half-way across the Mediterranean—"

"Or in the lap of an enchantress who does not quibble and demand verses about eternal love," said Niccolò.

"Or in the *lazzaretto* with something loathsome."

Niccolò laughed. "You are a prudent man, Luigi. You are never tempted."

"Oh, I am tempted," Germi admitted. "But not to roam, since I have everything I might crave within these walls."

"The best cook in the world," Niccolò ventured.

"And fat."

"And pretty."

"And willing."

Niccolò sighed exaggeratedly. "Not all of us are blessed with a Camilletta."

"To say nothing of a beautiful Amati, from which I shall never be parted. I am a violinist by choice, albeit a lawyer by avarice."

"It is also rumored you are not indifferent to politics."

Germi bowed in acknowledgement. "Let us wait for the situation to settle before proclaiming it. The city reeks of foreigners."

"You seem to have done well in spite of them."

"Some of us fall, like the cats of Genoa, on our feet," Germi laughed. "It does not matter who is theoretically master of the city. One can glean a small profit from those who come as from those who go."

"That is why I honor you," said Niccolò. "And why you shall always be treasurer of all my ventures."

"I thought you honor me for my prowess as a fiddler."

"Never."

"You cannot endure the competition."

In a more serious vein, Niccolò said, "Something will have to be done about my family. An income. A house, perhaps. My father grumbles, and my mother suffers."

"It will always be so. We are born either to grumble or to suffer. But something will be done, Don Croesus."

Niccolò examined the delicate Amati, turning the instrument to appraise its rotundity and glow. "The name, Cavanna," he said guardedly. "Is it familiar to you?"

"There is a tailor by that name," said Germi. "A bad one, I am told."

"He has a daughter?"

"Aha! He has a flock of daughters."

"A young, lovely one. About seventeen. Angelina."

"Seventeen is not an interesting age in a woman," Germi declared. "Where did you find her?"

Niccolò hesitated, then blurted, "Along the waterfront. She is a seamstress, she was returning—"

"Plying her trade, no doubt," Germi concurred with tolerant skepticism. "Along the waterfront. Ah, my friend, to what men can be reduced! You, who once cavorted with princesses …"

"For my purposes, a beautiful seamstress will do."

"Or a beautiful tradeswoman in other commodities."

"The differences are not as great as you would suppose, dear Luigi, between a princess and a seamstress."

"Or a tradeswoman?" Germi would not be ignored.

"Or a cook," Niccolò concluded firmly.

He had come to believe this, at least from time to time. A convenient philosophy, it dispelled confusion and convinced him he owed nothing of substance and spirit to any woman. Any woman of this world, at least…

❋ ❋ ❋

SCARCELY SEVENTEEN, Angelina Cavanna had an oddly infantile, conventionally pretty face, bovine eyes, and a skinny, unwomanly body. For a few moments, she had reminded Niccolò of Eleanora, the young Eleonora of flesh and blood. Then he realized that Angelina's ingenuousness was as calculated and false as Eleanora's was intrinsic and true.

If scarcely the seasoned tradeswoman Germi had indicated, Angelina had intermittent knowledge of the ways of the waterfront and had not been too proud to supplement her income with whatever opportunities arose. However, impressed by the identity of her avid, woman-starved wooer, she feigned great naiveté, permitting herself to be seduced and simulating fear, remorse, and pain. Niccolò found her pretenses amusing. He had possessed the gamy little body an hour after he first encountered Angelina, who might indeed have been soliciting near the dock. He found her able, sexually fluent, and not without charm, and consoled her sympathetically when she reproached him, in a outburst of free-flowing, automatic tears, for deflowering a maiden.

"Now you will never marry me," Angelina wailed. "My saintly mother—God keep her soul—told me that once a man has taken your innocence, the wedding is off."

"Oh, I wouldn't generalize," yawned Niccolò. "I find you very pleasing."

Angelina squealed with delight, then once more collapsed tearily. "No, you will never marry me."

"Perhaps I shall never marry anyone. And then, perhaps I shall marry you."

"Our social positions—" Angelina babbled.

"I have no social position. Have you?"

"But you are the great Paganini, while I—I—"

"While you are not," said Niccolò. "Wouldn't it be complicated if there were two great Paganinis? Frankly, I would not find that at all to my liking."

Angelina giggled and clung possessively to his arm.

"We shall meet tomorrow, dove? At dusk? Here?"

She pouted and pirouetted, pretending indecision. "I don't know."

"I shall make arrangements at the *albergo*. We'll dine in a private room, wine and capon and—"

"You won't want to—want to—want—"

"No, I refuse to promise not to want!" declared the fiddler, mock-shocked.

"It's wrong, what we are doing—"

Niccolò enjoyed the little deception. It provided conversation, no easy feat under the circumstances. He demurred, ardently proclaiming the utter rightness of their deeds. After all, one could not be held responsible for such an avalanche of emotion; the love that had set each of them aflame on but beholding the other was surely greater than puny considerations of right and wrong. Niccolò did not tax his resourcefulness. He exploited threadbare platitudes from fustian operas and silly plays viewed throughout the years. Angelina gaped, profoundly impressed.

He met with her often and found himself, despite Germi's carping, appeased and peculiarly content. Without a doubt, Angelina was, as his friend maintained, dull, dishonest, untruthful, and common. Her endless chattering so bored him that he often wished her a mute, but then, he did not actually have to listen. This blessed inattention, he decided, formed the basis of his infatuation for Angelina. He had neither to court her nor to be on his mettle. From an early age, he had found the indifference of prostitutes offensive; he felt rebuked as a man. A princess of the Revolution, on the other hand, had to be accorded the prerogatives of entrenched royalty, and Niccolò found dancing to the scepter altogether exhausting. And the industrious ladies of the theater proved too honest, too forthright, too comradely and co-equal in the art of love.

This little goose found him perfect. While her postures of girlish innocence were transparently sham, her adoration was genuine enough, feeding on dreams of miracles and grandeur. He would marry her, fantasy prompted, and transport her to the grand world of fashion and concerts and splendid clothes and jewels and excitement. Angelina turned demure; her nocturnal prowling about the waterfront ceased. She made novenas, embroidered, and handed down priggish little judgments about the shortcomings of the world.

It leaked out that she had been confiding her misadventure to her father, the tailor blessed with many daughters. Niccolò was at first annoyed; then he forgot about it. His concerns were with the destinies of nations and the availability of concert halls throughout a stable and prosperous Europe. He could not excite himself about the views of an illiterate tailor.

Angelina became coy. Innately passive and giving, she learned to check Niccolò's attentions at the very brink of fulfillment. She could not, no, she would not; she would be punished from above. Oh no, she must not outrage the memory of her mother. Dear, darling Niccolò must believe her; she had always been very proper; no man had ever so much as touched her little finger; oh, no, she would have died of shame.

"We'll talk of it another time," Niccolò suggested vaguely, confident that the matter had been laid to rest.

But Angelina had become obsessed with the need to have her honor repaired. She wept, sniveled, and most uncharacteristically left half the food on her plate, tormenting her lover with wastefulness. Worse yet, she became erratic in bestowing her favors. Sunday might find her clinging, yielding, exquisitely affable. By Tuesday—prompted perhaps by the calculating tailor—she might distinctly prefer death to the touch of unchaste lips, and Niccolò's overtures would produce fountains and rivulets of tears.

"I cannot marry you," Niccolò explained. "The Genoese law would not permit it without the consent of my parents. And they will never give their consent."

Since Angelina persisted in the notion that his lofty social status poised this obstacle, he no longer tried to dispel her error. That he had spent years in the Luccan court Angelina had been told. She could see at once that he was a gentleman. And the local triumphs were so well known as to cause Niccolò great embarrassment. He could not move about Genoa, even grimiest Genoa, without being pointed out by the curious as he roamed with Angelina; his lean, intense face and wiry frame were easily identified. Even Angelina heard bits and pieces of rumors concerning his great wealth, his wizardry, his connections with the Devil. Most of all, she seemed impressed with his great wealth.

❀ ❀ ❀

Genoa was growing tedious. His family had long ago grown tedious. Angelina was tedium itself, although he still sporadically ached to possess and devour her child-like, submissive little person, unencumbered by the moral posturing and conflicts and the unsuccessful subterfuges imposed upon him by his native city.

The political situation was beginning to stabilize. Italy, craving peace, could not be inflamed into prolonged strife. The Emperor had abdicated in favor of his son; Genoa had learned from unerring albeit mysterious sources that he had tried to poison himself. He had been confined to the island of Elba after seeing himself burned in effigy by those who had but yesterday hailed him as Caesar Augustus. His archenemies, the British, had transported him from Frejus with full imperial and military honors, including a twenty-one-gun salute. The time was ripe for concerts.

"While we cannot hope to wed in Genoa," Niccolò informed the chronically teary Angelina, "Milan has more liberal rulings concerning parental consent. There is no reason why we cannot be promptly married there."

Angelina, startled by his sudden readiness to redeem her from the most delectable of sins and dazed by the prospect of becoming a splendid lady, covered herself modestly and listened.

"We must leave secretly," Niccolò continued, beginning to enjoy the deception. "At night. Seen by no one, or else my outraged parents will intercept the marriage. Once we reach Milan, the ceremony can be performed, and Angelina will not need to weep, for weeping makes ugly girls with red eyes and bloated noses."

The silly girl flung herself gratefully upon her benefactor, exclaiming of love and imminent ecstasy. The latter intrigued Niccolò more than the former. He hoped the detested journey would be rendered endurable this time, and punctuated by pleasant distractions.

Vowing absolute secrecy and maudlin with excitement, Angelina departed for the parental hovel. Niccolò waited until she had vanished, then retraced his steps toward *Passo del gato moro*. He was convinced she could hardly wait to convey her good fortune to the scheming tailor, who, in turn, would do all in his power to sustain the illusion of a secret elopement.

It was not to Milan that Niccolò ordered the carriage. For several months, the lovers lingered near drowsy Parma, already a familiar place to him. Excuses were not too difficult to fabricate and, as had been anticipated, Angelina's histrionics and scruples dissolved with separation from her mentor. Occasionally, she carped of marriage, particularly when he was making love to her and would have promised anything, however outrageous. By and large, she remained the uncomplicated, vulgar little baggage that she was. Niccolò could enjoy Angelina without remorse or a sense of wallowing in the gutter. After all, even Germi, the spotless advocate of ancient lineage, had spoken poetically of the unblurred pleasures to be gathered from a woman of the lower classes; hence his Camilletta, who cooked, mended, and marketed. Angelina, Niccolò conjectured, was a somewhat livelier article.

The inn was outside the city proper and not too reputable; there seemed little likelihood of their being discovered. Soon the time would be ripe, the small volcanoes extinguished, and Paganini could embark upon his conquests, which might take him—where? To Vienna, to Paris, to London, perhaps even to exotic Russia and the very borderline of the civilized world, America. Meanwhile, there ensued an indolent time for Niccolò. The nightmares were gone; the succubus had vanished. Perhaps, he began to think, he could do as well without her. He slept late, practiced silently—he had devised and refined a method of near-silent finger exercises, meaning to share as little as possible with an insatiably curious world—and watched political events.

True, Angelina proved a consummate bore with her obsessive chatter and observations. He had anticipated this, accepting the confines of her world and her wit. But her passivity was vastly comforting to him. It seemed altogether delightful not to have to prove oneself, to beguile or enchant, to be clever, to devise an intricate web of courtly language and strenuous lies, but merely to quench one's thirst. To Angelina he had to prove nothing. He was greater than Napoleon at his zenith, mightier than all the potentates of the world—and she had never yet heard him play the violin! Nor did it matter. She did not seem to possess the rudiments of an ear or a voice. She never hummed or sang when alone, as women are apt to do. Her speaking voice was startlingly rough, at times grating; the dialect she spoke discarded altogether or abbreviated numerous vowels, emerging with un-Italianate choppiness and an absence of cadence. But Niccolò did not actually feel obliged to listen.

❊ ❊ ❊

Angelina was ill. Very ill. Morning after morning, she looked jaundiced upon awakening, belched apologetically over her food, which she but pretended to nibble, moped beside the window. Slyly, she attempted to conceal her indisposition from him, embarking upon concealment with such thoroughness that he was aware of little else.

"What seems to be the matter, my dove?" Niccolò inquired absently.

"Worms, perhaps," she whined, seeking her pillow. "Oh, I shall never forget when poor Brigitta had worms! Little as she was, she was doubled over like a dwarf." The very thought seemed to intensify her sickness; she sought comfort on her pillow and reminisced no more.

In the female conversations that had surrounded childhood and in the twitter of the Bacciochi court, Niccolò had learned much about Angelina's illness. The court, as a matter of fact, from grand duchess to chambermaid, seemed obsessed with talk of fertility and its circumvention, pregnancy, and the correction of pregnancy. "What else is there to do here save look ornamental and copulate?" a courtier had explained cynically. Etiquette and politics complicated the activity, and boredom stimulated it, but the essentials never varied.

The court ladies patronized doctors, barbers, witches, and quacks; they bribed midwives and apothecaries, and engaged as lustily in snuffing out life as in creating it. When these efforts failed, they accepted their lot graciously, bearing their wee bastards with love and forbearance, and with such maternal dignity that many were assumed to be legitimate issue, even by their mothers' husbands.

It seemed wiser not to precipitate problems where Angelina was concerned. Clearly, she was either too dull, too sentimental, or too unworldly to confront realities. Dissimulation had always been the sole means of affecting her and her means of communicating with others. Perhaps she needed the myth of her unsullied virtue and his honorable intentions; it would be imprudent to jar her from her dreams, particularly since she was clearly aware of her self-deception.

He returned from the apothecary—a shrewd person of some experience and learning, with whom, after a few exploratory minutes, one could be quite frank—bearing a quantity of gritty powder in an envelope.

"This," he advised the languishing Angelina, "is a world-renowned cure for worms. I purchased it at great cost from the apothecary. It is the finest specific known."

"You have put yourself to so much expense," the practical Angelina worried. "Perhaps the worms will go away of their own accord. It does seem I feel stronger in the evening."

She wished to take the medicine at once, but Niccolò detained her.

"No, it must be dissolved in wine," he said. "Or in strong coffee or a little goat's milk. Since you are feeling so much better, there is little point in agitating your system with a cure just now. Let us wait until morning. Perhaps," he smiled, "you are already recovered. Or perhaps I can offer you such joy during the night as to make you well."

Whereupon Angelina squealed with delight and puckered kittenishly to receive his kiss.

In the morning, Niccolò carefully supervised a generous initial dosage of the pink powder, which dissolved readily in the tiny cup of coffee but apparently altered the taste, for Angelina's face turned ghostly, and she needed coaxing to swallow the frothing liquid.

"I know the medicine is not supposed to taste good," she gasped. "But this is the very death! I prefer worms; really, I do!"

For a moment, a hideous doubt assailed him. Could she actually be innocent of guile? Did she really believe herself subject to an attack of worms—a common enough disorder—and could it be that she was not pretending at all?

Niccolò quickly snuffed out so unpleasant a thought.

Again, he departed for the day, leaving Angelina at rest, patiently awaiting her cure and instructed as to its prolongation. What would surely ensue, Niccolò decided, had better be spared his artistic sensibilities and male fastidiousness. He had some important business in the city, he hinted cheerfully; perhaps they would soon be leaving Parma.

The nature and efficacy of the cure remained obscure, for on his return to the squalid inn, Niccolò was physically assaulted by its innkeeper (who generally had the good sense to take his money and remain invisible) and pelted with imprecations by the hysterical Angelina. He was called a murderer, a poisoner, a seducer of innocent maidens, a rogue fit for flogging, a vile, glib devil. Niccolò bolted the door against the loud charges of his landlord, dragging Angelina with him. He had to slap her briskly to procure acquiescence, for she resisted, screaming that she would not be confined with a murderer, a poisoner, the fiend himself. Once within the chamber, her outcries halted, and she wept inconsolably.

"What happened?"

"Oh, you do not love me; you do not love me," she sobbed.

"What happened?" he shouted, itching to slap her again.

"I retched and retched. Oh, my poor stomach turned quite inside out...I vomited; I wanted to die!"

"Is *that all?*" Niccolò was furious. "Did you not take the second dose or the third? Did you follow my instructions?"

"How could I? I was so sick, I wished myself dead. Oh, how could you do this to me, robbing a poor girl of her maidenhead—"

"Maidenhead!" Niccolò did not care if everyone in the inn heard him. "You polluted little wretch, have you forgotten where I found you, and how you were occupied?"

"And tore me from the arms of my papa and promised to marry—"

"And back to the arms of your papa you go, this very day! Already the police have given me notice to get rid of you."

"The police!" Angelina shrieked. Her reaction was instinctual; she knew the defenders of the law as the scourge of lower-class Genoa and the waterfront: sinister beings to be bribed, cajoled, beseeched, feared.

It took many sordid hours to achieve Angelina's departure. She wept, clung to him, and exploded in tantrums; she knelt before him, begging mercy, offering to crawl in his wake as his handmaiden, if only he did not banish her from his world. Each moment, she became more hideous and more distasteful to him. Niccolò began to deem himself grievously wronged. His nerve-ends were searing raw. He felt that if he did not blot out this abomination, he would die of it. He screamed at her and called her besmirched whore, guttersnipe, filth, disease-carrier…

He was too shaken, too drained by rage, to question Angelina's decision to journey not to Genoa, to her father, but to rural Fumeri, to the old peasant woman who had nursed the tailor's little ones when their mother had died. He would have watched stonily had she chosen to journey to the bottom of the sea. He wanted her gone; she was strangling him by her servitude, her tears, her cloyish love, her lies, her stupidity.

As soon as she had been seated in the carriage, clutching her bundle of rags and a loaf of spiced bread, he turned coldly away and departed, not waiting for the impatient horses to start. His last glimpse was of her stained, puffy face, lower lip thrust out rebelliously, tears zigzagging from her eyes to the corners of her mouth. He felt liberated and light of heart.

8
The "Duel"

The banner of Fortune, the flag of Europe, hung on the titan who had been hunted down, isolated, and confined to an island estate on Elba with an income of two million francs a year and a miniature army and court. Niccolò, like many Europeans, had accepted the Emperor's banishment—preceded by the humiliation of capture, the attempt on his own life, and the traumatic journey through Lyons and Aix, where he confronted howling mobs and his burning effigy—as the end of an era.

Napoleon himself remained unpredictable. Louis XVIII reigned modestly in Versailles, but proper restoration in the south was blurred and indecisive. Then, late in February, the casually guarded Bonaparte gathered twelve hundred men at Porto Ferraio, landed at Cannes, and began his march over the French Alps. "Shades of Hannibal," muttered the puzzled, agitated Italians. Grenoble dissolved tearily; the soldiers flung down their muskets and cheered. Lyons turned out to a man, weeping, cheering; and Marshal Ney, having declared ferociously that he would bring the hated Corsican back in a cage, fell into Napoleon's arms and escorted him in triumph to Paris. "Myself or chaos," declared the Emperor. The world, hot to support success, rallied—vaguely—and waited. Louis XVIII disappeared, but no one seemed to notice. And hotheaded Italians rioted in the streets.

But the hundred days trickled by as Niccolò waited anxiously, unsure as to which way his coat had turned. Soon the Emperor stood moodily on the deck of the British man-of-war, *Bellerophon*, pointed toward St. Helena, where he abandoned himself to lingering cancer of the stomach and his memoirs. Perhaps it rankled most that his captors saw fit to send him a priest, although—through some quaint balance of justice and irony—the intermediary of Providence turned out to be his fond, petulant, slow-witted uncle, Cardinal Flesch, to whose ecclesiastical fortunes he had so generously contributed.

Niccolò chafed to return to Milan; Venice beckoned, and august Rome and Naples; and from the time of the Saracens, Palermo had been a citadel of artistic ferment. But Italy remained lacerated, torn. Perhaps the Napoleonic vision led only to miasmas. Perhaps it had been a vision damaged and betrayed by human imperfection. He would never know. He would wait for his own strategic moment, and wonder, and grow older.

❋ ❋ ❋

THE TURNKEY PRECEDED GERMI down the crooked stairs to the dank tunnel, from time to time grinning stupidly back at the lawyer as though unveiling a pleasant surprise.

"I thought he was in the tower," asked Germi.

"No, *Eccellenza*, under the tower."

The hollow echoes were but of shuffling feet, magnified to a roar. Even breathing seemed exaggerated, rasping. Fetid moisture seeped through ceiling and walls, and Germi stepped cautiously on the slimy, uneven stones.

"We have seen some fine prisoners," boasted the jailer's assistant. "Noblemen, new ones and of the blood. They go there—" His waving thumb designated the upper stories of the tower. "Politicals," he added. "We're careful with them. Up, down, in, out: a blind business."

Germi sneezed, seeking a handkerchief.

"One day we arrest you on my orders; next day we arrest me on your orders. See?"

Germi nodded, acknowledging the see-saw of fortune.

"Who are you, a lawyer? Let me warn you. That one you're to see is the Devil himself. There's no scaring him. Better, I figure, keep out of his way. I'll open for you, but I don't go in. Never. Not if my bread depended on it. He's got the evil eye, that one."

"Don't give yourself unrest," said Germi. "We'll try to relieve you of his presence as soon as possible."

"But what prestige! This place has the best reputation in northern Italy. Not an outbreak in twenty-five years, and such gentlemen of distinction, such families, even Frenchmen with powdered hair. You won't believe this. One we had last year smelled like an actress."

"Oh, I believe you," murmured Germi, bending forward to observe and control each footfall.

The old man thrust a great key inside the lock and scratched carefully. "Wrong key," he muttered. "In the dark, it's not easy." He tried another. Soon the door creaked balefully, and Germi stepped into the semi-darkness of the cell. The great door slammed shut behind him. "Holler, *Eccellenza*; I'll wait outside. And only a short time—"

Niccolò's voice cut vigorously into the turnkey's words of caution. "Luigi, it's you?"

"I should have preferred a more felicitous meeting," said Germi. "I just learned of your collision with the brave little tailor's honor."

"Who told you?"

"Your lawyer, Figari."

Niccolò seemed embarrassed. "You understand, Luigi, why I went to Figari?"

"Perfectly."

"I did not mean a slight."

"I do not easily take umbrage."

"Perhaps you do not understand. Because we are old friends, because you have been engaged in previous litigation against Cavanna, because you were not at home when I sent my nephew—"

"But I understand perfectly, Niccolò. And Gian-Maria is very competent and an eloquent pleader. More eloquent than I—"

"Yes, yes, I'm sure you understand. I must get out of here."

"Take my advice, Niccolò. Settle with Cavanna."

"Never."

"What does Figari advise?"

"As you do."

Germi applied a handkerchief to his squeamish nostrils. In his vehemence, Niccolò seemed oblivious to the stench. Perhaps he had acclimated himself to imprisonment. He resembled a madman. With ravaged face and unkempt hair, he paced the square cubicle, waving his arms about, uttering growls of frustration and rage.

"I shall strangle him!" he vowed. "Once out of this hell I shall strangle him! And that contaminated daughter of his. It will be a pleasure."

"Peace, peace," admonished Germi. "You may strangle Cavanna and his beautiful daughter, if you like, but as night follows day, you will have the pleasure of dangling from a noose shortly thereafter. It is entirely up to you."

"Seduction! Coercion!" Niccolò sputtered. "Can you imagine anyone having to coerce that itching little slut?"

"It would be very difficult to imagine."

"Why, the filthy whore was inside my breeches before I had a clear idea what she looked like. Spread from here to here!"

"Why did you run off with her? Why did you give them an opportunity to say you abducted her to Parma?"

"Abducted!" roared Niccolò foaming. "Is that what he says? Abducted?"

"But why, may I ask, did you take her to Parma? What is so objectionable about Genoa?"

"Privacy, privacy! I cannot scratch myself in Genoa without it being common knowledge exactly *where*."

"The friend of my youth has become celebrated."

"Say it, Luigi: notorious."

"It appears there is little difference. By the way, rumor has it the Devil himself has stopped by the prison to give you lessons. Yet I see you have no violin."

"I shall never appear at the Sant' Agostino again!"

"Don't be so dramatic. *Never* is a long and dreary time. You will appear at the Sant' Agostino and reap many *scudi* as a result of your notoriety."

"It will kill me."

"It will make you rich," Germi concluded. "But first, settle with Cavanna."

"Never," Niccolò declared. "This is blackmail. He tried to approach me directly, you know, assuming I would gratefully pay him to keep the matter quiet."

"The girl is pregnant, Niccolò."

"The condition is not unique. Half the women in Genoa are, it would seem."

Germi tugged his mustache. He had no desire to prolong the interview, which had become disagreeable and hopelessly stalemated. The chill had penetrated his very bones. Aware of Niccolò's frailty and history of ailments, he was convinced that his friend would not survive even a brief confinement.

"You will force this to a trial?" he ventured, shuddering.

"I shall bring counter-charges. I shall prove her unchaste. I shall show that poltroon sent her out to earn money, that she cavorted with soldiers of all flags, that she received men under his very roof—"

"That will be difficult to prove, Niccolò. And, in any event, all this happened *before*."

"Then how do I know the child is mine?"

"How does any man?" Germi smiled. "Faith, circumstantial evidence, and the apparent absence, at the time, of alternatives. Well, I shall talk to Gian-Maria to see whether we can get you out of here to await trial. Our courts are so dilatory, I am actually worried you may produce a few more offspring before the case is heard. It would be a nuisance to have this hanging indefinitely over your head. I'd settle with Cavanna, were I you."

"Under no circumstances," said Niccolò. "After the anguish he has caused me, after the perfidy, the lies, the attempts at extortion—"

"God be with you," Germi concluded, striking the door to summon the turnkey.

He felt relieved when the tight, heavy door began to swing open slowly, just enough to permit his exit. He would be haunted, he knew, by the fury, the extinguished eyes, and the feverish cheeks of Niccolò Paganini, who could do no wrong.

❋ ❋ ❋

NICCOLÒ PROVED A POOR PROPHET. He strangled no one. While he held forth rabidly on justice, ethics, and the law, none seemed moved. After five days of incarceration, he had developed a full-fledged rheum and begun to spit blood. He prayed for succor from his phantom mistress, but his sleep went dreamless. He had betrayed her, and now he would pay the price, literally. For when Figari succeeded in obtaining his client's release, it was with the understanding that he would pay Angelina and her father twelve hundred lire. Niccolò promised, then balked, deeming himself the injured party. It was with great difficulty that six hundred lire were extracted. He would care for the child,

Niccolò proposed; he would even magnanimously pay the expenses of Angelina's confinement. But upon pondering his own generosity, he recanted. Surely the law, devised to protect the helpless unborn, did not condone unchastity and collusion. Tended by the doleful Teresa, Niccolò lay abed suffering, refusing to receive anyone.

❋ ❋ ❋

In the middle of the night he awoke to find the Devil in his room. She stood by the open window, a naked silhouette bathed in pearly moonlight, staring into the blackness of the *Passo del gato moro*.

"Eleanora?"

She turned and looked at him in silence. Unreal as it seemed, he knew it was no dream. She had come back.

"I…I've missed you," Niccolò stammered. "I thought you had abandoned me."

She moved toward him, into the inky blackness of the room. For a moment she seemed to disappear altogether. Niccolò rubbed his eyes and searched the darkness. She emerged all at once, standing before him, naked and magnificent. She gazed steadily into his eyes, a faint smile on her lips. Her tail played menacingly behind her; it seemed to have a life of its own.

Niccolò's voice quavered as he spoke. "She was nothing," he said. "Merely a distraction."

She slowly pulled the sheet from the bed. Niccolò, too, was naked. Her tail crawled up the bedpost, slithered between his legs. Niccolò flushed; the tail was not the only thing with a life of its own!

"You love me, don't you, Niccolò?" she asked.

"I do indeed," he said. "I was afraid—"

"That I'd abandoned you; yes, yes, I know." The tail coiled around his thigh. Niccolò dared not move.

"You must learn to trust me," she said. Her eyes were cold and black as the night. "And I must be able to trust you."

"Yes," he said.

"You don't want to spend any more nights in the tower, do you?"

"No," he said.

The succubus smiled. Nectar rolled like tears down her thighs. "I've missed you, too," she said.

Niccolò swallowed dryly.

Skillfully, she lowered herself onto him, taking him deep inside of her. She began gently to rock, her tail in the air.

"I've been traveling," she said.

Niccolò seemed content to listen.

"I've been to Vienna and Paris. Vengeance and retribution are loose upon the Continent. I have made the most of it."

"Did you visit *Herr* Süssmayr?" Niccolò asked. He had heard of the Austrian's marriage and return to the Church.

She stopped rocking. "Franz is a fool, and of no great talent. A waste of my time."

Niccolò smiled inwardly. She began rocking again, much to his delight.

"I hope to prove *myself* a more worthy ally," he said.

She shuddered at the depth of his thrust. "You may, by defeating your most worthy opponents."

"I am unaware of any."

"Then you are blind or deaf."

Niccolò thrust again deeply. "Lafont?"

"*Monsieur* Lafont is a pretty player. And a man of the Church."

"He is a cipher."

"Prove it. Destroy him."

"For you?"

"Yes, for me."

"With pleasure," he said.

❋ ❋ ❋

THE NEXT MORNING, fierce with energy, he sprang from his bed and announced his imminent departure for Milan. Even Antonio Paganini worried. Niccolò had already settled a pleasant annuity upon his parents, and Antonio had begun to believe, if guardedly, that in the future he might yet be compensated for his sacrifices and self-abnegation. For this glowing future to ensue, Niccolò had to be preserved. The unkempt madman with bloodshot eyes, a cracked voice, and a consumptive cough seemed determined to annihilate everyone's prospects.

But Niccolò could not be deterred. Lafont, the arch-rival, was in Milan. Surely, he had come to hear Paganini and to suffer by comparison; or to mock or challenge him; or for their talents and destinies to embrace in mortal combat. Niccolò desperately needed someone to hate, and here was an internationally acclaimed violinist, a Frenchman trained to revere purity, sweetness, sonority, classical evenness of tone, one who regarded the Italian school as primitive and in need of an example.

Niccolò's mother and sisters wept as he departed, waxen and shaky. Antonio recited orations on disobedience and talked of ancient Roman fathers, who knew how to obtain respect from grown sons. As Genoa choppily faded from view, Niccolò forgot them and poor Angelina, and the still unsettled business of Cavanna's lawsuit. He needed a duel with Lafont to pacify his queen, and as do warriors everywhere, he thought of patriotism, glory, and the wrongs he had sustained.

Charles Philippe Lafont, practically the same age as Niccolò, had reached the summit of a distinguished career that included official status in the courts of both Russia and France. Epitome of the polished, elegant, somewhat understated French method, he kept closely in touch with happenings throughout the world of music, and Paganini was known to him by repute, some of it surely distorted and bizarre. Good-natured, unstraining, genuinely generous and secure, Lafont would have been astonished to find himself the great adversary of Italian music and Italian genius.

Lafont performed twice in Milan during the bitter-cold February of 1816, and Niccolò sulked in the rear of the auditorium, peering into random faces to gauge the extent of the visitor's success. He felt at length he could afford to be gracious for, as he informed Germi concerning Lafont's debut, "He plays well but does not astonish." This, to him, seemed so raw and basic a lack that there was nothing more to say. For some inexplicable reason, Niccolò's distaste fastened upon *Mme.* Lafont, who served her husband as entr'acte singer; the Milanese received her warmly enough, though she had none of the grand manner or the temperament of even second-rate Italian vocalists. While she resembled a Flemish housewife and sang with the modesty of a shepherdess, terrible rumors darted about Milan that *Mme.* Lafont had emerged from the proving ground of Parisian prostitution. Niccolò enjoyed the stories and, indeed, helped keep them in circulation.

He resisted as he would a fatal dagger Lafont's attempts to meet with him. He was indisposed or asleep or keeping an assignation; he had promised to dine with friends. The Frenchman called twice to pay his respects and was twice turned away by a puzzled chambermaid. His notes lay unanswered. Where success and failure mattered, Niccolò was as superstitious as an old crone. Let him come hear my concert, he muttered ferociously. His very skittishness sustained him. He did not rest or eat properly and looked more cadaverous than ever.

Lafont did come to hear him play at the Scala, applauding graciously the peculiar demonstration unfolding before him. He, too, stared at the faces of the audience, who screamed in the overwrought Italian manner, as for a gladiator. Niccolò was aware of his rival throughout the performance. He thought he could see the very glitter of Lafont's eyeballs, hear his loud, uncomfortable breathing. And he played malevolently, wielding a lurid, quicksilver bow.

But after the performance, Lafont appeared, mild and fraternal. "You are undeniably of the first artists of the world," he said simply. "But you might have benefited from the enlightenment of the French school."

"I do not quite see how," Niccolò snapped more harshly than he had intended, for *Mme.* Lafont was standing by, as was the powerful Peter Lilienthal. "And I must remind you that the so-called French school has at least one Italian ancestor. Viotti, as you may recall, was no artisan."

"I came to be illuminated, not admonished," Lafont murmured. His voice had dropped to a whisper; he seemed very calm. "I hoped there would be only amity between us, as I have been trying to reach you with this suggestion: let us perform together."

"Together?"

"Both together and separately, the same evening."

"Ah, a duel?"

"Not at all. Let us, rather, take measure of our methods."

"French against Italian?"

Lafont hesitated. "I prefer not to view you as a competitor," he said gently. "But the decision must be yours."

"It doesn't matter. I am of no school."

"Jove has a broad forehead. We must not quibble over words. I, for one, like to think of my many, many violinistic progenitors. But the point is, you will play?"

"Of course."

The joint concert, immediately designated a duel, a competition, a combat to the death, plunged Milan into an hysterical scramble for tickets. Speculators sold and resold the same seats, as well as numerous others that did not exist, at exorbitant profits, creating further chaos when the theater threw open its doors. Tapers in the boxes flared early, and the fashionable arrived with unfashionable promptness. And suddenly, Paganini was transformed into a constellation of symbols. He was Italian liberation, he was nationhood, he was the Napoleonic hero, he was the force of rectitude that shattered scepters, he was the monumental glory of every father's house, and he was the Fiend incarnate.

Niccolò had reluctantly agreed that there were to be no shattered strings. As host, he was first to make his appearance, bowing (with the excessive humility that had annoyed his friend, Luigi) to thunderous acclaim; it was at once apparent where Milan's loyalties lay. He played his own concerto; Lafont, he knew, was a mere executant. The work had been heard previously in Milan, offering a thread of familiarity that can be a source of pleasure to great and little opinion-spouters, and setting a standard in brazenness and pyrotechnics that all but extinguished Lafont's chances. Indeed, the audience occupied itself mainly by visiting and gossiping during the comparatively sedate Rode *Concerto in A Minor*, Lafont's initial offering. Even the sprightly third movement seemed heavily shod and cumbersome after the dazzling fireworks of the Paganini.

The Kreutzer *Double Concerto* that followed unfolded a study in glaring contrasts. The work had been fastidiously rehearsed, and the two roles were equally weighted as to importance and opportunities for display. And indeed, in the duet that announced the opening theme, the voices blended so exquisitely, with such an abundance of sweetness and such disciplined unanimity of spirit that many were visibly moved, and many held their breaths for fear the sheer perfection would snag or crack, or reveal some hidden flaw. That one voice of such assertive glory sang forth from the soul of man seemed miraculous but credible; that two such glorious voices proclaimed their harmonious affirmation and unity seemed almost too abundant a blessing. Eyes and noses grew moist.

The first solo passage in F minor belonged to Paganini. Bold, yet of an abandoned and tragic quality, the theme was attacked with imaginative fervor and laced with extraordinary improvisations. It emerged studded with embellishments and brilliant accessory ornaments that visibly agitated Lafont, since they had not been discussed in advance and were nowhere indicated in the score. To make matter worse, the audience was excited; approbation rippled on smiling faces. Lafont's repetition of the melody emerged with beautiful forthrightness, a sumptuous tone (Niccolò scowled; it was a very *powerful* tone), and with absolute fidelity to its creator. The tension of the audience subsided. Ladies' fans appeared, as did the low buzz of unconcern that formed an aural backdrop in Italian theaters.

The artists bowed in unison after the Kreutzer, touching hands vaguely to suggest the confraternity of art. Lafont seemed confident and amiable when he returned with his Russian variations. His manner implied that if the Milanese failed to esteem him, or preferred another's buffoonery to his art, then the Milanese, alas, were in error. The crafty Milanese, for their part, waited impatiently for headier draughts. The Paganini voice had become a clarion call to arms, before which other messages faded.

The headier draughts came forth, sulphurous and inflammatory, from the simmering cauldrons of the dark sisters of Niccolò's very own sponsor. He played "*Le Streghe*" more brilliantly, more tantalizingly, and more weirdly than ever before.

Paganini began his introductory tune quite carefully, relying on a fine vibrato, perfect intonation, and a very sweet tone. He then underplayed the short cadenza and presented the theme he had borrowed from Süssmayr. Nothing extraordinary thus far, and yet…and yet everyone in the audience could somehow *sense* that something was brewing.

The excruciatingly difficult double and triple stops of the first variation came effortlessly and flawlessly, and Niccolò had already sealed his victory. However, he was not finished; his dark mistress required an absolute triumph, and he would give the audience what they had paid to hear. No other violinist on the planet could pull off the dazzling, one-handed pizzicati of the second variation or the rapid-fire harmonics. However, this was not mere technical bravura; the octaves in the

B minor section that followed were indeed brilliant, yet at the same time moving and almost tragic. He next restated the theme, this time *in harmonic double stops!* The effect was positively unearthly, but before the audience could interrupt with wild applause, he dazzled them yet further with an array of breath-taking arpeggios, often bowing *spiccato*, and finally concluding with yet more harmonics.

The dams of restraint disintegrated. Delirium took over. Niccolò had won a colossal victory for his queen.

9
A Friend in High Places

S INCE THE LEPROSY OF JACOBINISM continued to hover over his person, Niccolò moved carefully. Occasionally, he was interrogated at borders and city walls. In Verona, his printed music and greatcoat were rigorously inspected. He could not imagine what intelligence he allegedly concealed and spoke sharply to the officers who detained him. He had seldom entertained in his quarters, and now the longing for political purity—plus the benefits anticipated—encouraged him to shut his doors to friends, strangers, and the curious.

Under more benign conditions he would have, at this juncture, journeyed once more to Parma to pay his respects to its new duchess, Marie Louise of Hapsburg. Napoleon's second Empress, who was to have mothered his dynasty, had returned to Vienna at the first crack in the Bonaparte armor. Now she had been installed as sovereign of the duchies of Parma, Piacenza, and Guestalla, embracing portions of territories formerly ceded to Elisa and Pauline Bonaparte. To Niccolò, the presence of Marie Louise in nearby Parma seemed a rose-strewn path to Vienna, Prince Metternich, and papal honors. Nevertheless, the risks, at this early date, were too numerous and menacing, even if Marie Louise—in the ambiguous climate of a united Europe that had recently moved backward (in solemn congress) by a hundred years—deigned to receive him, hear him, and provide auspices for his conquest of Austria. No, it was not possible.

Count Neipperg, too, had to be reckoned with. The handsome, resourceful aide sat beside his archduchess, ruled in her name, and had, his critics said, a hunter's nostrils for the Jacobin taint, however corrected and cured. The brief patronage of Prince Eugene Beauharnais, Josephine's son, would have rendered Niccolò persona non grata in legitimist Parma; his long association with the Bacciochi rendered him dangerously suspect.

He was in Verona when the final verdict in the Cavanna case—this one from the Genoese senate—reached him. The affair had dragged from one court to another, always terminating in a judgment against him and invariably eliciting from him expressions of persecution and rage. The new verdict proved no exception; and Niccolò, who had exhausted several capable lawyers, instructed his most recent pleader to engage in elaborate subterfuge and delays while his holdings were converted into trust funds for his parents. He knew the matter would drag on and that he would be compelled to throw the Cavannas a pittance from time to time, but his bitterness remained acute, and he felt himself the severely injured party.

Angelina, he learned, had never been delivered of the child. It had smothered within her and, close to confinement time, had to be removed surgically. Niccolò was profoundly agitated to learn this some months later. He had insisted he would care for the child, though not its undeserving mother. He would have accepted the court's concern for an unborn babe, he declared; what nettled was that Angelina's unchastity had been upheld, blessed, gilt over by legal dishonesty and intrigue, while he was publicly declared a scoundrel.

Yet the death of the child haunted him. His sleep—always thin, tenuous, crowded with vague disaster—now filled with visions of the infant in a river of blood and his own dripping hands. He tossed; he cried out. Once he had to be awakened by passengers in a stagecoach disturbed by his twitchings and outcries. Eventually, the terror receded, but the disembodied sense of loss clung to him for a long while. He measured time by the child's death, calculating how old it would have been in such and such a month, measuring its talents and charms. He was ashamed of his strange tenderness and shared it with no one.

Relief came only when he learned Angelina had married. He began to dream recurrently of her feverish little body sniveling and panting beneath him; he would awaken, laughing diabolically.

❉ ❉ ❉

BECAUSE HE HAD been CRITICIZED for his behavior in the Lafont confrontation, he avoided a similar challenge from Ludwig Spohr. The stodgy Teutonic archangel of the sugary-sweet tone (a little blatant in the rapid and agitated passages and somewhat overbearing in slow ones, as though he possessed a monopoly of human sentiment) fine-combed Italy for glory and debased currency. He had heard all the Paganini legends, and Niccolò had heard the usual comparison, unfriendly to himself, concerning purity, moderation, classic reserve, tonal elegance: the familiar juxtaposition of values.

They met in an atmosphere of determined, if frigid, amity, conversed in stilted French, feinted at chamber music. Each insincerely praised the other. Spohr, Niccolò concluded, was a fussy, unimaginative precisionist, devoid of spontaneity and passion. Spohr mentioned regretfully to friends and noted in his *Wanderbuch* the Italian's bombast and questionable taste. He conceded Paganini to be a technical wizard. Niccolò had learned long before his encounter with the German that those who would denigrate him admitted his technical excellence. "Mere technique," they would suggest.

Paganini was amused. "As though technique were ever *mere,*" he scoffed. "Why, it is like condemning a poet because he employs mere rhymes and meters. Let these lofty ones show how much music, and what sort of music, they can produce with technique less mere! Give them a virtuoso passage, and they struggle like elephants in glue! Mere technique!"

And he regretted that he had been so caustic and clever with the generous Lafont, and now had to bear the penitential burden of extending courtesies to the stuffy German, who wore his sense of superiority like a divine right.

But this Niccolò knew: He had heard the century's pride, Italian, French, and German. He acknowledged random merits but no great system or exponent. Paganini remained peerless. No violinist, however schooled or disciplined, could aspire to stand alongside him. In this he felt secure.

The sweet succubus upheld her part of the pact. As he would his.

❁ ❁ ❁

HE CONCLUDED HE WAS TOO OLD for heroes and too cynical to seek inspiration in the examples of others. The lost years plagued him; yet Lucca, where he had mislaid those years, was all he had known of friendship and evanescent ease. Of the century's promising young men, he knew himself among the least youthful. He was thirty-four; he was ailing. The merry, robust, indecently successful Gioacchino Rossini, whom Niccolò met in Milan, was younger than he by a full decade. Rossini had written his first acclaimed opera at nineteen. Why, at nineteen, Niccolò had scraped dutifully in the municipal orchestra at Lucca and competed for an opportunity to play a *Kyrie* from the cathedral loft.

No, he was too old for heroes. The true hero of his youth raged within a rocky island fortress. Those who live in the aftermath of revolutions have no heroes, only the taste of ashes in their mouths where the phrases have died.

Beethoven, of course; there remained Beethoven. But Niccolò regarded the colossus of the north as a revered musical ancestor, deeply rooted in the last century. The last century? He grew morbid. For the venerable Beethoven, as he viewed him, was his elder by but a dozen years, even as he himself was the elder of the scintillating Rossini by ten! Did the latter look upon him as an old man, a scarce-acknowledged ancestor? No, no, that was not possible. They had laughed and caroused together, and Gioacchino had shared the most indelicate stories; then they vowed to meet often and seek diversion together.

"What I would not give for your lean, skeletal, singularly ugly appearance, Niccolò!" Gioacchino had exclaimed good-naturedly.

"It is not usually my appearance that is coveted. That fate is more often reserved for my talents."

"Oh, I've enough of that commodity for the pair of us," Rossini answered. "But I should like to terrorize the good, tedious bourgeois who hound and surround me. The matchmaking mothers and the available daughters. I'd like to strike terror into them."

"A most peculiar ambition. Surely not too difficult to attain?"

"Impossible," said Rossini. "I'm too fat. Have you ever heard of a fearful fat man?"

Niccolò had to admit he had not.

The day of his arrival in Venice, late that year, Niccolò had a strange encounter that absorbed and transfigured, in one giant thunderclap, his yearning for a human ideal and his undercurrent of fear that destiny might have bypassed him.

Venice shimmered, incredible and pearl-like, on lightly whipped water. The day was slightly overcast, giving the sky a lifeless, opaque whiteness. The Adriatic loomed murky green and grey, foaming, and St. Mark's rose ethereally light, intricate, iridescent.

Here on the great square, the English milord was pointed out to him: George Gordon Lord Byron, fervid revolutionary, madman, seducer, demon, anti-Christ, genius, singer of songs, lover of beauty and freedom…and vastly rich, honored, born to great wealth and esteem, lavishly eccentric, as only one who need aspire to nothing because he possesses everything can be.

Niccolò pushed a path through the curious Venetians gaping at the poet, who walked slowly toward the canal's edge with his companion. The most beautiful head he had ever seen—dark hair gently curling, a Donatello face with a slight suggestion of antique god and satyr—was placed somewhat archly upon a short, energetic body. The hands were small and exquisite, dimpled as a woman's. And the milord limped—quite pronouncedly, Niccolò noted—which but underscored his uniqueness and isolation.

There suddenly welled up in the Genoese a ferocious identification with the poet: a sharing of oceanic passion, a vision of heroic fate in which both were, somehow, participants.

He was ashamed of the violence of his emotion. Adolescents and bored countesses might properly fling themselves at the feet of the pretty milord, whose tragic aura and patrician disdain incited them to foolishness. Men might quote the poet's verses, pass judgment on his latest mistress, even imitate his stances. But Paganini was a celebrated artist, first violinist of the world. For him to have succumbed to the Byronic spell seemed mawkish and inappropriate.

He haunted the poet's hotel, seeking a glimpse of his idol. In a literary journal, he found excerpts from the incomplete, badly translated, *Manfredo*, understanding its brooding, tortured, heart-rending outcries and heroic quest even when the actual words and allusions evaded him. And the Byronic discontent became his own—at once a shell to protect him from the perils of a mediocre world and a crag from which to launch his assault upon its diffidence.

Niccolò forgot his frugality and turned domino for an evening at the *Teatro Fenice*'s magnificent masked ball. All Venice attended, mysteriously, recklessly gay in the heightened feeling that the illusion of anonymity brings forth. But this domino had little interest in all Venice.

He lurked in the shadows, unable to tear his eyes from a wine-stained Bacchus, club-footed or cloven, it seemed, adorned with garlands and surrounded by naiads, mermaids, goddesses, a shepherdess or two—a most preposterous mass of adoring femininity. And this Bacchus seemed to find life not quite to his liking, though his treasured wit was greeted by moans of ecstasy and appreciation.

The dancers whirled about domino and Bacchus, and the music told of joy.

SYPHILIS, THE GREAT Dr. TOMMASSINI DIAGNOSED, the Spanish sickness. Common, difficult or impossible to eradicate, an affliction shared with most of the young and not so young bloods of the land. One might avoid it altogether by unbroken celibacy, or by rusticating faithfully with one's old woman acquired in the cathedral at a tender age. Otherwise, one had to learn to live with it. There appeared no other course.

Niccolò knew he had a promise to keep; surely this was a gift to remind him of it. Let him forswear the temptations of the flesh. His pledge was to the power and ecstasy of art, beside which paled the minor pleasures of earthly love. Niccolò found unpleasant the very thought of love's attainment. The most exquisite woman grew dreary, suggestive of squalid domesticity, if she responded to him. He might suffer insomniac agonies—brief ones, to be sure—over the graces of Lauretta or Marietta or Francesca or Lydia, but even friendly consideration of his suit, to say nothing of physical surrender, made him suspicious, emotionally on guard, callous. Only diffidence inspired his interest: an interest, he felt, that could certainly be controlled.

ROME, GHOSTLY, WET, AND OLD, was utterly ravishing—a dominion, Niccolò wrote exuberantly on arrival, surpassing his wildest imaginings of it. He drifted among the stupendous works of the past, Roman and Christian, vibrating—unaware of his own presumptuousness—to a sense of immortality. Quite shamelessly, he began to exercise blandishments to procure a papal decoration, which might do much to erase the Bonaparte stain and ease the road to Vienna and the world. And he practically begged for admission to the St. Cecilia Society, that impeccable sanctuary of musicians respected both by the arbiters of the art and the adjudicators of the social order.

With frustration came patience, but weariness, too. And as injustice began to rankle, Niccolò's tongue and pen grew acid-sharp toward the hypocritical piety of the Holy City, where favor and intrigue wore toy halos. His determination to rout Roman smugness by the sheer impact of virtuosity—the stubborn defiance that had sustained him during earlier tribulations—was suddenly in jeopardy. For he could find no theater. All doors were absolutely barred to him. And the long arm of clerical and political interference had, he was certain, much to do with their slamming shut.

There was, indeed, no theater to be had. Suitable theaters, open for performances from the day after Christmas to the dawn of Lent, were unavailable. Niccolò anticipated damage to his reputation were he to appear in some improper setting—an old palace, a ballroom fallen into disuse—and these, too, required discovery, maneuvers, and a great outlay of money for cleaning, rubbish removal, furniture, music stands, effective lighting.

He learned, too, that a Vatican edict prohibited musical performances anywhere in Rome on a Friday; music and meat came under the same interdict. This was a terrible blow, for Niccolò had to torment himself with the knowledge that the great auditoriums stood empty and silent this choice day of the week. He had always planned initial appearances in a city on Friday, since conflicts were infrequent, and the attention of press and public would not be diverted elsewhere. Surely a way could be found around this archaic prohibition. And surely the one to show him the way was the iniquitous Eleonora.

❊ ❊ ❊

HIS PRAYERS, HOWEVER, WENT UNANSWERED. Since his arrival in the Holy City, she had been visiting him nightly. He would awaken in a sweat in the small hours of the morning, his heart banging in his chest, his body shaking with cold, the nauseous clutch of blood in his throat. The air in the room would be thick with her scent, and the sheets stained with the waste of his passion. One night he awoke howling, and could not stop, even when the old landlady came with her lamp. She finally managed to subdue him by pouring a hooker of brandy down his throat. For several long minutes, he lay in her lap, staring like a child at her wrinkled, prunish face. This woman is of the earth, he thought. Let no one doubt the comfort of strangers.

But he could not answer the landlady's questions, for he remembered nothing of the dreams.

That the Devil was in Rome he was certain, yet she gave him no aid. Following a final, futile appeal to the *Teatro Argentina,* a spacious hall he had long had his eyes on, he decided suddenly to quit the city, and return when the circumstances were more favorable, or his mistress more responsive to his supplications.

❊ ❊ ❊

HE DINED ALONE and late at the *Penna d'Oca,* a tiny trattoria blocks from the *Teatro.* The heavy *pastasciutta* reminded him of his friend back in Genoa with his mistress cook. "Spaghetti is no food for fighters," Germi

133

would protest, "and a weighty and encumbered stomach cannot be favorable to physical enthusiasm towards women." Then it is right for me, Niccolò thought, and he proceeded to indulge himself unsparingly. He finished off the brutal meal with a second liter of Barolo. The frail fiddler, unaccustomed as he was to such excesses, slumped into sleep at the candlelit table.

An absurdly obsequious waiter let him snore there for nearly an hour. Niccolò finally roused himself at the sound of a passing carriage. It was after midnight. He decided, given the acute state of his indigestion, that he would get a breath of air and walk back to his rooms. This soon proved to be a grave mistake.

In the moonless night, black as pitch, every street appeared as empty and unfamiliar as the next. Within minutes he was lost. He kept walking, certain he would come across someone, or something, recognizable. Had the city been deserted? Shop windows were shuttered, doors were bolted, and only the cats stirred on the streets. Across a broad and empty *piazza*, through a narrow medieval passage, past the black silhouette of ancient ruins, Niccolò walked through the city as if walking back through time. Or perhaps time had stopped altogether. His legs grew weary, his toe blistered. The bell of a church struck one.

He pursued the lingering sound of the bell to an open square with a fountain. The square was empty, the fountain dead, but there, before the stone steps of a towering church, sat the black-lacquered brougham of Eleonora.

Niccolò walked toward it like a man in a trance. The carriage was empty; the coachman, gone. The horses stood waiting, huge and silent, completely indifferent to his presence. Niccolò turned and faced the church. The great doors were open, and the dark interior beckoned. Niccolò mounted the steps.

At the top, the entrance gaped like the black mouth of Death. Passing through it, he was swallowed in Cimmerian darkness, the air thick and inky black, scented with the incense of a thousand holy rites. He saw nothing in the darkness around him; he could barely see the floor at his feet. He felt his way forward, slowly down the aisle, the whisper of his step echoing around him. Then he heard voices emanate from the dark: murmurs and moaning, and an animal grunt.

"Eleonora?" he whispered.

A young woman giggled.

"Eleonora, are you there?"

A man's groan filled his ears, a sound so close it seemed he could feel the breath. He stepped blindly forward and stumbled on something soft. A discarded robe, the vestments of a cleric. A marble Christ on a wooden cross loomed out of the dark above him. He strained his eyes into the darkness ahead, and pale forms began to emerge.

Niccolò gasped in horror.

A large, fleshy man, stripped naked and gagged with a rope, stood bent over the altar stone, his face pressed against the cold marble. Eleonora sat in front of him on the altar, leaning back on her arms, her legs bared, her knees up and wide, the coil of her slippery tail gripping the poor man's neck. Behind him, the yellow-eyed coachman in his long black cape stood ramming himself viciously into the rear of the man. Niccolò, stunned to the core, staggered back.

Eleonora smiled her welcome. "Ask and you shall receive," she said.

Unable to speak, Niccolò stared at her groaning victim, whose hands scratched desperately at the altar stone. One of his fat fingers wore a wine-colored ruby, the sacerdotal ring of the Church.

Niccolò turned back into the dark. He heard the scolding voice of his mistress echo behind him. "You've wandered into another man's dream," she said, and he tripped on the robes and fell.

He woke up on the floor of the *Penna d'Oca*. The waiter helped him back into his chair, apologizing profusely, as if Niccolò's passing out had been *his* fault!

❀ ❀ ❀

THE DEVIL WORKS IN MYSTERIOUS WAYS. The next morning Niccolò received a summons and was ushered into the presence of the powerful Cardinal Albani, rumored to be a pivotal power behind the papal throne.

Always uncomfortable before clerics, Niccolò felt the familiar unease slowly congealing into a kind of elemental awe. The mellow affluence of the cardinal's palace jarred the austerity of his own mode of life—stinginess, many called it—and the synthetic splendor of the theater he had come to regard as his second home. There was, in the very sumptuousness, an aristocratic contempt for wealth and an utter absence of ostentation. Not even a painting hung in the reception room to compete with the exquisite wood paneling and the giant tapestry in muted colors depicting a medieval pilgrimage. Niccolò became instantly aware of the solidity and worth of every object, however accessory: the snuff box over which Benvenuto Cellini might have labored with tenderness, the aged, fragrant leather and gold bookbindings, the letter opener encrusted with rubies and pearls lying carelessly upon an uncluttered desk.

Niccolò bowed to the cardinal, blinded with emotion, vaulting hope, and self-hatred. The pounding of his heart argued the nature of the world in which he found himself and the artist's perilous struggle for existence.

As Niccolò raised his eyes to those of the prelate, he was clamped in a strange chill. Confronting him was a head intended for stone, for the all-seeing hands of a latter-day Michelangelo: a monumental figure to haunt a darkened cathedral niche or to grace a sunlit square of a great city. Niccolò viewed the unyielding icy fire and angularity of the ascetic crossed with enormous physical strength, a luxurious, near-pagan musculature, and deep wisdom tarnished by a trace of accommodation to things as they are. It was a face harmonious in its contradictions; it conveyed an informed, utterly devastating serenity.

The cardinal wasted few words.

"You have powerful friends," he asked or stated. It was difficult, despite his crisp articulation and resonant voice, to decide how the remark had been intended.

"I am unaware of them, Your Grace."

The prelate smiled with half his mouth but showed little inclination to dispute so trivial a detail.

"You place yourself in opposition to our Roman abstinences," he continued.

"I am humbly aware of finding myself in the Holy City," Niccolò murmured piously, unsure where the conversation would lead.

"They tell me," Cardinal Albani said, "that you do not regard secular concerts on Friday and suckling pig on Friday as equally culpable."

Niccolò began to understand. Hope fluttered in his bowels; the great cardinal would not have summoned him for a scolding. He pressed his point nervously. "I have often performed in the northern cities on Friday, for it is their custom. And occasionally, a prince of the church has blessed my efforts with his presence." It would not hurt to make this point known.

"But in Rome it is not our custom."

"I now realize this, Your Grace."

"Yet you continue to petition, and most unpleasantly of late, for a dispensation."

Niccolò was embarrassed. "As a matter of fact, I am about to quit Rome. I have submitted."

It seemed precisely the proper sentiment, and he mouthed it unscrupulously. In truth, what now quickened in him was scarcely submissiveness.

Cardinal Albani smiled a crafty smile. "I commend your submissiveness," he said, pronouncing the word most affectionately. "The Church, a wise and merciful mother, needs many submissive sons." He did not fully conclude this notion. "There remain but four weeks before Lent," he noted.

"I realize this. In fact, my decision to leave Rome—" Niccolò had not meant to say so much. It was imprudent to reproach; it was even more imprudent to expose the baseness of one's calculations. Why, that would be like declaring one had better dash to Naples to gather in a few scudi in a more promising area before it was too late.

"Your petition will be granted," said the prelate. "The authorities of the *Teatro Argentina* have been instructed to permit your use of their hospitality Friday next, on payment of the usual fee—"

Niccolò stammered, "Your Grace—"

"If Roman response warrants, you may repeat your exertions the remaining Fridays of the Carnival."

"I cannot thank—"

The ambiguous smile had frozen upon the fine, sculptured features of Cardinal Albani. "That is not necessary. It is, as you know, useful to have powerful friends," he said.

Then, standing to dismiss him, the cardinal held out his hand, palm down. Niccolò froze for a moment, staring at the sacerdotal ring.

"Is something wrong, my son?"

"No, Your Grace," he answered, and bent to kiss the scarlet stone.

PART THREE
ANTONIA

10
THE LION OF PRUSSIA

THE CRAWLING CANCER OF revolution had been excised. Europe lay draining from her wounds, the disease arrested. And in the deep spring of 1821, as if acknowledging the durability of the new old order, Napoleon Bonaparte died, causing scarcely a ripple. Those who had loved him and would continue to burn with the zeal he had generated had come to regard the Corsican as long dead, his deeds ennobled by distance, soon to be transfigured by myth.

The man who had reset the clock of Europe—perhaps the world—was no upstart spawned by the world's convulsions. With all his heart, Prince Metternich believed in the divine right of kings, in aristocracy's sacred mission to command and possess, and in the unity of the Holy Roman Empire as the golden age of recorded history.

Closer to his own day, the reign of Maria Theresa—unclouded by that uncomfortable triad, liberty, equality, and fraternity—represented a latter-day outpouring of divine bounty and a promise of the perfectibility of human institutions. Now that the revolutionary heresy had been snuffed out, the prince, in the service of his sovereign of the House of Hapsburg-Lorraine, Francis I, devoutly hoped to achieve such a restoration.

The Schönbrunn had become the political heart of Europe, and Chancellor Metternich moved decisively within its white, gold, and royal red interior, holding in delicate balance the conditions of arterial flow. All was to be as once had been, only immensely more so and for all time to come: such had been proclaimed by the Congress of Vienna, Metternich's masterpiece. Reaction, some muttered. Salvation, cried others. And some thought wildly, though silently, of betrayal, a long chain of treason and deceit in which few were uncontaminated by guilt. As for the liberals, they crept busily into their cocoons or learned to sing in different keys and voices. Liberalism had grown unfashionable.

❀ ❀ ❀

Prince Metternich was ill. He lay immobilized by the untidy scourge of voyagers the world over, bristling with impatience, frustration, and, in time, philosophical amusement at man's presumptuousness and frailty.

Between the Congress of Laibach and that of Verona, the chancellor planned a brief, ceremonial visit to Rome, accompanied by his daughter, Countess Esterhazy, and his sovereign, Francis I. The journey had been safely accomplished, all Rome welcoming the visitors with characteristic pomp and evidences of friendly homage.

Prince Kaunitz, Austrian ambassador to the Vatican and brother-in-law of Metternich, arranged a mammoth reception and ball in honor of the visitors. The affair, of imperial lavishness, was to culminate in a private recital by the incomparable Paganini, in whom—so ran the accounts—five hundred years of Italian musical art were contained, distilled, conquered, and outstripped.

Prince Kaunitz had exhausted language itself in describing the violinist's wizardry. "No other—no other—" he fumbled. "All that is human—ay, even all that is inhuman—" he had concluded, undiplomatically at a loss for words. The Austrian emperor nodded sagaciously; a cellist of sorts, Francis would judge for himself whether the Italian's virtuosity had been exaggerated. Everyone, of course, had heard of the bizarre fiddler; even distant Vienna clucked with rumors, the most exciting of which was that Paganini had been prevailed upon to visit and perform in the Austrian capital.

❈ ❈ ❈

THE APPEARANCE MARKED a subtle breakthrough in his relationship with Roman society. This remained clear: he would not, now or later, be received as an equal by the ancient families of Rome. In the regard of the old aristocracy, he would remain a clown: a gifted one, to be sure, a rich one, which altered premises, but a creature whose purpose was to amuse. Still, after this reception by the Austrian monarch and the princely champion of legitimacy, certain barriers would inevitably wither. There would never be for him, as for so many great musicians, the back stairs of servants, the low screen beyond which one dared not venture, separating jester from guests. He was being endowed with a special status, an invisible order or decoration, something that would, hopefully, forever qualify and set him apart.

Six hundred assembled to do homage to the Austrian emperor and to hear the Italian fiddler. The evening blazed triumphantly: thousands of candles, brilliants, jewels, new waltzes by the new Viennese waltz king, a profusion of coifed, perfumed, magnificently exposed femininity. Despite an interminable wait, which never failed to annoy him, and the excessive heat, Niccolò had seldom displayed his art so advantageously or with so delicate a balance of pyrotechnical magic and caressive emotion. An Austrian lady sitting close to the violinist uttered a convulsive moan and fainted. Niccolò nodded respectfully as she was carried out but did not interrupt the performance. He assumed her to be an Austrian; Roman ladies did not faint at concerts, even when flanked by an emperor and the very Prince of Darkness.

But his triumph was flawed; nowhere could he find Metternich. No one had informed him, of course, of the chancellor's indisposition. And of the two—emperor and chancellor—as Niccolò viewed matters, Francis I, before whom he bowed to the polished floor in a gesture of adoring humility, might have been a stodgy, watery-eyed, Teutonic innkeeper, while Metternich was the prime mover whose word became history, demolished revolutions, and ordered the flood tides of progress to recede.

Countess Esterhazy spoke graciously to the violinist in impeccable French. "You are all that you are reputed to be, *Monsieur*. I can think of no greater tribute."

Niccolò once again bowed his head, his eyes seeking the absent chancellor.

"I shall convey to my father an account of this evening," continued the countess, "and declare at the outset that it would be impossible to exaggerate your talents and accomplishments."

"*Madame* is magnanimous," Niccolò said, as he had schooled himself to say, feigning acceptance, indifference, the bland gratitude appropriate to clowns who have succeeded in amusing their masters.

❉ ❉ ❉

In the morning he awoke to biting abdominal pains and a familiar nausea. He crawled from the sweat-stained sheets to the half-filled chamber pot, vomited the remains of bisque and champagne, and then, trembling, laid his febrile head down on the cold wood floor. As he stared at the cracked glaze of the porcelain pot (blue lines of wind on a white sky), tatters of his dream flickered past like painted leaves. A rosy bed of flames, he remembered, the bristling erect nipple of her breast, the icy touch of her wandering hands, and the sound of her voice, indelible, like words penned in blood. "Trust me," she had told him, while the quickening lick of a leather whip seared his shivery flesh.

He heard heavy footsteps in the hallway, and a delicate knock on the door.

"Who is it?" he asked, hauling himself to the edge of the bed.

"A message for you, sir," came the stony reply.

Niccolò bade him enter, and an obese, glassy-eyed courier in foolish livery pressed open the door. The man's vacant gaze gave him the look of a sleepwalker, and for a brief moment, Niccolò wondered if he had again stumbled into another man's dream.

"Prince Metternich requests the honor of your company," the visitor recited dully. "This morning. Now."

Niccolò was at once flattered and resentful. But his curiosity was stirred even more than his vanity, and the voice of the succubus echoed in his mind: "*Trust me.*"

He told the sleepwalker to wait outside. The man nodded imperceptibly and shuffled away. Niccolò closed the door and went to his wardrobe, raised his nightshirt over his head and tossed it to the floor. He began to dress, then noticed something in the mirror. His abdomen and thighs were streaked with welts. He traced them with his fingers, and the crisscrossing lines of raised pink flesh sang to his touch.

"*Trust me.*"

Paganini carefully left his violin in his quarters when he walked out to the waiting carriage. He had been summoned, not his skill; he would go as a person, and if the chancellor had failed to make himself understood, let the burden of explanation fall upon him.

As he stepped out the entrance of the pensione, Niccolò stopped abruptly. Before him stood the black-lacquered brougham of the succubus, the hooded demon at the reins. Beside him sat the stone-faced courier, staring trance-like at the street ahead. The carriage was empty. The demon turned to face Niccolò, shrouded in the shadow of his cowl. Paganini hesitated for only a moment; he opened the door and climbed inside.

The familiar crack of a whip sent the horses off, and still with the bitter taste of vomit in his mouth, Niccolò was on his way to the see the most powerful man in Europe. As the horses' hooves clopped upon the cobblestones, he remembered Marlia and the carriage of Elisa Marianna Bacciochi. The velvet seemed the same, the polished brass, the painted wheels, the very scent. Only the fiery emblem was different.

And the era, and the destiny.

❊ ❊ ❊

Niccolò approached guardedly, but Prince Metternich seemed genial and relaxed, slipping from impeccable French into correct, slightly accented Italian.

An irrelevant conglomeration of thoughts and associations had crowded in upon Paganini as he was ushered into the chancellor's presence. Uppermost, quaintly, lurked an awareness that he and Clement Metternich had each, in a younger and vastly different time, been accepted lovers to sisters of Napoleon Bonaparte. The thought eased Niccolò; a vague, ironic smile, nearly fraternal, met the hearty greeting of the host.

"Envy commands you," Metternich smiled in return. "I have been prevented by illness from experiencing the delights that attended Prince Kaunitz's feast. Thus, I have devised a scheme to summon the greatest of these delights to my side. I thank you for coming."

Niccolò bowed his head. The third deadly sin had apparently been his mistress's weapon of choice.

Countess Esterhazy extended her hand. "I fear I have yet to cease jabbering," she confessed. "Perhaps my father's loss might be less keen were he not himself a fine violinist."

"It is my secret vice," said the chancellor.

Niccolò thought of his old patron, Prince Felix, and shuddered, remembering the poor intonation, the tangential chords, and the ragged beat.

"We shall strike a bargain," suggested Metternich, while the countess laughed in anticipation. "Either I play for you or you play for me. Which shall it be?"

"I am without ammunition," said Niccolò.

"Not so I," declared the chancellor. "And I shall share with you, if you will but perform in my stead." He had already motioned a servant, as by a prearranged signal.

To Paganini's astonishment, several fine violins and a collection of bows swiftly appeared. It seemed incredible that the chancellor had traveled with such treasures; they must have been hastily, though most discriminately gathered, in the urgency of a single morning, and prepared for him. The instruments were Italian, most of them of excellent quality—a fine Ruggiero, a Bergonzi, several by Amati and the copious Stradivari family. The bows were not strung as tautly as Niccolò preferred, though none could have been expected to appreciate his own delicate prejudices. Niccolò inspected first one violin, then another, fondling each deep reddish or glowing golden-brown belly, caressing each with his chin, silently fingering and adjusting strings. He held each bow critically, gauging its thickness and weight.

"Perhaps we can exchange diversions," he attempted lamely. His was no courtly tongue, Niccolò knew; the years of vagabondage had spiced whatever etiquette he had acquired with bluntness and candor.

"It might be more prudent to deploy my skills as a threat," said Metternich, and one could understand the effect of his elegance, diplomacy, and wit upon the nations.

Countess Esterhazy protested. "Father is only timid before Paganini."

"Yes, indeed," agreed the Prince. "Before czars and emperors he roars, my darling."

Niccolò had made his choice of violin and bow, eliciting a quiet exclamation of concurrence from the chancellor. "Yes, yes, that particular Amati—sweetness and strength, more than one dare hope for."

Paganini bowed. He felt the excitation, the quiet madness, that seized him upon confronting an enormous audience. He saw distant Vienna, a cluster of rotund turrets rising out of the Gothic wood of the mind's eye; and the papal decoration; and the clink of gold and silver, the happy sound of the forging of his empire.

"These I have dedicated to the artists," he muttered, consciously ambiguous. He raised his bow.

The chancellor proved as insatiable as he was gracious.

❈ ❈ ❈

So, THIS WAS NAPOLEON'S NEMESIS, the anti-hero, the scourge of European nationhood! It occurred to Niccolò suddenly that the polished, worldly chancellor was not so much the enemy of the new nationalism burgeoning everywhere as superbly beyond its specificities; that he was absolutely unable to understand the aspirations of peoples in terms of physical conformation or language or geographical accident; that as Europe's minister, he would successfully, alone if need be, hold back time and tide and the revolutionary avalanche itself.

Not, Niccolò shrugged, that it actually mattered. An artist, like a sailing vessel, must look to the prevailing winds.

11
ROSSINI'S STREET CARNIVAL

"ONE THING COMES, ANOTHER GOES; that is history," declared Gioacchino Rossini, recently ensconced in Rome after abandoning Naples. "As for me …" He flung an arm heartily about Niccolò's shoulder. "I have changed towns and changed friends three times a year without fail since the day I was born. And why should I complain? Does not the Pope himself seem content to live here?"

With thirty operas behind him, more than one for each year of his life, he had taken to bed to work on *Matilde di Shabran.*

Niccolò visited his fat friend each day and watched the creation swelling into a whirlwind of papers sprawled over bed, chairs, and floor. "Careful, Genoese, your boot rests on my trio," Gioacchino would shout.

"Why are you in bed?" Niccolò asked, feeling a touch of envy at the composer's robust good health.

"There is no other way of keeping warm in Rome," said Rossini. "Moreover, once here, I am forced to write out of sheer boredom. At liberty, I should find more interesting things to do. But tell me—how fares my nightingale?" The lively Spanish coloratura soprano, Isabella Colbran, had accompanied Rossini to Rome, along with his unscrupulous impresario, Barbaja.

"She prefers the Neapolitans. At least they listen, if only to heckle.

Here, there is so much social intrigue in the boxes, she is certain no one knows what is being sung."

"Splendid. A good omen for the new opera. I shall reuse an ensemble or two, perhaps an overture. None save a visiting Englishman will be the wiser. I've banished Colbran, you know. She mislays pages, wrinkles my bed, and deprives me of strength to complete my tasks. Rehearsals start Tuesday."

"You will be finished?"

"Oh, probably not. But I don't stir from bed until then, even for necessities. Barbaja will see that I am well fed; else how can he turn over his knavish profit? Tell me, friend. Is it true that Haydn was in exclusive charge of the chamber pot of his patron, Prince Esterhazy? *Ohimè!* What we composers must endure! Theaters, impresarios, chamber pots ..."

"The new work?"

"I am unenthusiastic about it. One does not write a *Mose* or an *Otello* every week. And I, alas, must write every week. We have obtained Liparini for the heroine. She has little talent and less voice, but she is formidably pious and has a slender waist. And accept this from an old man of the theater: for some operas, the prime requisite is a slender waist."

The old man of the theater had returned gaily to his labors, pausing only to consume the groaning trays carried into his room by Barbaja's lackey and a sympathetic maid. The flood of pages continued without abatement, Gioacchino resisting his hostess' attempts to introduce order.

"Out, my sweet angel, my lovely one, my tender little pigeon," he implored, while the crone giggled, her many chins quivering gelatinously. "I do not need fresh linen today. Niccolò, explain to this rare Tuscan rose that Hercules cannot leave the Augean stables till his labor is done."

"It is as he says." Niccolò broke into a spasm of coughing, muffled by a handkerchief stained pink with blood.

"My dear man," said Gioacchino with sudden concern.

"I'll fetch you some water, sir," said the maid, and she went off to fill a glass. Niccolò settled into a chair.

"You'd think the Devil himself had you by the throat," said Gioacchino.

Niccolò looked up at him but didn't respond; some things were best kept secret, even from friends.

The maid returned with a glass of water, and Niccolò greedily gulped it down. "Thank you," he said, handing her the empty glass. She nodded warily and left the room.

Gioacchino then yawned mightily and said, "Look under the bed and see whether there is anything at all suitable for a third-act ensemble. A quartet, perhaps, or quintet. I seem to remember something stored away for just such a drowsy afternoon . . ."

❀ ❀ ❀

THE OPERA WAS FINISHED practically on schedule; the composer doffed his soiled nightcap, replaced it with top hat and tail coat, and escorted his lover, Isabella Colbran, through a night of gastronomic celebration. Barbaja honored him with a huge dinner, where Niccolò encountered the prim little Caterina Liparini, to whom the principal role had been entrusted, as well as the singers Fusconi and Fioravanti.

"Perhaps we should have waited till after our opening for the celebration," suggested the superstitious Liparini.

"Nonsense," said Gioacchino. "We shall celebrate again when *Matilde* triumphs."

"Oh, do not tempt fate!" cried the soprano, crossing herself against calamity.

"I never tempt fate. I lead it around by the nose," Rossini declared.

Not this time, as it turned out. As the opening performance approached, a veritable epidemic of disasters broke lose, culminating in the shockingly sudden demise of the conductor, Antonio Bolle, found dead of a stroke on the very morning of the dress rehearsal. No other conductor in Rome seemed available or willing to undertake a dubious new score on such short notice. And so it came to pass that Rossini's lean and loyal friend, Niccolò Paganini, following a chaotic dress rehearsal, conducted the premiere performances of *Matilde di Shabran*.

❋ ❋ ❋

Niccolò AWAKENED TO AN APPARITION in the room. A shapeless and bloated figure wrapped in a black cloak approached hesitantly, with arms outstretched like a sleepwalker's. Niccolò sat up swiftly, now fully awake and aware of his terror. Into what abomination had his mistress been transformed?

"Alms! Alms!" the visitor squeaked in a racked, eerie voice.

No mistress this! "Out!" Niccolò quavered. "One does not force his way into an honest man's chamber!"

"I should have preferred an honest maid's," whispered the ghoul.

Niccolò sprang from his bed. "Gioacchino!"

"Don your trousers, *Maestro*," commanded Rossini. "And make haste. Only babes and ancients lie abed at this hour. Why, the night is barely begun, and this is the last Thursday of the Carnival."

"I was but napping," said Niccolò, feeling ill as always.

"No need to apologize. It will get noisier as the night progresses, so you would, in any event, soon be awakened. Now, how to disguise you?"

"Disguise me?"

"You have a face that is difficult to forget. For our adventure, Paganini, we must travel incognito."

"Our adventure?"

"Now, raise your arms that I may slip this over your comeliness. Ah, yes, that will be splendid."

"It is a dress. It is female apparel!" Niccolò protested.

"Precisely. Now stand quietly. I am going to transform you." And firmly, over Niccolò's wriggling and objections, "One of my nightingale's favorite wigs, a magnificent auburn with only a few places eaten by moths, made in Naples especially for *Elisabetta Regina d'Inghilterra*. The virgin queen—what could be more appropriate?"

"I don't want it."

"Now you must stop struggling, or I shall cease to be your friend. This fine headpiece leaves you vastly improved; you must take my word for it. Would that we could so easily disguise your nose. Now, come. Here's your basket."

"My basket?"

"To beg alms."

"Go without me."

"You are so piteous a figure—lean, gaunt, undernourished—you will be the fortune of us all."

"All? Who is all?"

Rossini grabbed his friend's shoulder. "The singer, Pisaroni, in Rome for the holiday. And Massimo d'Azeglio, a young man who may yet do Italy some service—and me. He is Manzoni's son-in-law. Can you sing?"

"*Sing?*"

"Certainly. We shall all sing. We are poor *ciechi*, caterwauling for alms on this merriest of nights. The whole city celebrates; on Wednesday, we go into sackcloth and ashes, and for forty days Gioacchino will have to forego gaiety and love. Spanish women adore penitence. Take that guitar, you will need it." And since Niccolò stood, sulking and uncertain, Rossini seized the instrument and twanged roughly. Paganini clapped his hands over his ears and then claimed the guitar.

"Are you drunk, Gioacchino?"

The composer of Matilde di Shabran roared with laughter. "I have, indeed, enjoyed some wine today, my friend, but I've also had something much better," he said, taking out a tiny little pipe. "Spoils of Napoleon's Egyptian campaign. The hemp plant, whose lovely, dried leaves can transport a man to utterly blissful realms. Enhancement of love. Solace for want of love. Would you like a toke?"

"Gesu, no! You know how sensitive my lungs are. And besides, I'm tired anyway. You have torn me from sleep. How can I possibly go through this mad caper of yours if I get drunk on top of that.

"Peace, Niccolò. Actually, the effect is quite different, though I'd forgotten about your consumption. But have no fears! Rossini's pockets can nobly compensate you for your lost sleep." Whereupon, the speaker reached into his coat and pulled forth a small packet.

"But you know I cannot smoke."

"Hemp, you smoke. But this is the ground dust of leaves from a strange medicinal plant unknown to our Italian doctors. I've heard that some people can go five days and nights without sleep if they have enough of it. Here. Just chew a little pinch. It should keep you going until the morning."

The other conspirators were waiting outside Paganini's dwelling, ludicrously attired in old clothes, with great colorful patches sewn on seats and elbows. "This promises to be more profitable than singing Rossini operas," announced Pisaroni, clearing his throat and pretending to vocalize. Paganini began to execute clever arpeggios, which caused several persons to stop and listen, exclaiming curiously that the blind old woman played so well. Several coins dropped into the beggars' baskets.

"You will soon have us picked up by the gendarmes," said Massimo d'Azeglio. "No *ciecha* plays the guitar so diabolically. Let us have some wretched tune, and please, for safety's sake, let Gioacchino sing."

"Yes, then they will pay us to go away," agreed Pisaroni.

Niccolò remembered the blind stroller's song, "*Siamo ciechi*" ("We are blind"). He began to sing in the slow, wobbly manner of the Roman beggars, strumming an oom-pah-pah accompaniment in a conflicting key. The quartet shuffled out of the narrow side street and toward the fashionable boulevard. Music and laughter assailed them. Gioacchino joined in a gluey bass voice, defacing the ditty with elaborate vocal ornaments, all exaggeratingly sentimental, and all out of tune. Coins began to clink on coins.

"I told you it would be profitable," whispered Pisaroni.

"Good, now I can retire," Rossini said, and bellowed yet more lustily.

"Paganini, you are supposed to be a woman, remember?" d'Azeglio reminded him. "Jump an octave, just for appearances." Niccolò, feeling a sudden stimulation from whatever it was he had been given, obligingly continued in a falsetto squeak that caused all heads to turn.

The quartet serenaded aristocratic balconies and were sent food and money. "My worthy patrons," Gioacchino designated with a broad flourish. "This is the first time we have really enjoyed one another."

They stuffed themselves with sweets and distributed the night's haul among the beggars, some blind, squatting on the stairs of Santa Maria Maggiore. "Who knows?" said Gioacchino hopefully. "Among them may be as great a knave as you or I."

Niccolò pressed coins into outstretched hands. One of them suddenly grabbed hold of his wrist. Startled, Niccolò found himself staring into the hooded eyes of the demon carriage driver.

"You have the Devil to pay," the fiend whispered with a grin.

Niccolò, trembling, dropped his coins, sending the beggars scrambling. He staggered back, then ran off down the street.

Rossini stared after him in puzzlement. "Too much of the magic powder," he said to his friends. Behind them, the figure in the black cloak stole away into the dark.

12
THE WAGES OF SIN

PURGING, DRAINING, AND BLEEDING: These attended his labors and blighted the fantastic triumphs. The nightly visitations of the ignescent succubus, Vesuvian fuel to the fires of his fame, left him increasingly sick and debilitated. Her demands, at last, proved exorbitant. Niccolò collapsed—surrendered totally, lay weak as a newborn and as wanting in will. Germi, hastening to Milan with Teresa Paganini, regarded his breakdown wholly as a failure of nerves and lectured his friend severely.

The distinguished Dr. Ciro Borda took matters into his own hands. First, he had his patient literally conveyed to Pavia, so that treatment might be sustained without interruption to his own activities. At the medical school of Pavia's great university, Borda, regarded by many as Italy's first physician, lectured and treated affluent patients.

It was Borda's extraordinary view that European medicine remained too conservative about dosage and too guarded in its applications of purgatives and bleeding. The time-honored methods had proved helpful for centuries but were approached too cautiously. If a given measure of a specific produced limited relief, it was only logical to conclude that illimitable help might be available, though scarcely to the timid. "One must rid the organism of polluted blood or there can be no healing," he insisted.

Opium and mercury, standard medicaments for the unpredictable Spanish sickness, could be tolerated in far greater quantities than physicians supposed. "The violence of the treatment is often the source of the cure," he emphasized. And if the patient grew perilously ill or developed symptoms hostile to treatment? "One does not die of pain. Pain is but the struggle for supremacy waged between doctor and disease."

Borda's epigrams had become accepted science. No physician in Italy was more esteemed, quoted, emulated.

The chronic colitis that had plagued intermittently now joined with tuberculosis and the ravages of syphilis. Feeble and trembling, Niccolò lay contemplating the ceiling and his ironic destiny. This year, he was to have journeyed to Vienna to start his conquest of the world. His emaciated, jaundiced face in the mirror terrified him; he wept. Yet he spoke optimistically and assured his friend that he was on the brink of recovering "*perfettissimamente*," stretching the excellence of language to emphasize the excellence of that recovery.

Teresa wondered whether he ought to be better fed. He was pale; he was weak; his bones could be counted. "Pig's blood, they tell me, strengthens and gives new vigor. Or red meat, nearly raw." The elegant Borda recoiled in horror. Starvation and the purges would prove cleansing, he declared. The hidden poisons would be eliminated. "One does not die of starvation—why, look at the ubiquitous poor," he scoffed.

Niccolò drifted into a lassitude that was, of itself, a living death. He prevailed upon Teresa to return to Genoa, promising to join her there as soon as he felt capable of undertaking the journey. Even in bed, the violin fell from his hands, so extreme was the quivering, so erratic the alternate waves of determination and feebleness. The opium and mercury cure, which had at first filled him with hope, had but created a debilitating stasis. He was lashed by spells of coughing; his inflamed joints ached; he could swallow nothing without penance.

Borda was outraged when he learned his patient had been clutching a violin and endeavoring to produce sounds. He forbade him to play, threatening not only repudiation but sudden death. Germi asserted that his brain, the seat of the disorders, had overreached, and now carried him, body and soul, to hideous death by each member's corrosion.

Niccolò knew different. The source of his illness was not in the resolution of his mind, but in the corruption of his soul. The pact with the succubus was bringing him fame and making him rich, but it was also killing him. Yet he could not find a way to break the enthrallment; her Tartarean enticements exceeded the power of his earthly will. She came to him like a dream in the darkest hour of the night, and with the addiction of a dreamer he inevitably succumbed.

On waking, inactivity and the stodginess of Pavia brought a new dimension to time: inertia, a perpetual present that made each hour many hours. His body was clammy-cold yet racked by fever; the taste of death's offal hovered in his mouth, loosening teeth, making him repulsive to himself. And so he endured the ravages of treatment, mercurial ointment rubbings, opium stupor, the half-death of near-starvation. Day's end found him desperate in the screaming silence.

At long last, as if in answer to his prayers, the succubus withdrew. Blinded by the fiery blaze of her own ardor, she had been the last to recognize the perilousness of his condition. Now, seeing that she might indeed lose her favorite if she continued her indulgence, she decided to leave him, for a time, to the care of an earthbound devil in the mountains of Lombardy.

13
The Cure

Cernobbia nestled luxuriant, subalpine, and furry green on the edge of its crystal lake, so clear even at dusk that the great villa of General Pino reappeared, inverted in the waters, as though painted on glass.

The general had managed to emerge unscathed and greatly improved in fortune from his generation's wars and political upheavals. He possessed a subtle genius for equivocation and for extracting the greatest gain from a given situation. As an elderly bachelor, he had also had the good sense to make a brilliant marriage. Union with the aging, eccentric Vittoria Pelusia had made him master of the most beautiful estate in Italy, one periodically coveted by Europe's scattered nobility. The villa seemed much too splendid for a Napoleonic general, long ago put to pasture, and a crotchety ex-ballerina, whose rise in the world had been accomplished by plying a still more ancient trade shrewdly and well.

But more than his magnificent fiefdom on the lake of Como, more than his handsome and intelligent animals, more than the memories of an age of heroes, more than the purse of his Vittoria, General Pino loved music. To his agitated ear, his own fiddling suggested the very stuff of greatness. The general often mourned the passing of youth and regretted the seductions of military glory and tangible wealth. He became a patron of singers and violinists, an activity viewed as suspect, even slightly disgusting, by his spouse. Having herself been a woman of the theater, La Pelusia, as she had been known in her prime, was content to forget her past, demanding that others forget, too.

The general loved Niccolò Paganini with something fiercer and more tender than friendship and quite different in quality (despite the age-span) from fatherliness. Perhaps he unknowingly identified with the Paganini career, seeing himself acknowledged musical wizard, rage of Italy, first violinist of the world. Several times, he had offered hospitality and smothered Niccolò with advice. Now, he was overjoyed that his friend was actually coming to Cernobbia, and suitably challenged that he was coming as a convalescent after nearly two years of harrowing illness and inactivity.

La Pelusia, who had changed radically from the days of her triumphs in ballet and in bed, muttered crossly about feeding an unending train of beggars unearthed by her spouse. She was even more annoyed that the lean, diabolical fiddler was an invalid who had to be offered an enriched regimen—veal and fresh eggs, tender fowl and asses' milk, creamy confections and delicate filets of fish. Had she been aware that the prescription was of her husband's devising, her displeasure might had been even more intense. The general, who did not hold with the Borda cure, set himself diligently to the task of strengthening and fattening his visitor.

As for Niccolò, he tried to stave off the general's purposes as gently as he knew how. He, too, had begun to question the efficacy of the Borda cure. His new doctor, a Viennese, Spitzer, had suggested that perhaps the famous physician (Borda) tended to think too dramatically—in terms of total recovery or death, superb health or debility—whereas Northerners preferred to regard results of their calling as calculable in infinitesimal degrees. In other words, it was better to be relatively less ill than to gamble for such perilous stakes. Unless death seemed the only alternative, each risk had to be measured prudently against the likelihood and extent of gain.

Niccolò had begun to nibble furtively, cautiously, after considering this advice; but the general's zeal proved almost past endurance. The old martinet swooped down upon his guest at dawn, tore him from bed for a first breakfast of *chocolat au lait,* and bullied him into trailing after his own energetic pathfinding in a walk along the edge of the lake. "Fill your lungs with the good Swiss air. It is magnificent air, cleansed by mountain winds. Breathe deeply! Deep breathing is the secret elixir of longevity. And walk more quickly, more vigorously. Before I am finished, you will be a titan."

"I shall be a corpse," Niccolò gasped.

The exertions temporarily done, the general now helped his guest attack a real English breakfast. Niccolò nearly swooned when he first saw the buffet decked out as for a fiesta at ten in the morning.

"One of the advantages of being a turncoat, which my enemies claim I am, is that one learns to accept the best of all worlds," he explained. "You have ingested your austere Latin breakfast, somewhat prettified, it is true, after the manner of the French. Now it is time you learned the true secret of Waterloo. A race thus fortified so early in the day is invincible."

"Eggs? At this hour, eggs are injurious," Niccolò insisted. "And meat? I shall not survive such an affront to the blood."

"I shall have you court-martialed. I demand absolute obedience in this. Believe me," he added, with the certitude of a man who had yet to experience a day's sickness. "If you become ill, I shall admit I am wrong; I shall continue to humor you and that madman from Pavia."

"Eggs and meat should be eaten at night."

"Superstition! At night we sleep," boomed General Pino.

"Can't you see he doesn't want it?" screamed La Pelusia, who had been expressing disapproval of the feast in not too subtle grumblings. "And do you know what this debauchery costs?"

The general ate heartily, filling his plate several times and urging more lavish participation.

"What is that?" Niccolò pointed.

"Porridge, a favorite of Lord Wellington. He never let a morning go by without a large bowl. One day, dear friend, I shall write a learned history of the great wars and of the effect of food on military strategy and military success. Why did Napoleon come to grief? It is really very simple."

The post-breakfast rest was a brief one spent silently browsing in the general's library. Niccolò found a volume—alas, in English—by the traveler, Leigh Hunt, who had lingered to talk with him in Rome at the premiere of *Matilde di Shabran*. He discovered Petrarch. He found a fine collection of Nordic myths, tales of stentorian and icy gods and goddesses as violent in their passions as the warmer, more predictable deities of the Mediterranean. The windows of the library faced the gem-like lake of Como, sloping lawns, a profusion of flowering foliage, the pearly iridescence of the air, hills heavy with fruit and blossoms.

She's gone, thought rejoicing Niccolò, in respite from the diabolic dreams.

THE GENERAL ORGANIZED CHAMBER MUSIC. Everything was in order: stands, music, and a pedestrian accompanist with a fine goatee, Professor Vanni from Como, who waited patiently, making plain he was being paid to render a service and would not venture to address his betters with familiarity. These sessions Niccolò dreaded even more than the eating orgies. Consistently nerveless and feeble, he could hold a violin only briefly and had dissipated his meager strength stomping about the lake with his enthusiastic host. Moreover, he had to listen to General Pino's lacerating musical efforts and was expected to comment rapturously or constructively. When he ventured to express himself with candor—this happened infrequently—his old friend wagged a remonstrative finger and advised, "One must be free of jealousy, Niccolò. You are the greatest fiddler in the world, true, but occasionally you will hear a divine cadence even from an amateur. Do you realize that I am virtually self-taught? Think where I should be today—only think—had I enjoyed your opportunities!"

Niccolò did not bother to disillusion the old gentleman. It occurred to him, and he had to suppress his mirth, that the general sincerely regarded his friend as privileged and himself as a victim of wars and circumstances. Why, Niccolò wondered, was it his wretched destiny to fall in so frequently with zealous amateurs? Surely, despite benefits accrued, an evidence of cosmic wrath!

Paganini had to cry for mercy, blaming Borda's treatment and his debilitating illness, before the old man would be done. But by this time, the enormous noonday meal was ready and General Pino had developed a lusty appetite accompanied by the conviction that Niccolò's protestations and pleas ought to be regarded as reticence. The first dinner was gluttonously Latin. It presupposed a long morning of semi-starvation and an imminent siesta, without which survival was out of the question. Even the acidulous Vittoria, so contemptuous of English breakfast, ate heartily at this repast, indulged an occasional bawdy story, and retired to an airless, darkened room, as did the others, to sleep away exhaustion.

On awakening, the general resembled a runner who has just heard the signal to begin: eager, competitive, impatient for laurels. He called for his horse. Exercise, he informed his guest, is the true elixir of youth. As soon as one neglects exercise, there ensue brittle bones and congealed joints; the body's fluidity evaporates (the general confided these items as though caretaker of some occult formula), and the spine loses its ability to support the body. Senility, as stiffness, must be fought; in a crooked body, the blood that feeds the brain has been diverted.

In vain, Niccolò pleaded his incompetence to undertake a walk into the hills. "Nonsense," the general decided, having displayed his equestrian prowess and described certain exploits of his youth. "The path is not a steep one and the view of the lake is most impressive. I beg you to permit me to prescribe your treatment. Place yourself confidently in my hands. I shall convey the very essence of my own health." He struck his chest and pulled in his stomach, affecting a military stance. "Trust me."

The Devil's minion, thought Niccolò. He numbly and reluctantly trailed behind his ebullient host, oblivious to the scenic glories surrounding him, concerned only with conserving himself and surviving yet another obstacle. Once, he was so overcome with lassitude he could but sit on a rock while General Pino scaled a dizzy promontory, shouting down to him and waving with a youth's glee. Another time, he felt so inadequate to the venture that he stumbled back to the villa, collapsing on the great *piazza* and having to be helped to his room by a servant.

Yet, despite Niccolò's fears that he was doing himself irreparable damage in breaking completely with the Borda cure, the general's strategy began to produce results. Perhaps these were but coincidental, utterly unrelated to the prisoner/slave marches, the example of gluttony, and the fantastic consumption of asses' milk. The general faced his friend's ingratitude and skepticism as he did his Vittoria's grumbling: with effervescent indifference.

The evening meal, served late, proved another exercise in ravenous lunacy. While less sumptuous than the first dinner, it produced quaint regional surprises, rare wines, exotic samplings from the probably mythical travels of General Pino, who spoke often as though he were General Bonaparte. This late repast constituted the sole social gesture of the general and his lady. They never visited, but on occasion invited acquaintances to dine. These might be an ill-assorted, motley crew; Cernobbia was isolated and lonely, and no one, including the hosts, seemed sure of anyone's social position, not even his own. "In certain situations, it is better to be somewhat imprecise," General Pino decided. "Especially you, my adored one," he added, in response to an uncharitable snicker from La Pelusia.

THE GENERAL'S NEPHEW, Cesare, shared his uncle's dedication to the delights of the palate, though none of the old man's compensatory energy. From time to time, he appeared at the dinner table, usually in the company of an insignificant singer from Como, Antonia Bianchi. They were an incongruous pair, and Niccolò enjoyed observing them, while pretending to munch and nodding at the general's theories as to which delicacy would strengthen the heart, which the bones, the blood, the liver…

The stately Antonia towered half a head above her little escort. Her creamy, cameo loveliness, vivified by an earthy strain (a somewhat peasant quality almost conflicting with her symmetrical features), made her seem more intelligent and interesting than she could possibly be. Niccolò could not avert his eyes from her, even when intercepted by the muttering of his hostess. Toward Cesare, Antonia seemed diffident—she pretended not to hear half of what he said—though the smile she radiated upon Paganini and her hosts conveyed warmth, affability, and absolute attention. Cesare, fortunately, noticed nothing, beaming upon his mistress and the company as though demanding that all admire his taste and cunning.

For some inexplicable reason, La Pelusia liked Cesare, defending him vigorously when her husband characterized his nephew as a slow, plodding dunce, a lout, and a disgrace to his ancestors. Cesare, in turn, knew how to ingratiate himself with the old woman, squeezing her hand, pinching her cheek, confiding (in a hoarse whisper that seemed to convey that they harbored important secrets and games) that his parents wished to be remembered.

La Pelusia did not, however, share Cesare's fondness for Antonia Bianchi, viewing the singer with the animosity and chill that only an ancient dame of the theater can bestow upon a youthful female. "That kind I can smell through all the paint and the cheap perfume," she declared savagely. "They want a rich protector, that's that. Greed. And dirt behind the ears. And if there is talent, nobody has yet had evidence of it." Forgotten, her own notably successful career among a succession of protectors. The glare of Antonia's beauty, the fact that the three men made idiots of themselves heaping attention upon her: these were beyond sufferance. The general doted on Antonia and ignored his wife's carping. "If the perfume is unsuitable, you ought to prevail upon that clod, Cesare, to provide something better. We men do not have your discernment in such matters, *cara mia*," he ventured to suggest.

After one such endless dinner, the general produced the funereal Professor Vanni, actually a distant relative of Antonia Bianchi. Groaning inwardly, Niccolò at once understood his host's designs, but the simple pleasure in Antonia's eyes deterred him from making an issue of his reluctance.

"I have been wondering when I may be destined to hear Paganini," she smiled, her eyes softly moist. No excess of tribute had ever moved him as did her happy expectations.

But the general had begun to tune his instrument. His repertoire, vanity, and endurance seemed infinite; his guests, bloated at his table, were trapped, dozing fitfully where they sat, incapable of the supreme discourtesy of displeasing him. All applauded hopefully whenever the old man paused—for that very purpose—and he continued with enthusiasm. La Pelusia snored in her favorite Louis XV chair, chin bobbing, mouth half-open. Across the room, Niccolò noted that Antonia, calculatedly girlish in wide-skirted white, was blinking rapidly, fiercely attentive by way of combating drowsiness.

"An excellent concert!" General Pino adjudicated several hours later, wiping the sweat from his brow. "Next time, we shall hear Niccolò and *Madama* Bianchi as well. I do not know why you do not assert yourselves, yes, both of you. We are exhorted by the saints themselves, if I remember correctly, not to hide our light under a bushel."

Niccolò did, in time, perform, when at last General Pino subsided with exhaustion and urged his guests to carry on in his stead. Antonia's suppressed amusement, happily, went unnoticed by the others, but Niccolò grinned openly across the room. As he tuned, he became aware of her quickening pleasure and irrepressible, deeply felt anticipation. It was the first time, perhaps, that the presence and expectations of another confronted him as reality. Even Metternich had been a force, not a person. Always, he had viewed his hearers as mass, even when that mass contained crowned heads or knowledgeable ones.

And yet, as he was about to say a few words about his lengthy illness, the stalemated convalescence, his virtual exile from the instrument, the fact that restoration proceeded slowly…he realized that no explanation was needed. He would play well, better than he had played since being stricken; and if he played with less than his consummate mastery, Antonia would understand.

Surging vigor, such as he had long ago surrendered and half forgotten, poured from unclogged springs and buried consciousness. His broken-chord thoughts were of conquering the world, of blatantly loving and possessing this magnificent woman (no, no, he could not wait another moment!), and of gratitude for his extraordinary musical memory. For once an idea had been articulated, it was burned into him, to lie flawless and unspoiled in the recesses of the brain, sustaining inertia, waiting for liberation.

The Bianchi voice did not live up to his hopes and expectations. What right had he, after all, to expect that it would actually match her loveliness? Antonia's was a big, brilliant, somewhat unsubtle soprano, strained in the upper register, breathy throughout, and wanting in dynamic shadings and control. Her crystalline enunciation and histrionic instincts could not compensate for the thinness of her technical resources and the damage she had already wrought upon her instrument. Paganini listened in an ague of commiseration. The voice was, in essence, beautiful, he told himself; even the great Giuditta Pasta displayed occasional rawness and inability to focus all her tones with purity and precision. But he would help her. He would yet make an artist of Antonia, and she, in turn, would become his entr'acte singer; the sight of her would suffice. He applauded the pair of Sarti songs, suddenly speechless. Bianchi was almost too intense, somehow uncovered, and emotionally obvious. The general, his idiotic nephew, and La Pelusia (who, since a woman was performing, was kept awake by rudeness and her critical faculties) babbled incessantly.

Antonia bowed and seated herself beside Niccolò. She was very subdued; the gesture seemed at once proud and intimate. She did not listen, even when Cesare compared her with the incomparable Malibran and, a moment later, with an angel.

"Music, I have noted, tends to stimulate the appetite," General Pino observed. "The English, I am told—"

"Bah! One day you will explode at your own table, and it will serve you right," threatened his lady.

It was General Pino's view that Antonia Bianchi was available.

"No, I do not think there is a tender passion for Cesare," he advised, having carefully considered such a possibility. "You have seen him. How could there be? Even a mother would view such an error with regret and pity, no?"

"Then she has sold herself to him?"

"Buying, selling…Yours is a thoroughly bourgeois mentality, Niccolò. You consort with emperors and emerge a tradesman. Why must you categorize everything? The lady quivers deliciously when you are near. Is that not enough?"

Niccolò looked uncertain. Perhaps enough to lose everything, he thought to himself.

"A woman, my dear fellow-artist, must be viewed as a gift from the gods. One must not appraise a gift too closely, ferret out a freckle or a squint or a missing tooth. There are more interesting, more urgent matters. I need not, I hope, tell you what they are."

"How to begin?"

"It is difficult to believe you are so naive. Three times *Madama* Bianchi indicated her house address, slowly and carefully, *approximating* the distance from the church of Santa Maria Dolorosa, should you lose your direction."

Niccolò shook his head. "She was not actually addressing me."

"I am aware of it."

"And Cesare? What of Cesare? Suppose he appears at the very time?"

"You fear him? Physically I mean? He will murder you?"

"Don't be ridiculous."

"You will murder him?"

"Not if he behaves."

"*Madama* Bianchi will swoon, scream, repulse, perish with shame?"

"I doubt it."

"I think," said the general, "that your point, whatever it is, is rather weak. I suggest you call on *Madama* Bianchi tomorrow, if the weather permits, or soon, at her home in Como. Ludovico will drive you in the carriage. You must be comfortable; you must protect yourself against the elements and conserve your strength. Who knows how much of it you will be called upon to expend?"

And as Niccolò scowled with embarrassment and floundered for words of denial, the old lecher continued slyly, "Struggling with Cesare, I mean. I am sure he can be something of a wild boar when moved to anger. Or so I am told."

Today seemed endless and motionless as glass.

❋ ❋ ❋

SUDDENLY, HE WAS WELL, THRILLINGLY WELL. His body had sloughed off its residual lassitude; the bizarre symptoms vanished. Months had passed without a visit of the succubus; a fresh feeling of freedom and possibility suffused his being. His appetite, while irregular, amazed and delighted the general and disgusted La Pelusia.

He walked briskly and spontaneously, without being coerced, around the lake, viewing its shimmering movement and reflections with a sensuous delight never before experienced save vicariously, out of books; a delight he had, in truth, supposed to be a literary attitude, fashionable and effete. Now he was stirred by the physical world sprawled out before him, too blatantly beautiful, reminding him that this bit of earth would outlive his quest, his burdens, his want, and would endure when his sounds were stilled and his name had receded beyond echo or memory.

Since condemned to be eaten by worms, he must know, if but for an hour, victory. Pawn of the Devil, he would be godlike. Doomed to corruption, he would love.

The general, while deploring his snail's pace ("The virtue is lost if you do not walk briskly, agitate the blood a little."), sensed it would be indiscreet to interrupt the meditations with too concentrated a dose of his sermonizing. Instead, he retreated, nodding sympathetically, recognizing that something quite miraculous and tender was involved, as well as what the wife of his bosom cynically designated "the dog's itch." In this latter regard, the general increased the prescription of his own secret catalyst to the natural impulse: the asses' milk, long considered an aphrodisiac by the ancients of Egypt and Rome. Although "Cleopatra's milk" was already being administered in massive doses to his bewildered guest, the general insisted on boosting the amount until it became the primary ration of his daily regimen. "It will invigorate the flow of blood to your limbs," he told the unsuspecting Niccolò. "To *all* of your limbs!"

Barely a week had passed when Niccolò advised his host that he had business in Como on the morrow. With the utmost indifference, the general offered the services of Ludovico and the carriage, hoping that it would be a good day.

There had been no assignation, no understanding that he would now or ever seek her out, no reason to suppose he had been awaited. Still, upon confronting one another, the lovers fell into one another's arms, babbling and sobbing, uttering foolish remonstrances, promising hysterical eternities of servitude and love. Cesare had been forgotten; he had never existed, Antonia declared. Life began when Niccolò crossed the threshold of her world.

He was grateful that Ludovico had been dismissed and sent back to Cernobbia. For two days and nights, Niccolò did not leave the musty, scented chamber. Antonia brought him delicacies to eat; unbidden, she brought him a basin, a towel, a chamber pot. She was soft, buxom, unkempt, gurgling voluptuously over such of his notions that had incited other women to anger. In the midst of dedicated caresses, Antonia would rise and wash herself or comb out her long black hair, or rub perfumes into her armpits and behind her ears, or powder her face, throat, and shoulders. Watching her in the faded glass, Niccolò turned weak with such love-lust that could not in a century, he knew, be assuaged.

"Surely, by St. Judas Iscariot, yours is a peerless *culo*," he gasped, penetrating her anus like a stevedore.

For a moment, she seemed startled, almost shocked by the novelty. Then her body turned gelatinous, feverish to his touch, and that which he sought: marvelously and tightly receptive.

"Oh my love, my love," she panted. "Yours is the very key—the only key—for this chamber."

And later, wrapped in her arms, face sunken in her magnificent breasts, mouth pretending to forage for the wet, purplish nipples, Niccolò wondered, "Did you—did you—?"

Antonia laughed, her whole body vibrating like a tidal respite. "I have always preferred an aristocratic penis," she said earnestly. "Long and narrow. Curious. Strong as iron. And oh, *Madonna mia*, so expert! And when you remove from me this burden—you grow heavy, *Carissimo*—I shall kneel before your key to paradise and do it homage. With tongue and lips and all my soul. Despite the fact that it has—*ohimè*—collapsed a mite. Why, alas, it becomes as nothing!"

"That is a reversible condition," Niccolò assured her. "I am as you would have me and wholly yours, Antonia, wholly yours."

Antonia cried out repeatedly in bliss, so that an answering spurt of laughter from a neighboring apartment caused Niccolò to blanch with embarrassment and fright. Yet moments later would find her nuzzling and nose-rubbing, and licking his hands and cheeks like a playful, furtive kitten. She was lavish and voluble, expressed both great admiration for his manly prowess and a crude, graphic satisfaction with all his bodily proportions, and she called frequently upon God and specific saints to bear witness to her avowals.

The novelty of real emotion outraged and delighted Niccolò. Regarding women as quarry, he had in the past been obliged to pay a price in courtesies, in tedium, in promises. But this woman was different: languid yet intense, earthy, regal, blazing with adoration yet sensibly self-contained. She offered herself freely, because she wished it so, and because it was her nature, demanding neither promises, ceremonies of seduction, nor declarations of eternal fidelity. Indeed, he made these declarations, but she did not really listen. Only the present mattered, the fiery and fleeting moment: time-baited, suspended, and grasped in greedy fingers. And always, she was aware of his swelling, thrusting, and explosive male need, which matched the hot, oily pool, and convulsions of her own.

"I do not want you to leave me," he murmured at the close of the second day, feeling pangs of guilt and confusion toward the general, and convinced La Pelusia would henceforth find him unacceptable as a guest.

"Oh, I had no such plans," said Antonia.

"But I must soon leave Como. I want you to come with me."

"Why, I should not tolerate your leaving alone." Antonia bit the back of his neck like a possessive mother cat.

"Then you are quite clairvoyant."

"No, you are quite transparent."

"We shall one day marry."

"Oh, perhaps," yawned Antonia. She began to run a glittering comb through her hair.

Niccolò was startled. "You do not want to marry?"

"Oh, no, I am quite resolved to do so. It is you who are unsure."

"First to Genoa, then perhaps Venice. Yes, Venice is a good place to begin anew. And I must teach you to sing."

Antonia leaned over him and kissed his throbbing phallus and each shaggy eyebrow. She was absorbed in this and did not seem to hear him. Since he did not at once continue, she offered, "Now you are a *maestro di bel canto*, too," but her smile conveyed pleasure as well as amusement.

"I have not performed in public in more than two years. I have been sick, Antonia. I am newly risen from the tomb."

She traced the lines around his eyes and mouth with her comb, nodding gently, aware of the struggle before them.

"Poor Niccolò," she said at last. And she added, "Do you mind very much if we go to the trattoria? There is little left in the house, and I am terribly hungry. Hungry enough to turn cannibal and eat you. I shall start with your big …"

THE GENERAL EXPRESSED satisfaction with his errant guest and extended a welcome befitting the return of a hero who has surmounted great obstacles. He practically flung himself into the hired fiacre to embrace Niccolò. He led him into the great house with vigorous backslapping and loud, expressive chortles of laughter. "You are cured! My prescription has been a success!" he exulted. "Now, who knows better—the ass of Pavia or your good and devoted friend?"

"You are the greatest physician in Italy; there is no doubt of it."

The general nudged Niccolò and lowered his voice. "Smooth as satin and smoldering as Etna, that one, yes?" he demanded, smacking his lips. The very thought of her had the old man's blood boiling. "Oh, you are the darling of the gods, fiddler! Such a woman! All wet kisses and lava, the Bianchi! I have been dreaming of your good fortune!"

La Pelusia's voice cut in upon them like cannon. "Why don't you hire the Como band, *mon Général*?" she called out, descending the stairs. "Our lodger has just returned from an extended visit to the Como whore. There should be wine in the fountain and dancing in the streets. You old fool!"

"Not too old!" cried the general. He raised his broad palm and whacked his wife solidly on the rump, sending a high-pitched shriek of astonishment echoing through the hall. Struck dumb, La Pelusia began backing away as the giant lumbered toward her. "Not too old at all for the likes of you!" he bellowed. He stripped the belt from his trousers and tore the buttons from his shirt. "I've a sudden inspiration, woman! Enough of your tongue; I'm ready for the rest of you!"

"You wouldn't dare," trembled Vittoria, stumbling in retreat on the bottom stair.

"Wouldn't *dare*?" roared the general, baring his leonine teeth.

She crawled backward up the marble stairwell, cowering in his towering shadow. "Paganini!" she clamored desperately. "Stop him!"

Niccolò stared dumbly up at them, gaping in amazement.

The general grabbed at his wife. "Leave the fiddler out of this. He's had his fill, and I'll have mine!" La Pelusia lunged from his grasp and scampered up the hall toward the bedroom. The general bounded off in pursuit, shouting back to his friend down the stairs, "The hunt is on, Niccolò!" He disappeared, and shrieks rang out from the end of the hall. Niccolò heard the large wooden door of the master bedroom slam open, but not slam shut. He was taking her right there in the hall. Amidst muffled howls of protest and roars of lust, servants began peeking out like frightened children from various doors above and below.

Niccolò smiled deliciously as the clamor abated. "Love is grand," he said aloud, and turned on his heels for a walk by the lake.

Two days later, Niccolò and Antonia Bianchi left for Genoa. Niccolò embraced his host, muttering vaguely of eternal friendship, indelible memories, and gratitude. La Pelusia did not appear. Niccolò was disappointed, but relieved as well. The general tactfully refrained from noting her absence.

14
MOONLIGHT SPECTACLE

NICCOLÒ HAD EXPECTED his mother to show hostility and resistance to his open liaison with *Madama* Bianchi. He hoped uncomfortably that she would not refuse to receive Antonia, and he worked out elaborate stratagems and threats for staving off scenes, denunciations, and such crude humiliations as Teresa might choose, from her vantage point of virtue, to inflict. His sisters and Carlo's wife, Anna, would have to be included in the declarations of defiance.

Should Teresa prove intractable, Niccolò shrewdly decided, he would threaten to remove her from the fine, fashionable house he had had Germi purchase for her a forgetful distance from *Passo del gato moro*. He would threaten the others with an absolute end to booty, reminding them that even during his more than two years of draining agony, they had suffered no interruptions of subsidy and gifts. Germi had several times expressed indignation at their callous demands; as a matter of fact, he had repeatedly urged Niccolò to harden his heart to the unending begging and whining and the recitals of urgent woe. "They never inquire of your health," he had raged. "They do not care whether you live or die, as long as their sniveling demands are met."

Let live, Niccolò thought bitterly. Blood is a chain, lightly linked yet indestructible. But he was prepared to handle any affront to Antonia, from bland moralizing to less benign devices.

He had underestimated the flexibility and calculation of Latin motherhood. Teresa greeted Antonia as a daughter, warmly kissing her on both cheeks, exclaiming over her beautiful clothes and loveliness, welcoming her to the feast. The others cagily followed her example, Domenica fawning like a servant over the singer.

Nor would Teresa hear of her son bedding down with his mistress elsewhere than in her own house. "Nonsense, Niccolò *mio*, we have here enough rooms for half a regiment, and fresh, clean sheets that smell of the wind and the sea," she declared heartily. It took Niccolò several days to realize that an official inamorata, to his saintly mama, seemed less ominous than a legitimate daughter-in-law, who might consume more, linger longer, and ultimately inherit.

But this could not mar his joy in the lusty and demonstrative Antonia who, blooming in the apparent acceptance of their love, lavished upon him solicitude such as he had never known. She clung and doted, praised his generosity, and vilified his competitors, most of whom she had never heard. Brazen, uninhibited, and passionate as a gypsy, she conveyed in time total emotional dependence upon him, which Niccolò found flattering, as well as a stunning indifference to his future plans for her, which proved more than reassuring. It was he, not Antonia, who spoke vaguely of marriage. Perhaps it would be prudent, perhaps it would make procurement of a papal decoration more likely, and perhaps it would not prove disastrous.

Antonia's attitude seemed to be, "Do as you think best." It seemed to him that she was interested only in perfecting the charming little affectional rites, in ascertaining that Niccolò wallowed in a perpetual froth of desire, in enchanting Teresa and his sisters, as well as—ultimately—the serenely skeptical Germi.

The latter, having sustained Niccolò through numerous affectations of the heart and their ensuing indiscretions, took an initially dim view of Niccolò's intentions. "Not only do I not visualize you a bridegroom, my friend, but I am ready to wager that by the end of the next month you will be weary of the lady."

"When you see her, you will know why you are speaking like a madman or a fool," said Niccolò.

When he saw her, Germi promptly conceded his error. "In your stead, I should lead *Madama* Bianchi promptly to a priest. Hurry. Someone may yet steal her in the night."

Antonia laughed mellifluously and tweaked Germi's ferocious mustache. "I should have to be dragged away against my will, shrieking—like a Sabine woman—to be parted from my Niccolò," she whispered slyly.

❊ ❊ ❊

THE INTERLUDE IN GENOA gave him a taste of the joys of permanence. The draught was quickly quaffed, but the flavor seemed the more pleasing for its brevity.

He wondered whether a stable position might be made available in the home city—yes, as a conductor, for he craved helmsmanship, remembering the swift triumph of *Matilde di Shabran*. Carlo played in the municipal orchestra and knew, or could identify, certain patrons pledged to augment the local treasury, hence influential. No post was offered, though Niccolò sought out, hinted, inquired, made known what he would accomplish should an opportunity present itself. He dreamed of a good, unstraining life, a suitable house with a view of the sea, the joys of the connubial bed, numerous male progeny.

Niccolò spent many hours correcting his mistress's vocal defects and choosing her repertoire carefully as to display her assets and conceal her faults. Antonia, he admitted, tried hard to please, but tended to be a frivolous student, finding, in the midst of a disquisition, a stray look into his very core of being, a fly to chase from the room, or some other pretext for terminating the lesson. Exasperated, Niccolò managed to laugh at her failings and to find them delectable; he would scold, she would pout, he would crowd her into a corner and cover her tear-streaked face with frenetic kisses. Fortunately, she did not interrupt his own pursuits and listened impassionedly to hours of technical studies that must surely have bored her. "Oh, that was divine," Antonia would declare, suppressing a yawn. "It seems to have made us both sleepy," Niccolò would conclude happily.

From Germi, he learned that he was still solvent. His investments had proved felicitous, and despite drawing somewhat upon capital, he had not cut appreciably into his total holdings.

"As you see, money adheres to the rich," Germi said. "And now that you are returning to the concert stage, you will be yet richer." But Paganini thought gloomily on his sufferings and the expensive treatment he had undergone. Why, suppose he had continued, during the two years, to save and invest over and above what Germi had previously invested for him! He would be a truly rich man, secure and honored. The world, after all, respects riches. And riches, to Niccolò, always signified an as yet unattained sum.

In the end, since stability was not actually offered, he left Genoa, which had anyway begun to seem close and familiar. Teresa had kissed a white and lavender Antonia rather too heartily, and waved gaily after the lovers and their baggage. The sisters pretended to weep, praying that Niccolò would not forget them.

Only Carlo, poor, dull Carlo, clasped his brother's hand and wished him well.

❊ ❊ ❊

WITHIN A FEW DAYS, Antonia was dissatisfied with their Venetian quarters.

"There is a stink from the canal; the water does not flow freely in this alley," she complained, closing the lead glass window against a thin gray rain. "And to the world, we shall appear absolutely impoverished living here, where we cannot receive, while everyone knows you are a very rich man, one of the richest in Italy."

"Oh, everybody knows this? *Everybody*? Tell me, who is this everybody?"

Antonia wavered, looking down prettily upon her bosom. "Cesare," she admitted at last. Then, as Niccolò glowered, she draped her arms about him and whimpered, "We won't talk about Cesare. He is such a pumpkin—though *generous*, Niccolò; you must admit he is generous?"

"I suppose I am not," Niccolò countered.

Antonia considered this prudently. "Well," she said, and simpered.

Niccolò reopened the window and stared down at the canal. A glossy black gondola slid through the drizzle, its raven-cloaked gondolier perched at the stern. Something clawed at Niccolò's memory and then was lost; in its place rose a baneful thought. It occurred to Niccolò that Antonia was playing an intricate game with him; that within her resided neither love, acceptance, serene good humor, doting childlikeness, effusive warmth—the things that had moved him—but a calculated imitation of these. He felt an eerie suction-strength emanating from this woman. She had purposes of her own to fulfill through him. The disguise began to crack; though he tried hard not to see clearly, the fires of her design crackled smartly and singed him.

"You have brought me no jewels," she whispered gently, suggestively, coaxing him to sit beside her.

Niccolò pulled his eyes from the vanishing gondolier, and carefully closed the window. "You have jewels."

"But they were given me by—by others."

"But you have them," he said angrily, noting her mock demureness.

Her little tongue glided playfully over his jowls. "Of course, my Sweet. I have them," she agreed.

He thought he had seen a flame darting from her eyeballs before the heavy, dark-fringed lids extinguished, for the time being, her cornered rage.

❋ ❋ ❋

BUT THEY DID MOVE TO BETTER QUARTERS, not far from St. Mark's Square, where Antonia could watch the swarming throngs and respond to the liveliness of the bizarre city. Quickly, she found milliners and dressmakers; she had, after all, to prepare for the forthcoming concert, to share the platform and bring credit to him. She discovered with delight how awesome and revered a figure Paganini had become in Venice, where his earlier triumphs lingered like a good fragrance.

Antonia was gay and friendly. She occupied herself, during his cloistered practice sessions, by promenading in the great square and talking to strangers. Niccolò scolded her for this, but she eluded him.

"They will regard you as common," he shouted.

"Better common than bored. The four walls will make me mad," she snapped, holding back tears. Antonia, he learned, could not bear to be alone.

"What decent woman walks in the square unaccompanied?"

"The square is filled with tourists and women and children."

"And men."

"I do not talk with them."

"I should like to believe that," Niccolò said bitterly.

"Well, I shall not *go* with them," she discriminated.

He longed to strike her, knowing well Antonia's magnetic coquetry and its possible consequences. No, he would not deflect his energies quarreling. There were more important matters to attend to.

Vienna, as always, lay ahead of him. The cultural capital of Europe, ultimate destination and proving ground of its most celebrated artists, Vienna held the potent promise of supreme triumph. But he would not venture forth as a mere Italian fiddler; he would enter the citadel in the grand manner of a worldly conqueror, crowned with laurels of the continent's most ancient authority. Through high-ranking friends and aristocratic admirers, he had continued to petition the Vatican regarding a long-coveted decoration, the Order of the Golden Spur, for the greatest violinist of all time. Various objections had been raised, snuffed out, again confronted. On the advice of a titled mentor close to Prince Metternich, Niccolò prepared to visit the newly designated Bishop of Venice.

"What will *he* do?" Antonia inquired. The entire procedure seemed absurd and exasperating to her, and she did not conceal her views.

"I am not sure he will do anything. He will probably interrogate me, and if he is satisfied—"

"Don't talk in riddles, Niccolò. If he is satisfied?"

"He may convey his satisfaction to Rome."

Antonia laughed. "Is that all? And for that you cannot sleep?"

"I have no difficulty sleeping."

Her laughter now came in tuneful cascades. "It is the middle of the night now, and you are getting gaunt and gray before my very eyes."

"It is a weighty and important matter."

"Why?"

"Why? Why?" he mimicked. "That should be obvious, why. Much depends on it."

"What?" Her question rang out, stark and honest, a tall wall between them.

"There is no point trying to explain anything to you," Niccolò answered coldly.

"In that case, darling, come to bed. It is chill and damp, and you need your rest, or you will grow feeble. Come; I think I have a good medicine for sleep," she promised, touching him so there would be no doubt in his mind.

Angry, pent-up, and amused, he followed her. Antonia leaned over him, smiling, to put out the candle.

THE FOLLOWING DAY, crossing St. Mark's on his return from a failed visit to the Bishop, he spied Antonia in conversation with a man at the edge of the square. Niccolò quickly stepped behind a pillar to watch unobserved. The man, partially hidden in the shadows of an archway, towered over her, his hooded black cape flowing ink-like to the rain-puddled street. Niccolò recalled the gondolier, the one he'd seen from their window. Antonia appeared both enticed and dismayed by him, shooting coy glances in a tentative retreat. At last, responding apparently to some indelicate remark, she turned away decisively and marched across the square.

Niccolò stepped out from his concealment and approached the mysterious figure. The man turned, quickly retreating into the shadows. Niccolò headed after him through the dark passage of the archway and out into the sunlight on the other side. Across a green canal, he spotted the flare of a dark cape disappearing around a corner. Niccolò scrambled over a slender bridge, jostling between two startled priests, and hurried up the narrow walkway on the other side. Turning the corner, he found himself wading through a torrent of shrieking, giggling, uniformed school children. In the center of the small, deserted *piazza* beyond them, an obsidian obelisk stood glistening in the sunlight like a dagger.

The demon had vanished.

"YOU HAVE NOT SEEN this…this scoundrel before?" asked Niccolò, slamming the shutters tight.

"Never."

"How can I believe you?"

She watched him anxiously pace the room. "Perhaps you'll have to spy on me *every* day."

"I was not spying. You did little to conceal yourself. All of Venice might know of it."

"Perhaps I should have invited him to my room before rejecting his advances."

He repressed a sudden urge to strike her. "I warn you, Antonia, do not make light of this."

The tremor in his voice unnerved her. "I do not know this man. I swear I had never laid eyes on him before."

"Then why did he approach you?"

"He said he was a boatman. He asked if I might enjoy a tour in his gondola."

"The audacity! And what was your reply?"

"I told him I might, but not without *Signor* Paganini."

"And then?"

"He asked if I were the wife of *Signor* Paganini."

Niccolò was astonished. "And you *responded* to this inquiry?"

"Yes." She looked up at him. "I told him *Signor* Paganini has no wife."

Niccolò stared at her a moment, then collapsed into a chair by the window. "A gentlewoman does not talk to strangers in public places."

"Well," Antonia decided, "I am not a gentlewoman. And are you not glad that I'm not? Whatever should I be doing here in Venice with you if I were a gentlewoman?"

❊ ❊ ❊

The first concert dispelled all doubts, his own and those of the malicious.

Paganini returned to the concert stage in masterful fettle—god and wizard, artist and provocative charlatan. His long idleness had failed to mar his technique, as rumor had wishfully proclaimed; he suffered no impairment or damage. On the contrary, he had grown, expanded his resources, and emerged, if such were truly possible, more dazzling, more eccentric, more shatteringly brilliant than before. The succubus had left him, apparently, but had by no means abandoned him.

Those who had come to scoff remained to weep and cheer. Others, faithful and of more enduring memory, journeyed respectfully from distant centers to be present at the performance. They came from the Adriatic towns and the Lombard plains and obscure country seats in the Dolomites; Dr. Martecchini left his sizable practice in Trieste to make the Venetian pilgrimage.

Antonia Bianchi was delighted by the avalanche of attention Niccolò's new successes produced. Suddenly, they both became the rage of Venice, fashionable and courted. Her own contribution, as might have been predicted, proved uneven and inconsistent in quality, but Niccolò declared her vastly improved, and Venice found her beautiful and mysterious, the gem in Paganini's coronet, according to one admirer. Antonia had never experienced such success. The men who now approached her furtively had impressive titles and stations; sometimes Antonia half regretted her inability to explore their suggestions. The women who now envied her were younger, richer, more desirable, thereby compounding the tribute inherent in envy.

Antonia enjoyed the fanfare, though she recognized much of it to be hollow. She was being feted and fawned over—this she knew—for seeming to command what she did not actually possess: the love of Niccolò Paganini.

With adulation, which he surely craved, Niccolò's nature sloughed off the habits of indolence and uxoriousness spawned during his inactive years. He had no time to lie abed mornings and contemplate his mistress's creamy magnificence.

Victory made him cantankerous and small. Perilously nervous, he quarreled over any petty issue, from a few *soldi* to the size of a poster. To his hosts—and suddenly there appeared a stream of fashionable petitioners panting to offer hospitality to Paganini and his companion—he proved an ungrateful and uningratiating guest, loud and unmannerly if he so wished, invariably unkempt and improperly dressed, always ready to take umbrage.

At the house of Ernesto Naldi, an elderly Venetian with the regal bearing of a doge, Niccolò amused the party with the old animal noises, the staple of his youthful career, and which had so shocked the Ferrarese. He had gone on amidst great hilarity, to other vulgar sounds (one lady swore on the rosary that she heard the violin expel gas!). But when someone said that he was known to practice many hours a day, he tugged the reluctant Antonia by the elbow and departed in a rage, to everyone's astonishment.

He found incomprehensible the delay in the granting of his merited papal order. He did not hesitate to court influence and favor, yet could not, somehow, sustain that effort. The young Count Perruchini listened sympathetically, promising to add his voice to the urgent pleas filed in Rome on Niccolò's behalf. He entertained lavishly for his idol, bestowing upon him respect and adulation that musicians, however eminent, did not routinely meet among the nobility.

But despite an intense effort to retain the good offices of the count, Paganini grew hostile and carping when surrounded by the petty discourse, the feasts wanting in conviviality, the stupid amusements and outrageous pomposity of those who might best help him. While Antonia smiled and bowed and, on occasion, struggled with poor appearance, he became shrill, raucous, and frequently uncontrolled.

Trying to mollify, as to redirect the barbed, uncomfortable dialogue that ensued when some dolt laughingly repeated the legend of Niccolò's imprisonment, the count most courteously asked *Madama*

Bianchi to sing. Antonia swished grandly to the pianoforte, bowing to the floor before the company. Her Bellini airs compensated in charm for their want of accurate pitch and vocal bravura; the listeners applauded enthusiastically, begging for more. The count then inquired of Paganini whether he would share his great gifts with the company.

"I thought I had been invited as a friend," Niccolò sulked.

"Indeed, you are a friend, *Maestro*," said the young count. "A most esteemed friend and the pride of our ancient city, as of all Italy."

"Then why am I exploited like a servant? I am no gypsy, to play for an abominable supper at any strange table. I have not even been offered a fee!"

And Niccolò tore out of the splendid room, leaving Antonia to burst into tears and pursue him blindly, and the company to murmur its astonishment and shock.

❊ ❊ ❊

THEY RODE HOME IN SILENCE, Antonia sobbing softly as the silver-trimmed gondola pierced the fog-heavy waters of the Venetian labyrinth. Niccolò, drowsy with fatigue, watched the rotting stone walls, the black windows, and the ominous bridges all drift past through layers of mist, as though the boat stood still while the veiled world moved around them. The woman's blubbering filled his ears, and the cold fog clung to his skin like the sweat of a whore. Venice, too, was a woman, dissolving his will, quelling his fire in her watery embrace, taking him down with her, down to her dwelling in the adumbral abyss. "Antonia," he mumbled, succumbing at last, drifting into sleep on this river of Styx.

Antonia stopped crying. Her inquisitive eyes, suddenly tearless, turned to observe the sleeper. His mouth hung open, his breathing was heavy; the thin skin of his face lay taut across his skull like the mask of death. Niccolò would not awaken, she was sure of it. Not after the potent brew of passiflora she had slipped into his wine at the home of the count.

They were drifting in the bay now, the vessel concealed in feathery fog. Antonia crept silently to the opposite end of the vessel and arranged herself comfortably on the satin-pillowed seat. She opened her legs, and clawed at her skirts, raising noisy silk over soft and slender limbs. She barely looked up as the gondolier came to her, moving like a winged dancer down the rim of the hull, his black cape billowing, his arms out wide, his bird-like face cracking through the shadow shell of his cowl. He swooped down upon her and—hunching his back—dug for the dagger that throbbed at his legs. Antonia glimpsed the shaft a moment before it entered her, blood-red and raw, like some internal organ burst forth from the demon body. She whimpered, suddenly terrified, and then she could not speak. For the incubus penis was cold as ice, an icicle prick, frigid, rabid, alive, and spewing her hot chamber with freezing venom. She stared up in horror at his sulphurous eyes, cold orbs of dying suns, and from the pit of her soul rose a blood-curdling howl, a scream as racked and terrifying as all the chorus of Hell.

❉ ❉ ❉

NICCOLÒ TRIED TO SHAKE HER AWAKE, until at last a bright slap across the face brought the screams to a stop and the woman to her senses. "Oh, " she cried, grabbing at him, yanking at the bed sheets, frantic to hide from the ubiquitous presence.

"I am here," he told her, as her eyes flitted about the shadowy room. "You've had a nightmare."

She held him, her breath rapid, the blood pulsing palpably through her veins. "The horror of it!" she said, trembling. "So real!"

"What was it?" asked Niccolò.

She envisaged again the sweeping form. "He came to me."

"Who? Who came to you?"

"The boatman," she replied.

"The man in black—the one from the square?"

"The same," she said. She held herself, as if chilled to the bone. "We were…on the water." She stared off vacantly, then her eyes suddenly filled with dread; she began sobbing and buried her face in his chest. "It was horrible!"

Niccolò held her in his arms. "You must never speak to this man again. I forbid you." She continued to weep. Niccolò held her shoulders, looked into her eyes. "He is *evil*, Antonia."

She stared back at him, confused and afraid. Too afraid to question him.

Niccolò pulled her close, peering over her shoulder into the darkness of the room. *The succubus,* he thought to himself. *She has sent him to destroy us*!

❈ ❈ ❈

ALL THE DAY HAD BEEN OVERCAST AND TROUBLED. By noon, the sun had vanished. Twilight fell quickly, the streaked purple turning to black. The Adriatic cast up strange seaweed odors and a rawness more suitable to northern waters.

The populace had gone mad, as in the time of Carnival, journeying to the cemetery in the Lido in gondolas and flat-bottomed boats, laughing, cavorting, rearing weird flare torches throughout the cemetery.

"Thrice this week already, and each time half of Venice in his wake," explained a nobleman, addressing his friend. Both carried masks but had decided the night was dark enough to risk detection. Besides, those they feared offending were also here, as exposed as themselves.

"They say he has never played better," said the other.

"Certainly," concurred an old man, who had been eavesdropping on the conversation. "He plays to ghosts and devils, to the witches that haunt these places. They are surely closer to him than fat, well-fed Venetians pressing their bottoms to rows of wooden chairs."

"His fallen angel is nearby," croaked an old woman with a candle holder in one hand and a tray of scapulars, charms, and medals to sell fastened round her neck.

"The Devil; she means the Devil. The hag knows her master!" Several youths pelted the old woman with walnuts and laughed as she hobbled away from them, clutching her wares.

A white-garbed Dominican with a ravaged face gleaming bluish-green in the torchlight cried out in a hollow voice, "My children! My children! Cast evil from your hearts! Banish Satan, turn from him!"

"Quiet, jabbering ape!" cried a voice from the aristocratic group, supported by peals of merriment.

"Turn back from abomination! Holy ground is being desecrated! An outrage is being committed in the name of the Prince of Darkness!"

"The old eunuch thinks he is John the Baptist."

"Listen to the neighing and the braying."

"Perhaps Paganini will answer him in kind."

"Obscenities before the dead."

"They will vomit down from heaven."

A high-pitched voice squealed that her thigh had been pinched and that she was a virtuous woman.

"A virtuous woman!" shouted a wag. "Where? Where? This, surely, is the eighth wonder of the world."

"Quiet, Venetian, this is the Lido; our women are respectable."

"Proof! We demand proof!"

At once, an odd hush broke upon the ribaldry and noise, extinguishing conversation. The lapping of waves could be heard on the Lido shore and the hoot of a passing cargo ship, wailing into the night. Then the agitation began, muted whispers, tense expectancy.

"There he is! I knew he would come!"

"He is ghostly; he is at once alive and dead."

"*Madama* Bianchi is beautiful tonight. She is like a goddess."

"Her jewels glitter like the eyes of many cats."

"She is a witch. She has had carnal connection with the Devil. One day they will stone her before the Duomo."

"Her gown is red flame and blue flame."

"Hush! Now he will play for the dead!"

Paganini was tuning his instrument. The wind carried the whimpering notes over the tombstones, into the hills. Then there was silence: choked, suspended, ominous. Everyone waited.

"My children!" Again, the cracked voice of the Dominican rose beseechingly, and a flare-torch was lifted to his face, so that his eyes seemed to send forth pinprick sparks. "Do not let this criminal insult your dead. Leave them to their holy repose! This rite is homage to Satan—" The exhortations ended in a muffled grunt. The torch moved on, borne elsewhere.

Sound, dissolving gold and penetrant quicksilver, poured over the multitude. They had come for sport: to amuse themselves, to view a celebrated eccentric who chose to perform symbolically for the dead, wherever they might now find themselves. The music sang of mortality and the end of days. The music sang of the triumph of the senses. The music loved and wept, suffered, mourned, knew renewal. And many were moved. Many knelt on the damp ground and shared the bliss of the happy shades, their burden spent. Peace and victory, wind-born, lived invisibly before the fluttering testimony of ears and heart, while the agitations of sulphurous evil, brewing, spitting, retching, piercing the sea air…The transfigured voice of man sobbed aloud in cat-gut and horsehair; it sobbed that he must die, that he must praise, that his remained the unceasing immolation.

"Paganini has never played more beautifully."

"*Madama* Bianchi is moved. She is weeping."

A tall man turned his black-hooded head toward the admirers. "She does well to weep," he said, his rich voice resonating deeply in the dark. "Hell is eternal fire."

❋ ❋ ❋

Paganini was replacing the violin in its case. His face, washed by the cold greenish light of the torches, seemed that of a specter, so hollow were the sunken, cadaverous cheeks, so feverish the smarting eyes, so diabolical the bony nose. Even as he put his instrument to rest, the inhuman flexibility of his hands, with their thin, elongated fingers, glowed against the blackness of hill and sky like winged birds fluttering about the tombstones.

He locked the case, raised his gaze to the sickle moon, and mouthed a silent prayer to his dark mistress. *Forgive me.*

Antonia stood staring at him, frightened, her cheeks wet with tears. The memory of the nightmare had continued to haunt her.

Niccolò turned to her, and his eyes softened. He offered his hand. "Do not be afraid, my darling."

But how could she not, with his growing strangeness and deepening obsession? She hesitated, then took his hand. He laid it gently over his arm and walked away with her toward the pier and the gondola, not even glancing at the stunned crowd waiting to render homage.

❋ ❋ ❋

The crowd dispersed, some dour and gloomy, others oddly elated. The boats were quickly filled, and the swish of oars mingled thickly with the talk and laughter. When the Dominican spoke again of satanic powers, the impatient Venetians dumped him overboard, watching with mirth as his white cassock flapped in the night waters; and, satisfied that he was able to swim ashore, bade the sinister boatman row on.

❊ ❊ ❊

"WE NEED NO LIGHT," Niccolò said hoarsely.

Antonia blew out the candle, continuing to stare at it while the wick glowed. Distant church bells rang, the timeless bronze tones vibrating slowly. In the darkness, she could feel the searing-hot, wild boar desire that waxed in her lover when another would be exhausted, broken by sheer expenditure. The irrational graveyard oblations made him crudely ravenous for her flesh, as though some dark compulsion had been spawned within him.

Niccolò tore at her clothing. "Kneel for me. Kneel upon the bed," he commanded. His words were dense and indistinct, like those of a drunkard. Impatiently, quite without tenderness, he pushed her before him and bent to bite her shoulder, lifting the heavy black hair to seize the scruff of her neck, like some enraged jungle cat, flinging himself violently upon her, kissing her roughly and with a terrible need.

"Be careful. I think I am with child," Antonia gasped. But she gurgled as he encompassed her smooth waist, and her soundings turned to avid, wild sobs as she let herself be carried into a dark land.

And before she was completely submerged and torn asunder, she thought (thought emerging without form or clarity in the writhing of great sea serpents) that she was surely damned, even as they said, cohabiting with the very Devil.

15
A Son

Antonia's impending motherhood was not, at first, regarded by either as a reality. Niccolò had heard; the words lodged in his brain like a burning coal. But he refused to talk or even think of such a possibility, for beneath it lurked a most terrifying thought: that if indeed an incubus had entered her bed, might it not be his seed that grew in her womb?

As the days passed, he grew wary of his mistress, more detached, more automatic in his physical relationship, as though extreme pleasure and abandon were degenerative and must be avoided. When he did succumb, it was with a viciousness and brutality grotesque and unfamiliar to him, as though he himself were inhabited by demonic forces. Antonia, infected with ill-boding dreams and disturbed by her lover's vague moroseness and aberrant lust, grew resentful, sarcastic, defiantly cold, desperately impassioned. Due to the delicacy of the problem before them, the usual quarrels could not be articulated. The tension between them grew unbearable; the malignancy seemed to fester and spread, as though the rot and decay of the city itself were seeping like a plague into their lives.

They abandoned Venice for Rome.

It was here, finally, in a *pensione* near the ancient Forum, that Antonia turned upon the barrier between them. The two were still abed, lying chastely apart staring at the ceiling, the mid-morning sun filtering wanly into the room between the double slats.

"It will be warm today, for so early in the year," Antonia ventured in a still, artificial voice. And suddenly, her pretense broke, and she said softly, without inquiry, on a scarcely suppressed sob, "You are unhappy about…about the child, Niccolò?"

He was taken aback. "I do not really know," he said truthfully; then, feeling compassion for her, embraced her with more tenderness than he now usually indulged. "It is not your fault," he conceded.

Antonia sobbed bitterly. "I did not want to displease you. I washed carefully—yes, I did, each time, as soon as I could."

"Are you certain of that?" he asked. "Every time?"

"Why yes, of course, always." She noticed a sudden darkening of his mood. "But you know that I am careful," she pleaded. "Why would you have reason to doubt me?"

He looked at her a moment, then lightly kissed her tear-stained face. "I do not doubt you," he said in a flat, neutral voice. "If there is to be a child, why, there is to be a child."

Antonia smiled and yielded prettily, in the confused, tremulous manner of a young girl. Niccolò smiled, too, in spite of himself. Nothing was pure: not love, not hate, not rejection, not uneasy acceptance. The extenuations always ate away at one, undermining truth and vitality.

❊ ❊ ❊

He had come to Rome to escape the draining decadence of Venice, and to perform, to keep his coffers filled, and to continue the dialogue with the representatives of Prince Metternich about the long-threatened, oft-postponed visit to Vienna. But looming over and beyond these considerations was the matter of the papal decoration, the coveted Order of the Golden Spur, without which any victory in Vienna would be provisional and pitiably incomplete. This now obsessed him to the point of desperation. He carried his petition everywhere, without modesty or shame; he talked of little else.

"The Cardinal Secretary of State has read my petition," he related excitedly. "He is eighty-four years of age; he borrows time to plead my cause."

Antonia recognized the hyperbolic touch and the wishful thinking. "Why is it so important to you, Niccolò *mio*?" And promptly, she wished herself tongueless; for now, of all times, she was not to antagonize her lover and render her situation the more precarious.

"Why! Because only three musicians have been thus honored, that is why."

"Who?"

"Gluck," said Niccolò. "And Mozart." The name was still a torment, as in boyhood.

"Oh, perhaps it is only for Germans."

"And Morlacchi," Niccolò said bitterly. "Of all Italian musicians— Morlacchi! That is what it means to have a proper advocate."

"It will all end well," Antonia promised confidently, as one might humor a small child who seeks a missing toy.

The next day, Niccolò returned from a session with his banker in an explosive rage and announced that he was going to fight a duel. Antonia burst into tears and demanded to know the name of his imminent murderer.

He proved to be a scabrous and decadent Frenchman called Henri Beyle, a scribbler whose excretions, in self-defense, appeared under various names, including Stendhal. This vile charlatan, liar, and character assassin numbered among many affectations a shallow, pompous interest in music, setting himself up (for profit, naturally) as an authority, though in truth he knew nothing. Since knaves of this sort can only survive by constant pen-dribblings, being quickly forgotten, Beyle had taken to writing on music and musicians. He had just published a *Vie de Rossini,* full of the most scurrilous errors, filth, and lies.

"Let Rossini fight his own duels," sobbed Antonia.

"They tell me he actually flatters Gioacchino," Niccolò said. "No doubt he expects some favors in return."

"Then why are you insulted?"

"Because now, now that I am so close to the Golden Spur, he publishes for the entire world that I am a criminal, that I learned to play in prison!"

Niccolò had, on his way from the bank, lingered at a bookseller's and been shown the offensive footnote. He had tossed the volume into the air and left yelling such imprecations that the astonished bookseller could but conclude he was a madman.

"When did you challenge him?"

"Who challenged him?"

"Then you did not challenge him to a duel?"

"He is in Milan...in Paris...who knows where he is?" Niccolò answered fretfully. "But I shall find him," he threatened.

Antonia smiled. "Why do you not consult Germi? I am sure he will give you excellent advice."

Woman-wise, she assumed Germi's advice would be to ignore the entire matter, that people would buzz and forget, that the charges had been heard so frequently as to be common property and common belief. To her astonishment, Germi shared Niccolò's enormous indignations, suggesting a lawsuit against the scribbler for defamation of character. Niccolò now added a series of conferences with lawyers and embassy officials and miscellaneous gossips who might inform him of Beyle's financial circumstances.

Antonia could have announced almost from the outset that the matter would dissolve in threats and speeches. But she had long ago learned that men must dissipate themselves over trifles, thereby being made to feel important and in command of their destinies. Her own problems were larger and more immediate.

"Niccolò," she said abruptly. Both were dressing for a concert and Antonia viewed herself critically in the glass, refining her coiffure, adjusting the lace at her breast. "You used to talk often about marriage."

He did not immediately answer, and Antonia, with an almost knotted effort and a swift flush of mortification, repeated her overtures in a more deliberate tone.

"Oh, did I?" he inquired absently.

"I have never pressed you," she reminded him. "But now—now that there is to be a child …"

It was very difficult to continue, and she was unable to do so. But since he made no answer, none at all, she persisted somewhat sharply, "Niccolò?"

"Oh, we shall see, we shall see," he answered, lifting the violin to his chin for the pantomimic session that always preceded a concert. She knew the matter stalemated and recognized that she would have to begin anew at a more strategic time.

Both were strangely silent on their way to the theater. Niccolò felt the lightheadedness that always filled him, like a mysterious drug, before a public concert. Antonia felt in him the aloofness that had trailed her announcement that she was with child, long ago in Venice.

She sang badly. Not analytical of her efforts, Antonia was aware of a deadness, a want of conviction, and only the most routine rapport with her audience. Supported by a small, scratchy orchestra, Niccolò played superbly, apparently unconcerned with their deficiencies and hers. Both concertos produced great enthusiasm and precipitated the suggestion that Paganini might, after all, be one of Italy's major composers. The variations on a Rossini aria, performed as a challenge, brought a stomping ovation. In a gesture of solidarity, Niccolò joined hands with his friend, Gioacchino (whom he had been ready to renounce for having elicited the scribbler's admiration), thus thumbing his nose at Henri Beyle.

Niccolò was furious with Antonia. She cringed guiltily. "I have not practiced. I am sorry."

"This is your last appearance, *Madamina*. You have made a fool of me!"

"Sh, they will hear you; there are students outside the door. Please, I shall study. I shall breathe exactly as you say."

"Do you take me for an idiot, and blind?"

"Quiet, love. Tell me when we are alone."

"From either side of the house, your belly hung like a washerwoman's. I am sure everyone saw you were *incinta*!"

"Is that all? Is that truly all?" Antonia screamed. "Well, I hope they realize who made me *incinta*. I did not know it is a secret. Or would you rather be thought impotent?"

"That is quite enough from you! I was merely trying to tell you courteously that it showed."

"Courteously! He tells me courteously! Merciful saints, what is discourteously?"

"...and that I must procure another singer immediately."

"You will do nothing of the sort, or I shall make life very difficult for you—and for her."

"I am bored by threats."

"I shall cut her gown with a scissors. I shall scratch her face with these fingernails!"

"Very amusing." He tried to laugh.

"I shall poison both of you!" Antonia shrieked, and this time Niccolò pleaded with her to desist lest all Rome know their problems by the morrow.

Outwardly composed, they appeared a dignified and harmonious pair at the palace of Count Origo, dining in a distinguished company of prelates, poets, and aristocrats. They had the supreme pleasure of kissing the ring of the aged Cardinal Secretary of State, and Paganini obtained for a few moments the venerable ear and undivided attention. Antonia had smiled proudly and possessively as she heard her Niccolò compared with Pindar, with Homer, with Phoebus Apollo. The child quickened in her repeatedly, perhaps as a result of her dressing room tantrum. She directed a swift prayer that no harm had been done.

❈ ❈ ❈

Trapped, furious, yet elated and proud, loving Antonia above all womankind for harboring his child, yet suspicious and doubtful, loathing the corruption that seemed to increase with her measure, Niccolò sailed from Naples to Palermo to await the birth of his son. He paced the deck of the small vessel like a ravenous, caged tiger.

Antonia lay feverish and ailing on the deck, where she had been carried. From the beginning of the pregnancy, she had been lethargic and weak, vomited frequently, and experienced discomfitures and cravings, as women often do. Following one of their senseless quarrels, she had collapsed and shown blood. And after consulting the famous Dr. Dellacorte, who had attended the Queen of Naples herself, Niccolò had decided upon the Sicilian journey. Naples, he had been advised, is quite unhealthy for childbearing in the summer. Antonia might very well lose the child, should the bleeding persist; in any event, she must be regarded as a fragile vessel until her confinement had been successfully accomplished.

The diagnosis enraged Niccolò and terrified him. He was no better than a peasant, or a serf, chained like an ox to the yoke, doomed by his own predatory manhood. And Antonia, the bitch—could she have taken something to cause the bleeding…to endanger his son? She would never admit it, he knew; nor would the doctor know. What, in the final analysis, was the wisdom of doctors? Calamities happen, Niccolò had been told with a shrug. But if the *Signora* would rest many hours each day and be served gently and not disturbed by male roughness and demands in the night, and if she were, above all, prevented from becoming agitated, there was no reason not to hope for a safe confinement, as scheduled.

Of course, the idiot had no way of appreciating that agitation was Antonia's natural habitat. She thrived on extremes of emotion. Her very languor deceived; assaultive and sensual, it was by no means the languor of repose. Deliriously happy or morose or furious or playful as a kitten, Antonia was not so much being this way or that as acting out, scaling great pinnacles of feeling. Now, she had to be kept passive and calm that his son might be saved; that he might not be expelled prematurely into the inhospitable world. Niccolò studied his mistress's protruding belly as she lay on the deck. Was she large enough? Would she become bigger? That lump could be but a puny infant. Yet he had heard of a Genoese woman delivered of a stillborn child of great size, strangled in the coils of his own efforts to emerge into the world.

And he wondered again about her dreams of the Devil.

"You are staring at my ugliness," Antonia wailed.

"I do not find you ugly."

"Oh, yes, be truthful. I am very ugly. I am as misshapen as a dwarf and bloated, and my skin is stretched."

"Don't be ridiculous."

Antonia's voice grew sharp and abrasive. "I saw you staring at the young girl who is returning from a visit with her relative in Sorrento."

"Quiet, quiet, you must keep very calm, *Cara*, for the child's sake."

"You are hankering for a woman. Oh, I know you, Niccolò. It is as though it were written on your forehead."

"I am wasting time trying to reason with you."

Antonia began to cry. "She is flat-chested. She has a squint. She is a virgin and will scream."

"I don't know what you are talking about." Not a lie, entirely; he felt her criticisms were exaggerated. The girl, while not beautiful, had a certain innocent grace that had reminded him, remotely, of Eleonora Quilici.

"Then why do we not marry? You used to talk of it all the time. Do you want a bastard?"

Niccolò stared into the purple waters streaked with the last liquid fire of the sun. "We shall see. We shall see," he murmured unhappily. "We shall see whether it is a boy."

Though this was not exactly his thought, it seemed a quite logical reservation. He could not understand Antonia's piercing, agonized wail, which brought several women, one clacking rosary beads, to her side.

IN HALF-ORIENTAL PALERMO, good lodgings were readily available. At not too great cost, they could live like gentlefolk in a thick-walled apartment with an ample balcony, not far from St. John of the Hermits.

Niccolò soon inquired after the finest doctor, who promptly referred him to the finest midwife, deeming it highly improper to be a participant in so intimate a feminine concern. As for Antonia, she rallied, but in a totally eccentric manner. She seemed to recognize her quaint power over him and ceased suddenly to be ingratiating. For hours each day, she stood before the glass, pouting, posing, simpering, contemplating her lumpy body and her strong, handsome face. She might let half a morning drift by placing a flower in her hair or contemplating her jewels.

She resented bitterly being banished not only from the stage but from the auditorium as well. Days and nights given over to the preparation of a concert were a torment to her, and on performance nights, she was nearly unbearable, weeping so wildly, so convulsively, that Niccolò several times supposed her on the brink of labor. But with respect to Antonia's public appearances, Niccolò was adamant. Lower-class women might indeed permit themselves to be regarded *incinta* by the curious. But respectable women do not parade their bellies before the world and call forth clever remarks about getting and begetting, joys and sorrows; respectable women remain discreetly cloistered, particularly when the learned Dr. Dellacorte commends tranquility and repose, for the boy's sake.

But Antonia never fully accepted these strictures. She would burst into tears and wish herself dead, or she would burst into tears and wish Niccolò dead or unborn, or that she had never set eyes upon him. Worst of all, she would plunge into wild paranoia concerning his infidelities.

Returning exhausted from a concert in the middle of the night, he was astonished to confront Antonia, sitting upright at the bedroom window, her eyes abnormally large, her face flushed and sickly.

"Why are you not asleep?" he demanded, more harshly than he had intended.

Antonia did not answer, nor did she stir. He noticed that she had arrayed herself in her finest gown of snowy white and purple, which could not now be buttoned or hooked; that her face was carelessly, freakishly painted; that she was bedecked with half the jewels she owned. The tightness, the hanging hooks and buttons, the gauche elegance, and the cosmetics and excessive glitter, combined to give her the aspect of an operatic madwoman.

Controlling his anger, he suggested, "Let us go to bed. Your Niccolò is weary enough to welcome death."

In a high, unfamiliar voice, Antonia declared, "She is surely a widow or an abandoned woman. I do not think she has a husband."

"Who?"

She continued in the same strange, artificial manner, as though reading aloud lines written in an unfamiliar hand. "Is she very beautiful? Is she young? Does she make love as I do? They say women are very different one from another. Tell me—is she lithe, slender? Does she kiss you often?"

"Who?"

"Your Sicilian *inamorata*," Antonia declared stridently. "Oh, you think I do not know; you think I am buried alive in this stench-hole guarding my belly; that my eyes and brain have withered. I know what you are about, Niccolò. I know why you are weary; why your eyes are extinguished."

"Indeed. I have been counting receipts. I have had words. I have almost come to blows with the slimy manager who performed the usual sleight-of-hand for my benefit. And I have given a concert, remember, and paid off my many leeches."

"I have heard that Sicilian men are very jealous, and that they slaughter one another over a woman. They are quick with the knife."

"And for the past week, my trusting soul, I have had trouble with the police."

Antonia's stage trance collapsed. "The police? What have you done? What has happened?"

"I am under surveillance and constantly followed."

"What have you done?"

He shrugged, mopping his brow. "Word of my youthful liaison with the Princess of Lucca has just reached this benighted isle. I am suspected of Bonaparte leanings."

Antonia stared in utter disbelief. "But Napoleon is dead."

"Perhaps word of that event has yet to reach Sicily," Niccolò said. He began to undress, scattering clothing everywhere. "And Byron died in Greece, I learned tonight. A hero. A savior. A fool." He buried his face in his hands for a moment, rage turned to grief.

Antonia regarded him possessively with a fond smile. "You know," she decided. "It pleases me, somehow, that you were loved so madly by a Bonaparte princess. I cannot quite explain it, but it pleases me."

"Madly is a slight overstatement of the case," he yawned. "And that was a quarter of a century ago, almost."

And it pained, it sickened, that time could not be arrested; that here he stood in middle life, looking for his nightshirt: a minor success, pitiful, withdrawing to his solitary bed, and the great world still at bay.

❋ ❋ ❋

"Almost."

"The child is kicking."

"That means he is healthy."

"Feel how he is kicking."

He winced, disgusted. "It is not becoming."

"Please. It is your child, Niccolò."

"I did not deny that. Go to sleep."

"Oh, he is kicking still harder—please put your hand here. It is very interesting."

"No," said Niccolò with finality. "It is not done."

"I should think you would want to."

"It is improper."

"You have done other things that are improper," Antonia whined. "If everyone were proper, the world would come to a swift end."

"You have slept half the day away, and I am exhausted," Niccolò shouted. "Now it behooves you to quack like a duck, and I must stay awake and listen."

Antonia began to sob loudly, sullenly. He patted her head lest she become agitated, although it began to occur to him that she was close enough to the time of her confinement to have considerably lessened that danger.

Late in July, Antonia's travail began in earnest. Palermo's finest midwife appeared immediately, accompanied by her two married daughters carrying mysteriously encased equipment. The old woman bore herself officiously, reminding Niccolò with amusement and a shudder of the omniscient Dr. Borda, who had nearly deprived him of life.

At the start, Antonia was affable and composed, smiling meekly and submitting to instructions. She seemed frightened but determined to show fortitude and a casual acceptance of natural phenomena.

"What any cat can do, I can do," she joked, walking up and down the room as the midwife had instructed to encourage the pains to recur at more frequent intervals.

"*Signor*, you are useless. I suggest you make your way according to your preference, to the church or the cafe," suggested the midwife.

"Oh, do not drive him away just yet," cried Antonia, to horrified exclamations from the midwife's assistants, one of whom turned her face in revulsion at the very notion of a lingering male.

"*Signora*, what are you saying?" murmured the younger of the two. "It would be a bad omen."

"He would not lie with a woman for a year," said her sister.

"Niccolò?" Antonia laughed. "Impossible!" And she doubled over under a fresh assault of contractions.

The midwife ordered her to bed and Niccolò out of the house at once. "We must help the *signora* bear down as to assist the child to push its way out. It is not a pretty business, the suffering of women. This will go on for many hours."

"I want to see my son."

"We shall not substitute another's," chortled the old woman. To Antonia she instructed, "Clutch the bedpost—it is strong; I have tested it—and tear at this towel when the pain comes." She turned to Paganini. "And if it is a daughter, she will be put to the breast just the same."

"A daughter!"

"Listen to the old goat," sneered the midwife. "Men, men: all of them alike. Joy in the night, a quick piss, and they demand sons. Make a son, there," she ordered Antonia, who had begun to writhe and moan. "It is very simple, is it not?"

"You should have seen my Augusto when he learned I had been delivered of a daughter," laughed the elder helper. "He cried, drank a liter of wine, and fell asleep in the stable."

"And which of his brats, now, can do no wrong?" asked the fond grandmother. "Giulietta, of course. Always the strap to the backs of his boys, answers to his prayers, small as they are. But when you are wriggling on a hot brazier and are torn apart in torment, when you have filled buckets with blood, they demand sons. Nothing else will do!"

Antonia uttered an unearthly shriek and grasped the bedpost; the room shook. A series of disembodied yells, sharp, staccato and wordless, were wrenched out of her throat; she stared at Niccolò with such loathing as he never imagined possible.

"Out, out, out, out!" chanted the old woman. "I cannot uncover the *signora* if you are about. Out, or I shall take a broom to you!"

NICCOLÒ WALKED THE SUN-BLEACHED STREETS while Palermo slept off its midday meal. The city lay deserted, a dream in daylight seen through squinting eyes. Out of the bone whiteness, like a dab of paint on a blank canvas, the tiny blue hotel appeared, leaning against the salt breeze blowing in off the sea, the lapping surf licking its paint-peeled wall.

Beneath a shuttered window in the lobby, on a wicker couch striped with lines of bright sunlight, the overfed hotelier lay asleep on his back, his belly rising and falling like the swell of the sea. No need to wake him, thought Niccolò. The month's rent had been paid in advance—at a price, he recalled with a pinch, that assured the fat man's discretion.

The girl had screamed the first time, just as Antonia had predicted on the boat from Naples. Blood had flowed and ruined the sheets, eliciting clamorous complaints from the hotelier on Niccolò's return a few days later. Lucre, of course, shut the man's mouth; now he lay snoring like a happy hippopotamus on a sun-streaked riverbank.

A black cat rose from its slumber at the base of the stairs, stretched languorously, and sauntered out the door. Niccolò climbed the narrow flight of steps, the tight walls still redolent with the girl's tender scream—a delicate, painful vibrato that had hung in the air like a pungent perfume. The memory warmed Niccolò's loins. He quickened his step.

The sound of his hand on the doorknob woke the dreamy-eyed girl from her slumber. Waiting in the wide, wooden chair beside the open window, she had drifted off with the slap-sound of the sea and the soft caress of the breeze. Now her face filled with an anticipatory tension; she did not smile, nor gesture, nor speak, yet Niccolò perceived a timidity in her manner and a glimmer of fear in her eyes—the trepidations of innocence at war with desire.

He held out his hand, and she rose from the chair. A trace of baker's flour dusted the falling curls of her raven-black hair. Her cheeks were pink porcelain; her lips, subtle and plump.

Niccolò took her arm and led her to the bed. She pulled back the coverlet, exposing cool white sheets. She turned, stood before him, her eyes downcast, her delicate fingers nervously fondling a button of her dress. The sound of her breathing filled Niccolò's ears; the sweet scent of her skin made him shiver. He pulled her hands apart and began unfastening the long line of cloth-covered buttons down the front of her dress.

He knelt to finish the task. The girl's breathing quickened, her chest heaving above him. He slid her pale silk underwear down to her knees, her white thighs opening before him like the petals of a flower. He nuzzled her dark pistil, his tongue probing deeply for the honey nectar. Soon the nectar flowed, the young body quivering in his hands like a plucked string, her tremulous voice fluttering off the empty walls. Niccolò turned the girl over onto the bed, entering her quickly from behind. He pressed deeply into her, reveling in the squeals of pain that came with every thrust. A fine fiddle this, he thought with a grin, plying her flesh with his blooming bow.

❈ ❈ ❈

HE DID NOT RETURN TILL MID-MORNING, at which time Achilles Cyrus Alexander (by his father's designation), red and blotchy, incredibly hideous, and squirming like an earthworm, was placed in his trembling arms. He did not even glance at Antonia till she informed him coldly from her bed that a wet-nurse recommended by the midwife was on her way.

Niccolò carried the tiny creature to the bed and placed him beside his mother. He stared at the newborn with uncertainty.

"There is to be no wet nurse," he repeated. "Those are my final words on the subject, and I propose to be obeyed."

He staggered to his bed and fell asleep almost at once, as drained and depleted as though he himself had given birth. Instead of elation, there had been a torpor so debilitating that he could no longer endure looking upon the world. He fell upon his face and knew he was quite dead, descending in a whirling vortex to a violent, infernal region where the dripping girl cavorted with devils, and witches danced to the tune of a bloody violin.

16

Knight of the Golden Spur

Domesticity remained a volcano's crater. Motherhood brought Antonia many tribulations and little bliss. She worried that lactation would make her old, pendulous, and fat. "Oh, I am developing udders; the little monster wants me to be ugly," she would protest, then inspect herself in the glass and discuss weaning with half the neighborhood. "We can try a little goat's milk soon," she hoped. "And some pastina, not hot …"

As their uncomfortable and suspended existence stretched out for many months in Palermo, Niccolò became aware of an uncomfortable stasis. The child, to be sure, became a central concern, a distraction from his obsession for the long-sought Golden Spur. Yet he could not actually feel for a puking blob of an infant who needed quiet at inconvenient hours, who failed to recognize his father, who howled with pain at the sweep of a chord or simple harmonics, who kept one awake at night. There were times when Niccolò felt certain the infant was not his.

Still, it infuriated him that Antonia did not bubble with maternal love. She did, indeed, experience moments of impulsive affection for the child, in her quaint way. "Oh, Holy Mary, what shall I do with you, you are so ugly," she would croon, hugging the little bundle, tossing him up and down till Niccolò trembled lest she drop him. "I think you resemble my Uncle Nino," she declared, tickling the infant's toes. "Of course, he was seventy years old when I saw him, and he looked like a puckered little monkey. But you are my sweet cabbage just the same." And she would make bird noises and frog noises, failing to notice that Achilles was wet, smelly, and fretful.

While the routine of domestic life chafed, rendering Niccolò sullen and rebellious, he harbored a particular distaste for that which he demanded Antonia regard as nothing short of beatific—the physical aspects of childbearing and child rearing. Parsimony, medical platitudes, and old wives' lore had combined to enforce his insistence that Antonia nurse the child herself. In truth, the procedure shocked and disgusted him. "Not here," he would shout whenever Antonia, pouting, displayed an engorged white breast, soft as satin and tipped with flame. Watching her suckling the child, whom she handled awkwardly and untenderly, Niccolò became convinced that he would never touch her again. Motherhood was a despoiler. When she smiled to him from her pillow and extended her arms, he could think only of her writhing, of her clutching the towel and the bedpost, of the midwife forcing her knees apart. He conceded himself unnatural, recognized that he had always been so; he remembered how revolting Angelina had become, many years ago, with her morning malaise, and how Antonia, in confessing her nightmare with the incubus demon, had snuffed out any remnant of his desire for her.

He suspected the Evil One still paid her visits. He often heard her murmuring in the night, trembling with fear—or pleasure—he could not be sure of which. Perhaps the she-devil had left him for good, and changed its sex for her. Nearly two years had passed since his last encounter with the succubus, and her absence gnawed at him. She was gone and yet not gone, hovering over his days and nights like some dark angel, menacing, alluring, and unreachable. He suspected it was she who thwarted his ambitions with domesticity, obligation, and the confounding denial of the Golden Spur.

Was this the Devil's retribution for love?

A stunning loss at the poker table seemed to confirm his suspicion. In an effort to escape Antonia's distemper and the sun-bleached boredom of Sicilian life, Niccolò had fallen back into his gambling habit, meeting a varying group of acquaintances at the home of Count Albieri for a weekly game of cards. They shared a camaraderie of sorts, a mutual respect which, however short of true friendship it might fall, nevertheless caused one to welcome the arrival of certain longtime opponents. To Niccolò's mind, the most notorious of these was the wealthy, wide-waisted Sicilian merchant, Girardelli, who on this occasion forced him into a most precarious wager. Unwilling to accept a promissory note, the fat man agreed to an offer of the fiddler's most treasured violin, a priceless pearl from the house of Stradivari. Niccolò, with four queens in one hand and an empty purse in the other, felt victory was both necessary and inevitable.

But the four queens were cardboard queens, ruled by the consummate Queen of the Dark. Girardelli's straight flush beat him flat out, and the famous violinist lost his famous violin.

WHY ANTONIA NOW TALKED INCESSANTLY OF VIENNA he could not understand; the demon must indeed have been whispering in her ear. "You are perhaps afraid to perform outside Italy?" Antonia would challenge. "Or are you waiting to become younger?" She seemed to know how lacerating he found such a taunt at forty-four, aware that many of the great names of Italian music had long reposed in their graves at his age.

Desperate at a crossroads, Niccolò found himself immobile. He had often admitted his own incapacity for action. The most indecisive of men, he had lingered at the Luccan court; he had lingered on his sickbed; and—most significantly—he now lingered within the confines

of his native land when the greater world cried out to him, and treasures awaited his mere grasp of them. Now, he feared that a long absence
might dispel forever remaining hopes for the papal decoration. He wrote
every bishop, cardinal, and bureaucrat whose name was known to him;
he wrote Germi, suggesting that documents be procured from Genoese
officialdom attesting to his law-abiding character and impeccable
morality, snuffing out the memory of his unjustified imprisonment.

Palermo palled, as did his changeling wife. Indeed, Niccolò suffered
a dramatic diminution of desire for her; Antonia's soft hand upon his
nakedness brought a shudder of revulsion; he heard her amazed gasp
and hated himself, but he could not soften toward her.

"IT IS PERMISSIBLE NOW," she whispered. "I am—as before." Her whisper
was calm, yet scratchy with impatience and lust.

He pretended not to hear, knowing she would never be as before,
knowing she was corruption, that something very precious had withered in him, quite irrationally.

THE GIRL STRETCHED her nakedness across the white sheets, reaching
for the black cat as it slipped beneath the bed. Looking up from lacing
his shoes, Niccolò paused to ponder the twin curves of the young woman's flawless buttocks. Perhaps he might be convinced to linger a while
longer.

No, he thought bitterly. Antonia's quarrelsomeness had increased of
late. She exploded out of sheer contrariness, often without waiting for a
reason; there was no need to give her a legitimate one now. She had not
discontinued her earlier charges of infidelity, suspecting a new affair in

every avenue and alley. Niccolò had come to regard an hour away from the house as a rare pleasure for which penance would be exacted; he did not often permit himself such luxuries. But the lure of the baker's daughter he found irresistible.

"Why are you looking at me," she asked, stroking the cat hugged to her breasts.

Niccolò paused before answering. "I find it remarkable that you need to ask such a question."

The girl eyed him curiously, then turned her back and lay on her side, head propped in her hand.

Niccolò's eyes swam down the cascade of her curling black hair. "You remind me of someone," he said.

She watched the cat wander off. "Someone you loved?"

"Someone…I wanted to love."

The girl clutched the cool tangle of sheets, drawing them up to her throat. She rolled onto her back and spoke to the ceiling. "Was she very young, this someone?"

"She was only a child."

"What was her name?"

Niccolò moved closer, sat on the edge of the bed. "Why should I tell you her name when you refuse to tell me yours?"

"You are the great Paganini. What can my name be to yours?"

"A mystery, if you will not reveal it."

"Have I not revealed enough to you?"

"No." His hand slithered beneath the sheet, slipping softly into the valley of her thighs. The warm flesh tightened, hotly squeezing his palm. Then she closed her eyes, and sucked in a fluttering breath, her legs parting ever so slightly. The violinist fingered her bristly labia, the tight, chubby lips still moist from their lovemaking.

"Tell me your name," he whispered, his long fingers sliding deeper. "Tell me."

Her damp eyes opened languidly, her golden irises swelling like fire feeding on the light of day. The pupils squeezed into vertical slits, feral doubles to the amber cat eyes watching from the sill.

Niccolò drew closer, a moth to her flame.

"*Who are you?*" he asked.

❀ ❀ ❀

The girl remained a burning secret, a fire in his pocket. With post-partum Antonia raving in one ear and the unquenchable Paphian panting in the other, Niccolò sought refuge in the cultured company of the DelSolars, mother and son, his warmest Palermo friends. Since he had made the acquaintance of the aristocratic Spaniards during the period when Antonia was not to be viewed by society, they had remained unknown to her; yet now that there was no reason to remain hidden, she seemed fiercely opposed to being presented to them. Repeatedly, Niccolò invited, begged, and even pleaded. Several times Dona DelSolar dispatched written invitations by a household servant. Antonia refused to go, offering neither excuses nor the courtesy of a reply, yet railed whenever he sought to visit these generous and intelligent friends.

"You are certain it is a son she has, a tender nineteen-year-old son?" Antonia nagged. "Not a daughter, Niccolò *mio*—truly a son?"

"You are free to come see for yourself."

"Oh, you say that pleasantly enough, knowing I do not intend to. If you supposed for a moment that I am actually planning to visit your stuffy *señora*, you might feel less comfortable."

"Come whenever you like. Come tonight."

"You know I would not stoop to spy on you. That is quite beneath my dignity. There are women who would do this, but never I. Still, I know what I know."

"Then you know nothing."

In profile, he could observe Antonia's lower lip quivering with conflict and self-pity.

"Since you do not plan for us to marry," she blurted, "I shall need a settlement."

He was simultaneously shocked, relieved, and cagily alerted. "Why? What for?"

"So I shall not have to beg for bread."

"You seem well-fed," Niccolò retorted, raising his voice.

She did not subdue hers. "So my child and I will not be at the mercy of men," she spat out.

He lurched swiftly. "You are going nowhere with that child; understand that. Achillino stays," he shouted.

"I go wherever I choose. You have no right to order me about."

"You may go precisely where and as you please, *Madamina*. But Achillino stays."

Antonia flung a figured majolica vase at him, overturning a crystal candlestick as she reached. She was a poor marksman, however, and joined him staring at the hundreds of tiny fragments that lay at his feet.

Achillino wailed.

❈ ❈ ❈

AND UNEXPECTEDLY, Antonia chose to accompany him to the house of Maria Ynes DelSolar and her son, Jaime. Serenely and graciously, she moved among the guests, and when she paid her respects to her hostess, the Spanish gentlewoman cried out in throaty, oddly accented Italian, "Oh, but she is beautiful, Paganini! Why have you so long concealed this rose?"

"So that others may not enjoy her fragrance," suggested a Sicilian dandy. Antonia accepted the compliments modestly, fluttering luxuriant eyelashes.

"And I am told you are a singer," said Señora DelSolar.

"Pale moon to Paganini's sun," Antonia murmured. Perhaps she had heard the phrase somewhere. Only Niccolò, apparently, detected her irony.

"Paganini tells me you have a small child," continued the enchanted hostess with a countenance suitably arranged for acknowledging very new motherhood. If aware that the union had yet to be blessed by the Holy Church—and who was unaware?—she carefully guarded the fact.

Antonia responded correctly; her face was positively seraphic. "Oh, Dona Ynes, he is my life's joy," she cooed. "And the image of Niccolò. It is uncanny."

The latter pronouncement, of course, was pure improvisation. For some reason, it delighted everyone and inspired a toast to the health of Achilles Cyrus Alexander, which made Niccolò uncomfortable.

Jaime, a slim, tall, intense young man, held his pale, luminous eyes on Antonia. "The child has brought a fresh beauty to your ladyship," he said.

Antonia did not respond. She had noticed that the young man's bony hands appeared much older than his years. She recoiled, her tongue silenced.

Jaime turned to Niccolò. "I have been wanting to ask you, *Maestro*. Why do women experience so much difficulty in mastering the violin? My sister—she is now married, but we are close to the same age and were reared, you might say, as from the same egg. She struggled many years, and under excellent tutelage. She is quick and musical, and I daresay would have played the pianoforte very creditably after so long a period of study."

Niccolò frowned, considering this. "Other than as singers," he began, "the results produced by women in all forms of musical art would seem meager. I attribute this to certain limitations of the sex—a want of vigor, to begin with, the fingers obviously of insufficient length and limited strength—as well as certain weakness or inconsistency of intellect."

"Oh, I am not at all in agreement with you," laughed the Spanish lady. "Women can be very strong-minded."

Niccolò had become distracted by Antonia's silent and uneasy withdrawal. "I do not mean strength in that sense," he explained, eyeing his lover warily. "It is a matter of dedication, to begin with. And the music, unlike operatic music, is quite abstract."

Antonia interrupted loudly, "Niccolò, I have had enough. Take me home."

"Music is quite abstract," he repeated. "It is not to be equated with certain thoughts or ideas, but is rather a different, far more complex form of—"

"I wish to leave this instant, Niccolò."

"Quiet," he said. "You are making a spectacle of yourself."

"Do you not feel well, *Signora*?" the hostess wondered.

"I ought not have come," she said, backing away from them. "I ought never have come! Please, let us return now."

"When I am ready."

"Don't you see who they are?!" she cried, becoming hysterical. She moaned, laughed, wept.

"I think she is ill," Jaime suggested politely, reaching for her arm. "I shall procure a carriage."

Antonia tore away from him. "I am well, thank you," she laughed, weeping copiously. With a panicky excess of energy, she pulled at Niccolò, dragging him from the room. Then, shrieking with teary glee, she followed him from the brilliantly illuminated hall and the gentle, astonished people.

Niccolò held her silently in the swift-rolling carriage.

"He is the demon," she murmured, drying her tears on the lapel of his coat. "The Devil of my dreams."

"Jaime is hardly more than a boy. Surely—"

"No, Niccolò. It is he; I am certain."

"And the dear *Madama* DelSolar?"

"She…she is the demon's mother."

"Of course," Niccolò replied, indulging her. "It would only be fitting that the Devil be born of a Spaniard."

Antonia pulled away. "Do you not believe me?" she asked, her teary eyes pleading.

"My dear Antonia," he started. Bristling, she turned away, crossing her arms, her tears suddenly vanished. "I believe you have seen the Devil," Niccolò explained, "but I do not believe Jaime is the Devil you saw."

"Hah!" she scoffed. "Your answer is as devious as the Devil himself."

Niccolò turned to gaze at the passing city and the round moon low in the jagged black sky. Yes, he thought with trepidation, the Devil is devious indeed.

❋ ❋ ❋

ANTONIA'S BEHAVIOR CONTINUED TO AMAZE HIM. While scarcely the conventional mother of Italian sentiment, she accepted her responsibilities, including the breast-feeding, quite philosophically. And despite her casualness and the press of other compelling interests, the boy flourished, growing more and more human, Niccolò noted, and happy and responsive, so one could actually begin to enjoy him.

Yet his doubts about the boy persisted, fueled in part by Antonia's recurring nightmares and aberrant moods. Toward her lover, now mere keeper of herself and her child, Antonia exhibited strange inconsistencies that made it impossible to know a day from its morning. She might be sugary, radiant as a bride, full of cheerful little homilies; yet an hour later would find her breaking dishes or screeching like a demented one. She would herself venture into the markets and haggle over the price of vegetables to save him a few coins; yet demand jewelry, elegant raiment, and extravagant amusements as a natural right, quickly degenerating into loud tantrums when she met his evasions and resistance.

She began to complain to others of her ignominious position, of promises made and flouted. Antonia was clever at this; she elicited quick sympathy. What she wanted, she informed Paganini coldly and repeatedly, was an annuity for her and the child. She had come to Niccolò in love and good faith, borne him a son, enhanced his reputation with her appearances. In return, he had but misused her, exploited her, and not even paid her the miserable stipend an auxiliary artist would have been offered with gratitude. Since she continued to feel for him—oh, he was the father of her child, after all, and so much of her life had been invested in him, so to speak—she was loath to drag his iniquities into the courts, particularly since he had set his heart upon some ribbon or garter from the Pope. And the vixen watched with shrewd glee as Paganini, congealed with dread, said yes, perhaps an annuity was in order; she must give him time to think about it.

It was Achillino he had to think about. Niccolò found himself unwilling to surrender his only son.

The boy had begun to walk and to babble at a prodigiously early age. A fiendishly inquisitive and active child, he had wearied Antonia, and had reduced a series of temporary nurses to nervous prostration. Niccolò began to boast about him, detaining acquaintances with tales of marvelous intelligence and precocity. "He fears nothing; he has the coordination and understanding of a child twice his age; he knows that an egg must be peeled; he weeps at the slightest *scordatura*, so perfect is his pitch," the great Paganini would declaim, oblivious to the yawns induced or the tedium of his recitations.

Yet Niccolò maintained a distance, a recurring suspicion that the boy might not be his, and a conviction that emotional involvement, while rigorously demanded of mothers, is somehow mawkish and inappropriate in fathers. And without admitting this even to himself, he felt unsure about the future of his unreal family, suspended in social and ecclesiastical limbo while he cogitated. Perhaps he would want to divest himself of all ties. Perhaps he would travel to strange, exotic lands, be admitted as an equal into the most aristocratic circles. He thought of Prince Metternich. His pulse quickened.

THE GIRL INFLAMED THESE WILD IMAGININGS, stoking the fire of his discontent. He divined his future in the landscape of her body, a pale continent waiting to be conquered—Europa, the virgin, plunder for the bull. Her heated scream became a calling cry, a trill that beckoned bliss; it ignited his passion, spurred his will, filled his soul with feverish ambition. He rammed her; she bit his neck and wailed. When her fingers tore his filmy flesh she licked the salty wounds, her long tongue lapping blood and sweat, her amber cat eyes flaring wild. Niccolò rose up, the bellowing white bull, arching his back and thrusting deep, losing himself in a dark whirl of abandonment and savagery.

He felt a tendril round his neck. Beneath him, the girl's creamy flesh turned silver and bright, her lupine eyes luminous, predatory. Niccolò, choking, grabbed the slithering coil, a thick muscle of leathery flesh tightening around his throat. He stared in horror at her glowing eyes. "*It's you!*" he stammered.

The succubus grinned. A web of saliva dripped from her lips. "I am glad you have not forgotten me, my Niccolò."

He sputtered, gasping for breath. "How…could I?"

Her snaking tail tightened its grip. "You have strayed, my love."

"I—"

"The pact. You've broken your promise."

"No! I ..."

She squeezed tightly. "Yes!" she insisted.

Niccolò could not breathe. His face turned dark with blood. "Yes—" he stammered.

The demon smiled and released her grip. The spaded tip of her tail played lightly across his chest, snaked over his shoulder, and slid down his back. Niccolò caught his breath, his hand feeling his throat.

"Is it your desire to languish on this island forever?" she asked.

"No," he answered, his voice quavering.

"I have laid the world at your feet. You mock me with your indifference."

"The Order of the Golden Spur—"

"The Golden Spur is yours, my love, but only if you honor your vows. Leave the woman, and I will force the Pope to kiss your feet."

He shivered at the tickle of her tail on his spine. A hound howled somewhere out in the night. "Antonia," Niccolò ventured, "has had... dreams."

"They are more than dreams, I assure you."

Niccolò recoiled.

"The demon has had his pleasure with her," said the succubus, slipping her hand between her legs, "and I have had mine—with you." She drew a wandering wet line across her belly and absently touched the finger to her lips. Then she turned away, her countenance darkening. "But I grow weary of such meager amusements."

"The child. Is the boy ...?"

She laughed in his face like a barking dog. "Would the great Satan waste his seed on a worthless whore?! Oh no, Niccolò *mio*. I'm afraid the child is all of your doing."

Niccolò sighed in silent relief; the boy was *his*!

The she-devil's eyes flickered. "You will leave him with the harlot, of course."

Niccolò paled.

"Do you think I'd allow you to be crowned on the throne of Vienna with that bastard of betrayal bellowing on your knee?"

"But I cannot …"

"You cannot? You cannot defy me. You are mine, and without me you are nothing. Remember that."

"I will leave the woman. You have destroyed whatever love existed between us. But the boy? Surely our agreement does not include the boy?"

"Perhaps I have misunderstood. Is it not love you feel for the bastard?"

"The love of a father for his son. He is of my flesh."

The succubus scowled. "And your flesh is your weakness, and so is it his."

"You must not harm him!"

"Oh, *I* will not touch him." She cocked an eyebrow, admiring her long, claw-like fingernails. "But the demon—who is having his way with your *bona roba* this very moment—who can say that he will not seek some diversion with the boy?"

"No!" cried Niccolò, staggering to his feet. "NO!"

❈ ❈ ❈

HE RACED MADLY THROUGH THE DARK, DESERTED STREETS, his clothes trailing in disarray, his heels echoing off high, hard walls. Bright stars streaked through the sky above him; he stumbled on his jacket tail, crashed to his knees on the pavement stones. The cackles of painted whores poured from a gaslit window and followed him down the twisty street like fluttering, bickering black birds. By the time he reached the house, the calamity had already occurred. Calamity? Miracle? Omen?

Later, much later, he was unsure. They never learned what had actually happened. Antonia had gone to bed early, complaining of some abdominal ailment, and had left the child to the care of their blubbery, bosomy, bow-legged nurse. Wailing and lamenting incoherently, the elderly woman called upon a galaxy of saints, wishing herself dead, and praying that he believe she had dozed but an instant. Antonia had ordered her to call for the doctor, so that by the time Niccolò appeared, Achillino's broken leg had been set and bound to a great wooden splinter. The old woman, fearing she had committed some crime and would be placed under arrest, was being counseled and consoled by half a dozen of her relatives, summoned by her outcries. The child wriggled fitfully in Antonia's arms, feverish and in pain.

How, how, the nurse keened, could such a pig's tail of a child (she did not mean this unkindly; he was a veritable *angelo da Paradiso*, but look how he squirmed, even in sleep!), how could he be kept quiet, that the leg might heal? He had health and strength, but as yet no sense. Begging their pardons, but he did not even understand danger, had tried to touch the hot stove, had been saved—and not a moment too soon, by her vigilance (remember that)—or else would have tumbled down the stone stairs and broken open his little head. He'd been babbling about seeing a prince in a black cape, and, upon being taken to the park for pure air, he had crawled under carriage wheels.

And finally, they were rid of her and of the chorus of relatives arraigned to protect her from Paganini's wrath.

Quickly Niccolò learned several things. He learned that Achillino's leg was indeed broken, a clean break above the ankle that would, hopefully, heal quickly, since he was young. And he learned that the child must be kept quiet and prevented from placing weight on the injured leg, lest more serious injury ensue.

He learned that Antonia was squeamish; that she could not endure looking at the swollen, bandaged leg. She wept and hugged the child and suddenly remembered texts of lost prayers, but she could bring herself to do little for him. In fact, her endeavors to be useful and make her small patient less uncomfortable proved gauche and unsuccessful, usually producing tears in both.

And he learned another thing: that he loved his child—his very own son—with a love shattering and total, beyond the narrow confines of fear and ambition, and with a commitment that brought cosmic order, as emotional chaos, to his world.

Night after night, stressful mornings, hot afternoons, whenever the child grew restive and tried to stand on the injured leg, Niccolò reached out to him, wearily yet perfectly content. He learned that love flowed from a deep spring; one may drink and drink; the source is continuous. He awoke with aching bones from a night in his chair, the child curled in exhausted sleep on his lap. He forwent sleep altogether, walking up and down with his beloved burden to dispel Achillino's disquiet. He learned to tell nonsense tales and to amuse with acrobatic feats and to sing songs out of his remote childhood, operatic arias, lullabies, old revolutionary airs, in his cracked voice.

And when the child grew better—young bones indeed knit quickly and well—Niccolò nearly caved in with exhaustion and sheer relief. Something had happened to him, he told himself as he tossed on his bed: something that would require him to rearrange forthcoming time and remaining life.

That something was love, selfless and pure. He understood now that this love was sacred, and that it must never be abandoned. For though it served neither his ambition nor his art, it nourished something deep within him, essential to his very being. Love fed the hunger of his soul.

Yet the threat of the succubus continued to haunt him. She had—with the help of the demon—corrupted his intimacy with Antonia, destroying their love forever. Might she not do the same with the boy? Already the demon had toyed with tiny Achillino's life. How could

Niccolò prevent another tragedy? How could he hold to his love without breaking his pact?

The answer, he decided, was to deal with the Devil on the Devil's own terms.

❋ ❋ ❋

THE SUCCUBUS LOLLED ACROSS THE BED as she considered the fiddler's proposition, her tail curling about her like an indolent cat. "I find your impudence most becoming," she told him. "It convinces me more than ever that you shall earn your place in hell."

Niccolò stood fully dressed, his back stiff against the bright slats of the shuttered window. The sight of her naked body in the darkened room pulled at him like a whirlpool, making him dizzy and weak in the knees. "I ask only for more time," he said, averting his gaze.

"What you ask is that I honor my part of our agreement while you continue to violate yours."

"But surely you can see that my feelings for Antonia have changed," he said. "It is the welfare of the child that concerns me now."

"And so you dote on the bastard and abuse your queen."

"If it appears so," he pleaded, "it is far from my intention. I ask only for enough time to establish my reputation in Vienna. I will then be in a position to bestow a reasonable annuity upon the boy's mother, so that the child will be properly cared for and the whole affair brought to a peaceable end." Again, he averted his eyes, wondering if a mere man could lie to the Devil and live to tell of it.

The succubus frowned. "Peace has no place in this," she said. "I recommend parsimony and abandonment."

"Of course, you are right," he admitted, being not entirely in disagreement on this matter. "But then, it may end in the courts, and I fear such notoriety will weaken my position."

"You are a coward and have no faith in me."

"Oh no, on the contrary …"

Her cat eyes narrowed. "You make me jealous of the boy."

Perspiration formed on Niccolò's brow; he tried to conceal the tremor in his voice. "My feelings for the child are certainly of a different nature than the deep love and desire I hold for you. Different enough to be exempt from our agreement, surely."

She stared at him with a menacing grin. "Be careful, *Maestro*, I warn you! Do not play tricks with the Devil."

"My destiny is in your hands," he said. "I would not dream of betraying your trust. I stand in awe of your power and your unparalleled beauty."

Her eyebrows lifted in mock surprise. "Flattery—another recommendation for a warm corner in the underworld."

Niccolò bowed his head, staring at the floor. "Time is all I ask, my queen. My love is all yours." For a moment, the room fell silent.

"Look at me," she said at last.

Niccolò lifted his face to gaze upon her. She moved slowly, seductively across the bed, a slash of shuttered sunlight playing over her body like the sinuous streak of the moon on the sea. She purred, creeping forward like a cat, eyes flashing, lips glistening, full breasts swelling beneath her, white thighs sliding forward toward him through the dim light of the room. She waited for him at the edge of the bed like the fabled offering of forbidden fruit.

"If you will indulge me, my darling," she whispered softly, "I may be persuaded to consider your request."

Blood pulsed madly through Niccolò's veins, his heavy heart pounding with dread and desire. He hesitated a moment, then moved slowly toward the bed, his mind burning with memories of past encounters, hellish journeys through the flesh-fires of ecstasy and pain, nightmares of obscenity and unspeakable perversion. What horror of transgression awaited him now? Surely the she-devil will devour me, he thought.

Niccolò stood trembling before her.

The succubus smiled. "You are right to be afraid," she said.

From behind him, a pair of long-fingered cadaverous hands slid over his shoulders. Niccolò stood frozen; he dared not turn. The bony hands lifted off his topcoat, dropping it to the floor. Hot breath warmed the fiddler's neck, while the cold hands unfastened the buttons of his shirt. The icy fingers wandered over Niccolò's flesh, caressing his nipples, sending chills to his heart. The hands moved lower.

The succubus seemed suddenly the lesser of two evils. "Please," he begged her.

And then he could not speak.

She slipped off the bed and stood before him. "Try to relax, " she whispered. Her tail wound like a python around his ankles. "Show me how you love me."

❄ ❄ ❄

ON APRIL 3, 1827, satisfied as to his stainless moral condition, past and present, and his suitability as a defender of the faith, His Holiness Pope Leo XII created Niccolò Paganini of Genoa Knight of the Golden Spur, an ancient honor accorded but three of his equivocal profession. The new knight might henceforth sign himself *cavaliere*, which he did, and receive whatever social advantages and spiritual benefits might accrue.

Knight, fiddler, father, lover, and servant of the Devil: Paganini was at long last ready for Vienna.

Part Four
The Cauldron

17
Viennese Triumphs

Artists, like mariners, need favorable tides. After the bungling and delays, the drawn-out apprehensions and precautions, Paganini arrived in Vienna at precisely the most auspicious moment. One might have supposed his journey had been plotted by astrologers; or perhaps, Niccolò darkly ruminated, the entire episode of the last two years had resulted, not from the earthly mingling of chance and choice, but from the sinister machinations of the she-devil herself, seeking amusement and distraction until the time was most ripe.

Whatever the cause, procrastination had conspired to aid him. The restoration of Austrian pomp and hegemony was complete by 1828. The imperial city was rich, stable, panting for innovation. The highest circles—the Emperor himself and Chancellor Metternich—had heard and been moved by the Italian wizard; others knew rapturous accounts of his feats from travelers, diplomats, journalists, and military sojourners. For years, Paganini had been on the verge of descending upon Vienna, and the newspapers had provided a perennial stream of information about his triumphs (musical and amorous), his criminal career and life in the dungeon, his reputed pact with the Prince of Darkness, his diabolical, otherworldly appearance, and his power over audiences, women, animals, and popes.

Niccolò's helplessness with the German tongue, however, left him indifferent to such notoriety as might have driven him straight back to

Italy or involved him in elaborate lawsuits. He arrived with Antonia, Achillino, half a dozen violins, Bianchi's not inconsiderable wardrobe, linens, voluminous correspondence, a hat box, the account book, and scraps of food for the infant. Flattered by the excitement that attended his forthcoming appearance, he remained felicitously unaware of its unsavory undercurrent.

As the carriage rolled into *Stefansplatz*, Niccolò's thoughts careened wildly on his idol, Beethoven. Overcome with a sense of loss, he burst into tears. "*È morto, è morto*," he realized, as one does not always realize the meaning of a departure from the world at the time one is told of it. "And I am too late, too late, too late!" Then *Madama* Bianchi nudged him wisely and said, "Calm yourself, Niccolò. They are staring at you. Smile; wave." And she set an example, her child asleep in her arms.

Vienna was Europe restored. But restoration is not merely return to a former condition; restoration honors the spirit of the time departed while transforming its body politic. The old aristocracy enjoyed great prestige—and economic eclipse. The new class that rose with Napoleon waxed richer and richer while he rotted in his grave. Never had music enjoyed such recognition, if little formal support. Strauss fattened and Schubert starved, as had always been the case, but the creative well proved deep, profuse, and generally misunderstood. Art and literature knew solemn lip service and all the ramifications of Teutonic earnestness: great columns in the newspapers and magazines, copious analyses, and (*Ach, Gott!*) commitment to exalted sentiments and ideas. But bulky Biedermeier flourished, and maudlin sentimentality and ugliness, with vigilant public morality (the Empress had the nude statuary of the ancients draped before making her annual visit of homage to art) and absolute self-righteousness. Vienna swarmed with sleek, overweight, neckless tradesmen, who judged the civilized world in their own image whilst belching, picking their teeth, and scratching their jowls. The world of Vienna was truly one of contradictions: enormous beauty and smugness, aspiration and foolish platitudes.

And the Paganini vogue erupted in Vienna like a great pealing of bells in the middle of the night. The city awoke, shuddering, screaming, and literally on its knees. Paganini became the rage, the current year's motif in gossip and fashion. Down with the giraffe; the Viennese had discovered a more picturesque beast.

Odes, sonnets, and songs of the most mawkish sort appeared to laud him. He was parodied in a musical review—his very themes plagiarized—to which the multitudes swarmed. Sketches, souvenir likenesses, silhouettes, lithographs, and portraits appeared by the thousand; he might be seen crowned with laurel and draped in a toga, or horned and hoofed like his dark master. *Wiener schnitzel* (disappointingly, merely *cotelette alla milanese!*) and sundry delights of the Viennese kitchen were served *à la* Paganini, with rolls and bread and tarts in the shape of violins. His eccentric dress was emulated, the stringy coiffure, soft hat, and loose cravat suddenly becoming fashionable. His beaked face appeared on the ivories of fans, snuff boxes, buckles, and the heads of gentlemen's walking sticks. Strauss wrote a "Paganini Waltz," which sounded exactly like all his other waltzes. Violins and arrangements of notes were ingeniously embroidered on everything from blouses to pillow cases to lace-bordered handkerchiefs. Impassioned love-letters arrived daily. A foolish girl who had seen the

's triumphant entry into Vienna tried to poison herself with perfume but succeeded only in falling into an alcoholic trance followed by vomiting.

Niccolò was flattered, though particulars of the flood of tribute eluded him. Distracted and sleepless from nightly visits of the succubus, he indulged his native moroseness and irritability, yelling at Antonia and the boy, although to no avail, for they yelled back and promptly forgot their contentiousness, whereas he took to bed with abdominal pains and could retain no food. Chills, fever, and debilitation returned, syphilitic gifts from his nightmare lover.

Antonia made herself gaily at home in their pleasant apartment near St. Stefan's Cathedral; she learned a few words of German from the young *Putzfrau* and each day returned to tell of the marvels of the great white marble city and the fantastic shops of the *Kartnernstrasse*, where amid a profusion of gowns and furs and gems, one could not escape constant reminder of the genius of Niccolò Paganini. Why—Niccolò would not believe this—not even a locket was being displayed without Paganini's solemn, intense likeness nesting within. Antonia wore a heart-shaped one of solid gold dangling from a huge chain, with no fewer than two tiny Paganini faces. She had been so touched that she bought the ornament at once, spending all the household money. She hoped he wouldn't mind.

❊ ❊ ❊

THE INITIAL CONCERT on March 29th was for the tastemakers. Genius or charlatan: that was the consuming question, and the Viennese burgher preferred to save his florins ("Piracy!" cried the press upon learning the price Paganini dared place upon his services) and let the matter be decided by the authoritative. He would wait and be sure.

Through the offices of Rossini's good friend, Domenico Barbaja, Niccolò procured the *Redoutensaal* of the Hofburg Palace, a coveted gem, white and gold, carpeted and magnificently chandeliered, where the ghost of Beethoven lingered. Barbaja spoke affectionately of both Rossini and Colbran, and wondered how Gioacchino was faring with so spirited a woman. "She is a Circassian, I think, and she is Jezebel herself," he chuckled, digging his elbow into Niccolò's ribs to underscore his meaning.

Though Barbaja's tenure at the royal theaters was about to end, and Count von Gallenburg had already been designated his successor, he seemed very cheerful about Vienna and made no secret of the fact that his experience had been satisfying and lucrative. "Yes, perhaps they have conquered us," he conceded with Neapolitan fatalism. "But Italian music has conquered them, and that constitutes a clean profit to your devoted Barbaja." And again, Niccolò felt an elbow energetically assaulting his thin ribs.

"We have a large Italian colony here," Barbaja continued. "This is useful. I have learned just enough of the abominable language of these Visigoths to drive a bargain and to reprimand a servant. But socially I do not employ it. Who can discuss a *fioritura* in German? Or make love? It is out of the question."

The finest musicians in Vienna, including a dazzling array of string virtuosi, made themselves available as an accompanying orchestra for Paganini's debut. Many had heard him in Italy; some he remembered from an exchange of friendly greetings or some special token or utterance.

Niccolò decided, in a gesture of homage to a fallen giant and out of deference to the assembled talent, to open his program with Beethoven—the *Overture to Fidelio* in its final version. And after much anguish and vacillation, he decided to permit Bianchi to participate, but to restrict her to two airs. The Viennese, he knew, had stronger stomachs for unbroken evenings of instrumental music than did the Italians. Moreover, he cringed from gossip, and he sincerely begrudged Antonia a share in his triumph. No longer did Niccolò fret that she might prove inadequate. On the contrary, he feared she might prove more compelling than the occasion demanded.

The Grand Duchess Marie Louise of Parma, erstwhile Empress of France, was in attendance with her husband, Count Neipperg; Chancellor Metternich with his pretty new wife and his daughter; all the more affluent Italian émigrés; the great and near great of music, literature, and art; every journal's scrivener, prepared to sit in judgment; and then came a group of the usual peripatetic Englishmen.

It was a glittering, affluent, yet highly knowledgeable audience, appetites sharpened by curiosity, fully prepared to beatify or to reject, to declare Paganini a demigod or a cipher. All the ordinary excellences became insufficient. Were he to prove himself merely the equal of any predecessor or contemporary, even the Teutonic idol, Spohr, he would be doomed. Fanfare proclaimed him no mere mortal, blessed with genius, educated to perform upon four vibrating strings. Paganini had become enshrined in a diabolical mystique. Satanic Majesty itself would hold forth in the *Redoutensaal.*

Paganini waited. The applause for Beethoven's overture lessened and finally died down. It was deathly silent. Still, he waited. Good that a pinch of anxiety be fused with the moment's exaltation. In regal scarlet, with a small tiara of stage diamonds and pearls, Antonia Bianchi sat with her head pressed against the mirror. Praying, perhaps. Frightened, moved, as she, veteran performer, had not previously had occasion to be moved.

Never had Niccolò allowed private ceremony to mar a public appearance—the presentation of amulets and charms, lopped-off invocations to mysterious good fortune, embarrassing sentimentality. He now suffered himself to glance once more in the mirror, affecting an expression of boredom and disdain. Then he moved, very deliberately, toward the stage door.

This opened onto a small balcony flanked by two short stairways leading to the platform. Niccolò had to walk from the door, which closed behind him, to the end of the overhang, then down the curved stairway. It was a superbly dramatic entrance. Proud, brooding, utterly ghost-like, the long, unkempt hair and feverish eyes contributing to his bizarre appearance, he did indeed resemble some odd creature from the spirit world come to wreak black magic.

And as he reached the first stairs, the orchestra, to a man, rose in homage; and then the audience, released from shock. Applause broke like a rain of artillery, and cries of welcome were followed by other cries—that one could not see, would the *gnädige Dame* please be seated, and cries that here was, indeed, a cadaver, a ghost, I. A. Hoffman's sinister Dr. Kreisler, child of some bearded witch-mother. A few aggressive ones stood atop chairs or ran out into the aisles. A woman cried that she was fainting; she quickly recovered, however, when an attempt was made to carry her from the auditorium.

He had chosen the second of his concertos, the B minor, composed a year or so earlier with a view to Vienna. Graceful, lyrical, rich with novel ideas, he felt it a most suitable introduction; and the florid rondo afforded a brilliant exhibition of the Paganini capers. This was to be followed by another relatively new work entitled *Sonata Militaire*, the third movement of which was comprised of dazzling variations on Mozart's "*Non più andrai*" from *Figaro*, surely flattering tribute to Mozart's countrymen. And as a conclusion, there would be a *Larghetto and Variations* in which a theme from Rossini's *La Cenerentola* found stunning elaboration. Bianchi's two airs, at strategic intervals, would round out the program, devised to be kept relatively short. The Viennese, he had been told, were accustomed to overlong programs and fully expected a short nap as legitimate part of the entertainment. It was Paganini's purpose, in this respect, not to give them what they expected.

Never had Niccolò experienced such an ovation. It was as though a dam broke, deafening, irresistible, carrying along prince and scrivener, poet and courtesan, and above all, every musician or aspirant or amateur within the *Redoutensaal* walls. Here roared everyone's submerged dream of perfect power, perfect beauty, perfect communication, and perfect love. In all his career, Niccolò had not confronted so emotionally charged an audience, one more ready to abandon itself to him.

They would never know, of course, that he, too, had been profoundly moved and had played almost beyond his powers. What after all, is the possible? Where the frail fine line, the mortal limit? The shadow of the Devil encompasses the world. He had touched the ocean depths, the sun's fiery crater. He had clutched infinity, stopped time, soared from the world's jagged edge into the immaculate realm of the spirit.

And when he stood, yellow and ravaged, in the dressing room, bathed in a clammy sweat that was turning to a chill, passively letting Antonia wipe his brow, not hearing the intemperate praises of the musicians, not seeing the lines of speechless men and babbling women who seemed to float in and out of the double doors, he rejoiced that he had sold his soul so dearly.

The turbulence continued. He was likened to a comet, a landslide, an apocalyptic storm, a volcano. As Pompeii had been buried in antiquity, the grave *Kritiker* wrote, all executant effort that preceded Paganini lay flat, lifeless, and invisible under the hot lava of his talents. Antonia laughed merrily at the journalistic metaphors.

He continued to perform in suitable concert halls throughout the city: the *Redoutensaal*, the *Kärntnertor*, the *Burgtheater*, the *Opera*. The emperor bestowed his august presence, a jeweled snuff box, and the title of chamber artist. Chancellor Metternich's fidelity and esteem could be taken for granted. And tickets of admission vanished the day they were offered the public. While the price of a seat to hear the Italian outraged his audiences, the latter were even more mutinous about the ensuing speculation in tickets that skyrocketed prices yet further. A malicious rumor reached Niccolò that the greedy paw at work in this conspiracy was his own. He denied this furiously, and that fury intensified when he began to calculate the profits reaped by parasitical middlemen.

Vienna had not only an apparent plethora of fine auditoriums, but capable and disciplined musicians as well. It was actually difficult to assemble poor ones, for the Austrian musical tradition was an instrumental one, and composers had begun to regard orchestras as independently serious and responsible bodies of musical expression. Niccolò listened with astonishment and awe to the last three Beethoven symphonies, stirred not only by their magnitude but by the difficulties they presented "ordinary" musicians performing anonymously as a group.

The Paganini repertoire, of course, bedazzled. But because it was of his making and smacked of mystery and magic—and because none could obtain or perform the work—some suspicion arose. Could he play *music*? Could he perform a standard concerto as effectively as his contemporaries? Probably not. Why, then, did Paganini play only Paganini? Perhaps there was a *reason*.

Not so, cried Niccolò, wounded that the issue had been raised not by the ignorant, but by fellow-musicians. Was not this, his offering, music—music of the highest order? The creator's arrogance, doubt, and self-searching gnawed; he had not, as charged, strained for exhibition and display, but to say things no man before him had said or known. Would his executant powers continue to conceal the scope and value of that which he had wrought? Granted; he had unique insights. Did they, then, diminish his offerings? Was this carping but envy?

However, the clamor continued, even as he resisted it. He must play a "standard" concerto, a work inferior to his own (as he viewed it), that direct comparisons might be made.

Did he not dare? Was that it? Was he afraid?

Niccolò presented concertos by Rode and Kreutzer—war horses done to death by a generation of fiddlers—condescending to improve, augment, and embellish both. To the Rode, which he regarded as fit for conservatory students, not mature craftsmen, he added an *Adagio religioso* "to make them look contrite"; to the Kreutzer, kept alive, he sincerely believed, by Teutonic dullness, he also added an *Adagio* (not characterized religious) in thrilling double stops, and a puckish *Scherzo*.

Niccolò did his best to squeeze eloquence and emotional radiance out of what he regarded as stale, shabby works. He added dazzling improvisations and interpolations, as was the custom, not bothering to concern himself that these emerged more fiery and complex than the works to which they were appended and were not always in character.

Once rid of the obligation of doing obeisance to violin literature not his own and of proving himself, Niccolò felt well rid of the debt. He acknowledged no obligation to the efforts of others. He read and gave himself dedicatedly to whatever music was placed before him at private chamber music evenings among musicians; these evolved spontaneously almost everywhere, with the easy camaraderie that artists, when not competing, can feel for one another. But public recitals for acclaim and money were of another category. Orchestral scores, entire symphonies by Beethoven and Haydn presented in separate movements, became part of his Viennese programs, replacing Antonia's offerings; but Paganini himself would play Paganini, and his scores would be guarded jealously lest they be stolen or debased.

For Niccolò was aware, as time went on, of the curiosity that attended his daily routine. This exceeded adulation; it ran over into greed. As the seat speculators profited in space, others wished to procure, in a simplified nutshell, his profitable "secret." For surely, there must be a secret, something that could be encased and sold, taught, doled out at an exorbitant price. He found spies at the window and the keyhole. One avid entrepreneur paid to obtain a position as manservant at an inn Paganini frequented. Antonia screamed that she saw faces peering out of dark hallway corners and heard furtive footsteps in the alley. "They hope for an obscene rite, for black magic," Niccolò muttered. But the Devil does not have to be called, he thought; she comes uninvited when one is asleep.

He found no mirth in these intrusions. While the wildfire of rumor raged around him, he remained silent on the matter of his dealings with the Devil. Unready to share either his method or his madness, and bitterly aware that mystery was worth more, in terms of receipts, than artistry, he resented all efforts to observe him at work, to penetrate his private world, to skim off details, however incidental, of his discipline.

His stance in performance and the size of his hands were subjected to labored diagnosis. He learned that he leaned to the right or to the left, that this shoulder or that was a trifle higher, that his hands were large or small, slender or plump, quite unlike everyone else's, of inhuman elasticity, and virtually jointless.

He read that his "race" contributed to his achievements, though identical membership tended to limit the capacities of others. Such diabolism had to be Latin, Romance, Italian. It simply did not accompany the deeper profundities of the Teutonic genius and intellect. Niccolò snickered. He thought of Goethe, the Sage of Weimar, reputedly involved with demonology; the Prince of Darkness, he had heard it said, actually dominated the great genius's masterpiece.

But when tales of Paganini's diligence appeared, of entire days and nights spent smoothing out the intricacies of a single passage, he grew furious. He had always harbored a distrust of labor. It seemed, in the telling, to erase the concomitant realities of his demonic inspiration. Diligence, however back-breaking, could not write or execute the *Caprices*, the concertos, the variations, or "*Le Streghe*." It was demeaning to be compared to a competent hack.

That he stood between the world and its dark powers: let them believe *that*, for it was true enough. After all, were not both Bach's God the Father and Paganini's Lucifer aspects of the same principle, part of man's journey for meanings and answers, the Janus masks of life's wholeness?

He extended a snuff box to an ancient fiddler in the orchestra at the *Opera*, who was fumbling in his pockets for snuff. The old man recoiled, letting the box drop to the parquet, its aromatic contents scattered over the pit. His lips moved to ward off a satanic spell; in his eyes lurked absolute terror. Niccolò left laughing, bitterly aware of the enigmatical nature of all blessings.

❋ ❋ ❋

HE DRAGGED HIS STRICKEN BODY to the chamber pot, dropped his head into his hands, and tried, in the all-consuming darkness of the small, silent room, to recall his dream.

He remembered vapor—the shifting of thin, nebulous streaks and cloud-ribbons, feeble light that gave neither heat nor day, a wreathing, an undulating, a slow massing of amorphous smoke.

It moved toward him, a strange, encrusted monster scraping across the rough floor of the dungeon on great claws, wondrously coordinated. And with the utmost precision, the slimy creature recognized him and focused to grasp, revealing its annihilating monster-mouth, ragged with black filaments of flesh. He saw pores, not a face but a surface with little holes in its skin and the strange, short hairs. He saw a ringed hand and a ringless one, and the hand turned to claws: an eel, an octopus, an oozy sea-creature; he heard deep breathing, a kind of oceanic heaving.

The clouds, sulphurous and misty, formed and re-formed; they flowed together; they disintegrated; they turned from white to swollen purple to inky black. Niccolò's dark master lurked within their convolutions, barely visible; she was sharpening knives. "You have promised me your soul, your heart, your manhood," she said. The knives glittered like stars, like streaks of lightning. Between her breasts lay Antonia's locket, dangling from its chain: heart-shaped, solid gold, its two tiny Paganini faces Janus-like within. "I have always been fond of jewels," she said.

The waters rose, blurring. Niccolò found his way into a small boat as the waves heaved him away. His black-caped steersman lashed the peaked waves with his whip; the little boat listed. The steersman plunked yearning chords and broken chords on a blood-red guitar. "I must carve out your heart; I must eat your entrails; I must have your hidden secret," he sang tunelessly. The wind and the rain whipped them on. Slimy sea serpents struggled to crawl into the boat; Niccolò cringed. He could hear the bubbling of distant cauldrons.

He felt a hollow scuttling, as of shell claws, over his heart; he put his hand to his throat to shield it from sharp fangs concealed within the whirlpool-cavern mouth. "I shall yet outsmart you!" he cried to the wind. "Ignorant old women have escaped their bargains with the Devil! My mother used to tell a story …" His steersman laughed, swishing his crimson tail.

"Do not touch it, do not touch it, Achillino!" Niccolò screamed.

He saw the skull beneath the child's plump cheeks and a spoonful of dust within the skull, and then a cipher, and then silence.

18
The Pact Broken

THE FOLLOWING DAY Niccolò returned to find Antonia and the child gone, the money cache gone, the diamond encrusted snuff box and other costly mementoes, as well as his favorite Guarneri del Gesu, all gone.

He roared like an enraged bull until he discovered the note Antonia had left behind, indicating the hotel where she might be reached, the very one where they had lingered for several days on their arrival in Vienna. He longed to hie himself there at once and wreck the place, murder her, recover Achillino and the possessions, and flee to some distant land. Instead, he became violently ill; then, as the situation began to clarify, he tossed half the night on his bed, penned two wild letters to Germi, and tried to decide upon his immediate strategy.

Niccolò was scarcely surprised at Bianchi's precipitous action once he allowed himself to consider it without rage and knotted feelings. Under the Devil's influence, the ménage had continued to crumble. Lovers no longer, Niccolò and Antonia found themselves bound by habit, material considerations, and a child. Both had been ready to terminate long ago, and the spurious intimacy had produced only tantrums and scenes. At Count von Gallenburg's, only a few days before, Antonia, hardly appreciative of the supreme honor of being permitted to show herself, had again departed, shrieking imprecations and charges of the vilest sort. Niccolò had forewarned her that she was no longer in a broad-minded Latin country, but to no avail. She had been rude to the countess and several grand ladies, either because she imagined herself insulted or because she simply sought to embarrass him. She had been publicly affectionate, knowing it would make him feel ludicrous. In general, her attitude seemed to suggest that, since she had lost everything, he must under no circumstances be permitted to extricate himself without mortification.

Several times Niccolò had ordered her from the house, only to be greeted by bitter laughter or a saucepan aimed at his head. She was free to go, he announced cruelly, only the child was to stay, his child, to whom she had no right. He would settle an annuity upon her. What else did she expect? He realized all the while that Antonia would refuse to vanish so conveniently.

Antonia declared herself ready to depart, but not without the boy and not without a far more generous settlement than Niccolò could coherently discuss. Thus, the situation continued to degenerate, each pronouncing himself hopelessly trapped. Niccolò shouted that his health was being gnawed away by a serpent (indeed, by two); Antonia shrieked that her career, the child she loved more than life, and the worldly rewards she deserved were being wrenched from her by a miser.

In the morning, Niccolò patiently waited for an acceptable hour—Bianchi, he knew, did not arise with the birds—and presented himself at the hotel. The concierge, a tall, gaunt, sallow old man, eyed him balefully. *Madame* was indisposed, Niccolò learned, and did not care to be disturbed.

Niccolò fumed, departing without a word. Something about the old man had disturbed him deeply: a familiar, fiery glint in his eye, the bony resemblance to the demon. Niccolò had little doubt that the succubus had spurred Antonia's sudden departure, but for what precise purpose he could not be certain. If it was the she-devil's intention to take the child from him, why had she not led them far away beyond his reach, leaving their whereabouts a secret? They had, in fact, traveled only a few miles, and Antonia had left a note. Perhaps it was Antonia's greed that kept her close, fed by the Devil's desire to see him suffer, to bestow a final punishment for his amorous transgression, to bleed him of money and honor before ripping the child from him forever.

Niccolò saw clearly the battle he faced. The line was drawn like a knife through his heart, a Janus-split of his mirrored self. He would fight to the death the Devil within, facing again the question he could no longer circumvent—whether to hold to a fate of fortune and fame, or to give it all up for the love of his child.

Niccolò trembled with uncertainty. He had reached the lofty pinnacle of artistic success, and in that rarified air saw more clearly than ever the white-domed splendor of those imperial heights, the stars that glittered like treasures in the night, and the unending promise of ever-greater glories to come. But from that same razored peak, he saw below the dizzying darkness of the abyss, the gaping terror of the black pit of Hell, where Lucifer waited with a sword for the word from his lips. Speak of love, and the fiddler would tumble.

But speak of love he must. Achillino, Achillino! The face of the little boy haunted him; he could hear the childish cadences, the pure, shrill, unknowing laughter, the sweet breathing of his son asleep on back or stomach, his tiny hands curled over his head.

Paganini steeled himself for battle. Vigilance, apprehension, continence, control: he fitted these cautions like armor to his heart and bridled his genitals with pious rebukes. To ward off the insidious influence of the Underworld, he decided he must avoid it altogether. He would keep himself awake, evading the dragnet of the Devil by shunning the deeper realms of sleep, holding fast to the day world, the surface world, where light and air and solid matter gave at least the illusion of certainty, if not the lie to deception. (He had learned all too well of the Devil's inclination to take form in the material world; she had made a habit of inhabiting his lovers.) And so, he spent the night on his feet, pacing beneath the candle-filled chandelier, his soiree of shadows dancing over the floor until they died, one-by-one, with silent sighs of smoke.

When he returned to the hotel the next morning, he was told that Antonia and the boy had taken advantage of the brilliant sunshine and gone to the country. He trembled violently, concerned that this might be a ruse, and that they might not return. But as he glared into the eyes of the insouciant concierge, Niccolò realized this was only another frivolous torture devised by his perfidious mistresses (for surely the two were in league, he thought). He stormed back out to his waiting carriage, and for several hours he combed the countryside in search of his child, joggling over decrepit roadways, suffocating in the pollen-heavy air, growing sick with nausea and the lack of sleep.

At last, he gave up and returned, ill and utterly exhausted, to the city. Fearing he would fall asleep if he went to his rooms, he decided to walk the streets in hopes of restoring his vigor. The thoroughfares coursed with late afternoon traffic of carriages and carts; sallow-cheeked, hunched like a beggar, Niccolò trudged up sidewalks amid scowling, parasoled matrons and fat-bellied burghers walking tiny, yapping dogs. On his way down *Kärnter Strasse* he was attracted by an agitated group of men and women gathered before the window of a small shop. Joining them out of curiosity, he quickened to confront an exhibit of lithographs and etchings of himself executed by various artists. Almost immediately—he had scarcely time to note what had produced such an impact—he was recognized, and the lively excitement and interest turned at once to horror. As though the proximity frightened them, they stepped back and recoiled, leaving him in a lonely circle before a huge likeness of himself—maniacal, deranged, in chains, fiddling away amid the leaping flames of Abbadon.

Many were the likenesses of the Devil, whose features were made the more malevolent by blending into those of Paganini concealing a violin beneath his cloak. One picture showed the Devil's fingers guiding those of the violinist. Another revealed a diabolical jailer with cloven hoofs and a long tail curled to resemble a G-clef, instructing Paganini, his emaciated prisoner. A small, uncannily knowing sketch, almost overlooked by Niccolò, portrayed him in the arms of a satanic mistress, apparently the dark muse of his inspiration.

A cry escaped from Niccolò's throat, raw rage beyond appearances or shame. He faced the group, which had suddenly become still as death, looking from one coarse face to another and recognizing that he stood condemned. How did they *know*? The crass, the ignorant, the scandal-mongering—how had they perceived what he himself had only barely understood? Why did they believe what he had never confessed?

The answer lay in the music itself. They believed because they *wanted* to believe. Genius outraged their mediocrity; unsavory stories about the great brought balm and titillation. The Devil lived where the common man feared to tread.

Niccolò fled the crowd, scattering lusty Genoese curses. By evening, back in his rooms, he had calmed himself sufficiently to start composing a long letter of protest to the *Wiener Zeitung*. That he had sold his soul to diabolical powers had become a common truth—a truth he must turn to lies. Fatigue, combined with a sense of utter futility—an awareness of the savage alienation of his life—slowed his hand, but anger and the desire to see his son returned forced him to persist. Nothing must be allowed to cloud his right to the legal custody of Achillino, particularly scandalous lies about purported intimacies with the Devil. Niccolò wrote righteously, sarcastically, and more or less truthfully, revealing his own vulnerability and his desire to be regarded as decent and conforming.

To perform was a nudity, a terrible exposure. Niccolò had concealed himself under the sinister black wings of his sheltering patron but had no intention of proclaiming his defection to the world. And certainly not now, as he struggled to free himself from the Devil's black embrace. Happy Jacob, who merely wrestled with an angel! Surely that heavenly creature had displayed only the most infantile wiles, compared with those of Niccolò's dark master.

As the night fell, he sensed her presence closing in with the darkness. The room had turned peculiarly cold. He felt imprisoned, surrounded by the disorder that always eventually claimed him—scattered man-uscripts, medicine bottles, syringes, poultices and pills, toys, books, pens, cartoons and press clippings, combs, Antonia's discarded brazier, legal documents, and correspondence—he seemed overrun by forces over which he had no control. The room began to spin around him as he paced beneath the dripping chandelier. He collapsed into a chair and fought the spreading fingers of sleep with bow and violin. He held the fiddle on his knees, later exchanging it for a guitar, which could be plucked casually, without the tension and muscular effort demanded by the bowed instrument.

Snatches of melody recalled his early predilections. Lucca returned in a kaleidoscope of lopped-off pictures and cadences and songs. The ladies of Elisa Bonaparte's court—the foolish, young, moist-eyed girls, the subtle, smoldering women—where were they? Some dead, no doubt; some grown old and ugly. All scattered, dust and ashes.

Doubt and self-loathing began nibbling away at him with little rats' teeth. His strumming sounded weak and pathetic; he set aside the sad guitar. "Without me you are nothing," the succubus had said. Niccolò shuddered, fearing men with long memories and sharp ears. He had been traduced by his own perfection. The superhuman had come to be regarded as routine; the miraculous, as possible and expected. How could he hope to attain those heights without the fiery magic of his hell-born queen?

In a fever of fatigue, he grew dizzy with defiant notions. He would write a violin method and convey to the world a system for mastery. He would complete, orchestrate, unleash music that would awe the immortals. Did he not have a treasure in the wilderness of paper and black dots that surrounded him? He would turn to America, and yes, he would accrue a new fortune. Many had described the majesty and scope of the young continent, its madness for European culture, and the stupendous sums that awaited the enterprising.

Idiot. Fool. (This, the voice of his father.)

Nothing was natural; nothing was neat; nothing flowed like a pure spring from God's earth; nothing soared on melodic wings supple as the outstretched wings of birds. (Nothing without her, thought Niccolò.) Antonio Paganini had disciplined his second son for greatness—by beating him brutally and leaving him in solitude to come to terms with himself. There had seemed no other way.

But it was the old man who had been the fool. For in that solitude Niccolò had discovered not himself, but only the shadow of himself. The shadow was long, deep, and dark, a black shaft into the earth, a hidden passage that opened nightly in the comfort of his bed, a burning path that wound through hell to all the riches of Golconda.

But with the riches came bondage and the butchering of his heart. The Devil had strangled him with the entrails of love. Love had become a nightmare, spewing intimations of death. Now he found himself struggling to close the passage, pushing a great black rock to block its entrance, to seal himself from the terror of the tomb.

Niccolò fought the seductions of sleep. He fought himself and lassitude and the fluctuations of desire to see the morrow. A high, hallucinatory fever made parchment of his skin and left his eyes sore and dry.

Was it day or night? He had grown accustomed to the Stygian gloom. Even the flicker of candlelight caused headache and waves of imbalance and dizziness. Perhaps the Devil had entered his head. Niccolò staggered to his feet; he must have lucidity and the use of his wits. He tore open the curtain. The window looked out upon a cramped courtyard, rain-drenched, gloomy, with a broken stone table like the ruins of an altar.

Dusk? Dawn? The world seemed an eternal Tophet.

Perhaps he had drifted off unawares. This torpor pierced by little daggers and wreathed in smoke—was this sleep? And were the grinning gnomes and monsters that flickered about him merely dreams? He should flee this place, he thought, order a carriage and run to his child. He tried to speak. He was strangely parched, as though the inside of his mouth were cracking. Hearing the drip of candle wax on paper, he peered up into the chandelier, its molten tapers wagging silent tongues of flame.

Eleonora had burned too, too brightly! *Shine upon me for I am cold,* Niccolò prayed to the receding vision of the young virgin. The abandoned never age. Like dead children, they are frozen forever in time and remain like graveyard statuary in the stance of our altercation with them. Angel cherubs wrestling with the unseen Devil.

A chill passed through him. The thunderclap and forked lightning that streaked the window were not emanations of sooty clouds hanging over the city. The creatures of darkness who ruled over him were displeased, roaring that no end of Masses or pieties or virtuous bequests would shelter him from his day of reckoning.

"You do not love me," declared the child Eleonora. Her eyes were large and beady, like the eyes of a doll. The thick, unreal lashes, arrested, did not once flutter. "You are wed to your violin, and I must be forever a virgin."

"No, no, it is only you I have ever loved," said Niccolò, seeing in a flash of lightning the sunny church square and the workbench of the crippled cobbler, Stefano.

"The artist belongs to a mistress not of flesh and blood," the girl quoted. "You must go where she leads and keep no pledge with another."

"I will cast my seed upon the sand."

The girl laughed. "No need of that," she said brightly. She lifted the hem of her dress. "Seven petticoats," she counted naughtily, demonstrating with a generous fringe of each and a girlish knee. "What will the great *maestro* give for the seventh?"

"He will give his heart."

"Now, what would I do with another heart? What else?"

"His soul, his immortal soul."

"I should not want to burn for both of us," she said, her voice cascading, then blending with the high, vibrationless voice of Antonia in a proper air by Purcell. The rising, interrogative thirds of the duet became an infant's wail.

"Hush! Achillino sleeps," he called out, seeking the cradle.

"It is my babe. He is dead," said Angelina. She wore a white nightrobe, like a shroud, and pattered about the room barefoot, clutching an empty candlestick holder. "And you never took me to the priest, though you promised, and now I have no virtue, none at all. He was strangled in my cord, and they would not let me have him and would not baptize him, so he, too, is damned—"

"Quiet, quiet, quiet," muttered Niccolò, covering his ears and shutting his eyes. The faces swiftly replaced one another, and cursing voices dissolved in the clatter of a rolling vehicle, the howling of a dog, the haggling of women on the street below: all grating on his thin-spun sensibilities till at last he fled the room, racing down steep, crooked stairs.

Niccolò found himself standing on the street, bewildered. A golden carriage emerged from the mist, and a crowd of Viennese gathered in prurient expectation. The carriage door was opened, and Elisa Bonaparte appeared. Her vassal threw over Niccolò a hooded domino with slit-holes for his eyes.

"For the Emperor's birthday," said the Princess. "A masked ball. And the beautiful English milord will recite verses. Shall we retire for a moment, fiddler? See, I spread my thighs—here, against the wall. It does not matter who sees us." Her fingertips were burning, lecherous.

"I do not like to be designated to dispel your itch," said Niccolò angrily. "And I will not be duped. I *know* who you are."

"Well, I should hope so," remarked Elisa. "I am a princess; you are a clown."

Niccolò ripped off his pointed hood. "I am the father of my child." The echo of his own voice terrified him; his ears vibrated and ached. "I demand that you take me to the boy at once."

"Christ is risen," said Eleonora, standing in the doorway behind him, fingering her small, black crucifix.

"Christ is dead," declared the Duchess, and tore her handkerchief. "He is eaten by worms and the Father of Great Lies. I read it in this beautiful manuscript, written in blood—"

"But suppose it is not so?" shrieked Niccolò. "Suppose we are, after all, punished for our sins?"

The crowd howled with laughter. "Oh, but you have grown tedious!" cackled Elisa. "You may go to Hell, if you insist, but please leave me in Marlia." She laughed and lifted her wrist, and a servant escorted her into the carriage. She turned to him.

"Come," she purred, "I will take you to the boy."

The carriage carried them away through the parting crowd. Like an innocent child, Niccolò pressed his face to the glass; around him, on hushed feet, revolved the world.

Haughty as a Saracen, the Grand Duchess of Tuscany reviewed her troops, riding the length of the great avenue of poplars that led to Marlia. "For two strings, for one string, for no strings," she said. "But now you please me no longer, and you must cut off your shiny buttons. Tell me: who is more beautiful, Josephine or I?"

"Pauline," said Niccolò dully.

The carriage rode on through drizzle and mist, an eternal twilight of lassitude. Niccolò struggled against his torpor, but eventually his eyes rolled back so that they showed bloodshot white, and his parched lips parted. The rolling, rocking motion continued. He was in a small, listing boat on a turbulent sea bound for the rocky crag of St. Helena; he could see the island, a sharp, coppery rock-triangle jutting out of black and purple waters. He swayed; he felt the treacherous seaweed washing his ankles.

His boatswain turned back to confront him, leering, showing sharp, appetitive fangs. He was tall and princely, and dressed in majestic black. Chains of flame hissed under boat and oars. Thin, filmy undulations of smoke arose, surrounding wanderer, boat, and boatswain.

St. Helena beckoned, rugged rock of doom. The little boat continued to list as the boatswain rowed recklessly, splashing his passenger with slime and flame.

"*Herr* Paganini?" a man's voice inquired, its tone dark and vaguely familiar.

Niccolò nodded, powerless to break the spell.

Oars slashed the brooding waters. "The lady is waiting," said the voice.

Creamy and quivering, Antonia emerged from the night sea, smiling her wise, furtive smile. She extended her arms, not in welcome or embrace, but as a sleepwalker might reach out toward an infinity of dream-wreathed, unbalanced emptiness. Very slowly, Niccolò became aware of her shimmering presence; and then, with an earthly shock, of her lavish, luxuriant hairiness (oh, had he never before noticed?), the masses of shiny black hair cascading to her waist, dense underarm thicket, the glorious mound of hers abundant with foliage. Her cheeks seemed strangely downy (or was it the mist, the pearly mist?); yes, to the touch, she had become the silken pelt of some magnificent wild creature, slain to warm the hands and feet of an aging emperor.

Niccolò felt a vivid resurgence of youth and manhood, and knew the honey-sweet pain of necessity. "Antonia," he muttered, aware only of his power, the glory of the overriding, insistent, burgeoning strength that swelled in him. Her voice answered his with tenderness and exclamations of unendurable bliss. The celestial heat roared within him, and his cloak dropped to the threshold. He had become a stallion, driven by hot whips to ride his mare, to force his swollen manhood into her dark waters. He bit her shoulder and laughed as she cried out with pain. But as they writhed toward inevitable bliss, Antonia suddenly began slipping away, her black mane streaking the mist, her purple-tipped bloated breasts and fine haunches turning to streaks of insubstantial smoke.

"Antonia!"

Niccolò awoke in a panting sweat, straddling the tattered seat of a rented carriage. Through the open door, a pair of coal-black eyes appeared out of blinding light.

"Are you all right, *mein Herr*?

Niccolò had arrived, inexplicably, at the inn of his fugitive mistress. He nodded feebly to the concierge, who offered his bony hand. Niccolò took it reluctantly, extracting himself from the carriage. Squinting painfully against the bright sunlight, he staggered, wobbling on his feet, and braced himself with a hand on the sash. He was told again that *Madama* Bianchi was awaiting him in her rooms. Niccolò furtively adjusted the stubborn protuberance in his trousers and followed the old man inside.

The velvet-draped interior of the inn was mercifully dim. A small, bright ghost of the sun preceded Niccolò up the stairwell, dancing impishly to Antonia's door. Niccolò rubbed his bleary eyes and knocked.

"You have been unwell, Niccolò *mio*?" Antonia inquired with concern. "Your face is pale and drawn. Is not Vienna lovely this time of year? Already in Italy it is quite hot." She seemed immodestly hale and serene; Niccolò felt the slow, rhythmic twitching of a vein in his front temple, leaving exquisite pain.

"Where is my son?"

Antonia dragged open an expanse of draperies, blinding him again. "I sent him for a carriage ride in the *Prater*.

Niccolò paled. "With *whom*?"

"With the kind Spanish Baroness who is staying in the rooms below." Antonia smiled craftily. "She claims to be visiting her nephew, but I suspect the young man is in truth her paramour."

Niccolò tried to control his panic. He remembered Jaime, the young son of the DelSolars who had so frightened Antonia; the Devil was nothing if not a master of illusion. "Are you in the habit of sending the boy off with strangers?"

"I did not think it good that Achillino hear our haggling. For that is why you are here, is it not? You must admit that is thoughtful of me. A good mother spares her child whatever unpleasantness she can.

He now noticed that she wore a new, *décolleté* dress of palest lavender, and that there were violets in her intricately coiffed black hair. She had prepared herself meticulously for the interview; the effect of her provocative beauty brought Niccolò's recent dreams flooding back, enticing and annoying him all at once. "Your cheap performance will get you nothing," he said, though he doubted the words, even as he spoke them. He had promised himself, particularly in the face of her composure, not to raise his voice; he now heard himself, shrill, cracked, jagged with emotion. "Achillino remains with me."

"I do not think so."

"Then you are in error."

They faced one another in absolute stalemate.

Antonia smiled brightly, her false warmth oddly disconcerting. He noticed something strange in her demeanor: an effortless, unworldly, almost divine elegance of movement and gesture.

"No court in the world tears a child from its mother," she said sweetly, her eyes continuing to smile at his. "And if you are unpleasant, Niccolò *mio*, I shall swear that he is not yours."

He made an abortive gesture to strike her, but she did not flinch. He stood frozen by her stare, her dark eyes emboldened with a mysterious inner fire. Against his will, Niccolò felt himself drawn to her. "You may find yourself without funds," he suggested weakly.

"Oh, no," she said, softly laying her palms on his chest. "You would not let Achillino starve. He is the only one you love." She gently caressed his neck and his long, stringy locks. "I used to be jealous of women when you did not make love to me. I did not realize then that you do not really need or enjoy the love of a woman and are not capable of loving one. I suppose that you must save it all for the boy."

Her open bosom pressed against him; he breathed the musky scent of her skin. "I am…more than capable of loving a woman," he said. The naked visions of his dream wrought havoc in his mind. If he could but touch her again…His hands moved up her arms to the bare white satin of her shoulders. "Antonia," he murmured, echoing the dream.

Her lips parted. Niccolò pulled her to him, kissing her full and hard on the mouth. They groped each other with a desperate passion, feeding a sudden, insatiable hunger. Niccolò felt her body against his, the press of her fingers, the soft wet caress of her tongue. He knew he must take her now, that nothing would stop him, neither Devil nor child.

Antonia gently slipped from his embrace, turned her back to him, and lifted her long black curls off the buttons of her dress. "I will need your help, *Maestro*."

As if in a trance, Niccolò began opening the gown, revealing the flawless ivory of her luxuriant back. He licked her spine with the tip of his tongue, slowly stripping down the shimmering cloth. The dress petals parted over round, splendid hips—and Niccolò recoiled.

Beneath the satiny folds of lavender stirred the serpent's tail, muscular, silver-scaled, leathery, and alive.

He stepped back, aghast.

The succubus turned to face him, a thin smile curving her lips. "I can manage from here," she said. She had taken again the form and visage of a womanly Eleonora, a ravishing young beauty in the full splendor of her sex.

Niccolò stood gaping as she lowered her dress, her large breasts plumping out before him, her perfect waist, shocking mound, arcing thighs and slender calves, knees bending as she raised first one foot, then the next, stepping from the pool of satin on the floor.

Niccolò shuddered, staggering back. Could it be he was still dreaming? Waves of dread and desire surged wildly through his blood. "Antonia? Achillino? Where—?"

"They'll return soon enough, my sweet." She began to unfasten the studs of his shirt. "Enough time for the two of us to—shall we say—renew our vows?"

"But the boy?"

"The boy is no longer your concern," she said, her long-nailed fingers groping. "Leave the bastard to the whore that bore him."

Niccolò trembled at her touch. "No," he murmured helplessly.

"No?" she countered, unhooking his belt. She slipped her cold hands into his trousers, warmed her fingers in his burgeoning fire. "What is a child, when I offer you the world?"

"He is my only son."

"And I am your only Queen," she said, stroking him gently, "to whom you owe the greater allegiance."

Niccolò stammered, unable to resist her. She slipped her thumb and forefinger around the root of his swelling shaft, and with a throttled moan, pressed it deeply into her, straddling him as he stood. She locked her legs around his waist, pushed her pillow breasts to his face, and began moving her hips slowly up and down. Niccolò slid tightly in and out of her, groaning with mounting pleasure. Her body felt light as a feather in his hands, yet cool and supple and real to his touch. He sucked a chubby nipple into his mouth, lapping the succulent swell of her skin. Warm juices trickled down his taut thighs; her slippery tail snaked through the wetness to tickle his anus and crawl up his spine. He joined the rising-falling rhythm of her hips, thrusting deeper and deeper, until the succubus, panting wildly, threw back her head and wailed.

Niccolò fell back on the quilted mattress of the canopied bed, the succubus pinned to his cock like a fluttering butterfly. She licked his neck and flicked her tongue in his ear, whispering throaty incantations. Rising to her knees, she rode him like a saddle horse, her hips rocking back and forth, her flame-tipped breasts quivering above him, her long locks thrashing like a willow in the wind. Niccolò watched her eyes grow bright, black cat pupils in a ring of fire. Flames rose up around the bed, dancing like demons, and the light in the room turned the color of blood. They lay on an altar of glistening marble, floating on a feverish sea of fire. Niccolò stared in awe at his queen, riding her steed through a starless night, her white face looming like a red-lipped moon. She rode him into the darkness, the vortex, the void, the hole in the world where the dreamless go.

They floated together like feathers down a well. Niccolò knew there could be no return; sin had offered its reward, without prejudice or sanctimony or confining expectation. The promise had been made; fate and fortune, sealed. His body lay locked with hers, throbbing at the threshold of ecstasy; no amount of feeble love could rein his burning ardor, no fatherly affection could slow the surging swell.

Yet Niccolò held back. He lay now with the succubus on the peak of a great black rock, surrounded by a chasm of vapors and flames.

"Come," cried the succubus. "Satisfy me. Offer your essence, surrender your love and will. I promise your deepest desires will be fulfilled."

Niccolò's passion burned at the brink: let go now and be damned forever.

The succubus howled for release. Niccolò began to give way. But on the verge of the moment, Achillino's voice echoed through his mind, falling like an arrow deep into his heart.

"Papa!"

The voice dissolved in the crackling blaze. Niccolò felt a bracing surge of defiance. "No!" he screamed, pulling himself from his nefarious queen. "I'll have no more of you!" He backed away to the edge of the rock and peered down in terror at the misty abyss.

The malefactress rose up, seething in the flames. "*You dare refuse me?!*"

"I dare it, and swear I do condemn you to the place from which you came!"

"Who are you to condemn me?!"

"A father who loves his child, and in that love am no longer yours."

"By your own tongue you are mine. I command you to obey me!"

"The love in my heart is all I shall obey. I damn you to hell!"

The devil-bitch rose in spectacular fury. Eyes flaring, outstretched fingers flaming, she advanced toward him, lashing her tail like a whip. The sharp, silver-spaded tip slashed at Niccolò, cutting bloody lines across his chest and hands. "It is *you* who are damned," she sneered. "Damned to the world and damned to hell!" Her tail whipped around his neck. "Without the darkness," she said, "your music will wither and die like a vine torn out at the root. Those who worship you now will scorn you, their delight turned to bitter disdain. Your music will be forgotten long before your days are through. You will die a beggar, and the child you so treasure will curse your wretched name."

Choking, gasping, Niccolò grabbed at the coil tightening around his throat. "I fear you...no more."

The hair of the blazing succubus became a writhing tangle of snakes. Her eyes burned like a pair of blazing suns. "Your lofty love disgusts me," she scoffed. "It wreaks of Heaven and the pieties of saints."

Niccolò gagged; the succubus was choking him to death. He grabbed at the flitting tip of her tail, cutting his palm on its razor edge. He grasped the blade in his bloody hand, and with a sudden jerk, slashed the edge across the coil, severing the tip from the stem. Black venomous blood spurted from the lashing end, splattering his face and chest. The succubus screamed in agony, and as the tail loosened around his throat, Niccolò slipped free. Sputtering, coughing, he fell to his knees.

The succubus reared up before him. "Die and be damned!" she raged, and charged toward him trailing fire.

Niccolò rose to face her. In his hand, he held the severed end of her tail. He raised the silver-bladed tip as the Devil fell upon him, her mouth wide with jagged fangs bearing for his throat. With a shout, Niccolò thrust the blade deep into her ribs.

The succubus staggered, clutching the severed tail at her heart; with a horrible gasp, she pulled the pointed blade from her flesh. The deep gash poured out black blood. She stared at the wound in delirium, touching the hole with her fingertips. She tossed the dripping tip soundlessly into the chasm, then looked at Niccolò and laughed. Stumbling toward him, she toppled into his arms. "You've broken my heart, Niccolò *mio*." Laughing maniacally, she slipped from his grasp, tumbling off the rock into the vapory abyss. Niccolò watched in amazement as she plummeted, her laughter echoing behind her, her body turning to flame as it vanished into the pit.

"Farewell, my queen," he murmured, and collapsed in a heap.

❈ ❈ ❈

ANTONIA WAVED THE TINCTURE OF SMELLING SALTS under the fallen fiddler's nose. He came to with a sudden gasp, peering wildly about the room.

"You fainted. I said you looked unwell, but I had no idea…"

"I…I'm all right," he said, realizing he was back in her room at the inn. Antonia helped him into a chair, away from the bright light of the tall windows. She poured him a glass of water, which he drank eagerly. He saw that she still wore the lavender dress; indeed, not a stitch had been touched since he'd entered the room. Niccolò realized the whole dream had taken no more than a minute of time in the waking world.

"Perhaps I should send for a doctor," offered Antonia.

"No, no," replied Niccolò. "There is no need. It is only that I have been unable to sleep these last few days," he explained. "Your little escapade has taken its toll."

Antonia, feeling a touch of pity or guilt—or perhaps merely feeling her own lack of sleep—rang for tea. They waited in silence as a gleaming silver set was brought in on a tray, and the time-honored rituals were attended to.

"If you would like to postpone our discussion," Antonia began.

"I would not," replied Niccolò emphatically. "The boy is leaving with me." Apparently, the mere sight of the tea had renewed his vigor.

"No court in the world tears a child from its mother," said Antonia. "And if you are unpleasant, Niccolò *mio*, I shall swear he is not yours."

Niccolò stared open-mouthed at his mistress. Had she not spoken these very words only moments before—moments that had seemed like a lifetime ago? She is instructed by the very Devil, thought Niccolò. Perhaps he should fight the Devil with the Devil's own tricks.

"You may find yourself without funds," he admonished.

"Oh, no," she said. "You would not let Achillino starve. He is the only one you love."

"Not if you declare him not mine," said Niccolò suddenly.

Antonia paled before the rigidity of his logic.

"If he is not mine, I have no obligation to either of you." Niccolò rose, quivering, watching, hoping the deception would take hold.

Antonia lowered her calculating eyes. "Of course, he is. I—"

"Yes. Now, you are to return the money and the snuff box and the violin and Achillino—"

"Achillino?"

"I plan to legitimize him. I shall buy him a title—yes, that is the world, all rotten, nobility to the highest bidder—but not if he is with you."

Antonia muttered something under her breath. She seemed very tired; underneath the large, expressive eyes were little bluish pouches, almost like bruises. "No, I am afraid not," she said. "Achilles goes where I go. And as yet, you have offered me nothing."

"He will be well provided for. His life will be rich and comfortable. I shall have him legitimized and see that there is a title. Otherwise, nothing. Otherwise, he is your bastard: care for him."

"I can sing."

"Yes," Niccolò agreed. "You can sing." He snickered. "I don't know where or how much you can earn, even if you supplement your income by acquiring an occasional protector. But you can sing." Another devilish thought occurred. "As it happens, however, I have all your music."

"I need it, Niccolò. I need it!"

"And I need the Guarneri and the snuff box and the money."

"You have other violins."

He shrugged. "You have Achillino."

She was confused. The calm and self-confidence had vanished. Perspiration appeared on her upper lip. The perfume, insufferably sweet when he had first entered the room, had become rancid.

"What about me?" she said pathetically. "You are rich. You want to turn me out on the street. What about me?"

"I shall make it worth your while. Is that what you mean?"

"No!"

"What, then, do you mean?"

"Worth my while? Worth my while? What do *you* mean?"

They faced one another, raw and avaricious, each breathing dangerously, each distrustful and marking time.

"I am not yet prepared to say," Niccolò decided at length.

Antonia started to scream. "This is as far as one can get with you,
Niccolò; it is always the same! You are not prepared to say! You will
never be prepared to say! Parting with money really hurts, does it not?"

"Control yourself. You will be heard in Milan."

Her voice dropped as she continued, "There is no point in talking
with you if you are not prepared to say. And I doubt whether you will
ever be more prepared than you are now."

Vaguely, he recognized some justice in her position. "Bring Achilles to
me in the morning," he pleaded. "We shall see. I shall consult a lawyer—"

She smiled malevolently, shaking her head.

Niccolò frowned. "The snuff box. Where is it? It is a gift from the
Emperor."

"The diamonds are precious. I have already inquired about their
value."

He knew she was lying, so he did not become excited. "Listen carefully," he said. "If you do not return the boy, you have nothing, and I
shall accuse you of theft. Oh, yes, you know I can be cruel, and I shall
do it. I want Achillino and everything that has been taken from me, and
quickly. I shall then arrange a settlement and an annuity. You can go
find yourself a husband. I suggest a nineteen-year-old peasant who will
bring you the sacrament seven times a night until he is thirty, at which
time you will have the pleasure of burying him."

"I do not find you amusing today," stated Antonia coldly. "And it is
wise not to hold in contempt what one lacks. Some peasants are more
endowed than some violinists, no?" She grew very earnest and very
angry. "Until you are ready to go to court and sign, it might be better
that everything remains where it is."

"Achillino—"

"I think it is better this way."

"I need the Guarneri. It is my cannon."

"You have other ammunition. And I even more desperately need my music."

He hesitated. It was her sole possession, gathered over many years, difficult and costly to replace.

"Out of the question."

"Then I think," Antonia said, rising majestically, if somewhat unsteadily, to see him to the door, "that you had better leave now and do a little thinking. You know where to find me, for the time being. But do not come merely to quarrel, or you may find me less agreeable."

She slammed the door after him.

Niccolò paused in the dim corridor, took a deep breath, and headed slowly down the stairs. Lost in a stunned and foggy silence, he did not notice the concierge pouring over accounts at the desk; if he had, he would have seen that the old man no longer resembled the gaunt and ghoulish demon of Antonia's dreams, but looked more like the bumbling, truckling innocent that he was, peering curiously over wire-rim clerics at the famed Italian fiddler heading out the door.

It was not until Niccolò had boarded the carriage and begun the jostling ride back to the city that the impact of what had occurred at the inn finally took hold of him. After years under the spell of evil and the yoke of obsession, he had relinquished his ambition, defied the Devil, and broken his pact. He had risked everything that had ever mattered to him—career, celebrity, wealth, even his music—all for the love of a three-year-old boy. No doubt there would be punishment for his perfidy, but at last his dreams might be free of the Devil, and Achillino, he felt certain, would soon be his. To Niccolò's surprise, these shattering new truths imparted neither a sense of elation, nor sadness, nor fear, nor relief, but only a deep and ineluctable sleepiness, to which, rocking like a babe in the curtained carriage, he willingly and peacefully surrendered.

19
CHEATING THE DEVIL

PRINCESS METTERNICH, DELECTABLY PRETTY and several years younger than her stepchildren, adored her precious Klem and guarded him like a good Austrian nursemaid. She could think of no more fitting present to mark his fifty-fifth birthday, for which a regal celebration had been arranged, than to engage Paganini.

The leonine chancellor was aging. Surprised, he wept before his guests and kissed the pretty hand that wiped away his tears.

When Paganini received word of the Princess's request—the very day after his encounter with Antonia—he fell into an immediate and debilitating panic. Certain that the Devil had had a hand in the matter, and that a very public and humiliating catastrophe awaited, Niccolò thought immediately of concocting some reason not to perform. Given the wave of nausea and tremors that now overwhelmed him, illness seemed the logical excuse. But after the initial terror subsided, a second thought came that pushed aside the first: a sudden, liberating realization that his fate no longer need depend on the whims of the Devil; that his ties to the succubus had been broken for good; and that the future of his career, and of his life, lay now firmly in his own hands, hands as yet quite capable of wielding instrument and bow. The Evil One may have engendered the fiddler's grand success, but it was Niccolò alone who had developed his talent; the Devil had only exploited it. And however vain Niccolò might be, he would not forsake his gift merely to preserve his reputation. He would instead have to put that reputation to the test, as he had always done with every performance.

What greater test than to accept the princely invitation and perform in direct defiance of the she-devil's curse? There seemed, in fact, a symbolic and inevitable logic at work. Aristocratic Vienna, content that history had been so neatly resolved for all time, would render homage to the chancellor, because he had brought Europe and the world to such a comfortable juncture, and to the violinist, because he was renowned, unique, and released their spirits to spheres uncharted. The master of history and the master of music together would bring the world to its knees.

He accepted the invitation, and in an impulsive gesture, refused a fee.

❊ ❊ ❊

Revitalized by sleep-filled nights and improving health, Niccolò pressed vigorously for severance with Antonia and custody of the child. Germi's aid was enlisted, as was that of the astute Milanese banker, Carlo Carli. Both served him well, though in both cases, Niccolò felt their distaste of the proceedings and an absence of sympathy for his point of view. Indeed, Carli wrote him on at least one occasion in defense of Antonia and her parental rights.

That Antonia ought to be regarded as a mother, and that she might actually harbor attitudes and emotions in the remotest sense maternal, had simply never occurred to Niccolò. His model remained Teresa Paganini, whose stance, at least during the little childhood of her children, had always been that of the traditional *mater dolorosa* immortalized in Latin religion, art, and lore. Throughout the years, he had become aware of Teresa's latent shrewdness, her most gentle talent for extracting benefits for herself and her brood from the Croesus she had brought into the world: her meek deviousness. But his sentimental recall of her remained that of visibly suffering, sacrificial motherhood.

Antonia, on the other hand, was vivid, skittish, sensual, and gay, interested, at least sporadically, in the vanity of a career, in jewels and finery, and frankly bored by such domestic responsibilities as were Teresa's whole world. How could she be a suitable mother to his child? It was out of the question. True, she feigned fierce love, but this was merely because Antonia knew how to drive a hard bargain and knew, too, that despite threats, he would never abandon Achillino or leave him to suffer want. Why, surely the vixen realized that having the child was as good as having a livelihood for the rest of her days. And there was little doubt in Niccolò's mind that the Devil's vengeance whispered in her ear.

THE VIOLINIST HAD CONSIDERED CAREFULLY what he might offer the most scrupulously bred blue blood of the old Empire gathered virtually by fiat. In open defiance of the Devil, he chose *"Le Streghe."*

Never had the weird sisters danced with such shrill abandon; never had their master whipped them with such glee. As the last vibrating note faded into the air, Niccolò found himself drenched with perspiration, teeth chattering with undulating waves of nausea and chill, his shirt limp and stained under the arms. Numbed and unsteady, he nearly fainted.

The royal hall remained utterly silent. Niccolò slowly lowered his bow, and in a flash of terror, wondered if the realm from which he had just emerged—that atmosphere of almost unbearable exaltation which accompanies a conviction that one is perfectly understood—had been an illusion, an elaborate fabrication of his vengeful queen.

He waited, eyes shut. Out of the silence, an ecstatic groan of "Oh God!" welled up out of the great mass of listeners. There followed an exploding ovation, loud shouts of joyous adulation, demonstrations even more sincere and more keenly felt than his initial Viennese salvos. The Princess showered him with panegyric praise; the hoary, sentimental lion wept; and the *hochgeboren* elite, clamoring to add their voices to the chorus of history, concocted paeans, extravagances, outlandish tributes.

Niccolò's fears of satanic retribution—the "withering" of his powers, spectacular failure, public humiliation—all dissolved in the thunderous acclaim. The newly-liberated violinist had performed in the full splendor of his talent, erasing all doubt and strengthening his resolve. Bowing deeply, he thought of his son.

It is said that fatherly affection is the purest form of love, untainted with selfishness, vanity, or desire. Such true and tender feeling stretched beyond the Devil's grasp. Ultimately, it was this love, pure and simple, that had set the fiddler free.

EVENTUALLY, AFTER MONTHS OF BARGAINING, the rupture with Antonia was legal and complete. In the end, she drove him to the wall, as he anticipated. Renouncing legal claim to Achillino, Antonia accepted a lump sum of 3,530 florins (nearly eleven thousand lire, he thought bitterly) plus the full proceeds of a forthcoming benefit concert—Paganini's tenth in Vienna. The separation contract ambiguously afforded her the privilege of occasional visitation, a provision Niccolò had no intention of honoring. Antonia had added to her lavish wardrobe during the weeks of sordid haggling and saw that her collection of jewelry was enhanced by a few sizable and precious items including a ruby necklace and earrings. Niccolò, however, did not surrender her music until ordered to do so by the court. He regarded the mound of literature as his hostage, and he resisted.

When all arrangements were complete, he called at the hotel in the company of his local manager, Domenico Artaria, whom he suspected of being treacherously friendly to Bianchi. Perhaps he'd had a visitor in the night, but no matter…

Antonia, pale as death under the paint and peculiarly thin, nodded to Artaria but did not appear to notice her erstwhile lover. She sat at a low table hunched over the final document that had been so painstakingly formulated, nodding, muttering, counting off items on her fingers, moistening her parched lips. Without a word, she returned the papers, taking from Artaria the sealed draft on the Milanese bank, which she did not bother to examine. Nervously, Artaria prepared a pen for both signatories, handing it first to Niccolò, then to Antonia, whispering a truncated apology to her for forgetting his manners.

Antonia returned the pen, solemnly watched while Artaria restored clerical order, then pointed to the door of the bedroom. She nodded, almost too intently. Waxen and unattractive, she first stared at the pen, then, as they understood, turned her back abruptly upon them.

Niccolò cautiously opened the door. The child lay upon his bed in adorable unkemptness, curled in deep sleep. He wriggled, distressed by the light that shone in upon him, and turned over on his stomach. Achillino's lips puckered; he emitted thirsty little sucking noises. His straight dark hair fell to his shoulders.

In an impulsive gesture, Niccolò seized the child, cradled him in his arms, shaking off a blanket clutched in the small fist. Supporting Achillino, who had begun to whimper, he now confronted the others.

"Our business is done. Let us go," he said harshly.

He did not once look up at Antonia who, with a sleepwalker's solemnity, handed Artaria a stuffed giraffe that was matted, eyeless, and nearly decapitated.

"You will send his clothes in the morning," the good Artaria began, then gave her a wild and helpless look and followed Niccolò swiftly from the room.

Both were grateful that the child did not awaken and was safely ensconced in the moving carriage before calling out, still tightly asleep, in an odd whimper, "*Mammina? Mammina?*"

Niccolò rocked back and forth in a strange anguish. He had beaten the Devil, but at a cost that could not be counted in florins or lire.

20
Helena

ACHILLINO GREW AND FLOURISHED. After the first few days, he ceased wailing for his *Mammina* and seemed, actually, to have forgotten her. Niccolò helped blur the child's memory by designating any woman who looked after him for a few hours or a few days *Mamma*. Thus, the little boy had many mothers, all casual and tentative, and a perpetual father who was stable and loving, and provided amusements and toys.

"The child exhausts me. I am ill from fencing with him and running about being his bear," complained Niccolò in a letter to Luigi Germi. But down on his hands and knees he would drop, seizing a pair of shoes to delight the squealing boy to yet louder expressions of glee. And soon Achillino was climbing upon the haunches of his skinny bear, resting upon the aching backbone, digging small feet into Niccolò's ribs and beating the sagging shoulders of his dragon or his horse.

The three-year old's energy and motility never ceased to astonish. Achillino was like a wild colt, forever prancing, impatient of restraint, striking out jubilantly out of sheer aliveness, voraciously consuming his father's time and health. In Niccolò's eyes, the child remained a miracle of precocity and perfection; the restiveness, understandable (for the child, after all, was so confined); the destructiveness, altogether excusable.

For the remaining months in Vienna and for more than a year of the travels that followed, he struggled as Achillino's sole nurse, amusing the boy, telling stories out of his own childhood, caring for him when he had measles, getting up at dawn to make the foaming chocolate the child had learned to love in Vienna. On cold days, in traveling or walking, he carried the boy inside his greatcoat, stroking him like some furry little animal who sought shelter from the elements and rewarded him by nibbling upon his heart.

"Oh, you must not strike your poor Papa so brutally, or he will surely fall upon the ice."

The child laughed gleefully. "Oh, I want to see you fall. I want to see you fall," he cried in German and Italian.

"Then you will fall, too, little squirrel."

"I shall fall upon you, Papa, and it will not hurt."

"Better wait," Niccolò gasped with the utmost patience, for the child was plump and heavy. "When we reach home, we can play with swords, and perhaps this time you will kill me."

"I shall kill you, Papa! This time I shall kill you!" cried Achillino.

"Very well. Only do not wriggle so," Niccolò begged.

❊ ❊ ❊

THE GREAT GOTHIC WORLD loomed before him (and to Paganini, the term embraced Slav and Saxon, and indeed, all non-Latin, non-Catholic Europe): gold and alienation, glitter and barbarism, and glory such as he had never dared imagine, but coupled with unceasing travel, misery, and inconceivable cold. He was uncomfortable and ill-fed, yet joyfully free of the Devil, and with his loving son at his side, he experienced great heights of exaltation and accomplishment. Each city—Prague, Dresden, Breslau, Berlin, Leipzig, and Nurnberg—brought singular honors. In Warsaw, he performed at the coronation of the Russian Tsar as King of Poland, this time receiving an enormous diamond ring in place of the ubiquitous snuff box. He ventured into society, pleased to find himself

adored despite parsimony, crotchets, quaint dress, and most unorthodox lodgings; great carriages pulled up before his squalid rooms, and
aristocratic arms welcomed him, while coachmen held their noses.
And for the first time since Vienna (and there Antonia had hovered
ominously in the background), he enjoyed salon flirtations, suggestive
glances, and the blandishments of beautiful women.

❖ ❖ ❖

Suddenly, he remembered Antonia's bitter word, "capon." Its full impli-
cations reached him belatedly; pride and anxiety about money had
shielded him then from the searing fact that his powers had waned.

He was shocked; he tried to rationalize. He reminded himself that
he had been ravaged by disease, that the artist's course is a priestly one,
and that the voracious Muse disdains to share. But he only half-believed
these weavings, and he began to suffer from an Italian distrust, as contempt, for a sexually inert male. Had he dared, had he not felt blinding
shame, he would have run to the nearest quack for a cure for dwindling
desires. One could not live out one's years in a perpetual twilight. As
long as he needed a woman's soft flesh to molest, tear, engorge, shape,
and relieve himself upon, he would stave off death's lassitude.

Yet, suddenly he was at a loss, gauche as a young boy, puzzled, terrified of being spurned. Perhaps the language presented difficulties;
perhaps his very eminence prevented him from moving about freely in
a strange land. He could no longer easily approach women of the lower
classes, or minor actresses and singers. The mere thought of a prostitute
had become odious and distasteful. He must be loved to madness or, at
least, dallied with for empyrean pleasure; he would not buy surcease,
like a cheap and untidy sweetmeat, to be hurriedly eaten.

And he, Niccolò Paganini, in unknowing youth the lover of a sovereign princess (the Emperor's sister!), found himself unable to negotiate

the transition from *politesse*, suggestive glances, the furtive hand-pressures and eloquent smiles of the salon to the joys and intimacies of the bedchamber.

What had Antonia told him bitterly, when at last ready to renounce him? He could not remember the exact words, but it was something about how he seemed to find love onerous; that even as he crested in triumph with a woman who adored him, he experienced little more than relief, little more than awareness that the itch had been dispelled, so that he could for a time be happily free of it and proceed to realities. "You do not love; you *piss!*" Antonia had spat at him shortly after the birth of Achillino. He had, at that time, blamed the outburst on a Sicilian midwife and overwrought nerves. All new mothers, it is common knowledge, suffer from overwrought nerves.

He encountered her first in Nürnberg, Achilles' "toy city." The crooked charm and medieval aspect of the place suggested Assisi, though in a secular, Nordic version, without the all-pervasive presence of the saint of poverty the world so venerates and ignores. Here Niccolò lingered for a week, buying toys, music boxes, and red-cheeked figurines for the ecstatic child and performing twice in recitals attended by all the surrounding area. From Ansbach, the fat, earnest Baron Ludwig Friedrich von Dobeneck had journeyed for the first of these, accompanied by his twenty-three-year-old wife, Helena, whose zeal had prompted the journey.

Though as splendidly proportioned as Antonia and nearly as tall, Helena did not suggest the latter's sensuality and perpetual, brooding amorousness. Her strong, full face radiated intelligence, enthusiasm, and wit; coupled with an aristocratic grace, wide green-gray eyes, and fine, regular features, the effect was startling and magnetic.

Somewhat timidly, she had followed Baron Ludwig into the presence of the wizard who had so deeply moved her. At first, Niccolò thought she had come reluctantly, upon being coaxed by her husband.

After a few moments' conversation—Helena spoke excellent French and very good Italian—he recognized that she was trembling, overwhelmed, unable to view their meeting as the routine bagatelle between a great lady and a great artist. There was an intensity about the young baroness that lent the familiar post-concert interview, with aggressive townspeople and musicians swarming about the untidy room, a quality of having been arranged by ancient deities.

Helena begged the baron to permit her to linger the week with local relatives rather than return with him to Ansbach on the morrow. "I shall be devastated if I do not hear *Herr* Paganini again," she said candidly. Then, turning to the fiddler, added, "My *Tante* is an invalid and goes nowhere, but she will be delighted to receive you. Tomorrow, she will invite you in her own hand!"

"She will do whatever Helena asks," smiled her husband. And it seemed to Niccolò that the good-natured Baron Ludwig, too, would do whatever Helena asked, though he seemed somewhat baffled by her earnestness, her odd exaltation, and the decision to linger in the shadow of the skinny, hollow-cheeked Italian who looked like the Evil One and issued sounds that could not be wholly virtuous.

But Baron von Dobeneck supposed such affinities not unusual in women, particularly overeducated and artistic ones who talked of moods and spiritual matters. The women of his own family, he was proud to say, had not been burdened with too much learning and too much sensibility. They applauded any music performed for them with the utmost courtesy but were unable to carry a tune. They wept at funerals, as one ought, not over poetry and romances, and did not turn upon an itinerant fiddler (albeit a rich one) the shining, ethereal countenance that properly belonged in church.

DURING THE DAYS THAT FOLLOWED, while they were never really alone—the ancient *Tante* with her fleshy St. Bernard face, mourning clothes, and arthritis always hovered about or pervaded the great house with the mustiness of her presence—there was a sense of intimacy, even of intendedness.

They talked softly, hours on end, scarcely touching. Helena's fingertips might alight for a moment on his shoulder as he sat facing the fireplace and glittering, upright coat of mail, the reminder of a Feuerbach ancestor of more enterprising days. "How small they were," she murmured, designating the hollow knight. "We think of them as giants and heroes, but they were, in reality, tiny men, and lived in a very little world."

She adored children, particularly little boys. "Tell me of your darling child, Achillino," she would demand, turning her beautiful, understanding eyes upon him. The union of the von Dobenecks had produced no issue; this was her great, great sorrow, she informed him crisply.

Helena's father, of whom she talked incessantly—though she seldom mentioned her husband—turned out to be the first legal intelligence of the century. Paul Anselm Feuerbach, recipient of every knightly honor known and an intimate of his sovereign, had shaken humanitarian Europe to its foundations by exposing the prevailing penal conditions and setting forth the theoretical framework for a sweeping reform of the criminal code, beginning with the abolition of all modes and instruments of torture. Head of the city government of Ansbach, Feuerbach was known in predominantly Catholic Bavaria as the Shield of Protestantism, being not only devout (sprung from a long line of pastors) and materially independent, but having defended embattled writers and thinkers whose utterances had involved them in censorship or personal hazard.

As the daughter of such a man, Helena had enjoyed many advantages, enhanced by her father's radical notion that women have brains, even as men, and that the intellect is not hampered by femininity. She had undergone as rigorous and demanding an education as her brothers, not only in languages, painting, and music, but in mathematics, philosophy, and the classics as well. She was, indeed, disconcertingly learned while remaining disconcertingly feminine; perhaps her excessive emotionalism helped offset the severe effect her intellectual strengths and eloquence might have induced.

"You have been married five years," Niccolò counted, after Helena had talked of her girlhood, of libraries and courts of law, and of visits to distant cities where her father was respected and consulted by sage and sovereign alike.

"But not for love," she explained quickly. Her polished hair glowed burnished red and gold before the open fire; she parted it in the center and gathered it into a soft bun, a coiffure as simple and unvarying as a Roman matron's.

"I mean—" Helena continued, blushing at the effort her candor called forth. "It was my mother's desire. Von Dobeneck—the family, the title. She feared I would be good for nothing but to become a governess if I grew older and read more. I was eighteen, you see, a suitable age. My papa seemed reluctant. He took me aside and said he was growing too fond of me, that he would be content to have me at his side in the study for many, many years, but must not be selfish."

"Did you agree with him?"

Helena smiled mirthlessly. "The night before my wedding, I begged him to spare me, to send the guests away, to withdraw the dowry so the irate von Dobenecks would depart."

"And what happened?"

"He seemed broken and distressed. He called my mother—"

Niccolò waited, drinking light and shadow from her face, feeling the quiet blessedness of being with her.

"—who listened like a pillar and slapped me furiously on both cheeks. The next morning, we proceeded with the wedding."

"You have...regretted?" Niccolò asked, peculiarly moved.

"Yes. No. I have not been a...participant," Helena admitted in an awkward spurt of candor. "The baron is good to me. He likes to ride and hunt. He has many friends. I am often alone. And when I am not alone—"

Helena stopped suddenly in her narrative and slipped a small hand with but a single ring into his.

"He does not concern himself with my regrets," she said quietly.

Her light eyes shone.

Helena talked of music with sensitivity and surprising wisdom, amusing him by shrewd accounts of her concert going and humorous ones of her efforts as a performer. No, she would neither sing nor play for him. Since she did not aspire to be heard or admired—indeed, her aspirations were of quite a different order, she advised significantly— it did not matter that she had a pleasing little voice or had learned to tinkle expressively on the pianoforte. But he—Niccolò—was Orpheus.

The baroness displayed an unexpected knowledge of the technical problems of the violin. Her questions as to his devices and effects were precise and sound; her descriptions, devoid of the maudlin undertones that had previously characterized discussions with ladies who declared them- selves impassioned by his playing and proceeded to ask idiotic questions.

Niccolò had never encountered so erudite a woman. The Duchess of Tuscany had been shrewd as a cobra and possessed the creative Napoleonic intelligence, but it was difficult to imagine her actually immersed in the process of learning. She had acquired early in life all she had to know, and demanded merely to share the fruits of enlight- enment with others, whether or not they wished to accept her gift. But this paragon spoke with gentle familiarity and without the slightest ostentation of Dante and Shakespeare, of Homer and the Eddies and the *Minnesänger*; she recited great chunks of Byron, Leopardi, and Heinrich Heine, whose fire and rhythms (or perhaps the ardor of Helena's recitations) stirred Niccolò even when he understood not a single word. He was awed, entranced, excited by this peerless creature, so unmistakably, as day succeeded day, in love with him. He dared not talk of love as yet, certainly not in the house of the Nürnberg *Tante*; not to the virtuous highborn wife of Baron Ludwig von Dobeneck.

But Helena dared. The afternoon of his final concert, she burst into tears and flung her arms about him. Emboldened by the thought of an imminent separation, Helena babbled of fatal love beyond her mortal power to arrest. In one swoop, she renounced her title and the baron's money, proposed to talk to her father about an immediate divorce, and promised to change her religion and be a good mother to Achillino.

Niccolò was touched, torn, and above all overwhelmed by such oceanic emotion. He found himself speechless; the lovely Helena had words and sentiments enough for both, it seemed. He wiped her eyes and kissed her fingers and hands, her throat, and eventually her lips. He muttered incoherently in Italian that he had been rejuvenated, reborn.

But he worried about being overheard by others, something that did not occur to the impetuous Helena. And he felt that time, and time alone, would suggest ways and means of resolving their problem.

Niccolò grew dependent upon her letters, melancholy and ailing when they failed to arrive, comically elated as he perused their declarations and reassurances. He went nowhere without his packet of letters tied with strong strings. Many times during a journey, he groped in his greatcoat to ascertain they were with him, fondling, even smelling the pages. One letter he neatly and accurately copied, to the very idiosyncrasies in punctuation, and sent to Germi in Genoa. He wrote distant friends that he might marry, though not in the immediate future, ecstatically describing Helena's assets and talents, as well as the immensity of her passion for him. His own letters, while lacking the verbal imaginativeness and loftiness of hers, were deeply affectionate, replete with courtliness and bravura sentiment.

Yet he remained immobilized. In the back of his mind, he was still haunted by one chilling clause of the satanic pact: "No love—except your love for me—will be possible." He had renounced the Devil, but could he dare imagine that the entire contract was truly null and void?

Time seemed fragmented, never adequate or whole. He was bone-weary, lacerated by travel, committed everywhere; the sordid details of arranging concerts, housing, and Achillino's care could never be satisfactorily delegated. He corresponded with Moscow and St. Petersburg, with London, Dublin, and Edinburgh. His homeland beckoned. Someone wrote of fabulous wealth to be amassed in distant America, but could he endure an ocean voyage? And as yet he had done nothing to legitimize Achillino. What if Niccolò were to die suddenly, as Carlo, his brother, had died, leaving his child stranded without legal rights in a barbaric country?

Yes, yes; he loved and desired Helena and would marry her—some day. Unwittingly, she became an additional harassment. He dreamed of her—not of her kisses, not of her body, not of the serenity of living with her, but that she reproached him for his failures or for her rupture with the affable Baron Ludwig, which for some unclear reason caused Niccolò immoderate guilt and anguish.

Obstacles grew ominous. Religion! Niccolò, who had not set foot inside a church in fourteen years (save for the purpose of hearing a rival's composition), found himself troubled by Helena's strict Lutheran upbringing and by the notion of being the husband of a divorced woman. He poured out his conflicts to Germi, who answered that while he did not regard himself as an expert in canon law, it seemed that if the lady became a Catholic—as she had offered—her marriage to Paganini might well be regarded as her first, with the former vows not binding. "If, ecclesiastically, there was no marriage, there would, of course, be no divorce," he wrote cautiously. Niccolò felt a twinge of disappointment; the inquietude lingered.

Helena's childlessness, hitherto a source for gratitude, now became sinister. A barren woman? Surely the Baron von Dobeneck desired progeny, and yet five years had yielded none. True, Niccolò already had a child, yet what if something (Heaven forefend) were to befall Achillino? Of course, there was a possibility that Helena might yet conceive. Perhaps the baron was impotent? No, he was burly, masculine, fond of the hunt. Sometimes (Niccolò had heard it said) the Spanish sickness left men bereft of the power to impregnate. But then, if Helena had children, Achillino's inheritance might be jeopardized. And surely, she might not honorably reclaim her dowry, the divorce being prompted by her desire for another.

Dubiously, he approached Achillino and wondered whether the little boy might prefer a permanent mother, like other children.

"Oh, yes," said Achillino. "And a horse."

"You would not be unhappy? You would not weep, even if forced to take naps and eat green beans?"

"Of course not. I have always wanted a horse." The child jumped up and down, pounding Niccolò's breastbone with his small fists. "Maybe *he* will eat the beans!"

In Frankfort, Helena attended his concert with her handsome, high-strung brother, Karl Feuerbach, and yet another dowager aunt with a St. Bernard face. She seemed thinner, more ethereal and exalted, and did not chatter so freely. In the presence of her relatives, she informed Niccolò that she had already left the Baron and returned to her father's house in Ansbach; that she had, at length, been forced to tell her husband of what she rapturously designated "our love," although she had tried to spare him as long as possible. Now Feuerbach was to take steps to procure a civil divorce for his daughter, which would require some time and much money, but leave them free to begin a new life.

Niccolò was desperately agitated. He loved her, he told himself during the sleepless nights that ensued. There lurked not an iota of doubt in his mind that here was the world's most dedicated and perfect creature; that he would never find another comparable to her. Yet, was she capricious? Would she one day tire of him or find him wanting? Would she again look with romantic fervor upon another?

Accustomed to the mores of the Latin nobility, and aware queens and princesses took lovers as they chose and did not confine themselves within the morality promulgated for the lower classes, Niccolò was nonetheless shocked that Helena had actually left her husband. The gesture seemed preposterous, almost indecent. With belated horror, he realized that according to Helena's rigid northern code, she could not, while loving another, continue to live with Baron Ludwig von Dobeneck. Honor and honesty, as she viewed them, were inextricably involved and never compromised; she would have felt contaminated. All this Niccolò found somewhat too rarefied and fine. It would have seemed less outrageous for him to visit her when her husband had gone hunting—and somewhat more moral, too.

Yet it was the recurrent thought of Helena, fleeing from the righteous connubial embraces of the baron, that prompted Niccolò toward Ansbach. Achillino had been deposited with a family of Italian artisans in Frankfort. The journey was made over frozen, rutted roads in a bleak land of stripped, winter-naked trees and congealed marshes.

This time he took rooms at an elegant inn—he haggled but briefly over the cost—just outside the town. He suspected that he had been recognized but gave the assumed name, as planned. He sent a sealed note to the baroness, directing his messenger to the Feuerbach house; he then ordered a fire and additional firewood. And for hours, he paced the spacious chamber, looking up at the high, canopied bed, immense and regal, and the gigantic, incredibly ugly, *echt* Germanic furnishings. He waited.

Early in the evening, the first snow began to fall. Niccolò loathed winter. Snowy roads, however trafficked, created fear and anxiety, and when caught in a blinding snowstorm while traveling, he huddled, sick and terror-stricken, in a corner of the coach, unable to open his eyes.

Now his concern was that Helena might be unable to come, or would use the ominous weather to bolster her scruples. Yet surely, she would appreciate the enormous pains he had taken to come to her, virtually interrupting his tour, engaging in superfluous, hated travel, risking his life on the glazed roads. He stood mournfully at the window of his warm room, looking out on the bleak, unscarred ribbon of road, now white with new-fallen snow. Fortunately, there was little wind, and the flurries thinned, showing signs of abatement.

The snow had ceased to fall when Helena appeared, hesitant, heavily veiled, wrapped in magnificent furs. Niccolò ran to the public room of the inn to receive her, pressing sums into the palms of the innkeeper and the flunkies who sprang to attention as he showed himself. His forefinger crossed his lips in a quick signal to them, and they bowed and scraped, grinning. Gently, he led his trembling, deliciously perfumed love, as overlaid with black lace and veiling as she might have appeared at an ancestral funeral, into his chamber.

Helena halted, confronting the commodious bed. She stood in the little alcove, divesting herself of her veil and outer clothing. "The snow—" she began. Her abortive laugh ended on a vague questioning note. "Take them, don't stand there like a ghost," she commanded in an unfamiliar voice, handing him her fur cloak and veil, both wet with snow.

Like a sleepwalker, he obeyed.

Helena walked tragically, self-consciously, to the great open fire and stood before it, warming her fingers, rubbing them through wet strands of hair. Niccolò stood watching, strangely numb. He started to speak and retreated, and when she turned toward him, her strangely transparent eyes widening, he forgot what he had intended to say.

"I did not know whether to come," she whispered, and then smiled. "Did you really expect me, Niccolò? Did you think I would?"

"I did not know what to think. Sometimes hope is enough."

"I did not know what to do."

"Yet you came."

"I wish you had not asked me," Helena cried. "It is difficult to refuse you, Niccolò. I do not understand entirely how it is with men. Or Italians. One may conduct oneself differently in your country, I am told. I do not mean this disrespectfully." She looked contrite, fearing she had offended.

"This I have learned in my years and my travels," Niccolò said. "Each province thinks its own women the most immaculate—with exceptions, of course—and its neighbors' in league with the Devil."

She laughed again, still ill at ease. "That is what they say about you!"

"Oh, but that is not so," he murmured. He began to kiss her cold hands, looking up to watch the fiery glow in her eyes and cheeks. "I love you, Helena," he said simply. "I am not young. I have been drained by disease. I do not know whether it is intended that I live or die. Then, there is Achillino."

He did not know what he had started out to say, but he was making a supreme effort to confront something with her and with all the truth at his command: something fundamental and troubling, something that would make plain what must be between them. He was trying to tell her, also, that he had not sent for her out of lechery or to exploit her love; that he was himself anxious and afraid, and that two years of celibacy had caused no suffering.

They sat before the fire, nervous, anticipatory. Softly and with great finality and sadness, Helena told of the baron's resignation, founded on gallant concern for her happiness, and of her distinguished father's hope of an eventual reconciliation. "But that is scarcely possible," she said. "We have not, you see, quarreled."

Niccolò shrugged. The excitement of Helena's presence dimmed the underlying clamor of her assumptions; one met each crisis as it arose. Besides, her status was still clouded, legally and ecclesiastically. It occurred to him that the baron's behavior had been almost suspiciously magnanimous. Perhaps he had wearied of his baroness's pedantry, a reproach to any man. Perhaps he found her irrational love for a foreign fiddler both timely and fortuitous. Perhaps he craved a more earthy spouse and a fertile one.

Helena leaned forward and placed her hand on his knee. Her eyes closed briefly; she was endeavoring to speak. The waning fire, sole light in the room, caught the agitation in her throat and bosom. He could hear her breathing.

"I love you chastely," she cried out, almost in protest, as though pleading that he believe her. And she covered her face with her pale hands, now devoid of even a single ring, and was racked by great convulsive sobs.

"Take me, since that is your desire," she wept.

She could have been a votive virgin presenting herself to a devouring god of ancient days, awaiting the slab and the sacrificial knife of the high priest. Niccolò pulled her upright, buried parched lips in her throat, and was suddenly maddened by a meek yet spontaneous loosening of her bodice. Her flesh was glaring white; the full breasts were still surprisingly upright. She trembled as he tore and clawed her clothes, offering neither help nor resistance. And, whetting his voraciousness, as she stood terrified and entirely exposed, waiting for Niccolò to fling his own clothes to the far corners, her hands fluttered feebly to protect her nipples and the reddish, hairy pubic triangle from his glances. He could hear her teeth chattering.

His exultation was surely the wilder, the more searing, for the interminable desert of abstemiousness he had endured. He became aware of a need to inflict pain, to punish. Even before penetration, he knew each monstrous thrust would be the thrust of a saber in her meek, uncomprehending body.

And the only word that raged in his brain during the long, barbaric night was *hochgeboren*—well born, high born; it did not matter. She was his social superior—and he had not for an instant regarded even the Princess of Lucca as his "superior"! He was amazed that this realization heightened his pleasure, appeased his quest for justice. But there would never be time to understand everything.

❊ ❊ ❊

Later, he remembered Antonia's flesh-fires and consuming ardor, her eager delight in bestowing. The baroness did not reach playfully for his nose, ears, toes, or throbbing genitals; she did not even slightly touch him, though she permitted, with a frozen little effort of a smile, his voracious and unending assaults upon her person, nodding tensely as he kneaded her, like a lump of clay, and declared her glorious. When the spasms of spent manhood overcame him, she wept quietly; he knew not and could not in those moments care why.

In the morning she rose, white as a sheet, and looked out upon the white world. Niccolò followed, jubilant over affirmation of his maleness, and joined her at the curtained window that rose from floor to ceiling.

"You are unhappy," he accused, not caring too deeply, though he would have wished it otherwise.

"No, I am not unhappy," she said at length.

"I see no indication of happiness."

"I am a woman, Niccolò. Have I not the right?"

"Oh, indeed. As happy, as ravenous, as greedy as I! He buried his mouth in her long hair.

She fluttered. "I like—when you do that. When you kiss my hair, my hands, my eyes; when you talk of love. Your Italian, it is pure poetry."

"When do you not like what I do?"

She hesitated. "When you are gross!"

"But that is *not* gross, *Carissima*. That is…that is what we are!"

"Oh, no," she sighed. "Aeons and aeons of civilization, centuries of progress, *culture*, my Niccolò: we are not, after all, animals!" She stopped, outraged, as he roared with laughter and, folding back her nightdress, reached with a small boy's smirk to squeeze her breast.

"I want you to joy with me," Niccolò commanded, biting her lips, forcing open her mouth.

She drew back, repelled by his morning breath and crude merriment. "You do not understand, Niccolò. You are a man—"

In a sudden spurt of elation, he flung her upon the carpeting before the window's snow-glare and mock wrestled with her. Helena's head fell back upon the fashionable false oriental rug; she exclaimed softly with alarm, rather than pain. At once he became aware of the obedient bonelessness of her limbs, and of a fresh little cloudburst of tears.

"Yes, thank God, a man!" he panted, himself somewhat hysterical.

In a moment, he had forgotten what had so displeased him.

Moments later, as the world floated back and took substance and form, and he became aware of an acute need for food, sweets, and coffee, he bestirred himself to look at Helena's puffy, stained face.

"Why are you crying?" he queried, exasperated.

"Because it is daylight and you have seen me…like this!"

"How have I seen you? Gorgeously alive!"

"Uncleaned," Helena sobbed.

He offered her a chamber pot, which she delicately spurned, and a comb. Then, singing in a quaint, falsetto voice an aria of Donizetti's, he rang for the flunky and ordered breakfast and a fire. It had begun, very finely and very uncertainly, to snow again. They would not leave the room that day, Niccolò decided happily.

❈ ❈ ❈

She recited verses by the Frenchman, François Villon, translating the archaic words so that he, too, might learn to revere them, sharing her deep feeling and enthusiasm. She sang in a shy contralto melodies she had herself composed to some of those lyrics. She chattered fondly of her many nieces and nephews, and questioned him closely about Achillino. Since Helena assumed the child's mother to be dead, he saw no need to burden her with explanations. And she was already planning for Achillino's future. He would need new clothes; he must meet his little cousins; she would send him marionettes and puppets; he must have a German Christmas.

Helena poured out love, regard, and affection. She begged for instructions as to how to please him. What did he like best to eat? Did he have a house in Italy? Where would he then buy one, so that she and Achillino might await him when he toured? On the other hand, if he went to Russia, perhaps she should accompany him, since it would be unthinkable to be so long separated.

In one sense, he experienced relief. Antonia's sensuality had grown oppressive; she had been forever wallowing and coaxing him into a dank, slimy, tangled denseness, a hot propinquity that knew neither beginning nor end. In sleep, she would entwine herself about him, even in hottest summer. With a sliver of distance between them, she grew cantankerous. Antonia had been vulgar, preposterously physical, and perpetually in heat. Age and habituation made no impression upon her; she had to be loved to desperation, regularly and demonstrably. Words were almost superfluous; words came later, when she started to prod him for his want of zeal.

The baroness, with aristocratic elegance, craved the ceremonies of love—that her hand be kissed and stroked, strands of hair fingered worshipfully, paeans of praise recited to her eyes and mouth, her pearly teeth, her soft little hands. Greater intimacy embarrassed her, brought on a martyred, almost cosmic sadness that Niccolò accepted without too much soul-searching as Gothic and essentially *hochgeboren*. As long as she was resigned to man's nature and man's unchaste needs and made no emotional demands upon him, he remained content. Ceremonial speeches at infrequent intervals did not comprise a hardship.

Besides, Niccolò felt the baroness's self-proclaimed modesty and scruples not altogether sincere. In the light of day, she was passive and humiliated, and spoke of woman's debasement. But eventually, after a dozen or so unions, with his absolute mastery established, she uttered little cries at night and clung to him; she scratched a bit and dug pearly white teeth into his shoulder. And since it was dark as pitch, the very windows snow-impacted, and they as good as sealed in a tomb, he was convinced it was not out of embarrassment!

Alas, that key provision of the Devil's pact endured, and it was not long before he tired of his *hochgeboren* mistress. Soon, the concert tour beckoned. Achillino would accompany him across the continent—but *not* Helena.

21
PREMONITION

A YEAR AFTER PAGANINI'S DEPARTURE FROM VIENNA, Germi wrote that he had heard interesting news from Milanese friends. Antonia Bianchi was about to marry or had married; they were not sure which. At once, Niccolò dispatched an urgent plea for the details.

Paganini was more than relieved that his volatile mistress had found herself a husband. He felt, in a real sense, acquitted; whatever injustices he had done her in the eyes of the world and of his friends had not prevented her prompt marriage. On the contrary, he had actually helped her by providing a sumptuous dowry. And it was now quite unlikely that Antonia would present herself at some future date to make claims on Achillino. She might even have other children.

Meanwhile, the necessity of securing Achillino's future had become the propelling force of Niccolò's life. Achilles' status had to be clarified, or else innumerable obstacles to inheritance might present themselves, and even the purchase of a title would prove an empty, doomed gesture. To the doting father, the child seemed faultless. His every small, spiteful act (such as hiding clothes and spilling ink) indicated intelligence and precocity of a high order. His undisciplined toying with musical instruments, which would have been odious in another, filled Niccolò with joyous expectation. His old Ferrarese friend, Giordigiani, visiting him in Bremen, was left shivering in the cold, with his trousers hidden under the bed and his boots dangling out the window. Niccolò found his predicament amusing; he joined Achillino in loud shrieks of mirth. "Oh, I cannot bear it; I cannot bear it. You look so funny standing there, trying to look annoyed!"

And even Achillino's delight in cards failed to distress his father. "Oh, the little squirrel is enthralled by games of chance," he explained with pride. "I fear he shares my depravity." And he would laugh heartily when the lad managed to outsmart him. "He does not yet know his letters, but is an old hand at faro," he boasted.

Niccolò arrived in Paris in 1831, during the early evening of a February thaw, after five harrowing days on wheels. He had left behind the Black Forest and all things Germanic, hopefully forever. His own mortality gnawed, and as on all voyages, he was plagued by what he had yet to accomplish.

Even more urgently, he was overwhelmed by emotions as improper, he felt, as an adolescent rash or a changing voice. Paris: youth, the strident slogans of the revolution, the crystallization of the hero and the heroic; Lucca with its toy court, emanating as it did from this luminous heart of Europe: everything seemed to float to the surface of memory with devastating clarity and a sense of tragic loss. *We grow old, we betray, we are betrayed.* The lights and rooftops of Paris, glittering through the mist, reminded him that all trivia would outlive him, the letters he perused, the cravat he wore, the soft toys Achillino clasped to his cheek. The stuffed bear, eyeless and limp-eared, would continue to stare vacantly at the sky if all makers of sweet music were to perish.

Thus, the great city lived on, a place of glory, squalor, intellectual agitation, and gross ignorance, quite like other cities except that, being

Paris, everything seemed heightened, intensified, more poignant and real than the realities of other places.

Niccolò arrived on the heels of the 1831 uprisings, but it mattered little to him whether Charles X resided in the *Palais Royal* or Louis Philippe. He knew he now lived among puny men, wee kings, miniature conquerors.

Yet, as he had somehow always contrived to arrange his entrances, Niccolò appeared at precisely the most strategic hour. The agitation of the new romantic movement had reached a fever-pitch. The novel, the unheard of, the audacious, the experimental, the tradition-defying: these, alone, were honored and relished. The tastes and attitudes of even the recent past were tossed into the rubbish heap, hopelessly irrelevant and out-of-tune. For the enormous energies of French literature and music, art and thought cut themselves off from their antecedents in a search for new directions. It seemed inevitable that the diabolical Italian would have something to say in Paris to the fashionable and avant-garde, to the bourgeois imitator, and in time, to each Parisian able to afford a ticket, despite the doubling and tripling of prices.

He settled in the fashionable *Hôtel des Princes* in the *Rue de Richelieu*, a departure from his practice of seeking inexpensive quarters. Meyerbeer had suggested this as the suitable address and explained in a patient and elementary way that the French tend to be somewhat overly attuned to appearances. If Paganini confined his initial visit to modest lodgings, he would save money, but would in turn realize less; his expectations would be promptly characterized as meager.

Niccolò had been convinced that to launch himself in Paris would demand more calculation and planning than the casual arrangements of Austria and Germany, where court theaters were frequently offered on the intelligence that he might be passing through. "In Paris everything is complicated," Meyerbeer warned. "And a false step may prove fatal."

Quite uncharacteristically, Niccolò heeded this advice and had his shabby possessions and precious instrument cases hauled into the *Hôtel des Princes.*

❀ ❀ ❀

DESPITE THE DAMAGES OF TRAVEL and the fatigue, Niccolò's first evening in Paris proved eventful. Unable to eat, he coaxed Achillino, scarcely awake, to swallow a bowl of soup; then carried the child, half clothed, to his cot. Still travel-stained and rumpled, Niccolò made his way to the *Théâtre des Italiens*, where Rossini, in premature semi-retirement, resided on the top story of the theater.

"Friend of my youth!" Gioacchino cried out, embracing his old Carnival colleague. "Oh, my nightingale will be beside herself—she is in Spain; some kinsman is dying—she has but recently departed. There is some difficulty about an inheritance, or will be."

"How is she?" Niccolò murmured awkwardly. He had almost inquired, "How is *Madame* Colbran?"

"There is nothing like a little visit to the magistrate and the church to make a scolding wife out of a loving mistress," sighed Rossini. "This, I now know, is true alchemy."

"And how is it with you, Gioacchino? Are you indeed a Parisian?"

"If the new sovereign continues to pay me a pension, I shall stuff my nose and cry, '*Mon Dieu.*' This is a lively place; each day I am introduced to a new genius."

"What are you writing?"

"I am no longer writing. I have put myself out to pasture."

"Then it is true? I can scarcely believe it."

"Oh," said Gioacchino, "the opera houses, providentially, do not forget me. Tonight, friend of my youth, if you are not too proud to wear appropriate clothing, which I shall be very glad to lend you, we go hear the great, great, great Malibran and Desdemona."

"But—nothing new?"

"Since *Guillaume Tell*, nothing. I have always hated work, you know. Pray God it will not again be necessary."

"It is hard to imagine Rossini inactive."

"Oh, it is very easy. I like to think of myself as of the world's nobility. What do the noble do? Nothing."

"Well," said Niccolò. "Since you have decided to have secrets, we must pretend to take you seriously."

"No, no, there is no secret," Gioacchino insisted. "A man's indolence should be respected if he does not make a nuisance of himself. Now, as to my friend who labors in the vineyard. Where are you going to play?"

"I hear there are complications in Paris. Much intrigue, no theaters to be had, and the king is a bourgeois and of little or no use."

"How would I know? He has occupied the *Palais Royal* so briefly. I have not yet been apprised whether I remain a favorite person, and this is important to me. But in the matter of a theater, my friend must be cautious. Let us first talk with Veron."

"Who is Veron?"

"Who is Veron? Veron has replaced God the Father, the Goddess of Reason, and the twelve Muses—or is it nine?"

"Please, Gioacchino. I cannot follow you."

"Very well," said Rossini, having found a hard salami and a loaf of extraordinary length, both of which he cut in half. "Now wine—where is wine? Do you know, my little nightingale turns out to be a respectable cook, as luck would have it, and she continues to dote on me. How I miss her! Yes, Veron. He is, actually, a doctor."

"Oh, I can always use a doctor," said Niccolò. "I hope he is competent and not a money-loving knave, like the others."

"He does not practice medicine," said Rossini. "He liquidated a splendid practice to devote himself to *belles-lettres* and published a fine review, which printed all the new writers—Sandeau and his inamorata,

George Something, and the young M. Balzac. But then he tired of it, and because he has the Midas touch—you must get to know this man, Niccolò—Louis Philippe has just made him a present of the *Opéra*."

Niccolò was confused. "A present?"

"Yes, the government is withdrawing its subsidy. Veron is to run it *profitably*, even contribute to the national treasury. While the government ownership has still a few more months to run, Veron has already taken over. Aren't you hungry, Niccolò? I am quite famished. His first official act was to throw out everything."

"Everything?"

"More or less. Cherubini at the *Conservatoire* is about to hang himself; there are already applicants for his job. Even the friend of your bosom has been declared anachronistic and *démodé*."

"What does he want?"

"If you won't eat, at least sit by the table, that I may. Oh, I found some cold scampi sent up by an elderly admirer. Not poisoned, I hope." He sampled gingerly, then smacked his lips. "What does Veron want? Oh, novelty! Something daring, shocking, original, romantic, expensive, and above all different. *Par example*, Paganini."

"You think he would be interested?"

"He will be delighted. Since he has banished the past, and Meyerbeer's new opus will not be ready for months—these Germans, you know, are so turgid!—he is but marking time. You can help him mark it advantageously."

"Meyerbeer has promised a new opera?" Niccolò had been so engrossed in his problems that he seldom asked, when the opportunity presented itself, about his friends' plans and activities.

"*Rover le diable*—I told you Veron is seeking devils! But poor Meyerbeer—I do him much injustice—has had many sorrows; he has been unable to deliver on time. The death of his small sons has shattered him."

Niccolò suppressed a twinge of guilt. Yes, his friend's sons had died; and now he struggles with a tune for the Devil. Perhaps he, too, had been caught in a battle with the Dark One—only, unlike Paganini, he had lost the battle. Niccolò remembered Achillino's accident in Palermo and for a fleeting moment, felt a pang of fear at the thought of him asleep back at the hotel.

Gioacchino chewed vigorously, waving his salami in the air to commend it to his friend. "Yes, yes, now that I am enjoying a nobleman's leisure, I shall learn also how an impresario lives. I must see Veron at once. How many concerts do you want to give?"

"As many as Paris is prepared to pay for."

"Bravo. An excellent answer. Two a week?"

"Two a week. But the terms—"

"It goes without saying they must be to your advantage. Let us say ten concerts in all. My Genoese colleague, I shall explain, needs to put away great sums of money. It is his plan to bribe St. Peter."

"You are a friend, Gioacchino."

"Prices can always be increased—that, I am told, is an old Paganini practice."

"I did not come to be mocked," grinned Niccolò, sipping wine.

"But there are leeches to be paid. The claque."

"I do not need one."

"But the *Opéra* does. A staff of sixty-six gorillas, headed by Auguste, who looks like a hangman."

Niccolò had heard of this gang of thugs. If they were not paid to applaud and cheer, they could wreck a performance with their boos and hisses. "They will want money from me?"

"*Mais oui.*"

"Out of the question!"

"We are missing the first act," Gioacchino yelled, jumping to his feet, the napkin still dangling under his chin. "The divine Malibran will come and go. No, it is too late to make you fully presentable, and you smell of Germany and horses. But wrap yourself in my black cloak—it has twice the capacity of yours. No one will be the wiser, and if they stare at you instead of Malibran, I shall swear I have never seen you before in my life."

"We shall meet Veron?"

"At the Italian theater? Such levity! No, indeed, my *Otello* is much too bland fare for his bourgeois palate. Veron wants pageants and spectacles and two hundred ballet girls and—" Rossini vanished to accomplish his hurried ablutions.

"And?"

"And the very Devil in person," he yelled over the gurgling and small splashes of the washbowl.

❋ ❋ ❋

ONE CAME TO FEEL CITIES, AFTER A TIME. They assumed a personal quality, differing one from another, not because of experiences encountered or landmarks viewed, or even personal associations, but in an almost abstract sense.

Thus, Paris. Achillino, too, responded to its uniqueness, becoming extraordinarily buoyant and aware, screaming of marvels to be seen in shop windows, skipping, jumping, and singing at the top of his voice in a jumble of tongues. Father and son played gaily at being tourists, and despite the inclement weather, traipsed about the boulevards absorbing the wonders of the metropolis and regarding the varied, exciting, singularly vibrant people. Everywhere, even in imperial Vienna, Niccolò had sensed a dullness and an absence of movement and charm. But in Paris, the contrary seemed true; every passerby was important, a prime factor in the revolution of personality that seethed and bubbled all about one. Every creature was wise, witty, and in superb control of his destiny.

Niccolò could understand why Rossini felt content to settle here, not for more money or more glory, but in relative idleness, because here he could feel most superbly at ease and among sympathetic souls.

And as Rossini predicted, Veron was indeed interested in the availability of the sensational Italian wizard. But all three parties to the arrangements—for Gioacchino suddenly found himself relishing his impresario's role and had no intention of officiating at introductions and retreating—needed to give, take, haggle, explain, compromise, and go through the elaborate machinery of disagreement and reconciliation.

Actually, each was in harmony with the other from the start, but after great feinting and the dissemination of many rumors, they agreed upon ten concerts at double prices, to be presented over a period of five weeks. The Paganini receipts were calculated in advance, barring unforeseen calamities, at so fantastic a figure that Niccolò lied to Germi in writing of his Parisian prospects. He felt it somehow wiser that nobody, not even his devoted friend and counselor, know accurately just how rich he was becoming.

Niccolò had some time earlier begun to prod Germi to start looking about for an Italian estate he might purchase, the future seat of his titled dynasty and a haven from the hazards and frettings of gypsy life. The dream, begun at Marlia, had been fanned by each visit to a great house. As at one time his fantasy life had been fed by the notion of being the greatest virtuoso in the world, he now aspired to country squiredom on a grand scale. He would buy a hereditary title and a vast estate to accompany it, where Achillino and his children and grandchildren could live out their years in abiding majesty. This would cost many fortunes.

It might be well to hide from Germi, as his middleman, the full extent of his power to pay, lest the costs mount beyond the limits of insane willingness. Niccolò loved Germi above all men and trusted him implicitly. In letters, he poured out his heart, revealing himself with a candor bordering on shamelessness. But it did not hurt, Niccolò became convinced, to keep from Germi knowledge of certain assets. That is why the world harbored many bankers and many banks.

Days before his first scheduled appearance at the *Opéra*—the journals had outdone themselves in intensity, excitement, and utter absurdity—Niccolò received the half-awaited command to play for Louis Philippe at the *Palais Royal*. This time, he experienced deeply mixed feelings. He knew that Ferdinando Paer, having given him half a dozen lessons (or less) now proudly regarded himself as Paganini's teacher and had exerted his considerable influence as *maître de chapelle* to effect the summons. Yet while mindful of the honor, Niccolò was reluctant to break the anticipatory spell by as much as a very private performance before the monarch and a few intimates.

"Now, how does one deal with a king, Achillino, particularly when one wants to say no?" he wondered, pacing.

"Will he give you a snuff box?"

"Very likely."

"Oh, then why don't you be sick?"

"A capital plan, Achillino. Already you are a great tactician. I am unwell. I deeply regret that I am unwell. I shall be honored to pay my devout etcetera respects another time, in the hope of affording His Grace a pleasant hour."

Niccolò sent his regrets and labored explanations. He was beginning to feel above this mode of obeisance; it no longer mattered whether a dozing king, a dilettante princeling, or a besotted duke found him good. Prudence alone tempered his language with respect and a tinge of servility. A guest must flatter his host.

"One king arrives, another departs," he declared when his letter had been sent off by messenger. "But we go on and on, don't we, Achillino?"

"When I grow up, I am going to live in a real house with a kitchen," said the little boy. And he added as an afterthought, "And with brothers and sisters."

❊ ❊ ❊

While the Vienna debut, with which he continued to make comparisons, had been stylish and an event for the cognoscenti and the court, Paganini's first concert in Paris proved even more dazzling and of quite a different character. Paris, beside itself, assembled to cheer him. Paris cheered so loudly, so frenetically, and with such exaltation that Niccolò wondered, and not out of humility, whether he was actually being heard or whether he had become Veron's symbol—new, scintillating, audacious, and radical, and breaking away from the crustacean past with its small certitudes.

The new literati were there, De Vigny, Musset, Sandeau and his trousered mistress, George Sand, and the peripatetic Heine, who had written so eloquently of Paganini on earlier occasions. Rossini and Donizetti sat with the French composers, Auber and Halevy; Baillot, the leading exponent of French violinism, greeted his rival, De Beriot, and the divine Maria Malibran.

The *Opéra* blazed with jewels on forthright bosoms, gold braid and epaulettes, the new vogue of manly mauve, the subdued, almost bourgeois decorum of the court (Louis Philippe himself was not present; he would wait), and the bristle and command of the military. Niccolò had quarreled strenuously about the claque, insisting he would not pay Auguste and his henchmen when spontaneous panegyrics were plentiful. Here Veron had stood firm, however, insisting that the claque would, if rejected, come to deride and hiss, creating absolute chaos. "We cannot risk it," he decided. "Each of the ten concerts must be an individual triumph. A little sabotage from Auguste, and we are undone." Paganini yielded.

He was moved most deeply, however, by an emotional young man who appeared after the concert and introduced himself in slightly guttural, heavily accented French. The stranger had to wait—tense, palpably affected, nervous—while the known and fashionable filed by to pronounce the usual banalities. Niccolò, observing him, had wondered whether some shattering experience had unbalanced him. When motioned at last to approach, the visitor began to babble, twitching and stammering so forlornly that after an instant's discomfiture (at which time he could think only of assassins), Niccolò felt an unfamiliar welling up of compassion, remembering his own youth and the fragility of all beginnings.

His life had been changed for all time, the young man explained innocently. He would not, after all, enter a monastery. He would defy the world and prevail; tonight, he had been shown this was truly possible. He would return at once to his piano. He would do for that instrument what Paganini had accomplished for the violin. Yes, he, too, would break boundaries, scale ecstatic heights, penetrate the depths of volcanic turbulence. Paganini had shown the way; Paganini would henceforth be his guardian angel.

Niccolò could scarcely follow the young man's French, barbarous to his ear, and the alien emotionalism. *So now I am a guardian angel*, he thought, too weary to laugh or to share the irony.

"You are called?" he murmured politely by way of reply.

"Franz Liszt," said his visitor, and turned awkwardly to go.

The arrival of spring in Paris brought with it the inevitable *affaires de coeur*, though all were brief, and few would be remembered. Niccolò's vision of an ideal mate, never wholly forgotten, but more dim and disembodied than before, had become focused around Achillino. Yes, indeed, if the Lord would but send a good, virtuous, high-born woman, who could love his child with a mother's love! She must be young, handsome, educated, and rich, and bring distinction of her own to the name Paganini; she must possess the passions to rejuvenate him and worship him beyond reason and moderation. Perhaps one day he would actually find such a woman. At nearly fifty years of age, wasted by disease, he recognized that celebrity would have to compensate, to an extent, for want of youthful vigor.

But of course, it was never to be. Beyond the vanity of his dreams and delusions, Niccolò retained little talent or tolerance for sustaining love or intimacy with a woman. He saw it as a weakness, and—more than that—an entree for the Devil. For although the succubus had been banished from his dreams, an evil seemed to linger at the edges of his life; he remained as doubtful and fearful of women's motives as he had ever been. Lovers came and went, through numerous short-lived and mostly unsatisfactory affairs. He remained somewhat worried about Helena, who had reportedly been pursuing him across half of Europe. The others, however, were of no consequence, mere dalliances; and in truth, Niccolò himself feared that his bond with the Devil had never been entirely severed. He lived with the constant and growing suspicion that the Evil One lay in wait; that one day, unannounced and unexpected, he would return to collect his due.

There were times when Niccolò thought he saw the demon, the same towering, black-caped figure he had pursued long ago through the labyrinth of Venice. The gondolier, the boatswain, the coachman, the sadistic sodomite: Niccolò had come to suspect that this dark demon had been Lucifer himself, and that the succubus was merely one of his minions. Once, outside the *Opéra* in Paris in the middle of the day, he thought he saw the shadowy fiend rolling by in a carriage, his yellow eyes aglint in the passing window. On a drizzly night, he saw a raven-cloaked figure standing on a bridge, staring down upon him. Niccolò approached, but the vision quickly vanished in the mist.

When, Niccolò wondered, would the Evil One show his face? When would he come to claim the fiddler's soul?

In death, no doubt: the Devil's door.

* * *

Niccolò tore open the white envelope and read in the small, careful, familiar hand: "Yes, Niccolò *mio,* I am in Paris. I am hearing you tonight and am close to you, and I live again, though you are unaware of my presence. I shall wait for you. H."

He calculated: it was now over a year since his assignation with the baroness, yet still she pursued him.

And suddenly, he was prepared to flee. Now, at once, into the night, anywhere. He would rush to the *Hôtel des Princes* to awaken Achillino and leave this very night for England. He would not remain here with the raw nerve-ends of irresolution and guilt piercing him, and perpetual fear of an encounter rendering every step hazardous.

He glanced at the address, which he did not recognize. Why, it might be any of the countless little streets pouring occupants into the *Rue de Richelieu* each day. Or they might meet almost anywhere; surely Feuerbach's daughter was being handsomely received, divorce or no divorce. Parisians tended to let live. France was the most comfortable and accepting country in the world, eminently accommodating to what Helena had designated man's grossness—and/or woman's calculations.

The valet, an Italian, cleared his throat and said, "*Signor*—the man respectfully requests your answer."

Niccolò crushed the white sheet in the palm of his hand. "Tell him: no answer," he said firmly, regarding his cadaverous face in the outside glass intended, no doubt, for the exploitations and vanities of the company's prima donna.

But he would not waste his life brooding on the predatory Helena and how he would, if he must, evade her. Clearly, it was time to leave Paris. London beckoned; Watson (his agent) promised a king's ransom, and perhaps the deranged Helena would leave him alone.

To Niccolò's relief, the baroness did not follow him across the sea. The painful obsession ended in madness and her confinement in an asylum.

PAGANINI'S ENGLISH TOUR WAS, AS EXPECTED, IMMENSELY SUCCESSFUL, but marred by yet another near-disaster. This came at the hands of Charlotte Watson, the sixteen-year-old daughter of his London manager. The cunning girl stole his aging heart and nearly brought him to public ruin, confirming for many the violinist's still-suspected satanic ties. Though Achillino adored her, Paganini finally recognized the danger. As soon as he had completed his contractual obligations, he made a hasty retreat back across the Channel, grateful to resume his series in the French capital.

IN 1832, PARIS WAS QUIETLY BESIEGED BY A LETHAL, if invisible, enemy. Trailing Niccolò from London, where it had reached near-epidemic proportions, the Asiatic cholera had begun to gnaw furtively upon its first victims. Disease lurked in alleys and stalked the shining boulevards. While, like all plagues, this one preferred the poor and the close squalor of their quarters, the poor could clearly not be confined; indeed, they swarmed about their business everywhere, followed gradually, then more swiftly, by the cholera.

Niccolò recalled the pest bells sounding in the morning and the evening of his boyhood Genoa. He remembered the glazed eye and ramrod limb of the dead—men, women, and even cats, sprawled out on the crooked, irregular stairs of the hilly streets overlooking the harbor. He remembered Teresa's gelid fright, the hushed talk of others' losses, and the shamed, quick-quiet ingathering of bodies. He saw the red sun of morning, the red sun of evening, and the red-striped sea.

"Pierre Robillard has gone to stay with his grandmama in Rims," Achillino said mournfully. "Are we going away, too, Father, so the pest cannot harm us?"

"No, indeed," Niccolò answered. "I returned to Paris to give ten concerts, which is what I propose to do. As for the pest? Listen carefully, my child. It cannot harm us."

"Don't you think, then, that we are very lucky?" Achillino was understandably proud.

"We are more than lucky. We are blessed."

The plague did not deter him. He took no precautions, not even on Achillino's behalf. And, indeed, save in absurd flight, what precautions were there to take? Rumors thrived: stringed garlic or amulets of a particular metal, or perhaps a novena to this or that intercessionary. Seeing so many ordinary people struck down, Niccolò could not seriously consider that he might be one of their number. He had survived a battle with the Devil, and now he flourished. He had survived innumerable lethal ailments, yet now he walked freely among the dying.

And he was not alone. Among the fashionable, the advanced, the intellectual and articulate, it suddenly became sportive to take an interest in the act of death itself. The visible process of dying (on the part of others, of course) came to be viewed as the most soul-stirring, erotic spectacle in the world, overflowing with unmentionable ecstasies and endowed with almost magical powers. Lost potency was restored at the sight of writhing victims clutching for a last gasp. Madness was smoothed into sweet reasonableness. Immunity from the plague itself filtered like an effulgence from the rattle of the dying and the stiffening of the dead. The revelers of decay ran merrily from the charity hospital, crammed with expiring victims in their final spurts of agony, to the charnel house to view the bodies slapped carelessly atop one another awaiting burial, and to the most eerie and distant parts of the grave-yards, where the cadavers were thrown stealthily into collective graves.

Niccolò was a leader of the new vogue. Death presented a sour-sweet, heady, distinctly ascertainable odor to his nostrils, like the bouquet of a rich wine. Nothing repelled or disgusted. Death was a pallid marsh flower, a murky flame. Niccolò gazed upon the swelling and the boils, the oozing pus, the retching and convulsions, and the fecal blood and vomit. The close sight of the dead and dying filled him with sensations of throbbing immediacy and bliss; his curiosity seemed bottomless. Alone and in the company of other students of horror, he sought out the stricken in the hope of viewing the naked mystery of life's leaving and the quick, imperceptible claims of corruption upon the shell so recently preoccupied with tears and pleasure and pain. He sought that hallowed moment when the soul tore away from the body. And he sought something else: a last word, a vision in the eyes, a terror. For surely in that final moment, the Devil would show his face, lured by the chance to steal the winged spirit.

Niccolò searched among the human rubble and the stench, holding a perfumed handkerchief to his nose as though it were a lantern. Was that the demon he saw in the dying eyes staring back at him?

22
THE FINAL PAYMENT

FOR YEARS HE HAD sought salvation in performance, yet as he grew older and his health worsened, he wearied of foreign cities and life on the road. He performed less and less frequently in public and permitted each tour to disintegrate or suffer curtailment. Living always within the garish light of notoriety, he found himself increasingly intolerant of his public, unable even to sustain affability and small talk. Conversation, particularly in travel, drained him. At each stop, however brief, he was assailed by callers. And as the news spread of his presence in a city where he was scheduled to give concerts, the stream became incessant—the curious, the awed, the respectful, the cranks, the vendors of cures and musical instruments, the expatriates, the beggars, the socially ambitious, the aspiring, the displaced, the desperate. Niccolò usually succeeded in hearing a few pleas before being overcome by lassitude or rage. He was certain that every charlatan and thief sought him out, as by magnetic attraction.

Niccolò had long ago lost interest in externals, however large, which did not immediately involve him or influence his fortunes. In youth, he had been stirred by causes and heroes. Later, living in the palm of the Devil's hand, he had calculated each man's worth in the unfolding of his personal struggle. Now he needed no one save Germi and his child, and a few repairers of precious bows and violins. It mattered not at all that his great contemporaries were embroiled in the struggle for nationhood or in passionate and boastful scrapes of one sort or another against a monarch or a social order or an art form. That Heine, his erstwhile shadow, festered in romantic exile in Paris; that young Victor Hugo had shattered the classical theater and now declaimed against the bourgeois monarchy; that d'Azeglio (with whom he had gone begging that wonderful night of Carnival a thousand years ago!) and Manzoni sang of a unified and aware Italy; that disorderly clouds were gathering over the august Metternich himself: none of these things impressed Niccolò or moved him to judge or commit himself. The world was a mound of mad ants, swarming, rearranging itself, yet always the same.

What did it matter, truly, which official patrolled a border, collected taxes, or put hand and seal to endless papers and some stupid face on the coin of the realm? The heroes, if they had ever existed, were dead: Napoleon, on his sea-splashing crag; Beethoven, alone in the stunning silence; the aged and godlike Goethe, who had known good and evil; the arresting George Gordon Byron, who had thrown his life away for Greek freedom. Perhaps, like the colossi of old, they had never been wholly real; they were the issue of half-truths blended with those greatly misshapen falsehoods of which legends are born.

In a rented room in a foreign city, Paganini found himself engaged in a struggle for life. Eight-year-old Achillino, terrified, rushed out into the street and accosted startled strangers, demanding the name of a nearby doctor. Bereft of speech, choked for breath, Niccolò had begun to vomit blood. The child's screams of mingled terror and nausea dramatized, for Niccolò, the swift worsening of his predicament. Achillino, son of an invariably ailing father, had always accepted the indispositions, symptoms, treatments, and interludes of suffering with childish indifference. Often, as Niccolò felt about to expire, the boy prattled of petty matters. In the midst of a raging fever, Niccolò would become aware of his son's demand, at once strident and whiney, to be joined in a card game or taken to the park. "I want to ride in the little boat," the child would shout.

But this time, even before the boy's screams had subsided, Niccolò identified his son's raw terror. "*What will become of me now?*" queried the great, moist, startled eyes of Achillino. And fear, the father's and son's, united them in an embrace as desperate as the struggle that separated life from death.

"You must not weep for me," Niccolò said hoarsely.

"I don't want you to die," sobbed the boy. "I don't want you to die."

Niccolò laughed soundlessly, too feeble to convey the absurdity of such a notion in words, as he desired. He pulled the blood-stained bedsheet over the basin into which he had vomited, now resting in the crook of his arm. Achillino must be spared. Achillino must not be offended or repelled. He tried to motion the child to summon a domestic but could not articulate or make his wishes clear.

He lay in his stench, vaguely aware of Achillino's almost disembodied, automatic sobs, until the doctor came and shouted for a chambermaid. He listened to the windy drizzle outside his window, which reminded him of the swishing of a broom, now near, now receding; he listened to the muted weeping of his son.

And for a lurid though quickly extinguished moment, it occurred to Niccolò that he would have been kinder, oh, so much more compassionate, to have left the child with his mother. Antonia, even at her most perverse, would have offered the normal joys and experiences of childhood: friends, games, schooling, an identity. As things turned out, Achillino was a gypsy's urchin, lone and thievishly selfish, immature yet knowledgeable beyond his age or needs.

				❋ ❋ ❋

They moved to Marseilles for the quiet and comfort of the sea. Hope simmered, if feebly. Death, after all, is a reality only for others. He remembered his childish horror on first confronting a dead cat, stiff-legged, stinking, with glazed eyes in which fat, iridescent flies buzzed. This could happen only to cats, he told himself, not to mothers, children, and lusty Genoans.

But death's realm had quickly widened, and eventually what happened to mothers, children, and lusty Genoans happened to everyone, although it could not possibly happen to him. Had he not defied death at the hands of the merciless Dr. Borda? Had he not repeatedly risen from the tomb?

Niccolò walked when he trusted himself to venture out of the room, stopping short of fatigue. He loved Marseilles, loving even its squalor and wharf roughness. The port, after all, was his natural habitat. In this city he had friends, yet was not generally known. His appearances sometimes called forth stares, but these were the stares of strangers, briefly arrested and incurious, free of gossip and malice.

While under the tutelage of *Monsieur* and *Madame* Gueron in Paris, Achillino had grown tall, strong, and detestably pious. In the gloomy *Église des Prêcheurs* in Marseilles, where he had earlier heard the divine *Missa Solemnis* of Beethoven and, more recently, a forgotten Cherubini Mass, Niccolò attended his son's confirmation. He thought: one must pity youth that cannot question, that knows only beads and catechism. For despite an erratic childhood, despite the wandering, skepticism, and irregularity that had nested him, Achillino emerged the very soul of complacency. Never would he shake his fist at the heavens, Niccolò thought. Never would he challenge the thunder and the lightning. He would not be an Olympian; he would merely be rich.

The incense and wavering candles nauseated, but the sight of his handsome, erect son brought him enormous strength. That Achillino lived at all; that he laughed, grasped, and inhabited his world remained an absolute and irrefutable miracle. Had he not, through his son—through his love for his son—an indirect claim upon God?

NICCOLÒ WAS AN EMBARRASSINGLY RICH MAN. Germi had tried to explain investment: the inevitable and wise ballooning of money—that wealth, properly bred, makes more wealth, even as a single pair of parents may breed children and grandchildren; and that even static wealth, sitting safely, manages to increase and grow fat. Despite the disaster of the *Casino Paganini* (in which he had invested) and despite overpayment for his baronetcy and the ruined estate in Parma, the Paganini fortune, placed in the hands of the astute Germi, had grown very fat indeed! Achillino would never need to worry about finances.

* * *

"FATHER—"

He heard, then heard the silence. It was like the echo of a hollow shell.

"Father. Please speak."

Words: then the rustle of leaves and the lapping of waves growing swiftly swollen, inimical. The language of scuttling creatures, of slimy extinction in the depths of bottomless seas, of tangling in oily weeds, of lungs overpowered, torn ragged by the watery pounding…

"Father, what will become of me?"

Niccolò's eyes focused suddenly. He became aware of a fearful thirst.

"We are in Nice. We are home. Count DeCessole has been twice to see you. Our maid is here."

"I am Concetta," someone said, rough and distant. "The cook will come this evening."

Niccolò struggled to sit. The room swam briefly, then crystallized, and then became stationary. "My son," he attempted in his cracked voice.

Achillino's forefinger was pressed gently to his father's lips. "Don't talk," he pleaded. "Save your strength. We arrived this morning. You were very ill. We had you carried into this apartment. Yes, it is the one you had arranged."

Niccolò nodded, conveying understanding and relief. "I thought—"

"I thought it was the end," Achillino said childishly. "I was frightened. I cried. I wanted to return to Genoa. Luckily, I remembered that Uncle Luigi had recommended a physician, the good Count DeCessole. Uncle wrote him, and he was waiting—"

"My instruments? My things?"

"Everything we brought from Genoa is here."

"Yes? You are—"

"Yes, I am certain. The count had a list, which he checked off at the dock. I guess Uncle Luigi…And again, when we reached *Grand Rue*. He even procured a litter to lift you to the third floor."

Niccolò sipped the bouillon spooned into his mouth by the maid. He gazed into her dark, snapping eyes. She was young—no more than twenty or twenty-one, thick-browed, and swarthy, but personable, in a strong and willful way. She had firm, conical breasts, a generous belly, a little moustache. There was ferocity about this Concetta, a capacity for passion. No matter, thought Niccolò. He stared into the tablespoon of clear soup. He was beyond bringing this creature or any creature bliss or vice, injury or innocent happiness. She would end by hating him.

"Take it. It's good for you," she said crudely, wiping his chin, as he found himself unable to swallow.

"Who sent you?" Achillino queried, reading his father's bewilderment.

"The countess," she answered briefly. Her glance seemed too hostile for indifference. "I am to remain as long as I am needed."

Since Niccolò had fallen asleep, she withdrew the cup and spoon with a loud sigh and started toward the kitchen. "Do you want something to eat?" she queried Achilles.

"Yes, thank you. I am very hungry."

"We have as yet little food. Cheese. Bread. Sausage."

"They will do. I can eat almost anything."

"What is the matter with him?" Concetta inquired, raising a huge bread knife. The long, thin, crusty loaf of bread was fresh, nearly warm.

Achilles joyously seized the end of the loaf and for a few moments was too preoccupied to answer.

"His throat—he rattles like a dying man. And that face! Like the Judgment Day in the church window. Will he die?"

"No," said Achillino.

"It is not contagious?"

"No. See? I am healthy."

She lowered her swarthy face to his. "Is he in a state of grace?"

"No…no. But he will not die."

Concetta cut a second triangular slab of cheese for him. The sausage began to sizzle in the skillet, blending its fragrance with the fragrance of the fresh loaf and the aged cheese.

"What if he does?" she asked sharply. "What if he does die?"

They stared at one another, woman and child, terrified of eternity.

❈ ❈ ❈

He lived to know Jovian rage. He writhed at night, scarcely sleeping at all, groaning, retching, flailing till exhaustion overtook. When movement was possible, he walked about the pretty, symmetrical streets of Nice like a madman harboring hidden caches of venom. Alternately explosive and mesmerized, he was pointed out by street urchins and vendors, recognized by some, and subjected to leering whispers concerning his devilish feats and his murdered mistresses.

DeCessole called often, uttered blurred and optimistic statements, and tried to engage his patient in matters outside himself. He spoke somewhat too heartily and wore an unfading smile. To others of the household, he smiled less frequently. His manner seemed secretive and dour.

Both the cook and the servant girl were from the count's household, and he made his instructions to them explicit. They were to remain where they were, procuring additional assistance as needed. The *maestro's* regimen had been meticulously arranged, and none dared alter a single condition. The old cook grumbled. Concetta's objections, on the other hand, could be heard throughout Nice. Niccolò was relieved to learn they were caused by separation from the count's groom rather than servitude to so ghostly and freakish a master.

"We shall both contribute to your dowry," DeCessole promised, pinching the girl's rump.

"Bah!" she retorted, sliding out of reach. "By the time I get away from this skeleton, I shall be an old woman, and Beppe will be ensnared by the seamstress."

❖ ❖ ❖

NICCOLÒ SUFFERED NOSEBLEEDS. His skin was transparent, spotted, sore; his throat felt razor-slit; often he vomited or coughed up blood. Breathing was the rack itself, and his joints had become brittle and unyielding, or so it seemed.

After a night of fitful sleep, Niccolò would awaken sweating and feverish, unable to call for help. Aware only of weakening, he became convinced that DeCessole was thoroughly ignorant of medical matters.

He sent Achillino to call on neighbors and learn the names of other local physicians, compiling a list of these. In desperation, he wrote his old friend General Pino, urging him to send Dr. Spitzer on an errand of mercy. But Spitzer sent his regrets, recommending several excellent doctors in Nice, including the unsuspecting count.

❋ ❋ ❋

ALWAYS THE PADDED FOOTSTEPS, the constrained sibilances, the flutter, muted and devious…He remained in bed, studying the shapes of the tousled blanket. Now it looked, where his feet were, like a squatting cat; and here a hunched hare with flopping ears, like the stuffed one he had bought Achillino in Nürnburg—when? Or a giant mushroom. The blanket stank. He must tell Concetta, who would scold him. The whole room stank. Perhaps DeCessole was drugging him. He must make it clear he would not be drugged to lie abed like a vegetable. Did the idiot suppose he felt no pain because he dozed occasionally? Niccolò recalled distant Vienna, and his somnambulistic struggle with the succubus. Better to lie awake in agony than succumb to the final temptation.

Why did this child repeatedly say, "Father?"

"Father," said Achillino, shaking him gently at the elbow. "You have slept away all the morning."

Sleep? Was this sleep?

"There is a priest here. He wants to see you, Father."

Niccolò wiped spittle from his chin. "Ask him—ask him what he wants," he whispered.

Achillino departed, admitting a painful shaft of light, then withdrawing it. Niccolò pondered this unusual visit with suspicion. He remembered the papal decoration. What had he done with it?

"Father?"

"What did he say?"

"He says he will hear your confession. It is nearly Easter."

Niccolò scowled in the dark. "Tell him to go away. I do not propose to die," he croaked.

"Father!" cried Achilles in anguish. He then quit the room without another word, shutting the door quickly to isolate the disturbing noise and light.

DeCessole arrived several hours later, pleased to find his patient propped against gigantic pillows, the linen fresh, his long hair combed and parted. A dog-eared manuscript rested on his knees: the *St. Matthew Passion*. The music had always moved him; the mumbo-jumbo of the texts had not. Bach's God the Father and Paganini's Lucifer: the Janus masks of life.

"Ah, spiritual cleansing has brought you years of renewed vigor," DeCessole babbled triumphantly, examining Niccolò's yellow eyeballs.

"Confine yourself, my dear count," Niccolò began. The rest was inaudible.

"You will sleep peacefully now," DeCessole purred, pleased with himself.

"... to the cure of my body." Niccolò stiffened with rage.

DeCessole shook his head, the hearty smile persisting. "In a day or two, then. You are already so much better."

"I do not intend to die." Niccolò formed the words with his lips. Sound had failed.

"Now, who talks of dying? Why, even Hercules ... *fait ses Pâques*," declared the count, lapsing into French as he often did in selecting a euphemism.

❃ ❃ ❃

WAS THAT LUIGI? Why was he walking through the clouds? And Gioacchino —where was Rossini? Why did he not write? Did it not matter to him that the Devil lay in wait for his Carnival friend, Niccolò? Lafont played well, and DeBeriot, yes, and even Spohr, but what did they know of Heaven, of Hell?

But perhaps they, too, had met up with the Devil. Would they also be punished with eternal damnation? What is death, really? Can one outwit it? If he had already endured so much pain, why should he now have to die of it? Pain was an old familiar, like the wrinkles around one's eyes or mouth.

Outside, the seas heaved and roared, thick with menace. In the northern waters, so they said, there were icebergs, great floating mountains of ice that accosted ships, splintering them, tossing fragments of men to the fish.

The fish was sacred. The hook was the true faith. *Nous pauvres pécheurs*…We poor fishermen; we poor sinners…Why should men be splintered by the seas and fed to indifferent fish? Why the Devil? Why the crescent? Why the cross?

He would never talk again. He would be mute, hence stupid, for his meanings would shrink and become very, very simple. Beethoven had lived in silence, but at least he could rage.

Why did she have to marry, Antonia, mother of his child, when everyone knew she belonged to him? She was velvet and satin; she was flowing wine. He could bend her as he willed, yet she always matched his madness and surpassed his lust.

And here was the poplar-lined drive to Marlia, with its mosaic gardens. The Princess of Lucca plucked an oleander, examining it closely for imperfections. If so many had died, perhaps death was not, after all, so terrifying.

In America were many rich cities: New York, Buenos Aires…

And suddenly, in the blinding doorway effulgence, the Evil One himself came to claim him. He was very tall, very severe, black as night, with shimmering coals for eyes in his leprous death-head.

Niccolò called Achilles, Concetta, Germi, his mother, but no sound came forth.

"I am Father Caffarelli. I am here a second time at the behest of the Bishop of Nice."

Niccolò shook his head. He would not quarrel; nor would he bestir himself. He would not die; he was not ready to die, and he refused to let the demon persuade him. The apparition grew blurry, elongated, with dark gashes where Niccolò's eyelashes seemed to interfere.

"He does not really understand," said Achilles. "You see, Father Caffarelli, he has been very ill."

"Unrepentant," said the sepulchral voice.

Concetta said, "Never have I heard him utter a prayer or the name of Jesus or of the Blessed Mother."

"The naked woman on the wall—"

"We saw the painting in the Vatican, Father," Achilles cried. "I think it is by Rubens. Perhaps not. It is very large." He was weeping copiously. "A whole wall, almost …"

"Repent," said the voice of death. "Make a good confession."

Niccolò continued to shake his head. The phenomenon was spinning now, cut into small irrational patterns. No matter; he would outstare the Devil! He was not afraid.

"… nor a crucifix, nor rosary beads," said Concetta.

"Look, I have rosary beads," said Achilles.

Niccolò waved them away. "Go," he whispered. He tried to say more but succeeded only in producing a grating noise. "No," he conveyed at length.

Firmly, with a stubborn smile, he turned to the wall. Perhaps the demon would go away now and leave him in peace.

When his Dark Master next appeared, days or weeks later, the very doorway shimmered like a sheet of cascading, gem-like fish scales. The room was fetid.

"I am here a third time," said the Devil sonorously, "by express order of *Monsignor* Domenico Galvano, Bishop of Nice. May I hear your confession, *Signor* Paganini?"

Niccolò tried to speak.

The Golden Spur. Where was the Order of the Golden Spur?

Even Achillino did not understand him, bending to embrace his father and to hear accurately.

"He is weak," the boy cried. "His legs are swollen. He is unable to breathe."

Father Caffarelli rebuked the dying man harshly, "Your soul is in a far more wretched condition than your body. I am here for your confession, to absolve you if I can, and to administer the sacrament."

Achillino held his father's shoulder, half supporting him while Niccolò whispered in his ear. "He says," fumbled the boy. "He says he will write it on a slate, that it may be erased."

"I am unmoved by his levity," the dark one declared severely. "Hell is forever. Tell your father his immortal soul is in jeopardy."

Two slow, sullen tears rolled from the eyes of the child, choked with his own bewilderment and fears.

"Who made you?" thundered the voice.

"God...Oh, God made me," wept Achillino.

Then Niccolò saw it: the demon's crimson tail; its spaded tip poked out beneath the somber flutes of his cassock. Niccolò raised himself painfully to a sitting position, leaning on an elbow, spurning with his grimaces the help his son offered. Because of the superhuman effort, because the words emanated from his very bowels, because he would surely be taken to Hell if he did not now address this demon, intelligible sounds somehow crackled out of his diseased throat.

"You are the fiend!" Niccolò articulated slowly. "I exorcise you and am free of you! You shall not have me! Merciful God, I have renounced this hellish bargain! Go! And do not ever come again!"

Achilles shrieked, "He doesn't understand! He doesn't understand!"

Then the blood and vomit came in rhythmic spasms, and Concetta fled, terrified, to summon DeCessole.

But the apparition had vanished.

"He understands," boomed a voice out of the empty air.

BY EVENING, NICCOLÒ FELT CALMER. After searching through dozens of boxes in storage, Achilles had uncovered the still-glittering Golden Spur in an empty, felt-lined violin case. His father grinned proudly as the boy pinned the yellow medal to his sleeve.

Occasionally, during the next several weeks, Niccolò was able to leave his bed and sit by a window. The view of the half-ruined court-yard displeased him, so he was instead often propped by the window of the enormous kitchen overlooking the *Grand Rue*. He would watch Concetta, Agata the cook, and Urico, the aging male domestic, who came as needed from the count's household. They fussed, worked, and scolded one another as though he were not there at all. Niccolò found them diverting. The activities in the street below now held him in trance-like fascination. Regarding the shopkeepers and fingering the dangling medal on his sleeve, he experienced a sense of accomplishment, of life's renewal.

He tried stubbornly to feed himself. Concetta, scolding all the while, placed a thick board across the arms of his chair. This could precari-ously balance a plate or a bowl of soup. Turned toward the hallway, his chair afforded a view of both the voluptuous Venus that had outraged Father Caffarelli and the lithograph of George Gordon Lord Byron.

Turned toward the window, Niccolò could see the rain, the sunshine—persistent, like himself—and all of Nice and the world.

And the world was good. Yes, yes, despite all contradictions and lies, despite death and injustices, despite evil itself, the world was good. He would cling to it. He would conquer it anew. He would make marvelous music out of silence, out of nothing.

Death came slyly as he dipped a piece of bread, to soften it, into the fish soup. He crumpled behind the board, looking very surprised. The warm bouillabaisse and the spoon clattered to the floor. Only then did the cook notice, shrieking that the count must be fetched, and Achillino sent for at school.

❊ ❊ ❊

For "various" reasons—religious, though ostensibly also concern for public health—the City of Genoa would not permit interment of its famous son. Marseille similarly declared him *cadaver non grata*, as did Cannes, although that city's administrators permitted Achillino to lodge the corpse in the rocky soils of Saint-Ferréol, an uninhabited island under their jurisdiction.

DeCessole, citing precautions taken with Napoleon's burial, recommended that Niccolò, too, be enveloped within three caskets: of hard wood, tin, and lead. "The Bishop's edict will eventually be overturned," the physician prophesied. "When that happens, Church authorities will insist on opening the casket before it is shut forever and placed back into the ground. I would like your father to look his best under the circumstances."

The body suffered the indignity of several relocations in the years that followed, until common sense, tempered with sufficient bribery (that timeless expedient, specifically designed to effect favorable decisions), prevailed.

Germi wrote to Antonia Bianchi of his friend's death before surrendering to his grief. Overcome with the loss, he did not participate in the ensuing struggle as to where the bones of Niccolò Paganini, unrepentant, might finally come to rest.

Epilogue

IN THE SANCTUARY OF Parma's damp, austere cathedral, on a tattered sheet of burlap, lay the unearthed, mud-caked outer coffin of Baron Niccolò Paganini. His son Achille's beloved wife, the Baroness Paola, who had never met her legendary father-in-law, stared in stone-faced boredom at the triple-caskets, while on the pew beside her, tiny Riccardo curled in sleep. Across the gaping central aisle slumped the three old gravediggers, snoring loudly. The wiry official sat behind them, his face buried in a leather-bound book. In a shadowy apse near the door to the vestry, the bald priest held a whispered conversation with the church pastor, an elderly man whose low, gurgling cough grumbled through the high-domed chamber.

The Baroness turned abruptly as the towering iron door at the entrance of the church noisily creaked open. In walked Achilles and his elder son, Attila, arrived at last from their long, wet walk. The Baron shook out his umbrella, showering silver droplets on the marble floor; Attila brushed a hand through his damp mop of hair. The two looked flushed and limber, and somewhat at a loss, as though their cheery excursion through the rain had come all too quickly to a somber end.

"We've been waiting for over an hour," carped the Baroness, glaring up at her husband as he came dripping down the aisle.

"Time spent in the service of your soul," said the Baron, gesturing airily toward the altar. His eyes drifted over the vaulted ceiling as he took his place beside her in the pew.

Attila reverently approached the coffins, his young face full of fear and wonder. After all he had been told of his grandfather's life, he could not believe it had come down to *this*. Slowly, he reached out toward the muddy lead box.

A door banged shut. Attila jumped. In walked the tardy magistrate, a fat and fussy functionary who had doubtless postponed his appearance until he was certain that the rain showers had more or less abated. The pastor departed to the sacristy. The dome-headed priest gathered the gravediggers, joined the magistrate, and approached the waiting coffins.

The screws that sealed the outer casket had rusted but offered surprisingly little resistance. One of the gravediggers pulled a solid metal wedge from his belt and pried it under the lid; after numerous jabs and accompanied by much creaking, he opened it.

The screws that secured the top of the tin casket were still functional. That box thus required considerably less effort.

The inner coffin—the baron could not remember precisely, but he thought it was some sort of pedunculate oak or comparable hardwood—had been nailed shut. Once again, the trusty crowbar sufficed to open it. And then—

The men stared in stunned silence. The magistrate lowered the handkerchief he had brought to his nose. Attila hurriedly squeezed between the men for a view into the casket.

"Oh, my God!" he exclaimed.

"It is a miracle," gasped the priest, drawing a cross in the air. The gravediggers slowly fell to their knees.

The Baroness, fearing the worst, shot up from her seat. "What is it?!" she cried. "Attila—come away from there, now!"

Baron Achilles rose behind his son and peered into the open box. Inside the velvet chamber lay the corpse of his father, dressed in black, his stiff white collar held by tarnished silver studs, his lapel pinned with the glowing Golden Spur. Beneath a cobweb of thin gray hair, the brown skin of his face had drawn taut across his cheeks, and his thin pale lips held a peaceful smile.

The body was perfectly preserved.

"It is a miracle," said the Baron, staring in awe at the wonder before him. "*It has been thirty-six years!*"

At last, the Baroness came forward, jittery with caution. As she spied the leathery face of the corpse, the uncorrupted hands crossed over its chest, her eyes widened with terror. She quickly crossed herself and backed away, pulling the curious Riccardo with her.

"Close it," she commanded anxiously. "CLOSE IT!"

The Baron looked at the priest and nodded. The priest gestured to the gravediggers.

"Wait!" shouted Attila, holding back the lid. He gazed down at the ancient face and reached to touch the Golden Spur. Then he touched the fingers of the dead man's hands, fingers that had once brought into this world such wonderful sounds, fingers that now lay still as death, silent for all of eternity.

Attila withdrew his hand and glanced at the men. The shadow of the lid fell over his grandfather, returning the old man to his peaceful sleep.

Attila looked up at his father with the calm expression that comes with certitude.

"*He was saved, Father. He was saved!*"

THE RAIN FELL STEADILY through the burial ceremony. Once again, Achilles stood beneath his umbrella with his two sons, as the priest prayed, and the coffin was lowered into the ground. Paola waited impatiently in the berlin, only steps from another carriage parked along the gravel road.

It was the black-lacquered brougham of the old woman, the one who had spoken to Attila that morning. Achilles found himself distracted, furtively searching the dark, curtained windows for a glimpse of her. When the coffin had disappeared and the prayers had ended, he turned to see a gray, withered hand reach out the window and gesture to the coachman. With a wistful ache of regret, Achilles watched the horses lower their heads and drag the carriage away.

"I wonder," he mused as he climbed into the berlin, "I wonder which one it was."

"Probably some notary's foolish widow," suggested Paola.

"Perhaps my mother," he said.

And turning from her sharp, shocked glance, he saw Attila still standing pensively at the grave.

"Come, my boy," he called. "Come out of the rain. At long last your grandfather has been decently laid to rest."

THE END—*FINITA LA MUSICA*

Afterword

MORE THAN ONE hundred eighty years following his death at age fifty-seven from a throat ailment, the name of the Italian virtuoso, Niccolò Paganini, continues to conjure up a variety of associations: those of a gaunt, nearly spectral showman and breathless daredevil of the violin, an inveterate gambler, an incorrigible womanizer, and—stated *sotto voce*—the Devil's collaborator.

His renown was comparable with that of the 21st century's most celebrated individuals; such was his fame in Vienna in 1828 that Paganini's likeness was used on portraits, silhouettes, the heads of walking sticks, cigar boxes, medallions, and other artifacts of the era. As with modern day celebrities, however, he was also subjected to tabloid conjecture and harassment. For example, he wrote a letter of protest after discovering that a Parisian vendor was selling lithographs depicting him in jail. The rationale behind this maligning characterization was that absences between concert tours were attributable to his having been jailed for murdering a mistress or a rival.

Paganini's appearance alone was mesmerizing: a narrow face framed by longish dark hair, a prominent nose, oddly flexible and elongated hands, and a thin body clad dramatically in black. His evidently astonishing technical mastery of the violin was perhaps aided by an affliction with Marfan's syndrome, a disease of the connective tissue characterized by disproportionately long limbs and an inordinate suppleness of the joints.

The violinist's fertile imagination and extraordinary physical capabilities led him to invent musical sounds previously unexplored, using a variety of new techniques that, even today, represent the pinnacle of difficulty. Harmonics in double stops, arpeggios spanning four octaves, prolonged staccato bowing, triple-stopped chords, and passagework played at breakneck speed: all of these devices are employed throughout his compositions. His own works are not merely technical vehicles, however, for Paganini's music is often characterized by an immense confidence that is combined with an acerbic wit and, frequently, the sweet sounds of his native Genoa. Whether in the nonstop fury of his fifth *Caprice* for violin solo, the effect of flutes playing a jaunty tune in the ninth *Caprice*, or that of a troubadour serenading while strumming a guitar—as in the center movement of his *Concerto in D Major*—his compositions frequently offer not only stunning virtuosic display but also interpretive depth.

Niccolò Paganini may have literally stumbled into the world of theatrical showmanship. An account by the historian F. J. Fétis quotes him describing in detail what took place at a concert in Livorno, which is summarized here:

> Having taken a nail in my shoe, I limped onto the stage—much to the hilarity of my audience, who did not settle down even as I began to play. Shortly thereafter, the candles on my music stand blew out, which further amused my listeners. Then my violin's E string snapped, which led to even more distraction in the audience. Rather than stopping to replace it, however, I continued to play on only three strings—to the astonishment of my public. This amazing feat was awarded a prolonged ovation and cheers, with many recalls to the stage.

Fétis then notes, somewhat acidly, that this "accident" of a broken string repeated itself many times in Paganini's future concerts.

A concert handbill from February 23, 1832, lists a program in Birmingham, England that featured a hodgepodge of works for orchestra and singers along with Paganini—then on an extended "northern tour" that also took him to Paris—performing several of his own compositions, among which was his "Scotch Air" ("Scots wha ha'e") performed on one string. A starring attraction of the concert was the virtuoso's *Imitations of the Farm Yard*, no doubt drawing from his repertoire of musical tricks and delighting his listeners.

Paganini's putative association with the Devil was a myth he encouraged, as it clearly increased his commercial appeal to his audiences at home and abroad. Indeed, the idea was not even novel; his predecessor, the great virtuoso violinist Giuseppe Tartini, wrote a famed composition called the *"Devil's Trill" Sonata*. Said to be derived from a dream Tartini had in 1713, in which beautiful, remarkably virtuosic violin music was played by the Devil himself, it is an inspired and passionate work that is in the repertoire of most of today's violinists. The concept of a violin-playing Devil endures in folklore and in both classical and popular music, such as in Camille Saint-Saëns' *Danse Macabre*, which he composed in 1875, and 1979's *The Devil Went Down to Georgia*, by the Charlie Daniels Band.

Although many of history's most illustrious classical music composers—e.g., Haydn, Mozart, Beethoven, Brahms, Stravinsky, Berg, and Bartok—have created beloved works featuring it as a soloist's instrument, the violin has been linked with some of the baser elements of humanity nearly since its inception as an instrument type in the mid-1550's. Its loudness, portability, and relative stability in tuning led to a great popularity for use by dance masters at weddings and other outdoor festivities, and its reputation was that of an unrefined and raucous instrument—unlike the lute, for example. Eventually, reform movements in both the

Protestant and Catholic churches led to a denunciation of dancing as a sinful act. Due to its strong association with dance—and, perhaps, Paganini's rumored pact with the Devil—in 19th-century Scandinavia, the violin itself was banished as an instrument of music. This banishment was relatively short-lived, fortunately, and the fact that the violin had been selected by extremely devout composers (such as J. S. Bach) as the voice for some of their most profound works helped redeem the instrument's sketchy reputation.

The myths and legends surrounding the violin extend to the instruments and makers themselves. For reasons that remain unclear, from the mid-1500's to the mid-1700's several families of violinmakers in the small city of Cremona, Italy produced what are unquestionably the world's finest violins, still unequalled by modern makers. Of these, the names Amati, Stradivari, and Guarneri represent the epitome of this craft, with the makers Giuseppe Guarneri *"del Gesù"* (1698-1744) and Antonio Stradivari (1644?-1737) held in the highest esteem today. Their instruments are in major collections or in use by soloists throughout the world, and are valued at millions of dollars.

Nicknamed *Il Cannone* ("The Cannon") because of its powerful sound, Paganini's preferred violin was made in 1743 by Giuseppe Guarneri. This famed maker (who was the son of another violinmaker named Giuseppe) is referred to as *"del Gesù"*—"of Jesus"—because he inscribed the maker's labels placed inside his violins with a cross and the IHS monogram, a symbol of Christianity derived from the abbreviated Greek spelling (iota = i + eta = h + sigma = s) of Jesus' name.

A "devilish" master performing his wizardry only inches away from the powerful Christian symbols placed at the very heart of his majestic violin! This, indeed, is the stuff of legend and provides the perfect vehicle for *Paganini Agitato*.

Stephanie Chase

Fomite

Writing a review on social media sites for readers will help the progress of independent publishing. To submit a review, go to the book page on any of the sites and follow the links for reviews. Books from independent presses rely on reader-to-reader communications.

For more information or to order any of our books, visit:
http://www.fomitepress.com/our-books.html

More novels and novellas from Fomite...

Joshua Amses — *During This, Our Nadir*
Joshua Amses — *Ghats*
Joshua Amses — *Raven or Crow*
Joshua Amses — *The Moment Before an Injury*
Charles Bell — *The Married Land*
Charles Bell — *The Half Gods*
Jaysinh Birjepatel — *Nothing Beside Remains*
Jaysinh Birjepatel — *The Good Muslim of Jackson Heights*
David Brizer — *The Secret Doctrine of V. H. Rand*
David Brizer — *Victor Rand*
L. M Brown — *Hinterland*
Paula Closson Buck — *Summer on the Cold War Planet*
L.enny Cavallaro — *Paganini Agitato*
Dan Chodorkoff — *Loisaida*
Dan Chodorkoff — *Sugaring Down*
David Adams Cleveland — *Time's Betrayal*
Paul Cody— *Sphyxia*
Jaimee Wriston Colbert — *Vanishing Acts*
Roger Coleman — *Skywreck Afternoons*
Stephen Downes — *The Hands of Pianists*
Marc Estrin — *Hyde*
Marc Estrin — *Kafka's Roach*
Marc Estrin — *Proceedings of the Hebrew Free Burial Society*
Marc Estrin — *Speckled Vanities*
Marc Estrin — *The Annotated Nose*
Marc Estrin — *The Penseés of Alan Krieger*
Zdravka Evtimova — *Asylum for Men and Dogs*
Zdravka Evtimova — *In the Town of Joy and Peace*
Zdravka Evtimova — *Sinfonia Bulgarica*
Zdravka Evtimova — *You Can Smile on Wednesdays*
Daniel Forbes — *Derail This Train Wreck*

Fomite

Peter Fortunato — *Carnevale*
Greg Guma — *Dons of Time*
Ramsey Hanhan – *Fugitive Dreams*
Richard Hawley — *The Three Lives of Jonathan Force*
Lamar Herrin — *Father Figure*
Michael Horner — *Damage Control*
Ron Jacobs — *All the Sinners Saints*
Ron Jacobs — *Short Order Frame Up*
Ron Jacobs — *The Co-conspirator's Tale*
Scott Archer Jones — *A Rising Tide of People Swept Away*
Scott Archer Jones — *And Throw Away the Skins*
Julie Justicz — *Conch Pearl*
Julie Justicz — *Degrees of Difficulty*
Maggie Kast — *A Free Unsullied Land*
Darrell Kastin — *Shadowboxing with Bukowski*
Coleen Kearon — *#triggerwarning*
Coleen Kearon — *Feminist on Fire*
Jan English Leary — *Thicker Than Blood*
Jan English Leary — *Town and Gown*
Diane Lefer — *Confessions of a Carnivore*
Diane Lefer — *Out of Place*
Rob Lenihan — *Born Speaking Lies*
Cynthia Newberry Martin — *The Art of Her Life*
Colin McGinnis — *Roadman*
Douglas W. Milliken — *Our Shadows' Voice*
Ilan Mochari — *Zinsky the Obscure*
Peter Nash — *In the Place Where We Thought We Stood*
Peter Nash — *Parsimony*
Peter Nash — *The Least of It*
Peter Nash — *The Perfection of Things*
George Ovitt — *Stillpoint*
George Ovitt — *Tribunal*
Gregory Papadoyiannis — *The Baby Jazz*
Pelham — *The Walking Poor*
Christopher Peterson — *Madman*
Andy Potok — *My Father's Keeper*
Frederick Ramey — *Comes A Time*
Howard Rappaport — *Arnold and Igor*
Joseph Rathgeber — *Mixedbloods*
Kathryn Roberts — *Companion Plants*
Robert Rosenberg — *Isles of the Blind*
Fred Russell — *Rafi's World*
Ron Savage — *Voyeur in Tangier*
David Schein — *The Adoption*

Fomite

9 781959 984023